The Best American SCIENCE FICTION and FANTASY 2020

GUEST EDITORS OF
THE BEST AMERICAN SCIENCE FICTION AND FANTASY

2015 JOE HILL
2016 KAREN JOY FOWLER
2017 CHARLES YU
2018 N. K. JEMISIN
2019 CARMEN MARIA MACHADO
2020 DIANA GABALDON

The Best American SCIENCE FICTION and FANTASY™ 2020

Edited and with an Introduction
by Diana Gabaldon

John Joseph Adams, *Series Editor*

MARINER BOOKS
HOUGHTON MIFFLIN HARCOURT
BOSTON • NEW YORK 2020

hmhbooks.com

ISSN 2573-0797 (print) ISSN 2573-0800 (ebook)
ISBN 978-1-328-61310-3 (print) ISBN 978-1-328-61886-3 (ebook)

Printed in the United States of America
DOC 10 9 8 7 6 5 4 3 2 1

Contents

Foreword

WELCOME TO YEAR six of *The Best American Science Fiction and Fantasy*. This volume presents the best science fiction and fantasy (SF/F) short stories published during the 2019 calendar year as selected by myself and guest editor Diana Gabaldon.

About This Year's Guest Editor

Diana Gabaldon is the *New York Times* No. 1 best-selling author of the Outlander series, which has more than thirty-five million copies in print worldwide and is the basis for a current hit show on the Starz network (on which she serves as a consultant). Eight volumes have been published so far, and the ninth, *Go Tell the Bees That I Am Gone,* is coming soon. There are also volumes one and two of *The Outlandish Companion,* a compendium of characters and lore for the Outlander series.

Diana is not exactly known for short work—her novels tend to be fairly mammoth tomes, and she doesn't often write short fiction (and when she does, it's normally novella or near-novella length)—but she's a writer who's been in the science fiction and fantasy field from the start of her career, though often seen as existing outside of it. Partly because of that perceived "outsider" status, and because she's not normally associated with short fiction, I thought it would be interesting to see what kind of selections a writer such as she would choose. (And boy, was it a good idea—we've got quite an array of stories this year.) She's one of the most voracious readers I've encountered during my time in publishing (and that's saying a lot), which factored into her selection as well, though when you read her introduction to this volume you'll see that her connection to short fiction goes back much farther and deeper than might have been known or expected.

Most of Diana's short work is part of the Outlander series or the other series she's most known for—the Lord John Grey series, which is itself part of the Outlander series and numbers nine volumes to date (including several novellas). Some of her novellas have been published as stand-alone books, but she's also published in a range of anthologies, including *Songs of Love and Death, Warriors, Legends II, Dangerous Women, The Mad Scientist's Guide to World Domination,* and *Down These Strange Streets.* Her stories are in two Arthurian anthologies: *Excalibur* and *Out of Avalon,* and a satirical story, coauthored with her son Sam Sykes, is included in the anthology *The Dragon Book.* Collections of her work include *A Trail of Fire* and *Seven Stones to Stand or Fall.* She is also the author of a graphic novel, *The Exile.*

In addition to her writerly qualifications, Diana has degrees in marine biology and zoology, as well as a PhD in quantitative behavioral ecology; she spent more than a decade as a university professor. She was the founding editor of the journal *Science Software Quarterly* and has written textbooks and scientific articles. You know, when I heard that Diana Gabaldon had multiple degrees and a PhD, I thought: Sure, sure, that makes sense. But I never would have guessed the subjects of those degrees.[1] Or that she'd been a computing expert who founded a science journal. Or that in her twenties she wrote several comics for Disney featuring Scrooge McDuck and other Disney properties.

All that is to say: Diana clearly contains multitudes. As do the stories she chose for this year's volume. It's a varied and fascinating selection, and I expect readers will be just as excited about this crop of stories as Diana and I are.

1. For the record, I would have guessed literature, history, and anthropology, with the PhD in literature.

Selection Criteria and Process

The stories chosen for this anthology were originally published between January 1, 2019, and December 31, 2019. The technical criteria for consideration are (1) original publication in a nationally distributed American or Canadian publication (i.e., periodicals, collections, or anthologies, in print, online, or e-book); (2) publication in English by writers who are American or Canadian, or who have made the United States their home; (3) publication as text (audiobook, podcast, dramatized, interactive, and other forms of fiction are not considered); (4) original publication as short fiction (excerpts of novels are not knowingly considered); (5) story length of 17,499 words or less; (6) at least loosely categorized as science fiction or fantasy; (7) publication by someone other than the author (i.e., self-published works are not eligible); and (8) publication as an original work of the author (i.e., not part of a media tie-in/licensed fiction program).

As series editor, I attempted to read everything I could find that meets the above selection criteria. After doing all of my reading, I created a list of what I felt were the top eighty stories (forty science fiction and forty fantasy) published in the genre. Those eighty stories—hereinafter referred to as the "Top 80"—were sent to the guest editor, who read them and then chose the best twenty (ten science fiction, ten fantasy) for inclusion in the anthology. The guest editor reads all of the stories anonymously—with no bylines attached to them, nor any information about where the story originally appeared.

The guest editor's top twenty selections appear in this volume; the remaining sixty stories are listed in the back of this book as "Notable Science Fiction and Fantasy Stories of 2019."

2019 Summation

In order to select the Top 80 stories published in the SF/F genres in 2019, I read and considered several thousand stories from a wide range of anthologies, collections, and magazines—basically, wherever there are stories, you'll find me there waiting to read them. As always, it was a tough process to decide which stories would make the cut, and so I ended up with several dozen stories that, in the end, were on the outside looking in, but nonetheless were excellent works.

The Top 80 this year was drawn from thirty-one different publications: twenty periodicals, nine anthologies, and two single-author collections (or, rather, one collection and one trilogy omnibus that included a bonus story). The final table of contents draws from thirteen different sources: nine periodicals and four anthologies. *Lightspeed* had the most selections (four); the anthology *New Suns* had three; and *Nightmare* and *The Magazine of Fantasy & Science Fiction* two each.

Six of the authors included in this volume (Adam-Troy Castro, Caroline M. Yoachim, Charlie Jane Anders, E. Lily Yu, Jaymee Goh, and Tobias S. Buckell) previously appeared in *BASFF;* the remaining authors are appearing for the first time. Sofia Samatar (not included in this volume) still has the most *BASFF* appearances all-time with four; Castro, Yoachim, Anders, and Yu have appeared in *BASFF* three times now, and this is the second appearance for Buckell and Goh.

This year marks the first appearances of two periodicals in our table of contents, both of which are long-storied genre publications that have died and been brought back to life more than once: *Amazing Stories* and *Weird Tales.* They are among those periodicals appearing in the Top 80 for the first time this year, and joining them on that list are *Anathema* and *PodCastle.*

E. Lily Yu had the most stories in the Top 80 this year, with three; several authors had two each: A. T. Greenblatt, Elizabeth Bear (both of hers were selections), L. D. Lewis, N. K. Jemisin, Rebecca Roanhorse, Sam J. Miller, Tobias S. Buckell, and Veronica Roth. Overall, seventy authors are represented in the Top 80.

Gwendolyn Kiste's story selected for inclusion, "The Eight People Who Murdered Me (Excerpt from Lucy Westenra's Diary)," won the Bram Stoker Award (she won an additional Stoker for her nonfiction writing). Caroline M. Yoachim's story, "The Archronology of Love," was named a finalist for both the Hugo and Nebula awards. Nibedita Sen's story, "Ten Excerpts from an Annotated Bibliography on the Cannibal Women of Ratnabar Island," was also a finalist for both awards, and Sen was a finalist for the Astounding Award for Best New Writer.

Among the Notable Stories, three were finalists for the Hugo Award: N. K. Jemisin's "Emergency Skin," Rivers Solomon's "Blood Is Another Word for Hunger," and Ted Chiang's "Omphalos." Mimi Mondal's "His Footsteps, Through Darkness and Light," A. C. Wise's "How the Trick Is Done," Karen Osborne's "The Dead, in Their Uncontrollable Power," and A. T. Greenblatt's "Give the Family My Love" were finalists for the Nebula Award.

Note: The final results of some of the awards mentioned above won't be known until after this text goes to press. The Sturgeon and Locus award finalists had not been announced at the time of writing, presumably due to the COVID-19 pandemic.

Anthologies

The following anthologies all had stories selected for inclusion in this year's volume: *A People's Future of the United States,* edited by Victor LaValle and yours truly; *New Suns,* edited by Nisi Shawl (*three* selections!); *The Mythic Dream,* edited by Dominik Parisien and Navah Wolfe; and *Wastelands: The New Apocalypse,* edited by me.

Several other anthologies had stories in the Top 80: *Forward,* edited by Blake Crouch; *Echoes,* edited by Ellen Datlow; *Current Futures,* edited by Ann VanderMeer; *If This Goes On,* edited by Cat Rambo; and *Mission Critical,* edited by Jonathan Strahan. The anthologies with the most stories in the Top 80 were the aforementioned *New Suns* (seven) and *A People's Future of the United States* (six); *Forward* and *The Mythic Dream* had three each; *Echoes* and *Wastelands: The New Apocalypse* had two each.

As always, there's a plethora of fine work published across a wide range of anthologies, but there isn't always room in the Top 80 for even very good anthologies to be represented. Here's a list of some of the anthologies that featured excellent work but nonetheless didn't quite manage to crack the Top 80: *Hex Life,* edited by Christopher Golden and Rachel Autumn Deering; *My Name Was Never Frankenstein,* edited by Bryan Furuness; *The Weight of Light,* edited by Joey Eschrich and Clark A. Miller; *Do Not Go Quietly,* edited by Jason Sizemore and Lesley Conner; *The Twisted Book of Shadows,* edited by Christopher Golden and James A. Moore; *Temporally*

Deactivated, edited by David B. Coe and Joshua Palmatier; and *His Hideous Heart,* edited by Dahlia Adler.

Collections

The standout collection from 2019 was—clearly, in my mind—Ted Chiang's *Exhalation,* which included the stunning originals "Omphalos" and "Anxiety Is the Dizziness of Freedom" (both of which are finalists for the Hugo Award); the former is in the Top 80, while the latter was too long to be considered. Strangely, this year only one other collection had a story in the Top 80 . . . and it's not even really a collection: it's a trilogy omnibus that also included an original short story set in the same world; I'm referring to *Binti: The Complete Trilogy* by Nnedi Okorafor, which produced the fine story "Binti: Sacred Fire."

Other 2019 collections also included excellent work. Some of these contained only reprints, and thus were excluded from consideration, but I note them anyway in order to shine a light on them: *Snow White Learns Witchcraft,* by Theodora Goss; *The History of Soul 2065,* by Barbara Krasnoff; *And Go Like This: Stories,* by John Crowley; *The City and the Cygnets,* by Michael Bishop; *The Girls with Kaleidoscope Eyes,* by Howard V. Hendrix; *Truer Love and Other Lies,* by Edd Vick; *All Worlds Are Real,* by Susan Palwick; *The Arcana of Maps,* by Jessica Reisman; *Memory's Children,* by Samuel Peralta; *A Cathedral of Myth and Bone,* by Kat Howard; *Laughter at the Academy,* by Seanan McGuire; and *Hexarchate Stories,* by Yoon Ha Lee. And not to forget perhaps the most surprising collection I discovered all year—that being *Someone Who Will Love You in All Your Damaged Glory* by *BoJack Horseman* creator Raphael Bob-Waksberg, which also happens to be just about my favorite title of the year.

Periodicals

More than a hundred periodicals were considered throughout the year in my hunt for the Top 80 stories. I read magazines both large and small and sought out the genre stories that might have been lurking in the pages of literary and/or mainstream periodicals.

The following magazines had work representing them in the

Top 80 this year: *Anathema* (two), *Asimov's Science Fiction* (three), *Beneath Ceaseless Skies* (two), *Clarkesworld* (two), *Fireside* (two), *Future Tense* (two), *Lightspeed* (nine), *Nightmare* (four), *Terraform* (two), *The Magazine of Fantasy & Science Fiction* (four), Tor.com (four), and *Uncanny* (eight). The following periodicals had one story each: *Amazing Stories, Escape Pod, FIYAH, Foreshadow, PodCastle, The New Yorker, The Verge (Better Worlds),* and *Weird Tales.*

The following outlets published stories that were under serious consideration for the Top 80: *MIT Technology Review, Strange Horizons, Catapult,* the *Cincinnati Review, Conjunctions, Factor Four Magazine, Fairy Tale Review, Futures,* the *Southern Review, The Sun, Three-Lobed Burning Eye, Tin House,* and a little venue called the *New York Times.* This last I'll expand upon a bit, because it was an intriguing project: the *Times* published a series of "Op-Eds from the Future," which produced very good material by contributors including Ted Chiang, Brooke Bolander, and Jeff VanderMeer. Being in "op-ed" format, however, they didn't necessarily feel like *stories,* though some of them were close enough to warrant consideration. They're worth checking out online.

And now we come to the periodical graveyard, or, in some cases, a temporary resting place. As noted in this space last year, the long-running magazines *Intergalactic Medicine Show* and *Apex Magazine* both announced they were ceasing publication, with neither publishing any new content in 2019. However, as I was in the midst of this writing (mid-May 2020), *Apex* announced that it would be returning in 2021. Other publications that ceased operations (or went on indefinite hiatus) in 2019 include: *Bastion, Factor Four Magazine,* and *Mad Scientist Journal.* Additionally, one appeared and then shut down in 2019, the interesting but short-lived *Foreshadow.*

In tribute to these magazines that have gone the way of the dinosaur, I implore you to support the short fiction publishers you love. If you can, subscribe (even if they offer content for free), review, spread the word. Every little bit helps.

Acknowledgments

It would essentially be impossible for me to do the work of *BASFF* properly without the able assistance of others. This year, much of that work fell to my newly minted assistant series editor, Christopher Cevasco (who used to edit a pretty great historical fiction/fantasy magazine called *Paradox* back in the day); bringing him on board feels like one of the smartest things I've ever done. Additionally, Alex Puncekar and Christie Yant again provided editorial support. Huge thanks to you all.

I'd also like to thank Jenny Xu at Houghton Mifflin Harcourt, who kindly put up with my delay in turning in this foreword, and otherwise keeps the gears turning back at Best American HQ. Thanks too to David Steffen, who runs the Submission Grinder writer's market database, for his assistance in helping me update the list of gone-extinct markets mentioned above.

As always, I'm most appreciative when authors alert me to their eligible works by dropping me a line or sending their work via my *BASFF* online submissions portal. Likewise, I'm grateful to the editors and publishers who do the same—particularly the ones who proactively make sure I get copies of their works without me having to ask (and/or ask . . . repeatedly!).

And finally, I'm eternally grateful to all of the readers of *The Best American Science Fiction and Fantasy*—both those who have read every volume and the newcomers. And a special thank-you to readers who have left positive reviews on Amazon or Goodreads or the like; reader reviews really do help bring attention to this series, as does talking about *BASFF*—or any book or story you love—on social media.

Submissions for Next Year's Volume

Editors, writers, and publishers who would like their work considered for next year's edition (the best of 2020), please visit johnjosephadams.com/best-american for instructions on how to submit material for consideration.

—John Joseph Adams

Introduction

THERE'S A HAUNTED room in my house. It's the back bedroom on the first floor—though I doubt there's ever been a bed in it. In fact, no one in the family has ever been able to use that room for anything, for long.

My grandparents built the house in 1938; I own it now. In 1952 my grandfather died in the house—suddenly, from a pulmonary embolism. My mother and I were there at the time, but I don't recall the circumstances, as I was two weeks old. Five years later, my grandmother died and my mother inherited the house. We lived there for the next nine years.

During that time, my parents tried repeatedly to use the back bedroom for an office, a writing room, file storage, a small library . . . but no one ever stayed in the room for more than half an hour at a time, and sooner or later, whichever parent was trying to do taxes or write lesson plans would be doing it on the coffee table in the living room or the kitchen counter.

The back bedroom is always cold. Its door opens onto a small central space where an old floor furnace supplies heat to the master bedroom, a small bathroom, the living room—and theoretically, to the back bedroom. Even with the door wide open and the furnace going full blast three feet away, the room is always cold.

We moved from that house when I was fourteen. It was another fifty years before it occurred to me that my grandfather might have died in the back bedroom.

His name was Harold S. Sykes, and he was the mayor of the city we lived in. He also wrote fantasy and science fiction stories,[1] some of them published in *Amazing Stories, Super Science Stories: The Big Book of Science Fiction,* and other magazines of what-wasn't-yet-called speculative fiction. My mother had kept several of the magazines, and as I read everything else in the house, I also read those.

Now, while reading through the eighty finalist stories submitted for this anthology, I'd noticed certain common themes and concepts among them, which rang a faint, subliminal bell for me. There were echoes from a long life of reading everything I could get my hands on, including a lot of fantasy and science fiction, but there were plenty of new themes, too. And as I was reading some of these stories in my old family house, it occurred to me to wonder what had (and hadn't) changed in the years between 1930 (when my grandfather's first story, "The Insatiable Entity," was published in *Science Wonder Stories*) and 2020.

"Fantastic" stories dealt (and still deal) with pretty much everything, but if you look at a lot of them, it's easy to see broad general categories. Let's look at a few.

First, there's Doomed Earth. This one has always been with us, apparently. As well it might be: it's an inherently human concept, heavy with hubris, and ever more engorged in later years. In the earlier part of the twentieth century, Earth tended to be doomed by external forces: asteroids, alien invasions, planetary discombobulations. In the modern forms, it's *always* humans. *We* are responsible for the death/destruction of the planet!

What's interesting about the differences in early and later doom stories is that in both types, the destruction/impairment of Earth is often merely the instigating factor for a second type of story—Escaping Spaceship/Seeds of Humanity—but in the more modern versions, you often see stories that don't deal with escape as much as they deal with entrapment. People stranded on a dying

1. "The Insatiable Entity," in *Science Wonder Stories* (Hugo Gernsback, ed.), March 1930 (n.b.: this was published nearly thirty years before the film *The Blob* appeared); "The Myriad," from *Amazing Stories,* December 1937 ("This story out-Lilliputs Lilliputia, for the action is carried on by the minutest kind of beings, who are decidedly able to take care of themselves!"—Editor's introduction); and "The Ancient Ones," from *Super Science Stories: The Big Book of Science Fiction,* vol. 7, no. 1, July 1950 ("Inheritors of an Earth they could not possess, they strugged [*sic*] onward toward a feeble glimmering of life, while Death incarnate stalked in their track!"—Table of Contents blurb).

world, meeting the notion of personal obliteration with everything from courage and unselfish love to pettiness and abnegation.

Now, even the Escaping Spaceship stories are less straight adventure and more psychology. One very interesting evolution is that many such stories involve extensive worldbuilding: the painstaking composition of a new onboard culture, frequently one whose Earthbound roots have long since decayed.

(One of the very interesting stories in this anthology is actually a twofer: "Between the Dark and the Dark" involves two parallel stories, one onboard such a multigenerational ship whose humans have long since lost direct touch with Earth—though their ship hasn't—and one on Earth, showing the equally changed culture of the people who stayed behind to deal with natural and political disasters, whose long-term hope lies in those deaf space-seeds, hurtling outward.)

One thing you always run into when dealing with SF/F is that slash between the *F*s. There's a rough rule of thumb for what's fantasy and what's science fiction, but there's often a lot of overlap.

Where do Aliens fall? It often depends on how the writer has drawn the specs. Invasion of Earth by (usually, but not always, inimical) aliens can be—and often is—straight SF, so long as the world of the story is drawn with internally consistent rules.

Invasion-by-hostile-aliens stories were much more common in the earlier days of speculative fiction than they are now. (I read a story in one of my grandfather's magazines called "The Bas-Relief," which dealt with the periodic invasion of Earth by a race of giant eel-men, who were using Earth as a breeding ground for food, i.e., humans. This one scared the pants off me when I read it. I was about eleven, I think, but still.)

Now, writers seem much more inclined to think that humans are the nastiest thing around, and thus much more likely to go invade, exploit, or ruin some hapless other planet. This may be the result of them growing up with the actuality of space travel, rather than merely the *concept* of it—and with a basic conception of humanity formed by social media rather than, say, philosophy or religion.

Putting aside invasion stories, though, aliens offer a kaleidoscopic view of humanity—particularly one sort of story that's almost completely modern: AI/Tech stories.

In 1930 computers didn't exist. You didn't start seeing stories involving machine intelligence until the late '50s (hey, ENIAC is only eight years older than I am), but such stories pretty much exploded through the last quarter of the twentieth century. And the major modern fictional innovation is that the tech often becomes real characters, rather than simply part of the worldbuilding.

This in turn led to more psychologically oriented stories asking metaphysical questions about the nature of intelligence—and of emotion (sometimes by contrast with a machine intelligence; sometimes by imitation or evolution of one). But a story lives or dies on its characters. Said characters may *be* "tech" themselves, but they still embody human preoccupations with themselves, and AI stories let writers do their favorite thing and explore themselves, while still dealing with novel situations that are disturbingly possible.

Another subset of Alien stories goes in the opposite direction, squarely into fantasy. These are the stories that are based on and drawn from extant folklore, magical beliefs, and history. Most such stories (as opposed to novels) deal with a particular human attribute—sexuality, greed, charity, identity—metaphorically expressed, and you'll see this particular story form going *way* back—perhaps the oldest form of speculative fiction. Homer, anyone? *Beowulf*? *Gilgamesh*?

As noted, one subset of folklore/myth crosses into the Alien concept. Another deals explicitly or referentially with real cultural beliefs and stories, and the third takes invented folklore/fairy story/myth material, but presents it stylistically in a traditional manner of storytelling.

I'm kind of putting aside discussion of stories written ostensibly as fantasy, but primarily for the purpose of political or social commentary, often using a standardized fairy-tale setting. There's a certain amount of this in many stories—in fact, a good story almost always includes a layer of social commentary—but in latter years, I'm seeing many more *explicitly* political stories. There's one included in this anthology—"Thirty-Three Wicked Daughters"—and I chose that one for its wit, elegance, humor, and heart.

Going on from the concept of using fairy tales and folklore as the basis for a story—whether merely as the setting of a world, or using the storytelling style—we come to the notion of Trope stories.

Trope stories are those wherein the writer deliberately takes on a popular style or trope and either uses it for humor ("The Galactic Tourist . . .") or goes further, into metafiction ("Another Avatar"). This is a fairly modern approach. You do occasionally see this in older mid-twentieth-century stories, but almost always in the form of a futuristic murder mystery (cf. Isaac Asimov).

So—is all writing essentially navel-gazing? Well, *yes,* but consider where that phrase came from: the Greek term *omphalos,* which translates roughly as "navel," but which referred originally to the "navel of the world"; i.e., the metaphorical center or hub of something. Good navel-gazing is the ultimate in speculative fiction, where a writer can express a greater truth by means of a microcosmic experience that takes the reader to the heart (or the navel . . .) of the matter.

Navel-gazing risks being boring by a lack of specificity. Someone contemplating the downfall of humanity is a bore (you'd think modern Twitter minds would realize this, but *nooo* . . .), whereas someone contemplating their own imminent demise is pretty fascinating.

Overall, in this very informal survey of trends, I'd have to say that twenty-first-century speculative fiction expresses a lot more personal anxiety than did older stories from the mid-to-latish twentieth century—though such writing has always been used as a means of dealing with Fear of the Unknown.

The major difference I see is that the unknown now openly and explicitly encompasses ourselves. One of the stories in this book, "Erase, Erase, Erase," could as easily be a literary short story dealing with alienation and powerlessness, or a straight psychological description of the results of child abuse. It's only fantasy because we don't know whether the first-person writer is mentally deranged or not; either way, they're telling the truth.

I don't recall much political moralizing in the older stories, either overt or veiled. (There were a couple of stories in the entry pool that so clearly were focused on Voldemort—you know, "He Who Must Not Be Named" because everybody already *knows* who you're talking about—that the authors were metaphorically jumping up and down in agitation, waving their arms and pointing a thousand-watt flashlight, wordlessly shouting, "Him! It's Him I'm talking about!" I mean it's *HIM!!!*)

On the other hand, there's a real place for what might be called Domestic stories: stories that take their shape from ordinary modern life and its historical imperfections . . . and run with it. There are three of those in this book: "Life Sentence," "Shape-ups at Delilah's," and "Up from Slavery." These all feature explicitly political/social commentary, but it's used as the springboard of the story, not the ultimate point. The stories are about real people, not animated megaphones.

As a final note, there are speculative stories that overlap with classic SF/F story types—ghost stories and horror stories. (See Fear of the Unknown, above.) There were a few entries along these lines, and while they were very effective, I didn't choose to include any of them. (Too many good stories, too few pages!) Not that all ghost stories are necessarily scary. After all, in the end, we make our ghosts; we haunt ourselves.

Last year, a house my parents had owned was sold, and my sister and I were obliged to belt up to Flagstaff, Arizona, and spend a frantic three days salvaging old family papers, photographs, dishes, silver, and What-the-Hell-Is-*This?* items from the storage space under the house. Most of this was carted next door—to my grandparents' house, the one I now own.

Among the salvaged artifacts was a big, very old, very battered leather suitcase. We hadn't looked inside it, but when I started shoveling things out of my living room months later, I stopped and opened the suitcase, out of curiosity. It was full of typed manuscripts; my grandfather's stories.

I took it to the back bedroom. One of these days, I'll take a chair and a lamp in there to read the stories, and meet again a man I haven't seen in a very long time. I'll leave the door open, though. For warmth.

— DIANA GABALDON

The Best American
SCIENCE FICTION
and FANTASY
2020

MATTHEW BAKER

Life Sentence

FROM *Lightspeed*

HOME.

He recognizes the name of the street. But he doesn't remember the landscape. He recognizes the address on the mailbox. But he doesn't remember the house.

His family is waiting for him on the porch.

Everybody looks just as nervous as he is.

He gets out.

The police cruiser takes back off down the gravel drive, leaving him standing in a cloud of dust holding a baggie of possessions.

He has a wife. He has a son. He has a daughter.

A dog peers out a window.

His family takes him in.

Wash is still groggy from the procedure. He's got a plastic taste on his tongue. He's got a throbbing sensation in his skull. He's starving.

Supper is homemade pot pies. His wife says the meal is his favorite. He doesn't remember that.

The others are digging in already. Steam rises from his pie as he pierces the crust with his fork. He salivates. The smell of the pie hitting him makes him grunt with desire. Bending toward the fork, he parts his lips to take a bite, but then he stops and glances up.

Something is nagging at him worse than the hunger.

"What did I do?" he says with a sense of bewilderment.

His wife holds up a hand.

"Baby, please, let's not talk about that," his wife says.

Wash looks around. A laminate counter. A maroon toaster.

Flowers growing from pots on the sill. Magnets shaped like stars on the fridge.

This is his home.

He doesn't remember anything.

He's not supposed to.

His reintroduction supervisor comes to see him in the morning.

"How do you feel, Washington?"

"Everybody keeps calling me Wash?"

"I can call you that if you'd like."

"I guess I'm not really sure what I like."

Lindsay, the reintroduction supervisor, wears a scarlet tie with a navy suit. She's got a bubbly disposition and a dainty build. Everything that she says, she says as if revealing a wonderful secret that she just can't wait to share.

"We've found a job for you at a restaurant."

"Doing what?"

"Working in the kitchen."

"That's the best you could get me?"

"At your level of education, and considering your status as a felon, yes, it really is."

"Where did I work before?"

Lindsay smiles.

"An important part of making a successful transition back to your life is learning to let go of any worries that you might have about your past so that you can focus on enjoying your future."

Wash frowns.

"Why do I know so much about mortgages? Did I used to work at a bank?"

"To my knowledge you have never worked at a bank."

"But how can I remember that stuff if I can't remember other stuff?"

"Your semantic memories are still intact. Only your episodic memories were wiped."

"My what?"

"You know what a restaurant is."

"Yeah."

"But you can't remember ever having eaten in a restaurant before."

"No."

"Or celebrating a birthday at a restaurant. Or using a restroom at a restaurant. Or seeing a friend at a restaurant. You've eaten in restaurants before. But you have no memories of that at all. None whatsoever." Lindsay taps her temples. "Episodic memories are personal experiences. That's what's gone. Semantic memories are general knowledge. Information. Names, dates, addresses. You still have all of that. You're a functional member of society. Your diploma is just as valid as before. And your procedural memories are fine. You still know how to ride a bike, or play the guitar, or operate a vacuum. Assuming you ever learned," Lindsay laughs.

"Did you do anything else to me?"

"Well, of course, your gun license was also revoked."

Wash thinks.

"Did I shoot somebody?"

"All felons are prohibited from owning firearms, regardless of the nature of the crime."

Wash turns away, folding his arms over his chest, pouting at the carpet.

"Washington, how do you feel?"

"Upset."

"That's perfectly normal. I'm so glad that you're comfortable talking with me about your feelings. That's so important."

Lindsay nods with a solemn expression, as if waiting for him to continue sharing, and then leans in.

"But honestly though, you should feel grateful you weren't born somewhere that still has prisons." Lindsay reaches for her purse. "Do you know what would have happened to you a century ago for doing what you did? The judge would have locked you up and thrown away the key!" Lindsay says brightly, and then stands to leave.

Wash gets woken that night by a craving.

An urgent need.

Was he an addict?

What is he craving?

He follows some instinct into the basement. Stands there in boxers under the light of a bare bulb. Glances around the basement, stares at the workbench, and then obeys an urge to reach up onto the shelf above. Pats around and discovers an aluminum tin.

Something shifts inside as he takes the tin down from the shelf.

He pops the lid.

In the tin: a stash of king-size candy bars.

As he chews a bite of candy bar, a tingle of satisfaction rushes through him, followed by a sense of relief.

Chocolate.

Back up the stairs, padding down the hallway, he pit-stops in the bathroom for a drink of water. Bends to sip from the faucet. Wipes his chin. Stands. A full-length mirror hangs from the back of the door. He's lit by the glow of a night-light the shape of a rainbow that's plugged into the outlet above the toilet.

Wash examines his appearance in the mirror. Wrinkles around his eyes. Creases along his mouth. A thick neck. Broad shoulders, wide hips, hefty limbs, and a round gut. Fingers nicked with scars. Soles hardened with calluses. The body of an aging athlete, or a laborer accustomed to heavy lifting who's recently gone soft from lack of work.

He can't remember being a toddler. He can't remember being a child. He can't remember being a teenager. He can't remember being an adult.

He stares at himself.

Who is he other than this person standing here in the present moment?

Is he anybody other than this person standing here in the present moment?

His wife stirs as he slips back into bed. She reaches over and startles him with a kiss. He kisses back, but then she climbs on top of him, and he pulls away.

"Too soon?" she whispers.

Mia, that's her name, he remembers. She has a flat face, skinny arms, thick legs, and frizzy hair cut off at her jawline, which he can just make out in the dark. Her nails are painted bright red. She sleeps in a plaid nightgown.

"I barely know you," he says.

Mia snorts. "Didn't stop you the first time." She shuffles backward on her knees, tugging his boxers down his legs as she goes, and then chuckles. "I mean our other first time."

The restaurant is a diner down by the highway, a chrome trailer with checkered linoleum and pleather booths and ceiling fans that spin out of sync, featuring a glass case of pastries next to the register and a jukebox with fluorescent tubing over by the restrooms. The diner serves breakfast and lunch only. Wash arrives each morning around dawn. The kitchen has swinging doors. He does the dishes, sweeps the floors, mops the floors, and hauls the trash out when the bags get full. Mainly he does the dishes. Dumps soda from cups. Pours coffee from mugs. Scrapes onion rings and pineapple rinds and soggy napkins and buttered slices of toast and empty jam containers and crumpled straw wrappers into the garbage. Sprays ketchup from plates. Rinses broth from bowls. Racks the tableware and sends the racks through the dishwasher. Stacks spotless dishes back onto the shelves alongside the stove. Scours at crusted yolk and dried syrup with the bristly side of sponges. Scrubs skillets with stainless steel pads for so long and with such force that the pads fall apart and still there's a scorched residue stuck to the pans. Burns his hands with scalding water. Splashes stinging suds into his eyes. His shoes are always damp as he drives home in the afternoon. He shaves, he showers, and he feeds the dog, a moody mutt whose name is Biscuit. Then he sits on the porch step waiting for the rest of his family to get home. His house is modest, with small rooms and a low ceiling, and has no garage. The gutters sag. Shingles have been blown clear off the roof. The sun has bleached the blue of the siding almost to gray. Across the road stands a field of corn. Beyond that there's woods. The corn stalks sway in the breeze. The dog waits with him, curled up on the grass around his shoes, panting whenever a car drives past. He lives in Kansas.

Sophie, his daughter, a ninth grader, is the next to arrive home, shuffling off the bus while jabbing at the buttons of a game. Jaden, his son, a third grader, arrives home on the later bus, shouting taunts back at friends hanging out the windows. His wife works at a hospital, the same hours that he does, but she gets home last since the hospital is all the way over in Independence.

Wash tries to cook once, tries to make meatloaf. He knows what a meatloaf is. He understands how an oven functions. He gets the mechanics of a whisk. He can read the recipe no problem. But still the attempt is a disaster. He pulls the pan out when the timer goes off, and the bottom of the meatloaf is already charred, and the top of the meatloaf is still raw. He hadn't been able to find bread crumbs, so he had torn up a slice of bread instead, which doesn't seem to have worked. He samples a bite from the center of the meatloaf, that in-between part neither charred nor raw, and finds some slivers of onion skin in among what he's chewing. When his wife arrives home, she surveys the mess with a look of amusement and then assures him that this isn't a skill he's forgotten. She does the cooking. At home, the same as at the diner, he does the dishes.

Other items that his wife assures him were not accidentally erased during his procedure: the date of her birthday (all he knows is the month, August); the date of their anniversary (all he knows is the month, May).

"Here's a clue. My birthday was exactly a week before you came home. Borrow a calculator from one of your delightful children if you need help with the math," Mia says, dumping a box of spaghetti into a pot of roiling water while simultaneously stirring a can of mushrooms into a pan of bubbling marinara. "If you'd like to know how long you've been married, your marriage license is in the filing cabinet in the basement. In fact, if you're really feeling ambitious, your children have some birth certificates in there, too. Heck, check your immunization record while you're down there, you're probably due for a tetanus shot."

There are moments so intimate that he can almost forget he's living with strangers. His daughter falls asleep on him one night while watching a show about zombies on the couch, her head lolling against his shoulder. His son leans into him one night waiting for the microwave to heat a mug of cider, his arm wrapping around his waist. Late one night after the kids are asleep, his wife hands him a rubber syringe and a plastic bowl and asks him to flush a buildup of wax from her ears, an act that to him seems far more intimate than intercourse.

But then there are the moments that remind him how much he must have lost. One night, during a supper of baked potatoes loaded with chives and bacon and sour cream, his family suddenly cracks up over an in-joke, a shared memory that's somehow related to mini-golf and bikinis. His wife is laughing so hard that she's crying, but sobers up when she realizes how confused he looks.

"Sorry, it's impossible to explain if you weren't there," Mia says, thumbing away tears.

"But he was there, he was the one who noticed," Jaden protests.

"He can't remember anymore, you ninny," Sophie scowls.

And then the subject gets changed.

Wash does know certain information about himself.

He knows his ancestry is part Potawatomi. He knows his parents were named Lawrence and Beverly. He knows his birthplace is near Wichita.

But taking inventory of what he knows isn't as simple as thinking, "What do you know, Wash?"

He has to ask a specific question.

He must know other facts about himself.

He just hasn't asked the right questions yet.

"Wash, were you ever in a fight before?"

"Wash, did you like your parents?"

"Wash, have you seen a tornado?"

He doesn't remember.

He tries asking Sophie about his past one afternoon. Wash is driving her to practice. Sophie runs cross.

"What was my life like before the wipe?" Wash says.

Sophie is a plump kid with crooked teeth, a pet lover, and has a grave demeanor, as if constantly haunted by the fact that not all kittens have homes. She's doing history homework, flipping back and forth between a textbook and a worksheet, scribbling in information. She's got her sneakers propped on the dashboard with her ankles crossed.

"Huh?" Sophie says.

"What do you know about my life?"

"Um."

"Like tell me something I told you about myself before I got taken away."

She sneers at the textbook. Bends over the worksheet, forcefully erases something, and blows off the peels of rubber left behind. Then turns to look at him.

"You never really talked about yourself," Sophie says.

He tries asking Jaden about his past one afternoon. Wash is driving him to practice. Jaden plays soccer.

"What was I like before I went away?" Wash says.

Jaden is a stringy kid with a nose that dominates his other features, a soda junkie, and constantly hyper, regardless of caffeine intake. He's sitting in an upside-down position with his legs pointed at the roof, his back on the seat, and his head lolled over the edge, with his hands thrown across the floor of the truck. He's spent most of the ride listing off the powers of supervillains.

"I dunno," Jaden says.

"You must remember something about me."

"I guess."

"So what type of person was I?"

Jaden plucks at the seatbelt. Frowns in thought. Then turns to look at him.

"A grown-up?" Jaden says.

Wash tries asking his wife, but her taste in conversation is strictly practical, and she doesn't seem interested in reminiscing about his life before the wipe at all. No photos are framed on the counter. No snapshots are pinned to the fridge. If pictures of his family ever hung on the walls, the pictures have long since disappeared.

But other artifacts of his past are scattered throughout the house. In his closet hang flannel button-ups, worn tees, plain sweatshirts, a zip-up fishing vest with mesh pouches, a hooded hunting jacket with a camouflage pattern, a fleece, a parka, faded jeans on wire hangers, and a suit in a plastic garment bag. Who was that person who chose these clothes? In his dresser mingle polished turquoise, pennies smashed smooth by trains, a hotel matchbook lined with the stumps of torn-out matches, an assortment of acorns, ticket stubs from raffles, a pocket knife whose blades are rusted shut, and the marbled feather of a bald eagle. Who was that person who kept these trinkets? There's a safe in the basement where his guns were stored before being sold. He knows a combination, spins the numbers in, and the handle gives. But aside from a bungee, the safe is empty. No rifles, no shotguns, no pistols. Even the ammunition was sold.

Who owned those guns?

And then there are the artifacts of his past that he sees in his family. Sometimes in the driveway, he'll glance up from the car he's washing or the mower he's fueling and see his daughter watching him from the door with an expression of spite. Was he ever cruel to Sophie? Sometimes as he drops his boots in the entryway with a thud or tosses his wallet onto the counter with a snap, he'll see his son flinch over on the couch. Was he ever rough with Jaden? When he sets his cup down empty, his wife leaps up to fetch the carton of milk from the fridge, as if there might be some repercussion for failing to pour him another glass.

He has a beat-up flip phone with nobody saved in the contacts except for his wife and his kids. Were there other contacts in there that were deleted after he got arrested?

At cross meets and soccer matches, the other parents never talk to him. Was that always the case, or only now that he's a felon?

How does he know that trains have cupolas? Where did he learn that comets aren't asteroids? Who taught him that vinegar kills lice?

Wash is at the homecoming football game, coming back from the concession stand with striped boxes of popcorn for his family, when he stops at the fence to watch a field goal attempt. A referee jogs by with a whistle bouncing on a lanyard. Cheerleaders in gloves and earmuffs rush past with pompoms and megaphones. Jayhawkers chant in the bleachers. Wash glazes over, he's not sure for how long, but he's still standing at the fence when his trance is interrupted by a stranger standing next to him.

"You did time, didn't you, friend?"

The stranger wears a pullover with the logo of the rival team. His hair is slicked crisp with mousse. He's got ironed khakis and shiny loafers.

"Do I know you?" Wash says.

"Ha. No. You just had that look. We all get the look. Searching for something that isn't there," the stranger says.

Wash cracks a smile.

The stranger grumbles, "I don't know why people even say that anymore. Doing time. That's not what happens at all. Losing time. That's what happens. Poof. Gone." The stranger glances down and gives the ice in his cup a shake. "I lost a year. Let's just say, hadn't been totally candid on my tax forms. Couldn't have been worse timing though. I'd gotten married that year. No joke, I can't even remember my own honeymoon. Spent a fortune on that trip, too. Fucking blows." The stranger turns away to watch a punt return, sucks a gurgle of soda through his straw, and then turns back. "How long did you do?"

"Life."

The stranger whistles.

"No kidding? You lost everything? From start to finish? How old were you when you got wiped?"

"Forty-one."

"What'd you do to get life? Kill a cop? Rob a bank? Run a scam or something?"

"I don't know," Wash admits.

The stranger squints.

"You aren't curious?"

"Nobody will tell me."

The stranger laughs.

"To get a sentence like that, whatever you did, it must have made the news."

Wash stares at the stranger in shock. He could know who he was after all. All he'd have to do is get online.

"We don't have a computer though," Wash frowns.

The stranger passes behind him, giving him a pat on the shoulder, and then calls back before drifting off into the crowd.

"Going to let you in on a secret, friend. At the library, you can use a computer for free."

Lindsay, his reintroduction supervisor, is waiting for him at the house when he gets off work the next afternoon. She's wearing the same outfit as before, a scarlet tie, a navy suit. She's sitting on the hood of her car next to a box of donuts.

"Time to check in," Lindsay says through a bite of cruller.

Biscuit stands on the couch, peering out of the house, paws propped against the window.

"Have a seat," Lindsay says brightly.

Wash takes a fritter.

"How are you getting along with your family, Washington?"

Wash thinks.

"Fine," Wash says.

Lindsay leans in with a conspiratorial look. "Oh, come on, give me the gossip."

Wash chews, swallows, and frowns.

"Why'd you have to give me life? You couldn't just give me twenty years or something? Why'd you have to take everything?" Wash says.

"The length of your sentence was determined by the judge."

"Just doesn't seem fair."

Lindsay nods, smiling sympathetically, and then abruptly stops.

"Well, what you did was pretty bad, Washington."

"But my whole life?"

"Do you know anything about the history of prisons in this country?" Lindsay reaches for a napkin, licks some glaze from her fingers, and wipes her hands. "Prisons here were originally intended to be a house of corrections. The theory was that when put into isolation criminals might be taught how to be functional citizens.

In practice, however, the system proved to be ineffective at reforming offenders. The rate of recidivism was staggering. Honestly, upon release, most felons were arrested on new charges within the year. And over time the conditions in the prisons became awful. I mean, imagine what your situation would have been, being sentenced to life. You would have spent the next half a century locked in a cage like an animal, sleeping on an uncomfortable cot, wearing an ill-fitting jumpsuit, making license plates all day for far less than minimum wage, cleaning yourself with commercial soaps whose lists of ingredients included a variety of carcinogens, eating mashed potatoes made from a powder and meatloaf barely fit for human consumption, getting raped occasionally by other prisoners. Instead, you get to be here, with your family. Pretty cool, right? Like, super cool? You have to admit. And the wipe isn't simply a punishment. Yes, the possibility of getting wiped is meant to deter people from committing crimes. Totally. But wipes are also highly effective at preventing criminals from becoming repeat offenders. Although there is some biological basis for things like rage and greed and so forth, those types of issues tend to be the psychological by-products of memories. And a life sentence is especially effective. Given a clean slate, felons often are much calmer, are much happier than before, are burdened with no misconceptions that crimes like embezzlement or poaching might be somehow justified, and of course possess no grudges against institutions like the government or law enforcement or former employers." Lindsay glances over, then turns back toward the road. "For example."

"So I'm supposed to feel grateful?"

Wash didn't mean to speak with that much force.

"Do you even know how much a wipe like yours costs?" Lindsay says, her eyes growing wide. "A fortune. Honestly, most people around here would need a payment plan for a simple vanity wipe. You know, you do something embarrassing at a party, you overhear somebody saying something mean about you that rings a bit too true, so you just have the memory erased. And then there are survivors of truly traumatic incidents, who often have to save up for years after the incident if insurance won't cover the cost of having it wiped. And alcoholics and crackheads and the like have no choice but to shell out, as a selective memory wipe is the only possible cure for addiction. Veterans with post-traumatic stress disorder are generally treated with wipes as well, although those wipes, as was the case with yours, are covered by taxpayers." Lindsay leans back on the hood of the car, propped up on her elbows, and squints into the sun. "It's a better deal for taxpayers anyway. Wiping your memory may have been costly, but was still nowhere near as expensive as paying to feed and shelter you for half a century would have been. That's the problem with prisons. They're overpriced, they underperform."

Wash scowls at the driveway.

"How are you feeling, Washington?"

"Frustrated."

"Tell me more."

"I don't even know what I did to get wiped."

Lindsay smiles. "The less you know about who you were before, the greater your chances of making a successful transition to your new life." Beneath her cheery tone there's a hint of uncertainty. "I would particularly recommend in your case that you avoid asking people about the details of your arrest."

Wash has to drive by the local library, a squat brick building with a flag hanging from a pole, whenever he drops off the kids at practice, and he tries to avoid wondering whether whatever he did to get arrested made the news. He notices that other parents stick around during practice, so occasionally he stays, watching Sophie stretching out at the track between intervals, knee braces on, or Jaden dribbling balls through a course of cones, shin guards crooked. Wash likes his kids. He doesn't mind being their parent, but he wants to be their friend, too. To be trusted. To be liked. The desire is so powerful that sometimes the thick fingers of his hands curl tight around the links of the fence out of a sense of longing as he watches the kids practice. Becoming friends with the dog was simple. Biscuit sniffed him and licked him and that was that. He's the same person he's always been as far as the dog is concerned. The kids are distant, though. He doesn't know how to jump-start the relationships.

On other days he drives home during practice. The wallpaper in the kitchen is dingy, there are gouges in the walls of the hallway, the ceiling fan in the living room is broken, there are cracks in the light fixture in the laundry room, but not until the constant drip from the sink in the bathroom has turned to a steady leak does he actually stop, think, and realize that the house must be in such shabby condition because of how long he was gone, in detention during the trial, when his wife would have been living on a single income. That faucet is leaking because of him.

He knows how to fix a leak. Leaving the light in the bathroom on, he fetches the toolbox from the basement. He's emptying the cupboard under the sink, stacking toiletries on the linoleum, preparing to shut off the water, when his wife passes the doorway.

"What exactly are you doing?" Mia says.

"I'm gonna fix some stuff," Wash says.

She stares at him.

"Oh," she says finally, and then carries on down the hallway, followed by the dog.

By the time the corn in the field across the road has been harvested and the trees in the woods beyond the field are nearly bare, he's got the gutters hanging straight and the shingles patched up again. He takes a day off from the diner to tear out the stained carpeting in the hallway, wearing a dust mask over his face with the cuffs of his flannel rolled. Afterward he's rummaging around the shelf under the workbench in the basement, looking for a pry bar to rip up the staples in the floor, when he notices a quiver of arrows.

Wash tugs the mask down to his neck and touches the arrows. Carbon shafts. Turkey fletching. He glances over at the safe.

Did he have a bow once?

Was the bow sold with the guns?

Turning back to the shelf under the workbench he sees that there's an unmarked case clasped shut next to the quiver.

Wash pops the lid.

Though he doesn't recognize the bow itself, he recognizes that it's a bow, even in pieces. A takedown. A recurve. And before he even has a chance to wonder whether he knows how to assemble a bow, he's got the case up on the workbench and he's putting the bow together, moving on impulse. Bolts the limbs to the riser, strings the bow, and then heads up the stairs with the quiver. Drags a roll of carpet out the back door and props the carpet against a fence post to use as a target. Backs up toward the house. Tosses the quiver into the grass. Nocks an arrow. Raises the bow. Draws the string back toward the center of his chin until the string is pressing into the tip of his nose. Holds. Breathes.

Leaves are falling.

He lets go.

The arrow hits the carpet with a thump.

The sense of release that washes over him is incredible.

Wash is already exhausted from tearing the carpet out of the hallway, but he stands out in the backyard firing arrow after arrow until the muscles in his arms are burning and his flannel is damp with sweat, and arrow after arrow buries deep into the carpet. Fixing leaks, hanging gutters, patching shingles, he can do stuff like that, but the work is a struggle, a long and frustrating series of bent nails and fumbled wrenches. But this is different. Something he's good at. He can't remember ever feeling like this before. The pride, the satisfaction, of having and using a talent. Biscuit watches from the door, panting happily, tail wagging, as if sensing his euphoria.

Wash is scrubbing dishes after supper that night while Mia clips coupons from a brochure at the table.

"I want to go hunting," Wash announces.

"With the bow?" Mia says.

Wash thinks.

"Do you hunt?" Wash says.

"No," Mia snorts.

She sets down the scissors, folds her arms on the table, and furrows her eyebrows together, looking up at him with an inscrutable expression.

"Why don't you ask your children?" Mia says.

Jaden and Sophie are in the living room.

Jaden responds to the invitation by jumping on the ottoman, pretending to fire arrows at the lamp.

Even Sophie, busy working on a poster for a fundraiser to save stray cats from getting euthanized, wants to come along.

"You're okay with killing animals?"

"I only care about cute animals."

"Deer aren't cute?"

"Deer are snobs."

Last weekend of bow season. Hiking off-trail on public land. The dawn is cloudy. Frost crusts the mud. Wash leads the way through a stretch of cedars, touching the rubs in the bark of the trunks, explaining to the kids about glands without knowing where he learned that's why deer make the rubs. Finds a clearing. Sets up behind a fallen log at the edge of the trees, Jaden to this side with a thermos of cocoa, Sophie to that side with a thermos of coffee, whispering insults back and forth to each other. Waits. Snow begins falling. The breeze dies. The kids go quiet as a deer slips into the clearing. A buck with a crown of antlers. A fourteen-pointer. The trophy of a lifetime. The arrow hits the buck so hard that the buck gets knocked to the ground, but just as fast it staggers back up, and then it bounds off into the woods, vanishing. With Jaden and Sophie close behind, he hurries over to where the deer fell. Blood on the snow. Tracks in the mud. Wash and the kids follow the trail through the pines, past a ditch full of brambles, down a slope thick with birches, until the trail disappears just shy of a creek. By then the sun has broken through the clouds. And no matter where he searches from there, the buck can't be found.

He's just about given up looking when he notices some trampled underbrush.

Beyond, on a bed of ferns, the buck lies dead.

Jaden and Sophie dance around the kill, doing fist-pumps and cheering, and that feeling before, shooting arrows into the carpet in the backyard, is nothing compared to the feeling now.

Driveway.

Weekend.

Icicles hanging from the flag on the mailbox.

Jaden, in pajamas, boots, and a parka, is sucking on a lozenge, occasionally pushing the lozenge out with his tongue, just far enough for the lozenge to peek through his lips, then slurping the lozenge back into his mouth, while helping him shovel snow.

Wash chips at some ice.

Jaden starts to wheeze.

Wash glances over.

"What's wrong?" Wash says.

Jaden shakes his head, reaches for his throat, and falls to his knees.

Both shovels hit the ground. Wash grabs him by the shoulders and thumps his back. Jaden still can't breathe. Wash spins him and forces his mouth open in a panic. Sticks a finger in. Feels teeth, a tongue, saliva, a uvula. Finds the lozenge. Claws the lozenge. Scoops the lozenge out with a flick.

The lozenge lands in the snow.

Jaden coughs, sways, blinks some, then looks at the lozenge.

"That was awesome," Jaden grins.

*

Backyard.

Weekend.

Buds sprouting on the stems of the tree beyond the fence, where a crow is perched on a branch, not cawing, not preening, silent and still.

Sophie, in leggings, slippers, and a hoodie, is helping him to clean rugs.

Wash holds a rug up over the grass.

Sophie beats the rug with a broom.

Dust flies into the air. Coils of hair. Clumps of soil. Eventually nothing. Sophie drapes the rug over the fence, being careful to make sure that the tassels aren't touching the ground, as he reaches for the next rug. Just then the crow falls out of the tree.

The crow hits the ground with a thud.

Wash looks at the crow in shock.

The crow lies there. Doesn't move. Twitches. Struggles up again. Hops around. Then flaps back into the tree.

"Was it asleep?" Wash squints.

Sophie stares at the crow, and then bursts out laughing.

"Nobody's gonna believe us," Sophie says.

Ballpark.

Minor league.

Chaperones on a field trip for the school.

His wife comes back from a vendor with some concessions.

She hands him a frankfurter.

Wash inspects the toppings with suspicion. Rancid sauerkraut. Gummy mustard. What might be cheese.

The meat looks greasy.

"You used to love those," Mia frowns.

She trades him a pretzel.

"Guess that was the nostalgia you were tasting," Mia says.

Basement.

Jaden is hunched in the safe.

Sophie is crouched under the workbench.

Biscuit is leashed to a pipe on the boiler.

Tornado sirens howl in the distance.

"This is taking forever," Sophie says.

"I want to play a game," Jaden whines.

"We should have brought down some cards," Sophie says.

"There's nothing worse than just sitting," Jaden grumbles.

Wash presses his hands into the floor to stand.

"Don't you dare," Mia says.

Wash freezes.

"I'll be fast," Wash says.

And then, after glancing back at his wife at the foot of the stairs, goes up.

Noon, but with the lights off the house is dim, like today dusk came early. Wash hurries down the hallway toward the living room. There's a pressure in the air. In the living room he pinches his jeans to tug the legs up, then crouches over the basket of games, digging for a deck of cards.

Rising back up, tucking the cards into the pocket of his flannel, he glances over toward the doorway.

He can see the door lying in the yard next to a can of paint, where he had been painting the door when the sirens had begun to wail. The windows in the door reflect the clouds above. Through the glass is flattened grass.

The screen door, still attached to the door frame, is rattling.

Wash crosses the living room.

He stands at the door.

He touches the screen.

Sky a mix of gold and green.

Leaves tearing across the yard in a rush of wind.

He can feel his heart beat.

The screen door opens with a creak.

Wash steps out onto the porch. His jeans snap against his legs. His flannel whips against his chest. Beyond the corn across the road, past the woods beyond the field, a tornado twists in the sky.

The anniversary will be their twentieth, but their first he can remember. Having to plan some type of date makes him nervous. He would just take his wife out to eat somewhere fancy, which he knows is the standard move, but aside from the diner the other restaurants in town are all chains: a burger joint, a burrito joint, a pizza place that doesn't even have tables or chairs. Besides, he feels like this anniversary should be special, something memorable, above and beyond a candlelight dinner. Wash agonizes for weeks, at a loss what to do, worrying that he won't think of anything in time, and then while leaving work after an especially brutal shift the week before the anniversary, he notices a brochure tacked to the corkboard by the door. Wash reaches up, fingers pruny from washing dishes, and plucks the brochure down from the corkboard. The brochure advertises cabin rentals in the state park at El Dorado Reservoir.

His wife looks shocked when he tells her what the plan is, but moments later she's jotting down a list of supplies to buy and gear to pack, which seems like a form of approval.

Sophie gets left in charge of watching Jaden, with cash for emergencies and a fridge full of food, and he and his wife clear out of town. Mia paints her nails teal over the course of the drive, her frizzy hair trembling in the breeze through the windows. Wash stresses, convinced that the cabin won't be as nice as the pictures in the brochure, afraid that his wife might secretly consider the plan too outdoorsy, but the cabin turns out to be just as perfect as promised, and his wife is beaming before the duffels have even hit the floor. He's never seen her like this. At home, she never drinks alcohol, she never plays music, she's stern and practical and tireless, emptying hampers and folding laundry and cleaning the fridge and washing the dog and checking the kids did their homework and helping the kids with their homework and scheduling appointments and reading mail and paying bills and organizing the junk drawer and lugging bags of garbage out to the bin without ever stopping to rest, as if the home, not just the house but the family and the lives contained within, would completely fall apart if she allowed herself to relax for even a moment. But at the cabin she's different, already loosening up, sipping from a can of beer, cranking up the country on the radio, dancing in place at the stove as she cooks up a feast of steak and mushrooms and roasted potatoes crusted with rosemary, giving him a glimpse of who she might have been when he met her twenty years ago, a twenty-year-old girl with a sense of humor and a lopsided smile and few if any responsibilities. He's liked his wife for as long as he can remember, but watching her dance around at the stove makes him feel something new, something powerful, tender, warm. He can tell that the feeling is strong, but even though he knows how strong the feeling is, and though he can't imagine how a feeling could possibly be any stronger, he's not sure whether or not there's still another feeling that's even stronger out there. He can't remember being in love.

Has no spectrum to place the feeling on. Doesn't know what the limit for emotions is. Does he like her, or really like her, or really really like her, or really really really like her?

After the meal he leans back with his bare feet flat on the floor and his hands folded together on his gut, stuffed with starch and butter and meat and grease, buzzed from the beer. His wife usually doesn't involve him in parenting decisions, just signs the consent forms and checks the movie ratings herself. But for once she's actually consulting him about the kids, leaning across the table with her chin on the placemat, toying absentmindedly with the tab on a can.

"There are these acne pills Sophie keeps asking to try."

"She gets like a single pimple at a time."

"Should we let her or not?"

"For one zit?"

"So no."

Then:

"Do you think Jaden is getting picked on?"

"What makes you say that?"

"He keeps coming home with ripped clothes."

"He's just wild."

"You're sure?"

Wash feels a flush of pride. He likes when his wife asks his opinion. Maybe it's only because of the anniversary weekend, but he hopes it signals a permanent change.

"I got us something," Mia says suddenly, pushing up off of the table to stand, looking almost giddy. She goes out to the car, pops the trunk, digs under a tarp, and comes back lugging an unmarked cardboard box topped with a silver bow. The present is nearly as long as the table.

Wash takes ahold of the flap and rips through the tape.

Lifts the lid.

A rifle.

"Whoa," Wash says.

The gun lies on a pad of foam. Carbon barrel. Walnut stock. A repeater. A bolt-action. He reaches into the box, but then hesitates, looking to her for permission.

"Take it out," Mia laughs.

The moment he picks up the rifle a sense of relief washes over him. Like having a severed limb suddenly reattached. A natural extension of his body. Automatically he pulls the bolt back to check whether the chamber is empty, then shuts the breech and raises the gun, butt to his shoulder, stock on his cheek, his eye at the scope, testing the sights. The smell of the oil. The feel of the trigger. He can already tell that he's skilled with this thing.

"Are we allowed to have this?" Wash says.

"You're not, but technically I'm the owner, I did all the research, and as long as you don't have access, we're in the clear, so we'll just keep the gun in the safe and if anybody ever asks then we'll say that you don't know the combo. And honestly, on my honor, I did want to have a gun in the house again just in case of intruders. A pistol or a shotgun probably would have been better for that, though. I went with this because of you. You can use it for target shooting out back, even use it for deer hunting if you want. I thought it all through. We'll just be careful. Nobody's going to know."

His chair creaks as she settles onto his lap.

He's overwhelmed.

"I love you," Wash says, without meaning to, the words just coming out.

He sets the rifle onto the table to kiss her, but an expression of alarm flashes across her face, and before he can lean closer she drops her head, with her chin to her sternum. Confused, he waits for her to look back up. Her hands rest on his shoulders. Her ass weighs on his thighs. She's trembling suddenly. No, he realizes, she's crying.

He can't remember ever seeing her cry before.

The sight scares him.

"What's wrong?" Wash frowns.

When she finally responds she speaks in a murmur.

"You're hardly you at all anymore."

"What does that mean?"

"You're just so different."

"Different how?"

Mia goes silent for a moment.

"You never did dishes before."

"Well, it wasn't my job back then, right?" Wash says.

"I mean at home," Mia explodes, shoving him in frustration, startling him.

"But after the meatloaf, you told me that's how things worked, was you doing the cooking and me doing the dishes," Wash says.

"I was kidding, I didn't think you'd actually do them, but then you got up from the table after we finished eating and you just started washing dishes, you'd never washed a dish in that house before in your life, you never used to play games with the kids, you never used to bring the kids along hunting, I always had to nag you to fix things around the house and even after you were done fixing things then you'd get on me for nagging you, I could barely get you to give the kids a ride somewhere without you throwing a fit, all you wanted to do was work and hunt and be alone in the woods, or rant at me about political stuff that there was nothing I could do anything about, we don't even fight anymore, I tried to pretend that you're the same but you're not, you're the same body, you move the same, you smell the same, you talk the same, you taste the same, but the rest of you is gone, you don't remember the tomato juice when I was pregnant with Jaden, you don't remember the fire alarm after I gave birth to Sophie, everything that used to have a secret meaning between us now is just a thing, to you a hay bale is just a hay bale, a batting helmet is just a batting helmet, a mosquito bite is just a mosquito bite, and that's not what they are to me," Mia cries, hitting his chest with her fists, "we lost our past, we lost our history," hitting his chest with her fists, "and you deserved it," a fist, "I didn't," a fist, "not me."

Wash sits there in terror, letting her beat on him, until finally she clutches his tee in her hands and sinks her head into his chest in exhaustion. His skin tingles with pain where the blows landed. His heart pounds from the shock of being struck. Wash glances at the blotchy sunspots on his hands, the faint scars on his fingers, the bone spurs on his heels, the brittle calluses on his soles, relics of years he can't remember living. He's never felt so much like a stranger in this body.

He's almost too shaken to speak.

"Which one do you want?" Wash says.

"Which what?"

"Which me?"

Mia heaves a sigh, then lifts her head, turns her face away, and rises off of him. She shuffles toward the bathroom. "I never would've gotten a gun again if you were the way you used to be."

Midnight. He lies next to his wife in the dark. The sheets are thinner than at home. The pillows are harder than at home. He can't remember ever having spent a night away from home before.

He's gotten so used to falling asleep with her nuzzled against him that trying to fall asleep with her facing away from him is intensely lonely. His feet are cold. An owl hoots down by the reservoir.

Does he love his wife?

Did he ever love his wife before?

Lindsay is sitting on the chair in the living room. She's wearing the same outfit as every month. She tucks her hair behind her ears, then bends to grab a toy from the floor, a plastic bone that squeaks when squeezed.

"This is the last time we'll have to meet," Lindsay says.

"We're done?"

Lindsay looks up with a smile.

"Next month will mark a full year since your wipe. By the standards of our justice department, you've been officially reintroduced to your life. Congratulations."

Lindsay tosses the toy down the hallway.

Biscuit takes off running.

Wash thinks.

"There's something I don't understand."

"What's that?"

"What happens if you commit another crime after you've had a wipe like mine? What else could they even do to me if they've already taken everything?"

"They took the memories you had back then. You have new memories they could take."

Wash frowns.

"If you're being sentenced to a partial wipe, a shorter sentence is better than a longer sentence, of course. But for a life sentence, the numbers are meaningless. Is it worse when a sixty-year-old dies than when a six-year-old dies? Of course not. The length of a life has nothing to do with the weight of the loss."

Wash settles back into the couch, folding his arms across his chest, tucking his hands into his pits.

"That's important for you to understand," Lindsay says.

Wash glances over.

"You have another life you could lose now," Lindsay says.

Biscuit drops the bone back onto the floor.

Lindsay reaches down.

"How do you feel, Washington?"

"I feel really good," Wash says.

Mia calls him into the bathroom. She's sitting on the lid of the toilet in drawstring sweatpants and a baggy undershirt. The pregnancy test is lying on the side of the tub.

"We're both going to remember this one," Mia says, smiling up at him.

His kids barge into the bathroom a moment later, already fighting about what to name the baby.

Wash goes shopping for a crib with his family, pushing a cart down the bright aisles of a department store as swing music plays over the speakers. Wash reclines on a checkered blanket at the park as fireworks burst in the sky above his family, shimmering and fading. Wash hunches over the wastebasket in the bedroom, clipping the nails on his fingers as his wife pops the battery from a watch on the dresser. Wash leans over the sink in the bathroom, tweezing a hair from his nose as his wife gathers dirty towels from the hook on the door. Wash shoots holes into a target shaped like the silhouette of a person as his kids watch from the stump of an oak tree, sipping cans of soda. And wherever he's at, and whatever he's doing, there's something that's stuck in his mind like a jingle, nagging him.

He sits on the porch with the dog. Rain drips from the awning. Silks are showing on the husks of corn across the road. Summer is already almost gone. Behind him, through the screens in the windows, sounds of his family talking drift out of the house.

Sometimes he does want to be alone. Sometimes he feels so lazy that he wants to refuse to help with chores. Sometimes he gets so tense that he has an urge to punch a wall.

But maybe all of that is trivial compared to how he used to be.

Is he a different person now?

Has he been becoming somebody new?

Or does he have some soul, an inborn nature, a congenital personality, that's bound to express itself eventually?

The academic year hasn't started yet, but the athletic seasons have begun. He's on the way to pick up the kids from practice when he passes the library. His eyes flick from the road to the rearview, watching the library fade into the distance as the truck rushes on toward the school.

Knowing who he was might not even be an option. What he did might never even have made the news. And he's already running late anyway. But still his hands clench tight around the wheel.

Swearing, he hangs a U-ey, swinging the truck back around.

He parks at the library.

"I need to use a computer," Wash says.

The librarian asks him for identification, registers him for an account, and then brings him over to a computer. All that time he's thinking, what are you doing, what are you doing, what are you doing, imagining his kids waiting for him by the fence at the school. The librarian heads back to the reference desk.

His hands are trembling as he reaches for the keyboard.

He logs onto the computer, pulls up a browser, and searches his name.

The screen blinks as the results appear.

Nothing. A pop star with his name. A goalie. A beach resort with his name. A monument. He's not there.

He skims through again to be sure, and then laughs out loud in relief.

The temptation was a mirage all along.

Wash swivels on the chair to stand, then thinks of something, and hesitates.

He turns back around.

Puts his fingers on the keyboard.

Tries his name plus his town.

The screen blinks as the results change.

His heart leaps.

He's there.

The list of articles seems to scroll on forever.

The headlines alone are enough to send a beat of rage pulsing through him.

Wash runs his hands over his mouth, glancing at the daylight streaming into the library through the door beyond the computer, trying to decide whether to leave now or to keep reading, flashing through all of the memories he has from the past year that he could lose. Jaden grinning in amazement after choking on the lozenge in the driveway. Sophie cracking up laughing after the crow fell out of the tree. Mia treading water at the reservoir in a white one-piece, glancing at him with a casual expression before suddenly lunging over to dunk him. Jaden lying on the linoleum in the kitchen in cutoff shorts, gripping him by the ankle, begging to be taken to the go-kart track. Jaden whirling around the yard with a lit sparkler. Mia swinging by the diner on a day off from the hospital, hair piled into a bun, trench coat damp with rain, splitting a slice of cherry pie with him while he's on break. Sophie standing under the light in the kitchen in pajamas, holding him by the arm, upset by a dream about a ghost. Sophie singing into a lit sparkler like a microphone. Mia arranging gourds on the porch. Mia brushing icicles from the awning. Mia sweating into a damp washcloth, deliriously rambling about how much she loves him, as he crouches by the bed with the wastebasket, waiting there in case she pukes again. The dog watching a butterfly flutter down the hallway, then turning to look at him, as if waiting for an explanation. His kids dancing around the dead buck, boots tromping through snowy ferns, gloved hands raised in celebration, lit by the dazzling sunbeams spiking through the branches of the trees, and afterward driving back to the house with the deer in the bed of the truck, the mighty antlers rising into the air out the window behind the cab, the kids chattering to each other on the seat next to him, hats both off, hair all disheveled, and later eating bowls of cereal in the kitchen in thermal underwear together as the kids recount the story of the hunt with wild gestures, while his wife sits across the table in a plaid nightgown, smiling over a mug of black tea. The secret experiences that nobody else shared. The joy of discovering the chocolate stash hidden in the aluminum tin in the basement. The habit he's made of visiting the glittering display of chandeliers and pendants and lamps and sconces whenever he goes to the hardware store, marveling at the rich glow of the mingled lights, filtered through the tinted glass and the colored shades. The sense of destiny when a bottle of cola suddenly plunked into the dispenser of a vending machine at the shopping mall as he was walking out of the bathroom. The fear and the awe and the wonder of seeing a monstrous tornado churn in the sky above the town, the funnel spiraling down from the clouds, the tip just about to touch the ground.

Wash sits back in the chair, looking from the door to the computer, biting his lip as he wavers, torn between the possibility of having a future and the possibility of having a past. But only for a moment. Because when he thinks about it, he knows who he is. He already knows what he'll do.

S. P. SOMTOW

Another Avatar

FROM *Amazing Stories*

The laws of nature are very much like the laws of Thailand; you can get around them if you know the right people.
—*The Tall Old Man*

ONE DAY, A tall old man stands in the doorway and says he has come for me. He says we shall go on a journey. When I ask him why, he tells me this: "So that one day you shall stand in a doorway, and you shall tell a boy that you have come to take him on a journey. And when he asks why, you shall tell him, 'So that one day you shall stand in a doorway such as this, and say these words to a child such as yourself.'"

My journey has been long, yet I have not reached the time when I shall stand in a stranger's doorway and call out to an unknown youth. It all unfolds in a continuous long present, yesterday and today all jumbled up like a basket of silk scraps in the fabric market.

Back then, to the twenty-first century. The breath of the Dragon Jade had not yet warmed the world. It was a time when children on street corners cried out that the world was ending, little knowing it had already ended.

Back also to a city. A teeming city, exotic to some. A city of metal spires and desolate landfills, of glass malls and porcelain pagodas, a city that, in those days, remade itself nightly in the moments before dawn so that you could sometimes wake in the morning not knowing where you were; if you've lived there, you'd know, and if you haven't, no amount of explaining will ever be enough.

I'll tell you everything I know, and it will all come out in one big jumble, and sometimes you'll believe me, and sometimes you'll say it can't be so, but stay with me. Every event in the world has at least two explanations: one that is fact, and one that is the truth.

Bangkok, the early twenty-first century. A Catholic orphanage beside a Buddhist temple, a Hindu shrine abutting an internet café, and all this sandwiched between high-rises and a shanty town; that's where the tall old man first comes to me.

April is the hottest month. The water festival, which proclaims the coming of the long monsoon, has come and gone; we're well into May, and it's still the hottest month. When our story begins I'm a hot little boy, sweating as I labor in a hot airless shed, because the corrugated iron walls keep the hot air in and there's not even an electric fan.

I'm an orphan, of course. To play this role, the tall old man once told me, you either have to be an orphan or at the very least grow up with surrogates, suspecting the whole time that you have a different parentage, perhaps divine. Usually, you had been given a dire prediction when you were born—you were going to kill your father and marry your mother, or you were going to bring about the downfall of the entire empire, so your loving parents, after shedding many a tear, wrapped you in a swaddling cloth and abandoned you by the mountainside, or floated you downstream in a reed boat. In my case, they leave you on the doorstep of Sacred Heart with a basket, a blanket, and a dagger.

Then, when you came of age, you'd learn who you really were, draw a sword from a stone, and go off to find your father's castle, marrying princesses, slaying dragons, and saving the universe along the way before attaining your rightful place on the throne.

When the old man told me all this, I smiled a little, because you should never offend an older person, but I didn't see how it applied to me.

Until—

The orphanage is run by the brothers, but they respect our culture, so early each morning they send us to the temple next door where a young monk named Phra Athit tells us the story of Buddha. After lunch, we learn about Jesus. We walk by the Hindu shrine, which is catty-corner from the Buddhist temple, and we always make a quick obeisance to Ganesha, the elephant god who lives there, just in case—although the brothers sort of lump in Hinduism under Buddhism, so we don't get three daily doses of religion.

Father Duvalier explained it thus, one day: "The Catholic Church is like a great big ocean liner taking you to heaven. Now, there are all these rickety little boats that could get you there, too. All your little pagan religions, not to mention the Protestants, but they're more like bamboo rafts lashed together with twine. Now wouldn't you rather be on the ocean liner than the rickety boat? Of course, it's up to you. That's what we call free will. Now, hands up who wants to take the big ship."

The hands went up rather unenthusiastically. Video night the previous week had been *Titanic.*

We also learn English, because, as Father Duvalier has told us many times, English is the key that will release us from the slum. Thai, he tells us, may be the language of love, that's true, but it's also the language of hierarchy and class and subjugation; English, which only has one word for "I" and one word for "you," is the great leveler, and with English any of us urchins could end up as a CEO in one of those glittering high-rises. With Thai, we'll be cleaning toilets in that selfsame high-rise.

It's a nice theory, but I never heard of any CEO in Bangkok who came from a slum, though if they did come from one, they probably weren't talking.

My name is Krit, but the brothers call me Kris. This is because they don't know that in Thai, when there's an *s* on the end of a word, it's pronounced as a *t.* You'd think that was obvious, but to them it's not. Nothing is obvious to them. (The Jesuits are the worst.) The fathers are all *farangs,* but though their skin is white (or in some cases pink) they all think they know everything about us Thais. The brothers are a mix of *farang* and Thai.

Father Duvalier, the head of the whole place, has explained to me the meaning of my name: it's a magical knife, he said, wielded by mythological heroes. Well, it's more a dagger or dirk, sort of, and it's all twisty. I was about to ask him for more details, but there was immediately a clamor in the classroom.

"What about my name, Father?"

"And mine?"

So, Father Du—that's a little Thai joke: *du* means strict, bad-tempered, ready to punish, and in fact Father Du beat us less often than any of the others, and often strayed from the subject completely—so, Father Duvalier spent a few minutes telling us the meanings of each of our names. But I knew mine was special because he'd named me himself. That's because I was abandoned on the doorstep in a basket, so I didn't come with a name already attached. Most of the others did.

This classroom I'm talking about, it's still there; it's more of a shed, really, and the desks and chairs are castoffs from a rather posh boarding school that a lot of children of politicians and CEOs go to. They're always upgrading their school desks, to our benefit.

Father Du is a high-profile father. He goes to social events, has an internet newsletter, and collects money from America. He's got a framed photograph of himself with the queen on his wall. He's written a couple of books about us, and they're not even that patronizing. In his own way, he does love us; that's why the orphanage isn't some soulless hole of horror with savage beatings and child abuse. Oh, it's grim, but we could be sleeping on the street, sniffing glue, and selling ourselves to tourists.

On the evening that my story starts, we've done the Buddhism thing, and we've done the Jesus thing; it's afternoon now, so many of the boys are off working. You may say, oh, it's child labor, oh, it's exploitation, but it's not like that: as long as it's not selling amphetamines, the brothers like us to have a sense of our own self-worth, our own money, even if it's just a twenty-baht note after a hard day's slog.

I'm in the classroom alone. And it's hot. That's where I started, isn't it? It's May and it hasn't rained yet. I'm collecting all the schoolbooks, arranging them in piles. I'm not a good reader, so I arrange them in stacks according to color. I've been doing that for years, and now everybody is used to my system. It's such a hot day that the air itself is sweating. Through the foul air that blows in from the stagnant canal, you can get a whiff of jasmine and incense from the temple. There's also a strong scent of bananas. That's because we've been collecting bananas from everyone in the slum. We're all going to offer a platter of bananas to Ganesha tomorrow, which is Wednesday, which is sacred to Ganesha, because my friend P'Waen has had a dream that he's going to win the lottery, and in his dream, there were a lot of mice, and everyone knows that Ganesha is the patron of all rodents.

The sun is going to set soon, and a tall old man stands in the doorway. I know before I see or hear him: I don't know how I know, but there he is.

"Krit," he says to me. When I look up, I am immediately surprised, because, although he is a *farang*, he knows how to say my name properly.

"Are you the new teacher?"

"Well, yes." He comes into the shed and I see that he's really tall; he stoops. I think he's old, but really he doesn't look old, he just has oldness somehow clinging to him. It's in his eyes. When he speaks to me, he does speak Thai, not badly either; he says the words funny, but he uses very sophisticated ones, like the ones you hear on TV soaps.

"Krit," he says, "I am Mr. Leopold Strange, the new English teacher. I'm here in Thailand because I'm fleeing an unsavory past. Maybe you can imagine what that might be."

"Yes, I can," I say. "When a *farang* shows up in Bangkok with an unsavory past, it usually means only one thing." I think about Gary Glitter, the English pop star, indicted in Cambodia for chasing the girls. "Should I worry about you?"

"Why, yes, Kris, you should."

I start to get nervous. I stop putting the books into piles and I look Mr. Strange straight in the eye. "I know a thing or two," I say, "and I don't think you're telling me everything."

"That's true," he says. Then, he tells me what I've told you: there are the facts, and there is the truth.

"The facts: I'm a washed-up writer of mediocre fantasy novels from England. Actually they're probably very good novels, they always got good reviews, but when it comes to sales, I was no J. K. Rowling, or I wouldn't be here. And okay, there was a scandal: I got a little too intimate with one of my readers. I should have known better. You know how pushy fans can be? No, I suppose you don't. But now, I am persona non grata. After the exposé in the *Sun*—oh, it was all lies, but who cares?—I couldn't have published a book if my name was Stephen King. So what could I do? Teach English in the third world, and that's where I've been: Colombia, Sri Lanka, and now here. But you know as well as I do that those are only the facts . . . they're not the truth."

"How is it that I know?"

"Because that's why I've come for you."

Sitting there in that dingy room with the stifling sweating air, I suddenly know there's more than one kind of truth, and that some people are more than they seem to be. I know that Mr. Strange and I belong to another kind of people, that we see things differently, and that we know things to be true that other people can only guess or have theories about.

And I find myself telling him the things he was going to tell me: "You're some kind of guardian, some kind of . . . I don't know what it's called . . . some kind of *avatar.* And um, well, there's a mission, and you've come to me because I've got . . . um . . . superpowers?"

I know that word "avatar" because in Buddhism school, the young monks also tell us stories about gods and demons, and how they often come down to Earth as avatars, to fight their cosmic battles in our world. I always loved those stories, but I never dreamed I would actually be in one.

"And how do you know all this?" asks Mr. Strange.

"I just know!"

"And what language have we been speaking?"

At this, I am struck dumb. Haven't we just been having a normal conversation? He's been using a lot of long words that I didn't think I knew. And everything seems, I don't know, vivid. But wait —did my lips move?

Did his?

"I think that's enough excitement for one day, Krit," says Mr. Strange. "Stay behind after class tomorrow, and we'll talk missions and superpowers."

It is at that moment that I notice he's eating all the bananas. Not peeling them, mind you, but scarfing them whole, positively inhaling them.

"Mr. Strange, those bananas are for Ganesha!"

"So?" he says. "It's already Wednesday in New Zealand."

It seems as though I look away for just one second, and when I look back he's gone. I run to the doorway, but all I see is a trail of dust. Who is he, really? Can he fly? Is it true that he's been speaking directly into my mind, showing me things that words can't possibly express? It's all too weird for me. I go back to cleaning the shed, and then, since it's just about suppertime, I traipse on down to the refectory, where the other boys are already starting to gather, arriving by twos and threes from their jobs or from their football practice. The boys have a team which they have, perhaps overreaching a bit, christened Man U. You might think that they were fans of Manchester United, but the boys of Sacred Heart actually favor Liverpool, on the whole; it's just that the two loudest jocks in the school happened to be named Man and Yu. (Or did they get those nicknames from playing football all the time and being pretty much attached at the hip?)

Next week, they are playing against an extremely snooty private boys' boarding school. The snooty school's board believes that having these games will make them appear to be "one with the people." The brothers, on the other hand, believe that by allowing such games, they are giving us opportunities to socialize with our betters, and might somehow become better ourselves because of the experience. This may not be a very Christian viewpoint, but it's pretty typical of the brothers. As for what the boys think . . . well, no one asks.

I'm waiting for my friend P'Waen, who is called Waen because he wears glasses. He is not nearsighted. He found the glasses on a seat on the Skytrain one day. Because they were on the seat, no one sat there, even though the car was crammed. He seized the opportunity. It's the only time a little nobody like him was ever able to actually sit down on the Skytrain, so he wears the glasses for luck. He can only see without them.

I call him P' because he is like my older brother and it's respectful. I call everyone in the orphanage who is older than me P', but the other kids think it's quaint and pretentious. If you are reading this and you don't speak Thai, this word is pronounced like the word for urine.

By the time I'm through, you'll understand how I got so good at English.

Let me get back to the refectory. It's a fancy word for a canvas awning spread over a concrete yard, with old plumbing pipes holding it up. There are some wooden trestle tables, and there is a big window into the kitchen, where Auntie Daeng cooks our slop in gigantic pots. The morning slop is rice soup with some ground pork floating in it and plenty of coriander and scallions; the lunch slop is usually noodles with fish balls and bean sprouts; the evening slop varies according to what Auntie was able to get cheaply in the market, but there's always rice and two side dishes: mystery-meat curry and fried mystery vegetable (extra salty).

Tomorrow, Mr. Strange is going to use the word "Dickensian" to refer to the eating arrangements in the orphanage, and I actually know what that word means because last year, the brothers showed *Oliver* on movie night. We all wondered why Oliver wanted to escape a perfectly comfy institution and enter a life of crime, but *farangs* see the world differently than we do. Now, one day a month, thanks to an American philanthropist, we get hamburgers and ice cream. Of course, Oliver didn't get that. But he lived in England, which is a dismal place where people don't even have rice to eat.

After supper, we all have to wear our orphanage regulation pajamas, which consist of blue shorts with an elastic waistband, and a white T-shirt with the logo of the orphanage, which is a red heart, like a valentine. We're told that it is not in fact a valentine, but the Sacred Heart of Jesus. So, supper is our last chance to look different from each other. It's hard enough with the same extra-short haircuts, but we all try.

The footballers are wearing a variety of football shirts from different teams, donated by kids from one of the British schools. When I see P'Waen, he's very smartly dressed for an orphan, with an actual shirt with a collar which he has found time to iron, and long pants. I'm impressed. I run up to him because I want to tell him about Mr. Strange scarfing the bananas, but he starts talking before I can.

"Sneak out with me tonight! You have to!"

"Why tonight?"

"Because you have to, that's why. It's my dream, you know, the lottery, the mice—"

"Look, P'Waen, something happened to the bananas. I'm sorry, I couldn't stop it in time—"

"You don't understand. I already have the number! I found it, you know, in the tree."

There is a big, ancient tree just beyond the refectory awning: they say it's a magic tree. The brothers say it's superstition, but well, look who's talking—pieces of bread that turn into human flesh without anyone even noticing, regular as clockwork every Sunday—if you can swallow that, and believe me, the brothers do swallow it . . .

Everyone is piling up to the window to grab their food, but Waen is so excited he doesn't even want to eat. He grabs me by the arm and steers me toward the tree, while I'm more inclined to gravitate toward the mystery meat (today it's in green curry, tomorrow it will be red, yellow the day after). But okay, I follow. Every old and twisted-looking tree in Thailand houses a spirit. This one must, because even though it's on a Catholic property, someone has been hanging garlands on the branches, winding colored ribbons around the trunk, and burning incense sticks nearby. I see the red, burnt-up stalks of the joss sticks poking out of nooks in the tree, and there's little scraps of yellow wax, too, from the candles people burn here when no one is looking.

"Feel, feel!" He kneels, and so do I; Waen takes my hand and holds it against the bark, a certain crevice, and tells me to rub.

I don't feel anything.

But I hear—inside my head—*919*. I say it aloud and he shushes me. "Quiet, quiet, it's our secret!"

Then there's a thundering voice: "No whispering in the refectory!"

It's one of the Thai brothers, Brother Poo (oh yes, that means crab, do you think his parents knew what it means in English?); he's walking grimly up and down the perimeter of the covered area, wielding a ruler to quell us unruly boys with. He even uses it. I see one of the soccer boys shaking his right hand ruefully. The *farang* brothers hardly ever hit us, though they threaten more. I think it's because, even if you have to pass some kind of heartlessness exam to become a brother, the warmth and easygoing culture of Thailand sort of corrupts them.

I don't particularly want to feel the sting of that metal ruler on my hand, so I go and get my rice and curry, as does Waen. We sit down at the farthest possible end of one of the tables so we can go on talking.

"Waen," I say, "I didn't actually feel that number in the bark of the magic tree."

"Of course you did, Krit!" he says. "You said it right out loud."

"But it wasn't in the tree. I think I . . . I somehow heard you."

"But I didn't say anything."

"But . . . it's like you did."

Right then and there, a chill grabs hold of me. It's more freezing than an upper-class shopping mall. Because now, I suddenly divine what the tall old man meant. *How do you know all this?* His lips hadn't moved! I heard Waen speak to me, louder than if he'd really been talking. Which means I was able to hear inside of him. This is scary. My instinct tells me not to say anything.

Anyway, I listen some more, watching P'Waen's lips, and it doesn't happen again. On the other hand, he's jabbering away and maybe that drowns out what he's thinking. He's saying, "Listen,

Krit, since I found out about this number I've been trying to buy a lottery ticket all day and I can't find nine-one-nine anywhere. But tonight, there's a major funeral over at the temple. They're bound to have lottery tickets. You've got to sneak out with me. If I go alone, I'll get caught, but somehow you never do."

When Waen says there's going to be a funeral, I know exactly which funeral he means. It's the funeral for this general who was very famous for fighting the communists, back in the days when they had communists, of course. All funerals have lottery-ticket hawkers, because everyone knows that being near a corpse brings good fortune; but a general this powerful is going to be particularly *heng.* I wonder why his family chose to have the ceremonies in this un-high-society part of town. If we can't find the number from Waen's head at this funeral, we won't find it anywhere.

"We'll sneak out when the brothers are on their way into compline," Waen informs me. Suddenly I understand why he's so well dressed. He wants to blend.

"I've nothing to wear," I say.

"So go scruffy," he says. "They'll just think you're a *dek wat.* You'll blend."

Sometimes I think the *dek wats* have it easier than we do. Most of them aren't orphans; they're country boys whose parents have sent them to the temple for a few years to learn proper manners and to earn merit for their next life by sweeping and dusting and carrying the monks' begging bowls. But they get the leftovers from the begging bowls, and everyone knows that monks get the best food.

We eat in silence for a while. Waen can't see his food clearly because of his glasses; he's constantly stabbing the table with his spoon. "Take them off!" I tell him. "Don't draw attention! Wait until compline."

Sneaking out during or after compline is always a good idea. Our brothers observe silence from the end of compline until dawn, which means that there's not much they can do about anything. The lay teachers don't live in the orphanage, but there's always one who stays to supervise the dormitory.

Tonight, the sleepers' watchman is going to be Uncle Wong, who used to be an orphan himself and now owns a Chinese restaurant in Yaowaraj. He made good, so he volunteers one day a week to repay the brothers. But since he used to live in this dorm himself, he tends to turn a blind eye. Or maybe it's just that he's always too drunk to notice.

We eat quickly, trying not to talk too much. Talking is actually forbidden during supper, but the brothers tolerate it as long as it's not too rowdy. When it's done, the brothers say a blessing. It's in very bizarre, "Catholic" Thai with weird words which no one understands, but in the end we all join in in a sort of boyish shout, making it sound more like a football cheer than a prayer: *decha phra naam phra bida lae phra butr lae phra chit amen,* which means something like "in the holy name of the holy father and the holy son and the holy mind amen" as far as I can figure. The brothers believe that these are three gods that are really one god, much like Brahma, Shiva, and Vishnu from the shrine across the street.

Then, Father Du has an announcement. "There will be no dessert tomorrow," he says, "because all the bananas are missing from the kitchen. Now, you know that these sorts of pranks just hurt everyone, so if one of you will confess, we'll stage a public caning and I will have new bananas purchased from the discretionary fund. You see, honesty will be rewarded, even if there's a bit of pain beforehand, just as our dear Lord was scourged and crucified in order to allow all of us to attain paradise."

I'm puzzled. I mean, Mr. Strange guzzled a plate of them without peeling them, but has he already been in the kitchen as well? They keep hundreds of bananas there. Deep-fried bananas with crunchy breading, stewed bananas in coconut cream sauce, sliced bananas, bananas wrapped in cheese—the things they can do with bananas on an orphanage-type budget are impressive. It can't have been Mr. Strange.

Another announcement: "Someone has tampered with the mousetraps in the video room. That person will be found and punished."

I can't help smiling at this. I know it's Waen. He fixed the traps after he had his little epiphany about the lottery. Tomorrow, if he wins the lottery, he'll confess and get six whacks. If he doesn't win, he won't confess. That's fair, isn't it?

"Finally, I want to tell you all we will have a distinguished English teacher who will take over from Brother Adam, starting tomorrow. English class will be right after Thai history, right after Jesus hour. Mr. Leopold Strange is a famous writer. He was once nominated for the Hugo Award."

"What's that?" a boy shouts.

"Quiet!" Brother Poo raises his rod of chastisement.

"You don't scare me!" comes another voice. Brother Poo whips around and scowls.

"Children, children," says Father Duvalier, "we're not actually sure what the Hugo Award is. It's some American thing."

After supper we are all supposed to bathe, a habit which Waen abhors; water frightens him. He claims that he had a near-death experience at the seaside. None of the rest of us have ever been there, so maybe it's true.

The communal bath at the orphanage is like this: there is a long trough in the middle of the room, which the bath monitor fills from a plastic hose. Each of us has a plastic bowl with our name written on it in indelible marker; they hang on a rack at the bathroom door. We also have a little cloth bag with our toothbrush and toothpaste. There is a little pigeonhole for all our clothes.

The brother on duty blows a whistle, and we take our bags and line up on both sides of the trough. On the next whistle, we start dishing up the water in the bowls and pouring it over ourselves. We keep our shorts on, of course; the Thais are much more modest than *farangs,* who parade around with it all hanging out (we've seen the brothers in their shower, which has hot water—who knows why, you'd have thought this country was hot enough already). We pour the water over ourselves in a regular rhythm. Then, whistle, soap; whistle, rinse. No talking, no horseplay of course, though you should see what happens when one of the less observant brothers is monitoring.

Brushing our teeth is much more of a musical exercise because the brother will insist on one tweet for every stroke of the brush . . . tweet up, tweet down, tweet up, tweet down. By the end of it, we feel like we've been working our way through a song and dance number at the transvestite cabaret down the road.

Speaking of transvestites, one of the boys in my dorm, Pek, is a *katoey.* He's in the orphanage because his parents didn't want to pay for the operation. He has decided to become a priest instead, because the vestments are as close to a dress as he will ever be able to afford. But more about him later.

I'm brushing next to Pek tonight because Waen is already hiding in the video-room closet. I can't help making fun of his mannerisms when he brushes. He says (between tweets), "Really, P'Krit. Don't be mean."

He's the only other boy in the orphanage who uses "P" as a form of address instead of "Hey, you."

"I'm not trying to be mean. One just can't help it, with you."

He knows I care about him, really, so he just giggles.

TWEEEEEEEET!!!!

Time to grab our towels and, oh, yes, a quick murmured recital of the magic mantra about the father, the son, and the holy something-or-other. Then, into the sleeping uniforms, and an hour for TV, reading, ping-pong, or internet. There's also a fifth favored activity: being beaten up by Man and Yu. Favored by at least two of us, anyway.

There are only two computers, but they are broadband, so the seventy-eight boys fight over them. In practice, a boy named P'Fat (the nickname is from babyhood, he is actually thin as a rake and really, really tall) is the guardian of the roster, but he can always be bribed. The brothers like him. He and Pek are the only ones who actually believe in any of this stuff and have even said they want to be priests. On the other hand, the brothers can't quite come to terms with Pek's reasoning . . .

Next year, I will be thirteen, so I will have one extra hour to fidget and fight over who goes online.

The brothers are off chanting to their threefold god. Uncle Wong has already arrived and has already hit the bottle. The video room is a big, messy place with donated plastic armchairs that don't match and three TVs that get louder and louder until someone yells, then start soft again. Boys are everywhere, wrestling, throwing things, seriously cussing (thankfully, the brothers never seem to know quite enough Thai to catch everything we say). The broom closet, I know, is where P'Waen is hiding.

I know the routine.

"Uncle Wong," I say, "can I be the one to close down tonight?"

No one ever wants the job . . . it's extra work.

"Sucking up, eh, Krit?" he says. "Sure." And takes another swig. It's Mekong whiskey. Deadly stuff.

I can't wait for the entertainment hour to be over. The constantly crescendoing noise from the three TVs, which show a soap opera, a music video, and a boxing match—the three main interests of us boys—gets on my nerves so much that I just want it to stop. I'm about ready to scream, but I can't scream, so I just keep thinking and thinking and thinking—

Stop! I think.

And it stops.

Just for a split second. Not just the TV sets. It's as if all the noise in the universe suddenly stops. Not for long. For a heartbeat.

And everyone turns around and looks at me.

I whip around to see who they're looking at. It's definitely me. I start to shrug, but—

Then it's all back again, noisy as ever, the whole chaotic madness. As though nothing happened. The computers are whizzing, popping, and clicking, and the boxing match is gearing up for a knockout.

But everybody knows something happened.

"Damn electricity," Uncle Wong says. "The church ought to pay its bills."

The ping-pong, the TV watching, the internet goes on. Only it's subdued.

What did I do?

Since meeting Mr. Strange, things have been strange. Do I really have superpowers? Am I really an unknown hero with a secret identity?

I think it's going to be an interesting English lesson.

P'Waen comes out of the closet blinking because he's been in the dark for an hour. "Brought you some civilian clothes," he says. I quickly slip on the white shirt over my orphanage tee; if I button it up, that will be enough of a disguise.

"Are you sure you want to do this?" I say. "You shouldn't believe everything a tree tells you."

In Canada, there's a Catholic orphanage where they beat you every day and the police run you down with sirens if you try to escape. We've all seen it on one of the video nights. The film won a lot of awards. Okay, Sacred Heart isn't like that at all. There are no locks. Once in a blue moon, someone even gets adopted!

Why would you run away? It's a jungle out there. Slip out for a lark, and if you get caught, take your whacks with a grin; that's all fine. But run away?

Bangkok is a city with ten million or more people, where the buildings transform themselves overnight, where the traffic gridlocks for hours yet everyone's in an infernal hurry; it's a dangerous place, and I've seen less of it than most tourists. My world is less than a kilometer square and, thanks, I'm happy to stay.

We have to hurry. We are only going to catch the tail end of the funeral. It's the back of the temple that abuts on our slum. The front is a grand facade where, I'm sure, all the general's well-wishers are pulling up in their long black cars.

We creep up to Pavilion No. 9 from the back. There are other pavilions with their own funerals going on—since every funeral in Bangkok lasts at least seven days, it's an assembly-line process in any major temple—but No. 9 is the biggie. The pavilion itself is air-conditioned, which means it has been endowed by a wealthy family. We don't get in, of course, because it's packed. We don't want to get in, anyway.

The alley between pavilions is lined with wreaths; they're arriving thick and fast and the temple boys can't hang them fast enough. As we get there, we realize it's only the first day, and there's a queue stretching out of the door of the pavilion practically to the front gate of people waiting to anoint the deceased's hand with scented water . . . the bathing of the corpse. But they're hurrying it along; this temple probably rents by the hour, like some hotels in my neighborhood.

Everyone's in black, but no one seems particularly sad. As they stand in line, they're all gossiping about their wives, mistresses, boyfriends, children, and so on. There are mangy dogs everywhere. Waen kicks one of them out of his way.

"Don't do that!" I say. "It could be your father."

"He ought to be reborn as a dog," P'Waen says, "for abandoning me like that."

"Don't be so unfilial."

"Unfilial? For God's sake, I'm an orphan."

"Shut up. Look for lottery tickets. Take your glasses off, no one knows you here."

The smell of incense wafts from everywhere. The already hot air is almost suffocating. In surround sound, groups of monks chant from each pavilion. The mourners move rapidly. Waen urgently waves me over to join the end of the queue.

"What? We didn't even know the general," I say.

"If the general is going to give us money," he says, "we owe respect to his corpse at least."

No one looks at us funny. It seems that so many people respected (or at least feared) the general that there are people from all walks of life, and now that the people with the black suits and ties and uniforms have all gone through, so can we. Almost before I can figure out what I'm doing, I'm inside the chilly pavilion and I'm on the ground, prostrating myself in front of a dead man with a chest full of medals, his face set in a grimace that suggests that he's about to have us all shot.

The atmosphere is choking because of all the perfumed holy water. The walls are piled high with wreaths. People are actually sobbing now, family members; as I get up, a weeping old lady thanks me for coming.

It turns out we're almost the last people. We haven't even left the pavilion when some soldiers come forward, wrap the body in a sheet, and hoist it into a coffin, then, a couple of burly truck-driver types start hammering the coffin shut and—

<<Let me out!>>

"What was that?" I look around in a panic.

It's a voice coming from the coffin. Not a gruff, tough, "execute them!" military-type voice, but a voice like a little kid's, like mine or Waen's.

"Waen, he wants out! He's not dead!" I whisper.

<<Please, Krit, tell someone to let me out!>>

"He's talking to me!" I say.

"Let's get out of here!" says Waen, pulling me toward the door. "The lottery-ticket sellers are gathering."

Sure enough, there's a whole army of them, each with a tray of lottery tickets slung across his shoulder: they've positioned themselves right next to the food, so you can't eat without being accosted.

<<Krit, little man, help me!>>

"Listen, P'Waen, I'm freaking out. The general's talking to me in my head."

<<I'm not ready to go yet!>>

A teeny little voice, more like a mouse than a big bad general. I'm afraid. Very afraid. I know that ghosts exist, of course, but meeting them is something that only happens to other people.

"Buy your tickets," I tell him, "and let's get back to the orphanage. I mean it."

"You're shaking!" Waen says. "That's not like you. It's not like you to be scared of ghosts."

“It’s not like me to be having a conversation with one,” I tell him. They’re hoisting the general up now on their shoulders. This happens every night of a multiday funeral; the body is paraded around and deposited in a special room, a dead-body holding area, not to put too fine a point on it; then they trot it out the next evening for more prayers, and so on. It goes on until the cremation. It could be a week, but for someone this important, it could even be fifty days, or a hundred.

Everyone is getting in line behind the corpse now as it is being hefted out of the pavilion, and it would be very rude to try to get away. Besides, the lottery-ticket vendors are swooping down on the funerary conga line and thrusting their wares at us. “Buy mine! Buy mine!” they’re all saying, “Guaranteed lucky!” There’s no money-back guarantee, of course.

The procession moves slowly and with grave dignity, though many people stop to pick up the elegantly catered snack boxes that are being handed out. These are particularly fabulous: they’re produced by the onboard dining service of Thai Airways, which makes a bigger profit on funerals, I suspect, than on passengers. Their chicken pies are famous throughout Bangkok.

Waen and I can’t suppress our smiles as we manage to get a couple of boxes each. We’re quite close to the coffin; I’m actually in the coffin’s shadow as it passes under the harsh fluorescent lamps that line the alley that leads from pavilion to pavilion. All the while that P’Waen is extolling the chicken pies, I’m hearing the general’s squeaky little baby voice and . . . worst of all . . . he’s tapping on the coffin lid, and nobody hears it but me.

“Anyone got nine-one-nine?” Waen keeps asking the vendors. He has to ask sotto voce, because if the news were to get out that someone has asked for a special number, everyone will want that number and there won’t be any prize money left.

They thumb dutifully through their books of tickets—with their garish antiforgery designs, you can go dizzy staring at a lottery ticket too long—and none of the sellers has one. The kids are quite perfunctory about it, especially as they don’t think they’re really going to make a sale to another kid.

You see, we’ve fooled all these high-society people into thinking we somehow belong—but you can’t fool a street urchin. They look right into our eyes and they know we’re trash, same as they are.

The procession moves along and a secondary procession moves

along with it—the lottery vendors, all trying to walk sideways so they can keep up their high-pressure tactics, all flipping through their ticket books and spouting their pitches—we look like a massive black millipede on its side, its legs wriggling insanely. We go down a narrow passageway; a wrought-iron fence separates us from a courtyard where a moss-covered old pagoda stands; a young novice monk and a *dek wat* are peering through the railings at us.

We're at the end of the temple that's closest to the Hindu shrine; these last pavilions, and the mortuary, lean against a thin stucco wall that separates the Buddhists from the Hindus.

As we get closer and closer to the storeroom, I get more and more nervous; I'm starting to hear other voices, faint voices, and they're all saying: <<Please, Krit, please, Krit, get us out of here.>>

We're at the door of the storeroom! It creaks open! It's a double door, and when both doors swing all the way out the whiff of incense and rotting jasmine leaves and the perfume they douse the bodies in comes rushing out and almost knocks me over . . . then the voices are clamoring, demanding my attention, trying to get me to do something and I don't know what I have to do . . .

Just at that moment, Waen manages to buy three tickets with 919 final digits. "We're out of here," he says to me, and grabs my arm. We're aiming to make a dash for the railings, squeeze our thin bodies through, and sprint across the courtyard round to the back door of the orphanage.

But they're pressing me into the storeroom, and a lady is handing out pomegranate leaves at the door (if you don't hold a pomegranate leaf when you're visiting a roomful of dead people, you're liable to be sucked into the limbo of the dead yourself); I have a twig thrust in my hand and the crowd sort of jostles me so I stumble over the threshold. Then, I'm standing in a corridor lined with shelves, three levels high, and the coffins are stacked on the shelves, plain ones, ornate ones, gold ones, wooden ones, each one with a little minishrine to the deceased in front of it, and a photograph, and decaying garlands, and flickering candles, and incense that makes me woozy from the whiff of it . . . and the crowd is propelling me farther and farther into the room but the corridor doesn't end, it's just coffin after coffin, receding to infinity, and always the voices, tugging at me, and now I feel ghostly hands, too, touching me, ruffling my hair, pulling at my T-shirt, and I'm fainting and fainting and—

Now what?

I'm falling into the floor. And the floor itself is dissolving. The dead people are pulling me down . . . I clutch the pomegranate twig, then it's as if something grabs me by the hair and I'm somersaulting up now, being hauled up through the ceiling by the hair and no one has even noticed . . .

Stillness. My eyes are closed. The clamor of the dead has died away. I'm sitting on something soft, fleshy. Slowly, I open my eyes. First, I see a pair of feet. They're big. I mean, my entire field of vision is these feet, and they are blue.

I look up. The stars are out. I seem to be in the courtyard, the one I was trying to run away to. I see a pair of eyes. Piercing eyes, with irises that are yellow, like sunlight. And they're big. I mean, the eyes are like two suns, and the face fills the whole sky. Or it seems that way. When I realize that I am actually sitting on the palm of a giant hand, a blue hand, I panic.

Soft laughter fills the air.

This laughter is like the ringing of the great big temple bells, and like the sound of the wind when the monsoon is about to burst.

I'm panicking even more now, because the hand is rising into the air and I'm clinging to the index finger which wears a ring that has a diamond bigger than my head.

Then, I see the lips, and the teeth.

This is it. Sucked in by ghosts and devoured by a monster before my thirteenth birthday.

"Oh, Kris," the whole sky seems to say, "you do have a quaint way of seeing the world."

I look up and I look down. This is no King Kong peering down at a scantily clad creature he can crush in the palm of his hand, this is no monster. This is human, a man, a deep-blue man, who is so tall that he seems to fill the entire world. And he calls me Kris, but not with a *farang* accent. It's more Indian, actually.

"What's going on?" I shout. "Did you eat all the bananas?"

The laughter again. It's a comforting laughter, but I have the feeling that this same laughter could topple mountains if it were just one or two decibels louder.

"No, not the bananas. That would have been Ganesha."

"But Mr. Strange ate a whole tray of them—"

"Exactly so."

"But—"

"Listen, Kris. About the dead. Get used to it. They're harmless. They can't hurt you; they really are dead, you know. Those voices are just faint echoes of what they were, or might have been. Sometimes, they can tell you something useful, but most of the time, it's just hot air."

"That's it? Ignore them?"

"It's hard, I know. The dead so want to stay attached. But when you answer back, they just stay longer in the world, and they have these long journeys to make, new wombs to seed, new lives to live. Of course, sometimes you're going to need their help."

"I am?"

In the last few minutes, I have gradually become aware of something extraordinary. I am sitting on somebody's hand, looking down at this little world of mine, and seeing, beyond it, the frantic, neon-strewn skyline of Bangkok, looking up into the face of some kind of supernatural being, and I'm not scared. It appears to be the most natural thing in the world.

I realize that this moment has been in my life all along, and that everything I've ever lived through has been a big setup for this conversation. It's the mystery of my birth, the secret identity, all that stuff.

"Quite exciting, isn't it?" say the giant lips. I catch a glimpse of a lapis uvula, its gold flecks glittering, and a tongue that rolls like a tsunami. I don't quite know what to say. Obviously he reads my mind.

But I read minds too. Isn't that what I've learned today?

And the dead talk to me, though I haven't yet learned how to answer.

"You're going to have to learn control. You've got an inkling now of who you are and what you can do. You're going to have to do it responsibly, too. It's a tough job, saving the universe. There aren't many who could even try."

"The universe?" Now, that startles me.

"You will have to learn about microcosms and macrocosms," he says. "A galaxy in a grain of sand and all that. And, you will have to learn that changing everything sometimes means changing one single heart."

"I see," I say, not seeing.

The laugh again. “I’ve whetted your appetite, I hope,” he says. “In a moment, I’m going to put you back down. In your dorm room, safe and sound. I shouldn’t really manifest like this, you know. It’s telling the story out of sequence. You should really only see me at the end. But you will soon learn that I’m playful. And listen to my banana-scarfing son; he’s one, too.”

“One what?”

“Be serious for a minute. Know that at any given time, there are only seven mortals in the world who can look me in the eye like this and live. These seven mortals have a mission. They keep the universe on track. Now, some of you are famous. I’m sure you’ve heard of Jesus, Buddha, Mother Teresa, and people like that. Mozart, too, and Einstein. You haven’t heard of them, but blame that on Thailand’s ethnocentric school curriculum. But others aren’t so obvious. Take you, for instance. Don’t be cocky, I’m not saying you’re Jesus. That would drive Father Duvalier up the wall for sure. I’m just saying that you’re here on a mission, and if you fail, everything collapses.”

“What’s the mission?”

“It unfolds as you go along. Goodbye now.”

He starts to lower me to the ground. I tell him, “Not so fast . . . you haven’t told me who you are.”

Laughter again . . . this time, it seems that the whole sky is laughing. There’s thunder and lightning, too. He says, “I am the uncreated one. I am Nataraja, he who dances the cosmos into being in the dawn and smashes it into smithereens at sunset and reshapes it the next morning. I am Ishvara, the very essence of things. I am Agni, the fire that lives in your soul. I am the universal Atman.” He’s like Father Duvalier when he wants to avoid the issue, like when you try to get him to answer a question about sex. Or like when the royal family comes on the evening news, and the news anchor goes into a string of fancified, polysyllabic, incomprehensible royal Thai, which nobody can understand.

“Yes, but who are you?”

I must be an idiot. I just don’t get it.

“Do I have to spell it out?”

“I’m just a dumb twelve-year-old kid, remember? Just tell me.”

“I’m God.”

*

I come to in my bed. It's barely dawn, but the bustle has started. My dorm sleeps forty boys in double bunks lined up end to end, five deep, eight across, with a single aisle just fifty centimeters wide. Almost everyone is already up, and I can hear water splashing from the communal bathroom. So I've missed the big crunch. I've been told that 5:45 a.m. in our dorm is very much like trying to get down the aisle of an airplane.

I rub my eyes. I can only half-recall last night at first; in fact, I'm sure it's some improbable dream. Then, I see P'Waen standing in the door waving a sheet of newsprint.

"No, no, no, no, no!" he's shouting, and hitting the nearest bedpost with a clenched fist.

Pulling on a shirt, I spring down from the top bunk. "How could I have been so stupid?" he says.

I want to tell him about my encounter with godhead, about the voices from the coffins, about plucking magic numbers from his head, but no, Waen's one-track mind can't hold anything but his disappointment.

"What's wrong?" I ask him.

"What's wrong? What's wrong? Look at this! Third prize, split twelve ways . . . thirty thousand baht . . ."

He sticks the paper in my face and I see the number 919 in huge, bold print.

"Congratulations!" I say. "What are you screaming about?"

He turns the sheet of paper right-side up.

"If I'd been standing on the left instead of the right," he says, "I'd have used my other hand to feel the bark. The number was written sideways! I'd have known it was six-one-six. I'm such an idiot!"

He takes the lottery tickets from his shirt pocket and he's about to rip them up when I catch his hand. I've noticed something a bit odd. The numbers . . . the figures . . . they seem to be wavering, shimmering.

"Give me those tickets."

I clasp them between my folded hands, as though I were praying with them. I wonder what it would be like if last night's vision were true, if I was, in fact, one of seven specially gifted human beings sent to the world of men on some divine mission . . .

"What are you going to do?" says Waen. "Change the numbers?"

I unfold my palms.

"You're double-stupid," I said. "The tickets were upside down when you bought them."

Because the serial numbers now end in 616.

I hand the tickets back. "You'd better go for your whacks," I say.

"Come with me," says P'Waen. "Make sure I don't cry."

Waen has put on two pairs of undershorts and he is wearing his thickest pair of pants. It is silly of him, because Father Duvalier never enjoys hurting us. He just knows that it wouldn't be a proper orphanage without a bit of tyranny and abuse. Wouldn't be Catholic without its share of repression and guilt.

So, we're standing in Father Du's office, which has wooden walls and a crucifix and, of course, the all-important framed photograph of himself with Her Majesty the Queen. There is a rattan bookcase with battered missals and a bible in Thai, which he's desperately been trying to slog through for as long as I've known him (all my life).

He sits behind his desk and says, "My boys, what brings you to me now? You haven't signed up for catechism, and that's not until eleven. Perhaps you have something to confess?"

Waen says, "Krit had nothing to do with it. He's just volunteered to be here with me."

"To make sure you take your punishment like a man."

Waen nods.

"Well, what's it to be this morning? Sneaking a handful of the host for a midnight snack? You're not, by any chance, responsible for the mustache on the statue of the blessed St. Catherine?" Father Du looks at Waen. "It's more serious, then. Impure thoughts, perhaps. Maybe you even . . ." he furrows his brow. "Touched yourself?" No answer. He thinks for a while longer and then says, "I've got it! You went out after bedtime!"

Waen nods again.

"Then it's very curious indeed," said Father Duvalier, not looking P'Waen in the eye, but fingering a little malachite rosary that hangs from his belt, "because it wouldn't be normal for a boy who sneaked out after bedtime to report to me in the morning for six whacks."

"I won the lottery," says Waen, "and I need you to go and sign for the money."

"Aha!" says the father. "You'd suffer one of my notorious scourgings for the sake of a few hundred baht?"

"Thirty thousand," P'Waen blurts out.

"He meant well," I say quickly.

"Yes . . ." Waen's mind is racing to find something that sounds noble. "I wanted to do something for my dorm mates. I wanted . . . um, yes, I wanted to give them all a day by the sea. Do you know, most of them have never seen the ocean? We're a country surrounded by water, and yet—"

And Father Duvalier begins to laugh. This isn't the divine laughter of God; it's an earthy guffaw that makes his jowls bounce around like the dewlaps of a bulldog. "So, so, so!" he splutters. "Your entire act of mischief was motivated by altruism!"

"Do unto others," P'Waen begins, but he can't finish . . . he never listens in religion class.

"As you would be done by," I mutter, hoping that Father Du doesn't realize that the sentence is being finished by someone else, which has the unfortunate effect of causing the director of the orphanage to look closely at me for the first time, studying my face very carefully.

"You know, Kris," he says, "I can't figure out your role in all this. In fact, I can't figure you out, period. Why would you aid and abet . . . wait. More fundamentally, why is it that I can read your friend Waen like an open book, but you, you strange little boy, you look at me and you can put up this shield, and I can't see what's going on in your mind at all?"

I don't answer him. Because I'm thinking about it myself. What Father Du is talking about is somehow connected with hearing the ghostly voices from the coffins. I know how to receive these voices, and I know how to block others from hearing my own. I've made a roomful of people go suddenly quiet just by thinking about it, and I've turned printed digits upside down on a lottery ticket. In the last twenty-four hours, I've completely lost track of who I'm supposed to be. I'm at sea.

"Well," says Father Duvalier, "I will tell you what I have concluded. First, you are to be commended for your generosity, Waen, in donating the money to give your friends a day at the beach. For that, I will remit you six strokes of the cane. However, you lied when you said that you were motivated by love for your fellow orphans, for which I'm afraid I'm obliged to whack you an extra six times. The sneaking out at night is the regulation six, so that leaves six. All right?"

"That . . . seems fair, Father," Waen says, gulping.

"As for you, Kris, I'm going to give you four whacks on principle. You did something wrong, I'm sure. Even if you didn't do it last night, I'm sure there's some crime you've committed that I haven't punished you for."

That's a bit much. I mean, of course I did sneak out, but didn't Waen carefully not snitch?

"However, before I administer this punishment," says Father Duvalier, "I have something else to say. I refuse to have you squander this money on a trip to the beach. It will go directly into a fund so that you can start college in five years' time, assuming, Waen, that you are able to pass the entrance exam." I am going to protest that we are now going to get beaten for no real reason at all, but he goes on, "However, I am touched by your statement that many of the boys have never seen the sea. The orphanage will therefore use its discretionary fund and we will all go next Saturday."

This logic, as you can see, was convoluted, but everything adds up neatly. It is Jesuit logic, of course. In the end, he doesn't hit us very hard, although he does make Waen take off his extra underwear.

Thus it happens that when we enter the refectory for lunch we are greeted by a huge cheer, and Pek runs up to us and pecks us both on both cheeks, which is embarrassing but typical of him. Everyone knows that we've willingly borne the lash so the whole gang can go to the beach on Saturday.

And when we go up to the window to get our food, we both have something extra: chocolate ice cream. Even though it's not hamburger day. Auntie Daeng grins when she ladles it out, and I realize that the staff are going to get to go to the beach as well. Despite my burning butt, which is even hotter than the sweltering Bangkok sun, it is turning out to be a good day, if I don't think too much about the supernatural.

Of course, there is English class.

The classroom where I first met Mr. Strange is now filled to the brim with sweaty boys; we've turned on the electric fan, but it hardly makes a difference. Our beautiful desks, donated by the international school, were not intended to seat three apiece, but there's a lot of us and not a lot of room. Man and Yu are trying to beat up Pek, which he quite enjoys, but P'Fat is rescuing him by tickling the soccer boys into oblivion. It's rowdy.

When Leopold Strange enters the room, it becomes oddly, unnaturally cool. The blast of cold actually makes the boys shut up, and they all turn around to look at him. The air also smells sweet, like banana syrup.

Mr. Strange is tall and fills the doorway; this time, he has a cane, which I believe to be a prop, because he didn't have one yesterday. He shuts the door, shuffles up to the front of the class, and mumbles, "English, English, English." Then he looks up at all of us. "Do any of you know why you're being made to study English?"

P'Fat, always the intellectual, says, "It's for our careers, sir, and to help us out of the gutter."

"True. But there is another reason. You see, if you know English, you will be able to read my books."

"You're a writer, sir?" says dainty little Pek.

"Yes, and I write about dragons, and princesses; gods, heroes, and monsters; I write about good versus evil, about rescue and redemption, beauty and betrayal, delight and despair."

"I see all those movies," Man says. "Especially the ones with dragons. Though the subtitles go by too fast."

"I'm not talking about movies," says Mr. Strange. "I'm talking about words. Words are all magic spells, and today, in the twenty-first century, the strongest magic resides in English. Not that there's anything inferior about other languages, but you see, the gods take turns, over time: they used to speak Sumerian, then Egyptian, then Greek, then Sanskrit, and right now it's English. For the moment, there's truth in English. But it doesn't work if it's your native language, you see; then it's just chitchat. You have to learn it, the way you'd learn a mantra. You have to form your tongue around those weird and wondrous words, imbuing them with a wild, inner vitality. Then they will become true speech, words that actually are what they describe."

He has everybody's rapt attention, but I, for one, am not buying it. On the other hand, he's already given me his talk about truth and facts, so I know that what he's trying to tell us is hidden. I only have to figure out—

Krit.

Huh? He's still talking, weaving a skein of texture and symbol so audacious that no one can stop paying attention, but inside what he's saying there's another voice, and it's speaking right inside my head . . .

<<Listen, Krit, listen! Remember, you and I have a private date after this little exhibition. And none of your friends are invited. This revelation's for you alone.>>

When? I catch myself. My lips did not move.

<<Sneak out again tonight. Yesterday was just an overture. Tonight begins the real adventure. Meet me when the moon is full.>>

But I just got four slices!

<<And it was worth every cut.>>

He's right, of course. I don't really have a choice. Big things are happening and I am a very great part of what is going to unfold. The coolness that emanates from Mr. Strange envelops me and comforts me.

I've never known what it's like to have a father or mother, never been hugged by a parent, never just sat down quietly with an older person I totally trust and just basked in that trust; today, in this crowded classroom with the sweat-drops hanging in the air, I feel like I'm resting beneath a vast tree, shaded and protected by a power too big to comprehend. Today, I know that Mr. Strange and I are some kind of kin.

Come moonrise, I suppose I will learn what kind.

I don't think I'm ever going to get to sleep, but the truth is I fall asleep instantly, and I fall into a kind of dream.

It's a sort of jumble of everything that's happened lately; of lottery tickets raining down from the sky, of gods cupping me in the palm of their hand, of generals trying to claw their way out of coffins. And through it all, there's me, and I'm prowling through this fantastical nightmare jungle, my right hand clenching the handle of the twisty *kris* that came in the basket when I was a baby. Yes, I'm just stalking through dense undergrowth, bones crunching beneath my bare feet, my heart thumping like a pile driver. I don't know what drives me. Fear, certainly. I'm being hunted. Who is hunting me? In the distance, I hear the footfall of something—someone—big. Like one of the demons that guard the Temple of Dawn beside the river. Or like a dinosaur. Or a dragon. I'm running now, heedless of the twigs that snap and dig into my soles.

<<What are you running for? Who are you running from?>>

I hear the laughter that's like the wind. I hear a voice, with a subtle Indian accent, whispering <<*Kris, Kris, Kris.*>> I'm wielding the knife but I also am the knife, I'm being wielded by something, someone much bigger than myself.

<<Kris, Kris, I twist you into the dragon's flesh, I turn you, I draw the glacial blood and stir it up to a volcanic heat. Turn, Kris, turn!>>

I stumble on a clearing. The moon is behind a cloud and there's only a faint radiance here. I stand in the silky half-dark and I cry out, "I want to see!"

All at once, the clouds shift and I'm bathed in moonlight. There's only me and the moon and the glistening dagger. I glow in the light. I'm so bright that if someone were to look at me he would go blind.

And suddenly I realize it's the moon that glows in my light. I am the source; the moon is only mirroring me. And it makes me lonely.

I wake up in the dark, all sweaty, floating on a sea of young boys' snores.

So, here I am, in my standard-issue Sacred Heart Orphanage pajamas, standing just outside the gate. It's late, terribly late, and I am in the moonlight as in my dream, and yes, I feel alone.

The moon is full and makes me glow. Behind me is the orphanage; to my right the Buddhist temple; to my left the Hindu shrine. This patch of ground, parched because there's been no rain, feels hemmed in somehow by the three places of worship. I wonder if I shall ever be free.

Father Duvalier did tell me once that the Jesuits believe that if they have a child before he turns five, they have him forever.

Where's Mr. Strange?

First, the sudden coolness. Then, the smell of ripe bananas, and the still air becomes sweet, as though someone has been spraying a sugar atomizer around. The sugar sort of ripples like a heat wave. I stick out my tongue and really, the air tastes sweet, like a delicate syrup ladled out over wafer-thin pancakes. It's a feeling of immense joy and calm.

But Mr. Strange's words are far from calm.

"You almost ruined it!" he says.

He's behind me. I never heard him sneak up.

"Ruined what?" If someone would only tell me the whole truth instead of always assuming that I can guess things . . .

"You've been listening to too many dead people. You've been slapping a great cosmic shut-up on the universe . . . do you know how much energy that cost? Probably killed off an entire star cluster in some backwoods galaxy. And that party trick of yours with the nine-one-nine and the six-one-six . . . personal gain, yet! You broke the cardinal law of the avatar code: never use your powers for personal gain!"

"But it was for P'Waen's gain," I protest.

He grabs my shoulders, stares me down. "I suppose it was at that," he says, and sighs. "Nevertheless, it is karma. Cause and effect. I was hoping to begin this adventure with a tabula rasa, but instead you're setting off with a hefty handicap: forty-two karmic demerits."

He lets me go. "Chew on that for a while. And no more sugar, you'll rot your teeth."

At once, the rippling syrup transforms into the bitterest of cough medicines, and I start to retch.

"Don't get sick on me yet. This is the moment you've been waiting for. The revelation. I'm going to tell you everything. Well, I'm going to tell you a lot. Keep your wits about you, because you only get to hear this exposition once."

"Why?"

"Oh, there you go. Stop whying or we'll be here all night. But since you ask, this is the answer. You are part of a great cosmic story. And in such stories, it is customary that the expository lump should be kept to a minimum, because we don't want to lose our audience."

"Our audience?"

"Yes. *Das Publikum.* The silent majority. The myriad inhabitants of the myriad worlds. We are doing this for them, not for ourselves. Before I start, perhaps you have questions."

"Only one. You keep using words and ideas I've never heard of, and yet I seem to get them right away. But I know I'm just an average kid. I don't do well in school. What are you doing to me?"

He laughs and jabs me in the middle of my forehead. "You have, my little disciple, a third eye. Yesterday, it blinked open. By next week, you will see far more than you ever dreamed."

He claps his hands and the taste of cough syrup vanishes. But the sugar doesn't return. Instead there is just the usual burning city air. "Illusion," says Mr. Strange. "All is illusion. It's simple physics. The universe is a mass of dancing waveforms that pretend to be particles that blip in and out of existence in a femtosecond or less, and the real world that you touch, feel, smell, taste, love so much, why that's just a diaphanous wisp of a thing that happens between the cracks of time and space. That's what the Buddha taught, and that's what Stephen Hawking teaches."

"Who's—never mind." I have a fleeting image of a wise but voiceless professor in a wheelchair, communicating by wiggling a single finger on a computer touchpad.

"Come, Krit," he says, taking me by the hand, "today I will give you the earth, the moon, and the stars."

He jabs my forehead once again. And yes, something happens. Wham! Colors I've never seen, planets I've never visited, quick images that flash by like cuts in a music video. He jabs. He jabs. And he starts talking again, quicker than a human being can talk, and my mind is opening up and taking it all in . . .

"Let's talk numbers first. This point you're standing at is zero, the still center of the careening universe. Do you see that pebble?"

He points to the ground. Sure enough, I see a single pebble set in the dried mud. "That pebble," he tells me, "marks the navel of the world."

"Sure," I say. I bend down to pick it up.

It's stuck in the earth. I try to yank it free but it's heavy. I'm panting. I get frustrated. I try again. Nothing doing.

"I can't pull the stone out of the earth," I say, remembering many an epic movie watched on video night, "which means I'm not the rightful king of England."

"To move that stone," says Mr. Strange, "is to move the whole world. And yet, there will come a time when you must do it."

"I think I'm ready for that expository lump now," I say. "I promise not to interrupt you again."

"Very well. Zero: the place we stand in. The still point of the turning world. The moment before the big bang. Now, listen carefully because this is all about numbers. You'll think twice before you ever dare change a nine into a six again.

"*ONE:* that is the Indivisible. The principle that guides the universe. The Atman. Do you know who it is?"

"Um . . . Ishvara?"

"Good boy. You don't miss a trick. Now *TWO:* two stands for karma. Cause and effect. You pick up this pebble here, well, somewhere out there, a pebble picks you up. This is the unbreakable law of the universe . . . as opposed to the many breakable laws. *THREE* is the ways that you can see Ishvara. You are standing at the exact conjunction between them. You see? You can worship Ishvara as many, like the Hindus; you can worship him as one, as the Jews and Christians do; or you can worship him as none, as do the Buddhists and the particle physicists."

"And four are the elements?"

Mr. Strange laughs. "Sort of. *FOUR* are the sleeping dragons whose bodies, locked together, are the world. Yes, they are sometimes called earth, fire, air, and water. They have other names too. You will be meeting one soon, the one named Jade. He's a bit of a problem."

"And what are five?"

"*FIVE* are the wise ones, or *rishis,* who guard all wisdom in this world. If you're ever in trouble, you must find one of them. He will not answer you directly, but will give conundrums inside conundrums."

"Are you one?"

"No. I'm one of the *SEVEN.* At any given moment in the world of men, there are seven guardians. They are gods, celestial beings, sometimes even demons, because *karma* isn't about good and evil, but about balance, about cause and effect. They have come to Earth as avatars. They have a mission here. But when you are born, you do not remember your past lives, unless something happens to trigger this moment of supreme gnosis; you must learn who you are, gradually, figure out your mission, and accomplish it. Do you know which being I am?"

The bananas? The sugar? "I'm guessing Ganesha?"

"And you're lucky it's me. I'm the god of creativity and truth. I cannot lie. Any other one wouldn't be nearly as straight with you about the nature of reality."

"And what is your mission?"

"My mission, Kris, has been to locate you, as quickly as possible, and it was a pain, let me tell you! I've been looking for you for almost a hundred years! It is to find you and to start you on your mission."

"Which is?"

"It seems that you are the only member of the *SEVEN* who is able to tame the *FOUR*."

And now I'm really perplexed. Nothing is sinking in. From a nobody living in a dorm with thirty-nine street rats, I've turned into someone quite different, someone I don't know. Mr. Strange looks at me, and I feel his concern; I've always been his special project, I suppose. And suddenly he says, "Let's go get some bananas. I'll tell you the rest along the way. Hop on."

Mr. Strange gets down on his hands and knees. Now I've seen it all, but okay, I jump up on his back and just like that, Mr. Strange is an elephant; not one of those mangy, pathetic creatures that parade up and down the street trying to earn a few baht from the tourists, but a magnificent creature, wild-eyed and trumpeting, with terrifying tusks. Actually, only one tusk; the other is broken. I remember the myth; Ganesha broke off one of his tusks and made it into the magical pen with which he wrote down the *Mahabharata*.

On his back, draped over his flanks, is a caparison of gold and silk. There are soft red pillows. I lean back. He's as smooth and as cushiony as a Mercedes-Benz. And he even comes with a built-in iPod and some minispeakers. "Mr. Strange," I say, "they sure named you well."

He sets off. And I will say this: no one has witnessed our conversation, or the transformation; no one but the moon. Beyond this little triangle of slumland and religious establishments, there lies Bangkok; I have to say that I have never left our neighborhood, except a few times, in Father Duvalier's car (he does have a Mercedes, though he says it was a gift from a sponsor) to help him carry groceries. But in thirty seconds flat, Mr. Strange has bounded through the alley between the orphanage and the shrine and has popped out in Sin City, with bars and women of ill fame (another Father Du expression) beckoning like sirens from every corner; with stalls huckstering everything from fake DVDs to fake Armani; with cars all crammed together and honking and motorcycles weaving between the gridlocked cars, with little children hawking flower garlands, and people, people, people. Neon in garish colors flashes everywhere and gas fumes clog my nostrils.

When they see us bounding down the sidewalk, people scurry out of the way. Tourists snap photographs. The food stalls, the ones on wheels, are shunted closer to the shop fronts. I see a woman frying bananas in a massive wok and Mr. Strange says, "Get me some. And if you see any sugarcane, I'll take it as well."

There's money in a pouch next to me on the silk rug. Mr. Strange bends down, bends his legs so I can clamber down, and I buy a bag of deep-fried bananas. I feed them to Mr. Strange, who gets impatient, seizes the whole thing with his trunk and shoves it down his throat, paper bag and all. It's one of those bags made from recycled old fashion magazines, and I daresay the ink is poisonous, but I suppose those things don't matter much to a god.

"That's better," he says, and his elephant body begins to shimmer and he just sort of morphs back into Mr. Strange the human being. No one in the street notices a thing. He's just standing there and the paper bag seems to have passed through his system, because he's scrunching it up and tossing it into a dumpster in a side alley next to a foot-massage parlor.

"You were going to explain about *SEVEN* and *FOUR*," I remind him.

"I feel like coffee," he says. He makes me follow him into a 7-Eleven, where he buys a large black coffee and gets me a plastic bag full of dim sum to munch on. Then, we leave again and we walk together, getting farther and farther away from the world I know; all the way, I'm acutely aware that I am walking around in a crowded street at midnight in my pajamas, but, as I've said, no one seems to see us unless we want them to.

"You're here to make the four dragons shape up. Because whenever a sleeping dragon wakes, it's almost certain to be a disaster. And Jade is a tough one: he's a fire breather. Why do you think it hasn't rained yet?"

"Oh, I know the answer to that," I say. "Father Duvalier showed us that movie with Al Gore. It's the pollution, and the carbon, and the greenhouse effect, and all sorts of scientific stuff."

"Those are facts," says Mr. Strange, "but we deal in truth. They will try very hard, all those activists and those well-meaning Americans, with their graphs and their carbon credits; but unless you can put the Dragon Jade back to sleep, you're soon going to be able to fry an egg on the pavement in Saskatchewan."

"So, my mission is to stop global warming?"

"Don't be so prosaic. You're going to assemble a team of stalwart adventurers. Mighty heroes, strong-thewed Amazon women, or maybe even just the dregs and rejects of society—who's on your team is completely up to you. You will fight your way to the dragon's lair, and you will drug, seduce, or sweet-talk him into going back to sleep, but on no account can you kill him; you need him to breathe, or there won't be any rain forest in Brazil." This adventure's becoming more outlandish by the minute. "And that's not your mission per se; well, just a small part of it. Your mission is dragon control in general."

"I've seen it in movies," I say. "I can handle it." I love those sorts of movies. "You think I can hatch a baby dragon and rear it as my own?"

"The Dragon Jade," says Mr. Strange, "has as a section of his spine the entire mountain range of the Himalayas. If he were actually to wake up fully, one of his wings would rip India in half. His right claw pokes out somewhere in Shanghai; one nostril is Krakatoa. Speaking of Krakatoa—you've heard of the big climate change in 535 AD? I guess not. The Dragon Jade had a nightmare. He stirred in his sleep. Fire shot out through that one nostril. The sun was blotted out for months—read your ancient history—droughts, famines, bubonic plague, the collapse of Byzantium—it was the end of classical times, and the world was plunged into the Dark Ages. That's what a single misplaced breath can do; that harks back to *TWO:* cause: effect. This isn't Siegfried versus the Giant Iguana. Get serious."

I don't talk back for a while. I'm thinking. Despite the supposed opening of my third eye, much of this is still going in one ear and out the other. This is all clearly a lot more than I can chew, even if I am some kind of divine avatar. There's a big difference between conjuring up a lottery ticket and fighting a dragon the size of a continent. And maybe Mr. Strange is a reincarnation of Ganesha, one of the world's most popular deities, but who am I?

We stop at a food stall so Mr. Strange can buy a bag of sugarcane. He doesn't suck the pieces; he just wolfs them down whole. He keeps walking; I can barely keep up and I wonder whether he will let me ride again. "Where are we going?" I ask him.

"A hero must have his weapon."

We turn down a side alley. It must be three in the morning by now, but people still jam the street and several of the shops are just opening up for business. An old Chinese lady is setting up baskets of fruit as another winds up the steel blinds of her grocery. A restaurant is hanging up whole boiled chickens in a glass case, getting ready to dole out huge helpings of chicken rice. Next to it lies a glittering array of cameras and electronics. "I'm lost," I say. I'm assuming this is somewhere near Yaowaraj, which is the Chinatown of Bangkok, but I know that it is nowhere near the orphanage, and I wonder just how far I have ridden on the back of the god.

"I know you are," he says. "Who wouldn't be? You were blind, but now you see."

"See what?"

"That we are all lost."

We stop in front of a pawnshop. There is a red neon sign in Chinese; I wouldn't have been able to read the sign as there was neither Thai nor English, but from the window display, with its used electric guitars, broken necklaces, and weather-beaten knickknacks, I can tell what kind of place it is. I'm about to ask why we're going in when suddenly it becomes clear.

We step into the shop; an electronic bell goes ping, and a huge man shuffles to the front. He seems to be a *farang,* but he speaks Thai with the most upper-class accent I've ever heard. The shop, which couldn't have been more than ten square meters when viewed from the outside, has become huge. It is lined with books, CDs, DVDs, and all sorts of repositories of knowledge like ancient banana-leaf manuscripts and ancient Roman scrolls. In one bookcase, hundreds of little clay tablets are stacked, filled with a fidgety, squidgy, wedgy kind of writing. It's not a pawnshop at all.

Or is it?

Music is playing. It's music I can't put my finger on. It sounds familiar and strange at the same time: a woman sings with an orchestra (Father Duvalier relaxes with CDs of opera, so that's what I think it must be), but her voice keeps soaring higher, higher, higher until it passes out of the range of human hearing, and yet I know it's still going on.

"Lovely, isn't it?" says the proprietor. I see he has been weeping. "It's the opera Beethoven would have written, about the nature of deafness, about love, about . . . oh, it's positively semiotic!" He looks up at us, doesn't seem to really see us until Mr. Strange clears his throat. "Yes, daring, isn't it, you say, stretching all the way into the range of canine hearing like that. Inaudible, you complain! But it wouldn't have made any difference to Beethoven."

"Customer!" says Mr. Strange.

"May I help you?" says the fat *farang*. "We've got a run on James Joyce right now, *The Secret Key to the Puns in* Finnegans Wake. And the *Lost Plays of Euripides* seem to be enjoying a bit of a renaissance, don't you know. And of course, the *Unwritten Beethoven Quartets* is a perennial favorite . . ."

"Later, Bob," says Mr. Strange. "Mr. Halliday, Mr. Krit."

"Krit, you said! Oh you mean Kris! Ah, you'll be wanting the dagger. Exquisite workmanship. Very ancient. Feel the raw power." He reaches under the counter and pulls out a kris. My kris.

"That's mine!" I say. "But Father Duvalier keeps it in his office."

Mr. Strange says, "My boy, the orphanage has been through hard times. When was the last time you saw the notorious knife that came in the basket you arrived in?"

"Why—" He was right.

I look at the twisty thing. It's maybe nine inches long, and it glitters, it writhes, it's alive. It occurs to me that my dagger may have a soul. That it may have lived with me before, in the other life, the one I cannot yet remember.

"Perhaps you recall," says Mr. Strange, "the time when you were eight years old, and the orphanage didn't serve supper for three days? The big stock market crash? Don't blame good old Father Duvalier. He has every intention of redeeming the dagger. But now, he won't have to."

Mr. Halliday holds out the kris to me, handle first. I clutch it for the first time. That handle: it molds itself to my hand. It is alive. It's warm, not like metal, but like an old friend. "Ooh," Mr. Halliday says, "he knows you." He offers me a cookie from a jar on the counter. It tastes like chicken.

"I was going to warn you," Mr. Strange says. "Mr. Halliday's day job is food critic for the *Bangkok Post.* Don't eat anything here unless you're expecting the unexpected."

"I see you remember the episode with the dragon's fin soup," Mr. Halliday murmurs with a certain ruefulness mixed with nostalgia. I bite down on the cookie again, and the next bite tastes like french fries.

"Next time you come," says Mr. Halliday, "let me know in advance. I'll order the oyster wontons from next door. You will think you've gone to heaven."

"This isn't a pawnshop," I say, "and you're not a pawnbroker."

I turn to Mr. Strange, desperately seeking confirmation. "Well, it's true! Pawnbrokers are wizened old men who look at your earrings and tell you they're worthless and cackle as they dole out a few miserable baht. This man, who's as round as the whole world, and who seems to know everything . . . I think he's one of . . . one of the *FIVE!*"

And Mr. Halliday begins to laugh heartily; when he laughs, he's like a jelly on springs, but it's a kindly laugh and it makes me want to laugh too. "The force is strong in this one," he intones in an uncanny imitation of Darth Vader. Then, switching to his soft-spoken, normal self, he says, "You're right. This isn't a pawnshop. It's a library that contains all the missing knowledge of the world. All the music Mozart didn't have time to finish. All the unmade movies still rotting in development hell in Hollywood. It's all here. All you have to do is know what to ask. Now, put away the knife before you poke someone's eye out."

In the distance, I hear a bell. "Matins!" I say. "The brothers are being called for the pre-dawn vigil. It's almost time to get up."

"No time to waste, then." Mr. Strange takes me in his arms and hoists me to his shoulders—like the father I never had. He leaps into the air and sort of unfolds himself, and the ceiling suddenly gives way—

And yes, I'm on the back of the elephant once more, but we're high above Bangkok. Far to the east, the Temple of Dawn rises in silhouette above the Chao Phraya River, and the Grand Palace and the Temple of the Emerald Buddha begin to glimmer in the twilight; the expressways twine and intertwine in a jumble with the elevated Skytrain, as to the west rise gaudy skyscrapers, some painted in rainbow colors, some topped with pseudo-Babylonian hanging gardens or Venetian cupolas, interspersed with clusters of spiky gold pagodas. Below me, the streets are not exactly springing to life, because they never really sleep. As we hover over the main road that connects to the alley that connects to the orphanage, I see the yellow-robed monks walking in single file, their begging bowls held under their robes, moving slowly as the early-morning devotees come forth from homes, from shops, from the vegetable market, standing in their path with folded palms, waiting for their offerings to be accepted; the *dek wats* scurrying behind the monks, staggering from their tote bags filled with alms, and this whole saffron-colored processional snaking down the street inside a long tunnel of utter silence and tranquility while the rest of the city jangles and honks and hawks and hustles. Mr. Strange spreads his ears like sails, catching the hot breeze, and he flies low, majestically, more like a zeppelin than an elephant; the wind cushions him.

The city in miniature sparkles; the world's problems seem distant for the moment. But I know I can't rest easy.

"What's the plan?" I crouch on Mr. Strange's neck and whisper just above his ear, and the wind almost blows me off.

"The plan," Mr. Strange says, "is up to you. I haven't come to lead you, but merely to hold up a signpost from time to time. It's up to you to save the universe, not me. It's up to you to find teammates and build up the expedition. There's no instruction manual, but there's a lot of fantasy novels, even translated into Thai, and of course you've seen all those movies. There'll be princesses to rescue, treasure to unearth, and gut-wrenching sacrifices you'll have to make so you can achieve maturity. And before you can even think of the Dragon Jade, you'll have to work off those demerits, but I suspect you can do that as you go along."

Then, in one of those abrupt disjunctions that I'm now starting to get used to, I find us standing at the entrance to the orphanage one more time. I can hear the monks intoning the matins service from the chapel, and I know that the boys in my dorm are going to be woken up in a few minutes and I have to get inside quickly. But there is still so much more to find out, so much more that I need to know—can't we talk a little while longer?

"See you in class," says Mr. Strange.

"Wait! Mr. Strange!"

"Can't. I have a grungy apartment in Upper Sukhumvit. Washed-up writers teaching English in orphanages are not well paid, you know. I have to go by Skytrain; flying in the daytime's much too conspicuous."

But something is nagging at me. I have to ask. "Mr. Strange, you've explained all the numbers from zero to seven . . . except for *SIX*."

It seems to me that dawn stops in its tracks. My heart just about stops beating; I've never felt so much sheer terror before. Mr. Strange's face freezes. This is not a metaphor. I mean that tears form on his cheeks, harden instantly, and break off like icicles; it takes him a few moments to return to normal temperature.

"It's not for me to explain that part," he says. For the first time, it is almost as if words fail him. "I am a creature of the light, a son of heaven. It's not good for me to talk about *Les Six*."

"But who are they?"

"You'll learn soon enough, Krit. For now, it's enough to know that they're the Bad Guys."

And he's gone.

DEJI BRYCE OLUKOTUN

Between the Dark and the Dark

FROM *Lightspeed*

TWO HUNDRED SHIPS moved through the stars, leaving an iridescent trail of transmission beacons in their wake. Five billion kilometers long, the beacons stretched all the way to Earth, a desiccated and shaken planet that the passengers once called home. Sometimes simple messages from the ships arrived in the data. After a long time, images came and—after an even longer time—clips of the passengers going about their lives. But the vast distances meant these clips were rare.

Normally an image arriving on Earth was cause for celebration, because it meant the crew was still alive, or at least the ship's systems were still functioning. Such moments affirmed they were still following their route to a habitable planet that could save mankind. But Steward Mafokeng recoiled from her module, and the image recently downloaded from the *Lion's Mane.*

"You think we should retire the ship?" she asked her fellow steward. The other steward was on the lunar base, while she was on Earth, buried twenty stories underground, protected against the torrential storms.

Steward Hutchins nodded his head on her communication module. "Clear evidence of cannibalism. Look at the missing hand. It was intentionally severed."

"The wound seems to have healed."

"Cauterized, I think. Look at the captain."

Mafokeng looked at the woman bringing a detached finger to her lips, as if about to eat it. The fingernail on the brown flesh was painted a dull gray. "How do we know that finger is from the missing hand?"

"What does it matter? They're eating fingers. That is cannibalism. We must assemble the stewardship council."

Thin, tall, and without a hint of congeniality, everything Steward Hutchins said always felt like a judgment.

"You've run the checks?" Mafokeng asked. "The image isn't doctored?"

"There's no evidence of tampering."

"And you're confident we can rule out murder."

"We *cannot* rule out murder—"

"—in which case, the internal justice system of the ship would punish the offender."

"Authority on the ship rests with the captain."

"Not on every ship."

"Not every ship has a captain, this is true," Hutchins sighed. "Some are run by consensus or by computer. But Captain Chennoufi is wearing official insignia. The insignia has changed somewhat, of course, from its original picture of a lion—after a hundred years, it would be natural for the heraldry of leadership to evolve."

"It looks more like a fish than a lion," Mafokeng admitted. "But she does appear to be the captain. Could it be a mutiny?"

"A possibility. There are many possibilities. All of which we have considered, and not one of them can justify the fact that the captain is about to eat a human finger, and she currently holds authority over the passengers on the vessel. That is a clear violation of the Exploratory Covenant."

Steward Mafokeng examined the image again, scrutinizing the face of the victim. Difficult to place his ancestry: He seemed to be a mixture of Mediterranean, with full West African lips, a long, slender neck, and eyes that might have been Korean or Japanese. He looked oddly resigned to his fate, raising his mutilated arm in the air over a sort of raised platform covered with shallow dark water. He appeared poised to say something, but it might also have been the pain causing him to grimace. The captain, meanwhile, was gazing triumphantly around her as she held the severed finger aloft like a trophy. Worse, the other crew members in the photo looked celebratory, as if attending an immaculate feast.

Steward Hutchins was correct. The evidence was alarming enough to consider retiring the ship.

"Convene the council," she said.

*

No one hides in the same way. I remember watching my elders being hauled away to the Renewal Pond. Elder Volker was cowering in his own urine as they came for him in an escape hatch. The following year, Elder Amina was hiding under her berth, the most obvious place in the world, when they discovered her. They were intimate lovers who had been born on the Lion's Mane, *and shared every confidence together throughout their short lives, but even though they knew each other intimately they still hid differently, as if they had never spoken about it at all.*

There is no shame in being found, you should know. Indeed, the most courageous elders celebrate the moment of their discovery, knowing that the Pond will forever preserve them in our journey. So I was embarrassed when Elder Amina clawed at me as they pulled her away. And I remember turning my head in disgust as Elder Volker pulled against his restrainers when they dragged him out of his escape hatch, thrashing about until they stunned him into unconsciousness. I felt ashamed at their desperation, as any child would. The Finding brought honor and fecundity to our voyage, and without it we would not survive. Didn't they understand that?

"You have my eyes, Rory!" Elder Amina shouted on that day, clutching at her bedsheets. "Look in the mirror and you will know!"

But the idea was preposterous to me. I hadn't spoken to either of them for four years, not since I'd commenced the initiation. None of us children had—we'd been sealed off from them. And we had learned during the mysteries that the seeds of our elders are intermixed by our ship system so that we have no parents and they have no children because all of them are our parents and we are all their children. We prize the health of the journey above everything else, and because I looked so healthy, the other elders and even my young peers always complimented me on my looks, how my face, skin, and hair were the perfect blend of all the elders on the ship. They said I had Elder Miyoko's thick eyelashes, Elder Anatoly's compact torso, and Elder Michael's curly hair, which grew so short that it rarely had to be cropped. To them, I was a marvel of our ship's gen-gineers. So I did not believe Elder Amina when she claimed I was her child when everyone else aboard considered me their own. Who did she think she was? Did she think she was more important than our journey?

"What a healthy child," people said as Elder Amina wept from fear in the dark waters of the Renewal Pond. I tried to hide my pity for her as the fight began. "He knows he belongs to our journey," they said. "Surely he'll one day be captain!"

*

They were the ones who forced us to consider cannibalism. They arrived as crystalline blooms on the mountains, first Kilimanjaro, then K2, McKinley, Denali, and the Matterhorn. It was as if smoked glass covered the peaks. The blooms were impenetrable and, according to the radiologists and chemists, completely inert. They spread down the snowy peaks, cloudy thick crystal, through the plunging gorges and foaming rivers all the way to the mountain's base. If the blooms were alien, they did not care to communicate. Sensors could not detect any readings inside or out, until the seismic activity began. Elemental earthquakes that shook the mountains and sent shock waves across the land and tsunamis raging through the seas.

The East River swallowed the United Nations headquarters in New York; London was swamped by the New Fens; and a tidal wave deluged Shanghai before world leaders agreed that the crystal blooms were threatening life on the entire planet. UN delegates reconvened in Geneva in the middle of a tornado, offering a last gasp of consensus before the international body was permanently dissolved in favor of the Exploratory Stewardship Council. The blooms could not be attacked, and they could not be stopped. Without the ability to communicate with them, there was no feasible way to understand their intentions or negotiate. The only solution was to leave the planet as quickly as possible.

The world would assemble two hundred ships to venture into the cosmos to find a new home. The ships themselves were made from different designs—lightsails, ramjet engines, liquid propellant, solid propellant, and fusion engines—developed by a mixture of private industry and government.

Twenty-five ships voyaged to Mars. The rest to the beyond, crewed with a range of peoples and cultures on voyages in which generations would rise and fall before they reached their destinations of theoretically habitable moons and planets. The ramjet engines lost contact almost immediately, warped as they were by constant acceleration and the limits of space-time. Even if they settled on new worlds, people on Earth wouldn't know for centuries, and then only if they could invent new methods of communication that defied our current understanding of physics.

But the conventional crafts *could* communicate—and were required to remain in touch with Earth at all times—through the beacons and relays they dropped behind them, which would boost their signals.

The Exploratory Covenant set forth many rules: pooling resources to build and launch the ships from the largest moonbases; shared ownership over any resource discoveries; military support, but not intervention; and then strict prohibitions: genocide, crimes against humanity, human bondage and slave labor, and its simplest article, a prohibition against cannibalism:

Art. 3. Cannibalism. Evidence of cannibalism, whether or not induced by starvation, shocks the conscience and warrants instant retirement of the vessel.

Retirement was defined as a pulse transmitted from a council base ordering the ship computer to automatically kill the crew, by asphyxiation, exposure to the vacuum of space, or conflagration. In no instance was retirement ever permitted to be slow or painful.

Sickness could be healed. Rights could be wronged. But not cannibalism. If in doubt, the Covenant held, kill the cannibals.

Before I entered the initiation, the crew often paid me compliments on my physical form and cool head under pressure. As I mentioned, people expected me to become captain of the Lion's Mane *one day. This assumption was so widespread that I visited the fish tanks at the age of just nine, an immense privilege reserved for the most trusted gen-gineers. We only learned about the trout in the mysteries—their biology, habits, and propagation—but I was able to see them firsthand as a young boy! The captain allowed me to scoop a handful of the most beautiful roe, thousands of little eggs that felt like I was slipping my hand through jellied diamonds. Such was their value that this was not far from the truth. My head swelled with pride, and I hoped I would one day be an excellent captain just like her.*

Everyone who survived the initiation had to take a genetics test before qualifying to enter the ranks of the crew. For most of us, this was a mere formality because the computer system already knew our parentage. The test was essential for the health of our journey to remove any anomalies. I remember feeling that it would be my final triumph after I had mastered the mysteries—everything from propulsion systems to mathematical languages to electrical maintenance to EVA walks, food conservation, and Finding-Evasion—the test would confirm my genetic health, one last blessing before I became a trusted elder.

Then, just like that, I was the one who was chosen for a Finding.

"I'm sorry," the chief gen-gineer said to me, reviewing my file. "But the results are clear. Look at your markers. You're missing some crucial haplotypes. I'm afraid you were the product of just one pair of elders." Before I could reply, he said seriously, "Would you like me to tell you who they were, Hiroko?"

I could barely force my head to nod. I was too devastated to move, as if my very breath would fail me.

"It was Elder Amina and Elder Volker," he said.

"No, it can't be."

"It's nothing to be ashamed of. They were good people. Friends of mine. I would even say you have many of their best qualities."

"It can't be!"

I was *ashamed. Very ashamed. I brooded over his revelation in my quarters, crushed. Elder Amina had told me herself and I had not believed her. I had genuinely thought they had been lying to me. And besides, didn't attachment convey weakness for the journey? That's what the mysteries had taught us. These were the attitudes that made me fit to be captain! Except now I knew I had been their offspring all along—two people bound by love and not the shared mission of the journey. There was nothing wrong with coupling, other than that they should never have conceived a child. Now I was the weakest link in the ship. The very definition of an unhealthy crew member. There was no way I could become captain now.*

"There are some people, Hiroko, who believe the Findings should stop," the chief gen-gineer whispered to me when he found me sitting at the cafeteria, absently stirring a bowl of tofu. "Everyone thinks you're fit to be captain one day. You were a standout through the initiation, from what I heard. Perhaps genetics aren't as important as people believe they are. Maybe things have gotten out of hand."

During the initiation we also learned that if we pushed a dead crew member from the airlock, their flesh was lost for the journey. It was a total waste of resources, when we had so precious few to survive.

"We can take on water in space," I said, keeping my eyes on my food. "We can harvest minerals. But we can't replace complex organic matter."

"That's from one of your mysteries, isn't it? From the initiation?"

"I cannot tell you that."

"I'm merely asking—" he insisted. "Look, I'm trying to say that it's all right if you miss Amina and Volker. I do too, from time to time."

I stirred my tofu. No Finding had ever been canceled, and he did not hold the authority to do so. What did he want from me? To weep like a baby? To grow weak when a Finding would require every ounce of my in-

genuity and strength? My self-pity had died on the Renewal Pond with the people who had created me.

"Findings are the only way," I said.

He gave me a disappointed look, a look not too dissimilar, in fact, from the look Elder Volker gave me when he was dragged away, as if he was about to say something that might upset me, and did not.

For practical reasons, the Exploratory Stewardship Council did not convene in person, because some stewards lived at lunar bases, others in low-Earth orbit, and several on Mars, even if most remained on Earth sequestered in underground filter domes. There were over two hundred stewards in total, one stewarding each ship, with responsibilities for tracking the movements of the vessel and the health of the crew. That was before the ships started failing.

Steward Mafokeng waited as the other stewards took in the image of the captain of the *Lion's Mane* raising the severed finger to her lips, some furrowing their brows, frowning, or shaking their heads.

"Savages!" one declared.

"Barbarians!"

After the delegates calmed down, Steward Hutchins spoke to the assembled group, displaying information about the vessel before them. "The image was transmitted fifty-five years ago, eighty-point-three billion kilometers beyond the Kuiper Belt. The *Lion's Mane* is carrying three hundred individuals en route to Tau Ceti. It's an Interstellar Galleon Lightsail, class four."

"Any deviations from the flight plan?" a steward asked.

"The *Lion's Mane* orbited a near-planetary object for two months, and continued on, with full crew remaining on board at all times. It took on water as it pushed through the Mars-Jupiter asteroid belt, and several times more through the Kuiper. All healthy deviations from the prescribed flight path."

"Signs of distress?"

"No emergency signals were triggered. The hull reveals full structural integrity. Oxygen levels are at optimal levels, perhaps even slightly elevated." Hutchins waited for these facts to sink in as the stewards cycled through the information. He wasn't repeating anything they hadn't yet read themselves. "This was a clear violation of the Covenant, which required decisive action. Accordingly, I move for a vote."

Steward Hutchins nodded assuredly, wearing a look of resignation. Mafokeng raised her finger to indicate an objection, but held it there, feeling indecisive. It was all happening so fast. The evidence was incontrovertible, but given the consequences, wasn't it worth prolonging the discussion? She had read the brief forwarded by Hutchins, like the rest of the stewards, but didn't three hundred souls deserve a little more deliberation? It was a chance she had never been afforded with her own ship, the *Medallion*.

"The council moves to retire," the council president said. The rotating president was chosen for their reputation for impartiality, and held final decisions on procedural matters. They largely stayed out of debates. "Any objections?"

"Yes. Steward Hutchins, are you not charged with the well-being of this ship?" It was a steward interjecting from a sealed cavern in the Philippines. Machines and blinking lights were interspersed among giant crystalline stalagmites that glistened from a trickle of limestone water.

"I am indeed charged with its well-being, Steward, as we all are."

"Then why does it seem to me that you are all too quick to condemn this ship to retirement?"

The Filipino steward had a reputation as a contrarian, for which Mafokeng was grateful at this moment. She stewarded a fusion vessel, which meant that she lived with the knowledge that it could melt down at any time, or send shock waves across the asteroid belt, killing the crew instantly. Like her, most stewards of fusion vessels tended toward the religious. She was a zealous advocate of her crew, a caretaker who delighted in every report that they were alive and well. "The *Lion's Mane* has traveled farther than any other ship, if I'm not mistaken."

"That's not entirely true," another steward chimed in. "The *Halios* is a full twenty billion kilometers beyond the *Lion's Mane*."

"But we are *certain*," the steward insisted, "that the *Halios*'s crew is dead, bless their souls. We haven't received a message or signal for fifty years."

"I am not sure I follow your reasoning," Hutchins said.

"My reasoning is this: If the *Lion's Mane* is the farthest exploratory ship of the council, then it deserves more than a rushed vote to destroy it. We owe a full discussion and consideration of the evidence before us."

"I have shown you the evidence," Steward Hutchins grumbled.

"It's all there in the dossier. It pains my heart to see the captain about to devour her own crew member. I've seen her grow up from when she was just a child."

"You mean you have clips of life on the ship? Couldn't they help us understand the context?"

"Sadly, Steward, we haven't received a clip for thirty-five years. The ship lost the ability to transmit large data packets in a radiation storm off Neptune. I've conducted my investigations through the automated still images sent by the ship, which we receive in bursts of eight bytes each. And telemetry, of course. The transmission speed is painfully slow."

Steward Mafokeng finally realized what was bothering her. "Steward Hutchins, you said that you were forced to take decisive action."

Hutchins gritted his teeth, the thin tendons of his jaw knotted and severe. "Steward Mafokeng, we know that you enjoy participating in these debates, but the *Medallion* was lost a decade ago—"

"—I was appointed by the Stewardship Council as lead crew-behavior expert."

"—expertise that did not help save your own vessel, the very one you were charged with protecting under the Stewardship Oath."

Mafokeng reeled at the accusation in the most public of all chambers. She had spent years rebuilding her career after she had lost the *Medallion*. She had utterly shamed her family. Not to mention what it had done to her soul, studying the images of the sheer terror of her crew as the ship ripped them apart, over and over again.

"The loss of the *Medallion*," she said, keeping her voice steady, "was fully investigated, documented, and confirmed by the council."

"And yet with no ship to steward," Hutchins went on, "you feel it's appropriate to intervene in this proceeding—indeed, every proceeding—when the most base, most heinous behaviors are evident before us, namely *people eating people*. I should remind you that the crew will be retired, but the *Lion's Mane* will continue on, sending us data about its discoveries as it follows the mission. Your ship offered nothing of value once it was destroyed. At least allow us to gain from the *Lion's Mane*'s discoveries through its automated systems."

Focus, Mafokeng thought. *Forget the* Medallion. "You did not answer my question."

"We have most certainly answered the question," Steward Hutchins said. "That this is cannibalism. And it must be stopped."

"No, about the decisive action. You said you *already* took it, Steward Hutchins. Now, please share with the council—before we vote: What decisive action did you take?"

Hutchins peered at the various delegates in view, as if assessing their opinion. Then he solemnly said: "An extraplenary body of this council sent the signal to retire the *Lion's Mane* yesterday."

The delegates roared back to life all around the solar system.

"How could this be!"

"You had no right!"

"They could still be alive!"

"There are three hundred people out there!"

Hutchins held up his hands as the council protested, waiting for the clamor to die down. Mafokeng was aware of how much he seemed to thrive in the tumult, even when the voices were turned against him.

"As you all know, the Covenant authorizes rapid action by the ship steward, the rotating council president, and the council judiciary for any crimes that shock the conscience. This is one of them. We voted unanimously in favor of retirement. The evidence is before you. Had we waited, you would still have voted for retirement. In my view, every day wasted is another day of descent into madness and suffering for the crew. Now I plead with you to affirm the vote. If we are to disclose this incident to the public—who deserve to know—we need full unanimity from this council. So I put it to you now, for posterity. Is there anyone among us who would vote to preserve this disgusting display of cannibalism, the basest of all human inclinations? Your voting shards are before you. Make your choice."

Mafokeng watched as the votes poured in across the council, a pile of blue-gray tridymite shards interlaced with each steward's DNA. Even the steward from the Philippines reluctantly voted in favor of retirement, signing the cross on her chest as she dropped in her shard. It quickly linked to the other shards already assembled, beginning to form the crest of the council.

Mafokeng could feel the eyes of the other council members upon her. Was Hutchins right, she wondered, and she was merely transferring the loss of her own crew on the *Medallion* to the *Lion's*

Mane, so desperate to avoid another tragedy that she would tolerate cannibalism?

She refused to believe this. She refused to believe that the council could so easily kill an entire crew without deeply studying the evidence. Killing three hundred souls with a rushed decision was not much better than the crimes retirement would punish. The Covenant had drawn a clear line that could never be crossed, but she felt they owed it a deep review, and she mistrusted Hutchins's motivations. He moved too quickly, too adroitly to have his word taken at face value. He had mastered the council and his swift rise in the bureaucracy attested to that fact. Mafokeng dropped her shard in the no vote. The crest of the council shattered before their eyes and she signed off.

To prepare myself for my Finding, I train while everyone else is sleeping, using the resistance machines to firm my muscles and the simulators to hone my reflexes. During the initiation, we learned that you need every skill available to you to evade a Finding for three full Earth days of pursuit—what we call Evasion. You have to be quicker than your finder in body and mind. It was one of our earliest mysteries. Only the most celebrated elders had ever achieved Evasion, and they inevitably became leaders on the ship. Not captain, but revered crew considered beyond reproach, with the caveat that they enjoyed no right to propagation.

I practice crimping onto the smallest handhold on the climbing wall with servo weights. I hold my breath for minutes on end and paint my face with antisurveillance makeup patterns before washing it clean and starting all over again. I study the devious ways elders have hidden before, and try to imitate them, remembering the mysteries. And when no one is paying attention, I visit the tanks, where the fish open and close their small puckered mouths as if waiting to devour my flesh.

"Not me," I whisper, "not me."

On the day the Finding begins, the entire ship comes out to watch as I am paraded through the corridors and galleys in ceremonial regalia. My short black hair is shaved bare and my naked body is adorned with preserved trout, their filleted skin sticky on my body so that I look like a glimmering, rainbow-colored being. I make my way slowly through the ship to the sound of a marimba fashioned from decommissioned exhaust piping.

My finder—a strapping woman in her twenty-second cycle—stays close to me, sobbing ritually, for she knows that if she finds me I am only mark-

ing a fate which could one day befall her, too. Anyone can be named to the Finding if the health of our journey demands it. I walk proudly through the open hatches and lurch at children with my teeth bared, causing them to giggle or sometimes run shrieking to the elders. The other initiates watch me amble by, some of them mournfully shaking their heads, others pleased to see my injured pride after the favoritism I had received. I resolve inwardly to prove them wrong—I will outlast my finder for three days and become an elder crew member. I will not stand on the Renewal Pond.

When I finally arrive before Captain Chennoufi, my finder strips me clean of the trout skins on my naked body. We each take a bite of a fish and force ourselves to keep down its pickled flesh, flush with carefully cultivated psychotropics. Then we retire to a berth and make love together, aroused by the substances coursing through our bodies, one last intimate shared moment before we become enemies.

She locks her legs around me and hisses like a snake, while I douse myself in oils until I am slippery, simulating the watered death that awaits me if I fail. Some initiates never make it beyond this point, overwhelmed by the sheer ecstasy—and there are worse ways to die. But I am determined to outlast her. After what feels like hours of this passionate embrace, she loses her grip over me and I escape.

Thus the Finding begins.

Hutchins will come for you, the message warned on Mafokeng's module. There was no information about the sender. The message could have originated from anywhere within the past hour—the Earth, the Moon, or Mars. She knew Steward Hutchins would be upset, but this disturbed her. Had he taken her vote as an insult? Did it humiliate him in some way? He sat on various committees within the council—so many, in fact, that she had lost track—but what would he do to her? What *could* he do? No steward had ever physically threatened another steward. Their weapons were words, reasoning, persuasion, and, above all, consensus, which meant everyone should agree, even if the agreement was a compromise. Even idle threats ruined such goodwill. But the message was clear: *Hutchins will come for* you. She had to move quickly.

The pictures from Hutchins's briefing popped up on her module. Each appeared to have been taken from a different part of the *Lion's Mane,* a four-hundred-meter vessel that had been assembled in space near the central lunar base. The first image depicted a crew member in motion, walking past an open area with exercise machines, a fold-down table, and a passageway to the next part of the ship. It was likely the mess hall or recreation hall. The second image showed the shimmering golden sail of the spacecraft, spread out to harness the Sun and patiently edge the ship forward. The third image caused Mafokeng to pause. The image was taken in the same corridor as the one with the severed finger, but she couldn't find anyone in the image. She could clearly see the pipes snaking down the corridor. This was a different angle, where she could clearly discern a tank of water. It would have been directly opposite where the captain had been standing when about to consume the human finger. And inside the water she saw something silver and snake-like.

A fin.

The fourth image was even stranger. Here, one of the crew was adorned in strange regalia, with makeup applied asymmetrically across his face. His hair, too, poked out at irregular angles, but appeared to have been intentionally fixed that way. It was difficult to spot him in the image, as he blended in with the machinery, and the jagged-edge makeup made his features unidentifiable. Who was he trying to hide from? Surely, he knew that the ship sent automated images back to Earth? Every ship had a duty to maintain its transmissions. Then who?

Fresh air, Mafokeng thought. She visited the closest atrium, a colossal biodome with a simulated sky. Her steward's cloak gave off a faint haze from its superconducting body armor. She took comfort in the slip of vision because it meant she would be protected—stewards didn't threaten other stewards, but there were plenty of fanatics who held grudges. Artificial clouds hung in the top of the dome, and bright-colored songbirds circled overhead in a geofenced aviary. This base was one of the finest on Earth, carefully excavated by the mining companies that operated near the Kivu Mountains of the Eastern Congo, supplying the spaceships with the rare minerals that powered their electronics. Her own family's mines had benefited from the way the blooms shook the land, which exposed minerals previously too deeply buried for regular extraction. People were going about their lives, shopping, sipping tea, courting, listening to music. They bowed their heads to her out of respect, for stewards were rare, and more trusted than domestic politicians, considered selfless servants of the human race, as coveted as an astronaut before space travel became commonplace. No one seemed threatening. Maybe the message about Hutchins had been wrong.

She *did* feel horrified by the notion of humans consuming each other, of humanity turned against itself. She hadn't seen any children in the still images, yet feared for their stunted lives, children she had never met and who would be adults by the time she even glanced at their images. But such was the lot of a steward—living vicariously through others, inspecting ancient digital transmissions like breadcrumbs. Light moved fast through the cosmos. But not data. Data was messy and it took the most powerful processors to reassemble the scattered transmissions into a coherent image, a herculean task that required unwavering patience and perseverance. Her training had included sociology, history, empathic awareness, astronomy, 3-D modeling, physics, engineering, and archaeology. But nothing about cannibalism, other than a strict prohibition against it. She had not expected to be confronted with its visceral reality.

Maybe this was why the words "savages" and "barbarians" kept repeating in her mind. The other stewards had used these words to justify destroying the crew, but she remembered how her own ancestors had once been described in those terms centuries ago, justifying their slaughter by the Gatling gun. *Barbarians. Savages.* Kill them all.

And she recalled how the media had covered the loss of the *Medallion,* focusing on Captain Trent Tieman Deng, a man born and raised in Canada and touted as humanity's hope until the ship exploded, at which point he became Trent Deng, the child of Sudanese immigrants, his stature stripped to its barest essentials.

Mafokeng searched the word "cannibalism" in an isolation pod of the council archives, sorted by word cloud.

Anthropophagy. Human sacrifice. Crimes against humanity. Genocide.

Then she looked up anthropophagy:

The eating of human flesh by human beings. Orig. Greek.

In one definition, anthropophagy linked the eating of human flesh with sexual pleasure. Hutchins had not mentioned anything about sex in his report, so she suspected she was going down the wrong path.

Next she looked up "human sacrifice," which led to a word tree that branched down the screen: Greeks (ancient), Aztecs (Mexico), Rome (ancient), Maya (Mexico), Yoruba (Nigeria), Shang dynasty (China), Ur (Iraq), Cahokia (United States), Israelites (ancient), Hitobashira (Japan), Inca (Peru), Igbo (Nigeria). The list included dozens of cultures scattered across millennia.

Here, she thought, *here is something.* Time to learn. But she had been sitting for hours already. She told the archives to read the entries back to her as she moved through some stretching poses, breathing deeply as the information washed into her. The archive compressed the information down into its essence, layering on olfactory notes to ensconce the data into her memory. Each inhalation affirmed the data; the deeper she breathed, the more it etched into her consciousness. It was not the same as remembering information in rote form, or even studying it closely, but there was an associative purity to it that she preferred over raw data. Besides, she didn't have any time to spare.

Mafokeng left the biodome as the clouds began raining, a light pleasant swish that turned into a deluge complete with thunder, which delighted the children as the water splashed about their feet, draining into a graywater system where it would be reused once again. Like the passengers aboard the *Lion's Mane,* these children had likely never experienced a real summer rain, for the torrential acid rains on the surface would burn exposed skin. This was safe, recycled water, purged of any dangerous bacteria or toxins but too sullied with particulate matter to drink. Not potable but usable. She could feel an insight beginning to take shape, as if the revolting image of the captain eating a finger, strung out over decades, was coalescing into meaning. Her deep breathing from the archives was stringing together the separate strands into a theory. Something about the water.

The attack came as three short flashes in the corner of her vision. She was thrown into the moist air of the biodome. She landed with a heavy splash in the French drain that ringed the foliage. When she opened her eyes, everything around her suddenly seemed crystal clear. Her shield was down. Its haze had disappeared and she was completely vulnerable. She threw her hands over her head, expecting a follow-up blast. But nothing came.

A family saw her curled up on the ground and the father ran over to help. "Are you all right, Steward?"

"Where did it come from?"

"Somewhere in that tree."

His little daughter pointed up. "The flower," she said, "it got very bright."

The police arrived shortly after to investigate, and confirmed that the daughter had been right. The brugmansia blossom was a short-range device, designed to short out any body cloak, placed there intentionally, apparently several weeks ago. Normally the device disabled any shielding for a blunt force attack, but she was lucky enough that no one harmed her when her shield went down. She thanked them and went on her way.

Safe, for now, Mafokeng returned to her dwelling, an expansive underground villa that her aunt had donated to stewards visiting from off-planet. Ten years ago, after the *Medallion* had been destroyed, she had planned to stay at the villa for a week to decompress before returning to the lunar base. She had never left.

The dark walls were interlaced with sparkling minerals with a central fountain that dribbled water over the rock, and national treasures donated from governments all over the continent—sculptures, tapestries, and bas-reliefs. The hope was that if the smoky crystal blooms covering the nearby mountains ever made contact, there would be enough fineries to impress them. The entire villa—like the underground biodome—was suspended within a jelly polymer, protected against all seismic activity save molten magma itself. Mafokeng had never prevented other stewards from enjoying the hospitality of the villa, maybe because her aunt's towering presence haunted every corridor. Watching her, judging her. Nonetheless, the villa pleased the council, since stewardship was psychologically taxing work. For her part, she spruced it up, refreshing it with eucalyptus and hardy succulents that responded to the inset biostrip lighting.

When she returned, a steward was relaxing on a chaise longue, sipping on a tincture of honeybush tea mixed with cannabinoids and electrolytes as a machine stimulated his muscles. He was a large man with an ample belly, which seemed to have grown after a six-month visit to the *Valles Marineris*.

"Ah," he said, "the lone holdout. Ms. Obstinance herself."

"Is that what they're calling me, Steward Kusago?" Mafokeng asked.

"Gossip to stewards is like water to the well. And some of them are quite thirsty."

"You're stoned."

He laughed loudly. "Everybody feels high after living on Mars for six months. Even underground. The air in here—it lends a certain delicacy to everything. Their habitations are getting better, but they really don't compare. This tea is delicious. Your family certainly knows how to entertain."

"This is the sovereign land of the council."

Kusago chuckled. "Quite the prickly one today. The council does *not* provide food of this quality. This is your doing."

"I do try to make visiting stewards comfortable, of course. That's my duty as an emissary. The villa was donated by my aunt. She's never set foot in it."

And thank the gods she hasn't, she thought. She did not feel charmed by Kusago's playful mood, and sat heavily across from him in an antique chair wrapped in kudu-skin shagreen. "I was attacked in the biodome."

Kusago raised an eyebrow. "Attacked? What happened?"

She told him about the blossom that had shorted her armor, and the way the family had saved her. The police still didn't have any leads.

"If it was placed several weeks ago," Kusago guessed, "then they could not have known you would vote against retirement of the *Lion's Mane.*"

"But it's possible Hutchins had already seen the photo then."

"I suppose that's true. That would have required remarkable foresight on his part to suspect you would vote against him. Do you suspect anyone besides him?"

"No one."

"Strange. I won't deny that Hutchins is angry with you. He's moving for the council to affirm the retirement again. When you broke consensus it makes his decision appear to be extralegal. He expects to be celebrated around the world, perhaps even nominated to the council presidency. You're ruining his plans. He wants to be known as the steward who sacrificed his own ship for the good of humanity."

"The wrong kind of sacrifice."

Steward Kusago, she recalled, specialized in living systems, moving between council bases to optimize their food sources. He was allowing his hair to grow out, and she was surprised to see white mixed with light brown. The stresses of interplanetary travel affected people differently.

"Steward," she asked, "have you heard of fish being kept aboard a ship?"

"Fish? I've heard of attempts. The early vessels did not have the technology to support lab-grown meats. Each one contained some form of hydroponics to provide food and sustenance for the crew. It was the only way to ensure a food source for a long voyage, with crew members trained to select the best plants that could resist the radiation from space, usually by manipulating the transcriptome and omics. Aquaponics were never successful."

"Why not?"

"Aquaponics were meant to be a symbiotic system. In theory, people could eat the fish. The fish droppings would fertilize the plants, which the fish in turn feed upon. The council abandoned plans to install aquaponics on the ships before launch. The systems failed because of the nitrate problem. You see, the fish droppings contained too many nitrates for the plants, and eventually killed them. Thus any aquaponic ecosystem would eventually collapse. The council modified various bacteria through gene sequencing to convert the nitrates to nitrites, but none were proven before launch. The cell-based artificial meats common today were not yet developed, and full of unpleasant mutations. It's a shame, too, because there was another benefit to aquaponics, which was the radiation shielding. Lead can shield the crew from radiation, but water is also effective. Water is useful. In an aquaponic system, the water would sustain the fish while protecting the crew from radiation."

Mafokeng thought it over. "My ship, the *Medallion,* had hydroponics but it depended on a seed bank for renewal, not the amount of water you're describing. What do you make of this image, Steward?"

He leaned in to look at her module. "I must have glanced over that one in Hutchins's dossier. Certainly a fish. An aquarium, perhaps?"

"That seems unlikely. It would be wasteful. This is the fin of a brook trout—meant for consumption, not display."

"It could be some sort of mascot. Or maybe a talisman."

"I'm not sure I follow."

"Like a parrot on a pirate ship. Something to boost morale. There was a glow worm kept as a pet aboard my transport to Mars. Hungry little fellow. Do you have a higher-resolution image?"

"No."

"Then Hutchins would be the most knowledgeable, given that he is the steward of the *Lion's Mane*." He took a long sip of his tincture and his eyelids drooped.

"I very much doubt," Mafokeng sighed, "Hutchins would share anything with me at this moment."

The quake began first as a light rattle and moved through the villa in waves, the magnetic force of it shaking the lights. The villa switched over instantly to a different source of geothermal power.

"Minor quake," Mafokeng said.

Kusago used his free hand to unclench a balled fist. His entire arm had locked in cramp. "I feel queasy."

"You get used to it. The nausea of the quakes passes after the first few days." Mafokeng peeled open his fingers and massaged his forearm, the first time she had touched another human's flesh in months. "You need potassium."

"I'll add it to my tincture," he groaned. "If only you would leave this lair of yours to join the daily affairs of the council."

Her eyes alighted on a ceremonial mask with bulging eyes and protruding lips wrapped in antelope sinew that had been donated by the Mafokeng royalty. It had graced her aunt's immaculate reception chamber as a child, when everything her aunt had touched felt perfect and gilded with elegance. That was before she had lost the *Medallion* and her aunt had disowned her for the loss of the ship.

"Being on Earth keeps me close to the people," she said. "They're the reason why we're acting as stewards in the first place."

"True, of course. But here there is a certain *kind* of people. The Martians feel somewhat differently, that people on Earth are inherently wasteful. I can't say that they're wrong." He took a big swig of his beverage. "But I also think they lose sight of the finer things in life. I will be more direct: I fear you may not be safe here, Steward. Hutchins has a nasty way of treating people who disagree with him, and you did so quite publicly."

"He should never have acted so rashly without consulting the full council. Not with so many lives at stake."

"That is not how he sees it, I'm afraid. And he sees things more clearly than most. You need only look into his eyes."

"His eyes?"

"Both eyes are augmented. It's subtle, but I've heard he uses heat and pheromonal data when addressing the council. He's not merely speaking, he's watching for reactions, very closely."

Mafokeng considered this. That would explain why almost all of Hutchins's motions on the floor tended to pass the council. If he could read his audience to the very level of their pheromones, he could swiftly change tack in the middle of an argument.

"It *is* worth my asking," Kusago went on, "if you don't mind, why you persist in this cause, if the pulse to retire the *Lion's Mane* has already been transmitted?"

"Integrity, Steward Kusago. And I would very much like to know where that pulse was generated."

"It's closely guarded information, of course. Don't want sabotage." He balled up his fist and relaxed, rotating his hand around. "Logic would tell you that it must be sent from a stable source of energy, unfettered by atmospheric pollution, which would be . . ."

"The Moon."

"That would be my first guess, although again, I couldn't confirm it."

"Thank you, Steward Kusago."

"I hope you can prove us wrong about the *Lion's Mane,* Steward Mafokeng. Godspeed."

"Only if the gods can travel faster than that pulse."

He took one last gulp of his tincture and drifted off into a deep sleep.

After I escape from my finder's embrace, I distract her with various trails which lead to nowhere. I trick her into entering the cargo bay, with its dozens of hatches and storage units, and even into the septic tank, where the stench alone delays her for hours, until I gain enough time to lower myself into the fish tanks in an EVA suit. I hook myself onto a section of the tank which bends around a corner, thickened like an aorta to protect against the heavy surge of current from the nearby oxygenation pumps, where no one can see me. The rainbow trout first swarm around expecting a meal but soon ignore me. I reduce my breath to the bare minimum and meditate to pass the time.

During the initiation we learned how the plants filtered the water, which sustained the trout, and the importance of the Renewal Vats, completing the virtuous cycle. I knew exactly how much protein and potassium each fish produced (30 grams and 800 mg per kilogram, respectively) and the exact wavelengths of light required for the various herbs and greens that fed us.

The captain and her most trusted gen-gineers were the only people who knew the formula for the Renewal Vats. I had always assumed, naively, I would learn the formula one day as captain. It was the most coveted mystery on the ship. The mystery that is never taught yet always known.

But I had learned enough secrets of my own to help me survive the Finding. Several cycles ago, I had discovered an old access hatch to the tanks that was partially covered over but still possible to open. Within minutes of being selected for the Finding I dropped extra air canisters inside.

I was so well hidden in the pipes that my finder would never have been able to find me. Except on the second day I realized I had packed one canister too little. I had not anticipated how much effort it would take to keep myself from being wedged into the tunnel with the strength of the current, even with the carabiner keeping me attached to the side.

Soon I'm struggling to breathe. Each flush of water loosens my grip against the side of the tank and the current tugs at my consciousness. The trout cluster now by my faceplate, somehow aware that I will soon be theirs, even in a different form. Before long, I give in and I'm swept away.

It takes several elders to extract me from the tanks, coughing and sputtering. In my finder's eyes I can tell she is disappointed.

"You would have evaded me," she confesses. "I was searching in the septic tank, and I would have continued looking for you there. The next place I was going to look was the entertainment hall. You shouldn't have to fight me on the Pond. It would be dishonorable."

I think of what the chief gen-gineer told me, recalling how the crew might have allowed me to refuse to participate in the Finding. But to do so would mean the death of everyone aboard. Of that I am certain.

"Didn't you find me?" I ask.

"Only because you ran out of strength."

"Isn't that what makes for a successful finder? The ability to outlast your quarry?"

"It does," she nods warily. I can see she remains unconvinced.

"The watered death is my right. Don't deny it to me."

"Are you sure that's what you want?" she asks. She touches me lightly on the cheek as she says this, seeking a tenderness that has long since left

my body with the psychotropics. Sober now, the only love that I feel is for the mysteries of my initiation.

"It's my right."

On approach to the council lunar base, Mafokeng could make out the solar collectors branching like golden sea fans into the darkness. The square habitation units wafered across the regolith, punctuated here and there by jutting observation towers. She felt the gentle tug of the Moon's gravity upon landing and could spot the coal-black entrance to a Helium-3 mine on the horizon; even after forming the Exploratory Stewardship Council, industry remained a core part of everyday life.

The flags of the council ships lining the arrivals hall had once thrilled Mafokeng, but she now saw how many of the flags had shifted to the opposite wall—another fifteen or so flags hung above the viewing window onto the Sea of Tranquility. These ships had lost their crews but were still operational as exploratory vehicles. And soon the *Lion's Mane* would join them.

There was no time to dwell on such matters; she had lost a full twenty-four hours traveling to the base. In two weeks, the high-energy pulse transmitted from the lunar base would clear the Kuiper Belt, and then there would be nothing capable of stopping the rest of the three-month journey to the *Lion's Mane.* The crew would be dead.

Mafokeng took a shuttle directly to the lunar archives and spent the time waiting for the council to reconvene sifting through its voluminous records. Hutchins may have been angered by her obstinance, as Kusago had called it, but he could never revoke her access to the archives. That was a coveted privilege held by all stewards—the ability to look at the archives of every ship without explanation. The council believed that transparency would help ensure the longevity of all the missions.

Hutchins hid his surprise when she arrived at the delegates hall, pretending as if he had expected her on the Moon all along.

"I heard about the attack, Steward Mafokeng," he said as she made her way to an empty chair. "It must have been quite traumatic. We would have been happy to grant you more time to recover. You could have cast your shard from Earth. Now that you are here, of course, you're most welcome."

"Thank you, Steward," Mafokeng replied curtly. Nothing in

his smile suggested he meant it. She paid closer attention to his eyes now, trying to determine if Kusago had been right, and that Hutchins was using enhancements to monitor her. But she could see nothing unusual other than his customary aloofness.

Hutchins immediately called for a vote after confirming a quorum of delegates was present. "Thank you for joining us at this emergency session. There are seventy-five ships with living crews that deserve the time and attention of this body. Accordingly, I move to confirm the retirement of the *Lion's Mane*. Let's end this aberration. There can be no equivocation over this decision, and the public deserves to know we're acting in their best interest. This is a stain on humanity, one that should be quickly effaced."

Mafokeng rose from her seat to stride into the center of the delegates hall. "I couldn't agree more, Steward Hutchins," she said. "It's a stain on humanity that we did not even give the passengers on that ship the benefit of the doubt. It's a stain on humanity that this council sent a pulse to kill them all. They cannot speak for themselves and they have traveled for over a century to find us a new home. Giving a few moments to prolong their lives seems like a worthwhile use of our time. I humbly ask you to delay their final death sentence for another Earth hour."

"This is pointless," a steward shouted. "The pulse has already been sent. Nothing we do here will change that."

"The point is integrity," Mafokeng corrected. "The point is justice. And I believe there is time to stop the pulse before it is too late. I ask that you allow me to speak."

"Seconded," Steward Kusago said from her villa on Earth, catching a nasty look from Hutchins. This was all Mafokeng could get Kusago to promise her. He had not said he would change his vote.

"To understand what I am about to propose," Mafokeng began. "I ask you to imagine yourselves aboard the *Lion's Mane*."

"We are Stewards," a steward observed. "That is the very essence of our duties. To protect and to serve our vessels."

"But not this vessel. The *Lion's Mane* is different. The passengers have traveled farther than any ship in our council. Much farther. They receive almost no news from Earth, the Moon, or Mars, or any other ships, to our knowledge. We have always known this could happen, which is why we encouraged all ships to be able to make their own decisions that would prolong the health of their crew and raise their chances of reaching their destinations. We are stewards. We are charged with the safe and prosperous journey of our ship. We do not send instructions; we send *support.* Aid. Encouragement. Meanwhile, they act alone. When they deviate from their assigned trajectory, we interpret that as a healthy act. It tells us they're still alive. These ships must be able to act without our interference, and to adjust to the conditions before them. Steward Hutchins, you explained that the *Lion's Mane* deviated slightly from its path several times, likely to take on water. Is that right?"

"It's in the dossier I provided to the council."

"What you did not include in the dossier was *how much* water the *Lion's Mane* needed to survive. By the telemetry we have available, the vessel took on water at least four times more than similar vessels before it moved beyond Neptune."

"There could have been any number of reasons," Hutchins said. "It was not my place to question their judgment."

"No, their water intake confirms what you failed to disclose, Steward Hutchins—that the ship used water for radiation shielding. And beyond that, the ship utilized aquaponics to feed its crew."

There were murmurs among the delegates as they took in this information. This meant, to Mafokeng, that they were at least paying attention. She glanced at her time counter. She had less than four Earth days before the pulse traveled beyond the Kuiper Belt.

"You make it sound," Hutchins protested, looking offended, "as if I deliberately omitted this information. It was not material to our decision. The ship relied on traditional lead-polymer radiation shielding, with the aquaponics system as an experimental backup. The aquaponics system failed, just as predicted."

"It did not fail, Steward Hutchins. Much to the contrary: it thrived."

"What evidence do you have?"

"The ship manifest details the aquaponics system. And I ask you all to look at the third image from your dossier. You will clearly see a fish. Specifically the dorsal fin of a brook trout."

"Even if it's a fish. It doesn't mean anything, Steward Mafokeng," a steward said. "It could be a pet."

"Possibly, but then look at the captain's insignia. In the dossier, Steward Hutchins told us that the insignia meant she was the captain, and she was the one supervising the eating of the finger in the image. Here, I have had the computer enlarge it for everyone to see."

The insignia appeared over their modules. The circular blue patch appeared to depict two fish, each eating its own tail.

"From afar, it looked like a lion's head, so it's an easy mistake, given the swoosh of the fish tails, but those are clearly fish."

"Get to the point," a steward huffed.

"My point, my fellow stewards, is that the aquaponics system was not just an experimental resource on the ship. I would argue that it was the most important resource on the ship—so important, in fact, that the very culture of the ship evolved to incorporate fish into its way of life. This is why the ship stopped much more often than other ships to take on water. It needed the water for the fish to survive. The fish provided protein to the passengers, and their droppings nurtured the plants, allowing for a rich vegetarian diet. This virtuous cycle fed the crew for decades. Indeed, I believe it is still feeding the crew today."

"Aquaponics have never been proven to be sustainable," a steward interjected.

"And you would be right to observe that, Steward. On Earth, the nitrates in the fish droppings overwhelm the roots of the plants, causing them to die. That's why we switched to cell-based meats. Isn't that right, Steward Kusago?"

"Steward Mafokeng is correct," Kusago acknowledged.

"The crew of the *Lion's Mane* would have known that there was natural entropy from the aquaponics system, requiring a source of renewal. Something to lower the nitrate levels, or convert them to nitrite. Our experiments in cultivating bacteria to convert the nitrate failed on Earth. But every ship had basic gene-sequencing technology aboard. So it's possible the fish were genetically modified, with the crew selecting out fish that excreted less nitrate. Or they selected plants that had a higher ability to absorb nitrate. Would you agree that's accurate, Steward Kusago?"

"You have described the nature of the problem. All are possible, although not yet documented by science."

"I do not know how, and I do not know why, but I suspect the rituals of the crew had something to do with it. I believe that the fish are thriving, and they are central to the culture."

"None of this explains the cannibalism in the images," Hutchins declared.

"I have been thinking about that quite a bit, Steward Hutchins. I believe we are not using the proper term. I would call the eating of that finger anthropophagy, not cannibalism."

"A semantic difference."

"Not semantic at all. I agree with the Covenant that cannibalism as practiced by an individual, for the purpose of inflicting terror or self-titillation, or even avoiding starvation, is aberrant and should never be preserved. Anthropophagy is a symbolic consumption of human flesh. It is not intended to provide real sustenance, but to signify the contribution of the flesh to society. Throughout human history, cultures have practiced human sacrifice, from the ancient Egyptians to the Druids of Stonehenge, the Hitobashira rituals of Japan, the Carthaginians, the Israelites, or the Igbo of Nigeria. It was a way to bring the spirit world in balance with the terrestrial world, often by culling the aberrant from society—when there was disease, overpopulation, or genetic mutations.

"But those that practiced anthropophagy went a step further and consumed the flesh itself. It was the opposite of the Christian Eucharist, in which bread and wine are taken to symbolically represent the body and blood of Christ. With anthropophagy, the devouring of the flesh reflects the culture. The Aztecs dismembered and devoured the body like the chinampa crops they depended upon. In the case of the *Lion's Mane,* I believe it was the dependence and cultivation of fish and their aquaponic ecosystem. What you saw before you, my fellow stewards, was a ritual sacrifice, not cannibalism. It was affirmation, not barbarism."

"There is nothing in the images that speaks to anything you just described," Hutchins objected. "This is all conjecture, completely unsupported by facts."

"I beg to differ, Steward Hutchins. I believe that the images sent back from the *Lion's Mane* were a signal from the ship revealing how the crew survived. We do not know how the fish lived—and yet they do. We do not know how the society is organized, yet the people survived. I believe there is a connection between the two. There was one aspect to your dossier that bothered me, Steward Hutchins—the lack of mundanity. As a steward of the *Medallion,* I looked at thousands and sometimes even hundreds of thousands of images of routine tasks on the ship, from the crews cleaning the hatches to images of them sleeping in their berths. Images of anything other than the ordinary were extremely rare. These were all automated images, transmitted from multiple cameras hidden about the ship without control or interference from the crew. Your dossier contained only five images."

"I already reported that the ship's antenna had been damaged in a radiation storm. It takes our most advanced processors years to reassemble the data. We receive very few images from the *Lion's Mane*."

"And the logs? Why don't we have captain's logs, or logs from the crew?"

"There was nothing of consequence."

"That may be so, if we take you at your word. I hope you don't mind that I decided to search the archives of the *Lion's Mane* myself. If the images were as rare as you suggested, then I wanted to view them in their totality, as is my right as a steward. You were right—there were comparatively few. And I didn't find any text logs. But I did find a clip which confirms my theories. The sound, unfortunately, has been lost. But we can still learn a lot by watching it."

"You have no right—" Hutchins began, but it was too late. The clip was already displaying before them. In their modules, the delegates could see an enormous corridor crisscrossed with large pipes. Two adults were addressing the captain in a strange, exaggerated manner above what looked like a small pond. Their hips swayed from side to side, and they stomped their feet. At which point the captain received something from them and dropped it into the fish tanks.

"This clip was sent deliberately by the crew," Mafokeng explained. "It was not an automated image taken by the ship."

"Why did you hide this from us?" a steward asked Hutchins.

"That clip was taken nearly fifty-five years ago!" Hutchins stormed. "It's completely immaterial. We analyzed it numerous times and learned nothing. We don't know what the captain was doing at the time. It could have been a pH test. It could have been an experiment!"

"Not an experiment," Mafokeng said, shaking her head. "Not an experiment at all. This was a ritual. Look at the way the people addressing the captain exaggerate their movements as they present the captain with whatever is in their hand. Look at the water she is dropping it into. It is like a raised dais—like an altar. That place is important to them. Important enough that they don't just hand it over; they're dancing, moving their entire bodies to underscore its significance. This is a symbolic act. They are feeding the fish that keep their crew alive, and whatever has been handed over is precious. This was a virtuous cycle, a cycle of renewal and sustenance, one that was essential to the mission. The images you shared with us, Steward Hutchins, were taken much later, several decades later, in fact, and we can assume that the culture evolved along with it. And I believe you left one important piece of information out—that the images you shared were *also* shared deliberately. They were not automated. We did not catch them in the act, as it were. The images were meant to show us the act in all its grim practicality. They were showing us how they survived."

Hutchins stood there contemplating Mafokeng's words, but she could see that he was not swayed. "Steward Mafokeng, if I may present my point of view."

"Of course."

"And the point of view of the council, and the president, all of whom voted unanimously to retire the ship. The Covenant is crystal clear on a prohibition against cannibalism. There is no exception for anthropophagy, or what you call human sacrifice. The reason is that we are not supposed to interpret their actions. When we spot cannibalism, we are supposed to condemn it. And we have. Your theories are fascinating—insightful, even. But they do not take away from the fact that these people are consuming human flesh. Your obstinance in the face of these facts makes *you* the barbarian. *You* will be the one who is blamed when the public learns that a council member wanted to permit cannibalism aboard one of our ships—the very ships designed to save civilization as we know it. They needn't know that a steward who lost her ship was driven crazy with guilt from the loss and would do anything to prevent the loss of another, even if its passengers embodied evil itself. Or that the steward herself was born into mining royalty and never knew true suffering."

Mafokeng reeled at the insinuation. Her family had already shamed her enough for her failures.

"Steward Mafokeng," he went on, "we are offering you our hand. You can join us and we will unite as one voice condemning the act together. No one need know of your dissent. Cast your vote for retirement and we can move, as a body, to focus our energies on the remaining ships so that they do not suffer such a terrible fate. If you don't, you will be overruled and the shame you feel will be of your own making."

Mafokeng considered Hutchins's offer, wondering if he was correct, that she was merely ignoring the evidence before her eyes. The guilt she felt was real, and her life had been shaped by the loss of her own ship, causing even her retreat to Earth, where she wallowed in her dignified isolation underground. What did he see with those augmented eyes? Which members of the council were leaning to his point of view? She felt hopelessly blind as she watched the impassive faces of the other stewards. She had no deep insight like he did into what they were thinking. Hutchins was right; she couldn't prove her theory—she could only trust in the evidence, see the correlations without being able to show the causation.

Except for the fish. The fish were still thriving, alive, and present.

"As stewards," Mafokeng responded, "our art form is making sense of the specific assemblage of data sent along to us across wide swaths of time and space. I would even argue that our highest duty involves interpreting these images in furtherance of the mission. I would argue that Steward Hutchins has failed this duty, not out of malice, or ill will, but because his emotional response to the images clouded a more rational one. Steward Hutchins is incorrect. My role here is not to prove my theory. My role here is to argue for the lives of the three hundred crew members aboard the *Lion's Mane,* and provide us with more time to make a decision, a truly informed decision with no evidence withheld from us. This ship has traveled farther than any other. Its crew appears to be alive and healthy, which means they have discovered some secret to prolong their journey. My theory is based on what we see before us, and it is no less compelling than Steward Hutchins's claims. I do not ask you to allow the crew to live indefinitely. I merely ask that we cancel the signal for retirement, and wait for further contact from the ship. Then we will have more information. *Crucial* information."

She waited for her words to sink in, looking for a sign from the delegates as to their feelings. Their silence made her feel as if Hutchins was right, that she was the lone dissenter in the face of overwhelming evidence.

"How is it possible to cancel the retirement pulse?" a steward asked.

This gave her hope, at least, something to speak for.

"Thank you for your question, Steward. It is not possible to cancel the retirement pulse. It is a five-gigawatt pulse traveling at the speed of light. And the pulse itself does not retire the crew, of course. It sends an encrypted code through a back door on the ship's systems to kill the passengers. However, our charts suggest that we can transmit a signal from the orbiting station on Io to several ships in the vicinity of the Kuiper Belt. These ships can scatter the retirement pulse by simultaneously activating their transmission beacons. The interference would weaken the signal so that it would be unlikely to reach the *Lion's Mane.* I urge my fellow delegates to act quickly, as the pulse is nearing the Kuiper Belt at this very moment."

She did not expect the council president to come to her point of view. Throughout the proceedings, he had remained silent, merely listening without objection. But his had been the crucial dissenting vote all along. Only he could prevent the council from overruling her.

The council had tolerated her up to this point, allowing her to remain active even after the loss of her ship, a privilege not afforded to any other council members. This would surely be too much. After her meddling, Hutchins would see to it that she was removed from proceedings. Strip her to an honorary nonvoting role, or worse, kick her off altogether.

"The answer is clear," the president declared. "We must jam the pulse. We must await further transmission from the *Lion's Mane* before executing retirement. And we appoint Steward Mafokeng, as well as an independent investigator, to examine the archives. Steward Hutchins is hereby suspended from stewardship of the ship until the next transmission is retrieved. We should have had all the available information before he persuaded us to order retirement. In this chamber, we uphold total transparency. It is one of our highest virtues, and through his actions we have ignored it. Move for a vote."

And it was done. Fifteen minutes later, Mafokeng watched as the council's transmission operators sent the new signal through. If they were fortunate, light would scatter light, and the pulse would not reach the ship.

Already her aunt was hailing her from somewhere, likely having learned about the vote from her sources. She would be concerned about her reputation. Mafokeng pondered what to tell her. That she had allowed the passengers to dance around their altar for another day? That they would sleep well in their berths, their bellies full of fish, believing as always that their journey would continue on?

On the Renewal Pond, I stand my ground in the shallow pool of dark water. The trout swirl beneath the thick glass I stand upon, their shimmering skins dancing in my vision. I wear only loose fabric to protect myself, carrying a thick rubber club, while my finder holds an electric trident with tips so sharp they can slice through the hardest stone. My boots are fixed to the bottom by weights that feel like nails have been driven through my feet. I am surprised when the crew cheers for me and not for my finder. Perhaps the chief gen-gineer was right. Maybe my peers still believe, somehow, that I can become captain. But no person has ever been captured during a Finding and survived. The odds are against me. My ceremonial role now is to prolong our struggle for as long as possible. I allow each breath of the ship's air to gather in my lungs, gathering energy. All I can do is fight.

She slashes at me with her electric trident and—whack! whack! whack! —I slam her across the jaw with my club so hard that she falls to the ground. When she turns back, her face is flush with anger, and she grits her teeth with determination. It's the same expression she wore when we first made love.

"Come again!" I shout, hoisting my club above me. The club is twice as long as her trident but designed not to be able to cause her real damage.

I hit her again and again until blood spills from her lips, dodging the point of her trident by shifting my feet. But the effort to lift the heavy boots depletes my energy for the next thrust. I manage to land several more blows, at one point slashing her arm so hard that she drops briefly to the glass in pain. Except she has learned my weakness by now—all she must do is wait. She knows I am losing my strength. A spark alights in her eyes and I can see that something has changed. She bides her time until I am so weak that my feet refuse to move at all. I swing my club limply at her, and she lunges at me swiftly with her trident, severing my hand from my arm.

As soon as my flesh touches the water, the automated systems of the Pond take over, immediately injecting my body with pain-numbing anesthetic. The crew erupts in the Ballad of the Pond, a delicate, mournful melody that celebrates the memory of all who have sacrificed themselves before me. I refuse to cry out from the shock, and raise my voice to join the chorus when I can:

When we arrive, when we arrive
The watered death, the silver scales
All for the journey
Together
When we arrive

The steady march of the drum keeps me singing. Finally, after so many verses that I can barely remain standing, we come to my verse, and it's my turn to sing:

When we arrive, when we arrive
Fingers slip through cool water
Hiroko will gather oceans
For our roe
When we arrive

My shipmates repeat the verse, and the system laser-etches it into the Journey Tablet. Soon I will be gone, too. The system will dismember my body, lasering my flesh into smaller and smaller pieces, until I am drained into the tanks.

Captain Chennoufi leans forward and whispers the mystery to me in my ear. The mystery that is never taught yet always known. She explains that cortisol induced by stress is what excites the bacteria. I induced it during the Finding, and I made more while fighting on the Renewal Pond. The missing ingredient of the tanks was in my own body all along. And it means that I will live on, and begin my journey again.

I call out one final time to the crew: "When we arrive!"

And they return it, their voices exultant in my ears. "When we arrive!"

Then the captain presents the finger of my right hand to my finder, who steps forward to taste it.

KELLY BARNHILL

Thirty-Three Wicked Daughters

FROM *The Magazine of Fantasy & Science Fiction*

IT STARTED WITH whispers, and if it had remained so, then perhaps King Diodicias could have contented himself with doing nothing. One can, he reasoned, build a fine career on doing nothing as a matter of policy. Indeed, it was a strategy that had served the King well all these years.

That his Daughters were, by all accounts, uniformly wicked was not a thing of particular concern. After all, what *was* wickedness, anyway? Wasn't it all a bit in the eye of the beholder? His Daughters, despite the whispers, did not seem particularly wicked to *him*. Indeed, the King felt his Daughters were—while numerous and chattering and a whirlwind of arms and legs and hair and minds and endless, endless *plans* . . . well. He thought they were rather marvelous, if he were to be truthful about it.

Albina, for example—his dear, dear Albina, the eldest of the thirty-three—who was, at this very minute, constructing a wealth-distribution scheme that would, within ten years' time, permanently erase poverty in the nation, removing the mandated tithes and tariffs to the Baronry, and, while she was at it, abolishing the Baronry. That didn't sound particularly wicked, now did it? The King was uncomfortable with the Barons anyway: they were, as a rule, an uncouth, bullying, brutish bunch. Perhaps it *was* better if they learned a trade.

The Barons disagreed. They lobbied to have Albina's documents burned and to have her banned from any official business. There was a vote and it was unanimous. And the King *supposed* he should respect such a thing . . . But he loved it when Albina sat by his side during the presentations of his economists and financiers and policy makers, and he loved listening to her argue, *and gosh darn it,* he said to himself, *didn't she just sound so reasonable?* So he did nothing.

Wicked, the Barons said. And they began to seethe.

And Arlene, who made it her habit to show up unannounced at Council meetings and invoke the wisdom of scholars and philosophers so numerous and obscure that by the time the Honorable Council Members finished finding enough corresponding quotations to even hope to contradict her, she already had new decrees penned, royally signed, and sealed, and had distributed each one to the relevant Ministries, Offices, and Bureaucrats, which meant that they could never be undone without endless meetings and processes and forms signed in triplicate. Arlene, better than anyone else in the kingdom, knew how government *worked.* And she worked it.

Wicked, the Council said.

And Aneis, the cobbler, who produced shoes of such beauty, comfort, and efficiency that she singlehandedly opened the market once scrupulously cornered by the Shoemakers' Guild. Similarly, she managed, through her own ingenious styling and construction, to create footwear for women that increased their comfort, well-being, and mobility, and suddenly, in the streets, market squares, trade floors, and halls of business, *women were everywhere.* And they didn't seem eager to leave anytime soon.

And to make it worse, she never bothered to license her designs with any of the Guilds, and instead widely distributed her drawings and instructions so that *literally anyone* could make them. On their own. Unlicensed shoes! How dare she?

Wicked, grumbled the Guildmasters. And the futures traders. And the business peddlers. *Wicked, wicked, wicked.*

And Andromeda, whose liturgical dances—all fluid movement and bare skin and ecstatic joy—caused temples full of worshippers to loosen their garments, shed their clothes, and begin dancing in delight and spiritual fervor for hours on end. It was said that even the universe sighed with pleasure. *Nudity,* the Priests' Union complained. *So much nudity.* Well, the King thought, readjusting the drape of his robes and wishing, once again, that he could shrug it off. If the clothiers would bother making their stitching less uncomfortable, maybe people wouldn't be so quick to undress.

Wicked, the Priests said.

And Althea, his favorite, who was right now in the slums of the kingdom, teaching reading and writing and mathematics to the children of laborers, telling their parents such pretty phrases like, "Knowledge and education are both categorized as a means of production, and their productive capacity belongs to you and your children and to no one else. And I should like to see you capitalize upon it." Nothing pleased the King more than watching his Daughter teach. And while he wasn't entirely sure what "means of production" meant, he simply loved hearing her say it.

Wicked? the King thought. *Surely not!*

And Alana, the tavern owner. *Do you have any idea what goes on in that tavern in the middle of the night?* the Council asked. The King didn't. He went to bed far too early. But how bad could it be?

And Annika, the boxer. Undefeated, in any category. Still, booking agents put the odds against her every time—because how could they favor her to win? Against giants of men? And there she was, barely a hundred pounds soaking wet. And yet she crushed them. Every time. It went against reason. She even bested soldiers who came to try their luck—well trained and highly skilled all—who then had to face the wrath of their Generals for being so foolish as to be bested by a girl so small. How was it possible?

Wicked, the Legion of Gamblers said. And the Generals, too. *Wicked, wicked.*

And Aurora, and Anastasia, and Ada, and Abigail, and Adele, and Amara, and Alice.

Wicked, wicked, wicked, wicked.

The Daughters heard the whispers—of course they did. They weren't stupid. And so they formed a Council of their own, and formed a plan.

"The antidote to rumors is action," they decided, "and the counterbalance to grumbling is positive change."

"We'll build schools," Althea said. "Lots of them. All over. We have money. More money than we need. We'll put them everywhere. No one can argue with a school."

"We'll create a community bank," said Albina, "and allocate an annual income for every man, woman, and child. Have you seen Father's treasury? No one needs that much. And anyway, it's just sitting there. Better to get that money moving."

"We'll distribute shoes to every child," said Aneis. "Winter is coming, after all, and far too many kids walk barefoot."

"Community dinners," said Alana.

"We'll teach girls how to fight and defend themselves," said Annika.

"We'll dance without ceasing," said Andromeda.

Each Daughter proposed a plan to do good, to be good. Each Daughter agreed that they must, as a group, insist upon being of service to the kingdom. That is what it meant to be a King's Daughter.

(*That is . . . while there are still Kings,* each one thought in the quietness of her heart. Because how could there be, in the future? It just didn't make any sense.)

And, without delay, the Daughters put their plans into action. Schools popped up like mushrooms. The poorest in the land had money to spend. Bellies filled. Tiny, cold feet found protection and warmth in brand-new shoes. Legions of girls learned how to throw a punch. And a spiritual revival swept across the land like a delicious breeze as people found the grace to express their devotion through song and dance, freed from the bounds of shame or tradition or convention.

And they were beloved, the thirty-three wicked Daughters. By the proletariat, at least. The Barons and the Guild-class and the Bourgeoisie, along with their friends among the Priests and Council and Generals, all were of another opinion.

Peasants carved likenesses of the various Daughters into the trunks of trees and the doorposts and lintels of houses. Schoolchildren painted their faces on placards and stones. Poor families named their own daughters Althea and Alana and Annika and Aneis, Andromeda, Aurora, Ada, and the rest. Villages venerated the Daughters as saints. They carved statues and placed them in temples and market squares. Blushing brides laid bouquets of roses at the feet of the wicked Daughters.

Wicked, whispered the Council.

Wicked, murmured the Generals and the Guildmasters.

Wicked, grumbled the Priests, Mages, and Clerics.

Wicked, challenged the Barons.

Had it simply been whispers, then yes, the King could have done nothing. Grumbles, too. But a challenge was another thing. And it was the challenge that kept the King up now.

He paced his quarters all night long. He visited his pigeons, asleep in the aviary, and asked their advice. The pigeons, of course, said nothing, and instead blinked back from the shadows of their lofts, their eyes bright and hard and keening.

He loved his Daughters. Of course he did. He didn't always remember their names and couldn't always tell them apart, but he loved them anyway—with their pronounced chins and their broad shoulders and their quick feet. He loved how they wrestled and built and climbed as children, how they would go from creatures of beauty and delicacy and ribbons and grace one moment to a horde of screeching, scratching, scheming harridans the next. He loved their loud voices and their strong muscles and their wildness. He loved how they could out-think, out-reason, and out-argue him at dinner. He loved the depths of their knowledge and the beauty of their faces and the bawdiness of their jokes. He found their inexplicable incongruencies utterly delightful.

But this challenge. It was tricky. The crown on his head was a necessary burden, but it wasn't pleasant. Still, it wasn't as though he could simply *retire*. Kings are Kings until they are not, and they leave their offices either aged and decrepit in sickrooms, or with their heads paraded through market squares and hoisted upon a bloody pike.

And what would become of his Daughters then? Would the Council protect them? Would the Generals? Or the Priests? The King didn't know, and he certainly didn't know where he could turn.

The next morning, he called his Daughters into the Royal Receiving Room.

When they arrived, the King felt his breath catch. How beautiful they all were! And yet. He could see by the darkness under their eyes and the thinness of their bodies that they were all working themselves far too hard. Was it wickedness that was causing this exhaustion? Was it possible that the Barons and the Priests and the Council were correct? The King decided to ask.

He cleared his throat.

"Girls," he said.

"Yes, Father," his thirty-three Daughters replied.

"Are you . . ." His voice trailed off. This wasn't an easy discussion. He tried again. "Are you, any of you—or all of you, as the case may be . . . Which is to say, I mean, I don't want to presume. Or assume. Still. As I was saying. Erm. You have probably noticed —unless you haven't, which is also perfectly fine. But still. Girls. I must ask. In case it is true—even though I cannot imagine that it is. You know your father loves you, and will continue to do so, no matter what. Without ceasing. And without question. So. What was my question? Oh yes. Very good. My question." He stopped and looked at his Daughters, an expression of painful desperation on his face.

Finally, Albina, the eldest, went to her father and took his hands. Her fingers, he noticed, were covered with paper cuts, and she had no fewer than fifteen quills stuck at random in the coiled braids snaking around her skull. "Father," she said. "You look worried."

The King sighed in relief. She understood! Of course she did. "Oh, Albina, I am *terribly* worried. There is so much whispering throughout the kingdom. People think you're wicked! As if you could be wicked—you! And not just you, darling. All of you together. And it's crazy, of course. You're not wicked at all . . ." He paused, and bit his lip. He glanced sidelong at the marvelous young women assembled in front of him. He loved them so much he thought he'd burst. "Unless. That is to say. I mean, not that I would judge. But . . . *are you?* Wicked, I mean."

All thirty-three Daughters rolled their eyes.

"No, Father," they said in unison. "*For crying out loud,*" they muttered as one.

"Oh, good," the King said. "I mean, I knew it." He pressed his hands to his heart, as though desperately trying to keep it inside his chest. "Oh, my dearest Daughters. Come give your papa a hug."

And one by one, the Daughters hugged their father, and as they did so, they caught one another's eye, and exchanged a grim expression. *This isn't going away,* their eyes told one another. *And it is probably going to get worse.*

The next day, Ada the archer was out in the green fields, shooting at painted targets, when one of the Council members arrived with a phalanx of soldiers, accusing her of slaughtering one of the nation's Sacred Hawks. He displayed the Hawk for all to see, with one of Ada's arrows shot through its heart. The punishment for the murder of a Sacred Hawk was death, of course, to be rendered immediately, as was the Law, and that was exactly what would have come to pass if not for a group of moss gatherers who happened to be in the field that day, who witnessed not only that Ada hit nothing but targets with her arrows, but also the Council member who scurried behind a target, plucked out an arrow, and plunged it into the heart of an already-dead Hawk.

"Look," the moss gatherers said. "There's no blood. And the bird's neck is wrung. And look at its eyes. So dull! The poor thing's been dead for at least a day." These were incontrovertible facts. The phalanx of soldiers turned their gaze to the Council member.

"W-well," he stammered. "I mean . . ." His voice trailed off and he said no more. A soldier's sword neatly removed the Council member's head from his wrinkled neck. The Law is the Law, after all. And, really, he should be grateful. The removal of the head is quick and kind. Had his offense been worse, he might have been sent to the Island of Giants to be devoured. There is no worse fate than that.

A week after that, Abigail the knife maker found herself accused of murder. Three of her knives had been found in the backs of peasants, murdered in the darkest of dark alleys. Three of the Barons hauled her in front of the King, who wept at the wickedness of it.

Abigail kept her composure. "Father," she said, "ask for the knives in question to be brought forth."

He did, and they were.

"Now ask one of your soldiers to unwrap the leather binding on the handles."

"This is nonsense," the Barons protested. "Surely she is only trying to buy time!"

Abigail remained unflustered. She looked at her father. "As you know, Father, when I first learned the skills of knife making, I fashioned beautiful knives for each of your Barons. Just like these. What you may not know is that I also inscribed the names of each knife's owner on the handle, under the leather bindings. For exactly this purpose."

"I MEAN TO SAY," the Barons shouted, but there, etched in metal, were their names: Baron Fraus, Baron Skulken, and Baron Malare.

With a heavy sigh, the King asked his soldiers to haul them to the dungeons. They pleaded for mercy. The King scoffed. "Feel lucky I did not have you sent to the Giants!" But this was an empty threat and he knew it. While this was the legally justified punishment for the worst offenders, the King had never used it. He had read what happens to people there, and it turned his stomach.

"Thank you, Father," Abigail said, kissing his cheek. She turned and walked out of the castle. She had knives to make, after all.

The King shook his head. "This is a dangerous game you girls are playing," he said as she retreated, but he wasn't sure if she heard him.

Sometimes, fathers lock their Daughters at the tops of high towers, the King thought desperately. *Or build high walls around abbeys and insist that their Daughters become nuns. Or marry them off.*

But the King couldn't bear to do any of those things. He'd miss them too much. Besides, he had no idea how he'd find a way to do it. They were tough, his Daughters. And wily. And they were much, *much* smarter than he. He had known that for years.

The accusations didn't stop. And then came the attacks.

Annika the boxer lost the first match of her life, owing to the fact that a man reached around the edge of the ring and grabbed her arms, allowing her opponent to wale upon her face, again and again, until she saw stars. The crowd roared and complained, but the referee did nothing. Everyone could see the bulge of coins rattling in his pocket.

Alana's tavern burned down in the middle of the night.

Althea's favorite school was suddenly infested with rats.

Arlene was accused of sedition.

Albina was accused of theft.

Andromeda's women's prayer circle was suddenly attacked by misguided young men, convinced by the Barons that a joyful circle of dancing naked women was somehow an assault on the delicate and fragile flower of the masculinity of men everywhere —their own, mostly—and was possibly the reason why they had neither jobs nor girlfriends, and that it was likely all a sinister plot, doubtlessly hatched by their mothers. They attacked with rocks and clubs and ugly words. Fortunately, the members of the prayer circle were also members of Annika's self-defense workshops, and all of them knew how to throw a punch. And land a kick. And all of them were quite good at it. The young men retreated. And then they threatened to sue.

The thirty-three Daughters ended each day tired and sore, bruised and brokenhearted. They did their best to hide this from their father. At night, they kissed his cheeks and squeezed his hands and retired to their quarters, sleeping like the dead.

The Barons had counted on this.

With the entire castle worn to the point of exhaustion, it didn't take much to tip the whole place into a slumbering stupor. A bit of poppy-tincture in the wine, henbane powder on the handkerchiefs, ground-up mandrake thrown on the fire, causing billows of sleeping-smoke to curl around the castle. Everyone would be unconscious for hours.

Thirty-three Barons snuck into thirty-three bedrooms and carried off thirty-three unconscious Daughters, each bringing one Daughter to his own castle, to a hidden, secret room within—a bridal boudoir, if you will. With no windows and no skylights. A heavy iron door at the threshold. And a very strong lock. Thirty-three Priests arrived before dawn, one at the home of each Baron, to mumble the wedding rites over the heads of the sleeping Daughters, and to sign the documents binding each one irrevocably in marriage to each scheming Baron. The plan, they reasoned, was foolproof. They locked their new wives into their prison-boudoirs and prepared to present themselves not as Barons any longer, but sons.

"Married?" the King said over his morning bowl of porridge. He had a screaming headache, and his thoughts were labored and slow. And not a single one of his Daughters had come downstairs to kiss him good morning, which had *never* happened before. It put the King in a foul, confounded mood.

"Happily so!" said Baron Yre, with a florid bow. "How happy are we to be part of your family, dear Father-in-Law . . . I mean *Dad.*"

"Let's just stick with *my King,* for now," the King said with a frown. There was something about this situation that didn't sit right, but his head hurt, and his thinking slogged, and he couldn't, for the life of him, ascertain exactly *what.*

One of the Barons called for champagne, and another called for strawberries, and another called for cake, and still another called for a bit of beef and perhaps some pickled onions and maybe a few loaves of bread, since one does get peckish after one's wedding night, doesn't one? And the sons-in-law ate and drank and sang and guffawed, and all the while the King kept glancing at the door, waiting for his Daughters to burst in like a whirlwind. Or a cleansing fire. Or a mighty wave.

But they didn't come.

The Barons left with bawdy jokes and burly man-hugs and

promises of grandsons. They pounded the King's back and told him to get used to being called "Grandpop." The King hadn't even considered grandsons. Or any sort of grandchildren. He just wanted to talk to his Daughters.

Days passed.

Weeks.

A month.

The King couldn't bear it.

"Please," he said to his sons-in-law. "Send me my Daughters. I miss them. Tell them to come around for tea. Or dinner. Surely you can spare them for one night. Their beds are made here, and their rooms are ready. I check each one each day, to make sure it was left exactly how they like it."

This was true. When they were home, his Daughters swirled and tangled in his mind and he rarely could keep them straight. But now that they were gone, his broken heart separated and elevated each one. He remembered things he did not even know that he knew—how many blankets each girl preferred. How they liked their breakfasts. What they liked to read. Whether they kept their rooms cool or roasting. The sorts of scents they liked on their pillows. He was, he realized, an encyclopedia of Daughter-knowledge.

"Please," he said again. "Tell them to visit their old dad. I yearn for them."

"No, no," the Barons said jovially. They winked and chortled. They were, the King felt, his cheeks growing hot, unnecessarily *rakish*. And deep within him, a fire started to burn.

"Whyever not?" His voice was even and sharp. Like a blade.

"Our wives are too busy. Wives cleave to their husbands, you know. It's in the contract. They belong to their husbands now. This is how it works."

"What are they busy with?" the King asked.

The Barons hesitated. "Wife things," they said at last. "And various wifely activities."

"I see," the King said. The fire in his belly grew hotter. He closed his eyes. He needed to think. He needed his Daughters. He was lost without them. He told his Barons that his strength was not what it once was and that he needed to take a lie-down. The Barons saw this as a hopeful sign.

"This is our time," they told one another. "Ours." And they started scheming, each man for himself, as to the best way to capitalize on the situation. They imagined the King's dear head raised upon a pike in the market square. They made sure to whisper their hopes and dreams to their brand-new wives, and listened to them pound upon the locked doors of their secret rooms, screaming all the while.

It was the screaming, they decided, that satisfied the soul.

They imagined their new wives coming around after a bit. Eventually. The marriages, after all, had not yet been consummated, given that the Barons relied on the locked iron doors to prevent their new wives from ripping out their throats. Still. Eventually. They would accept. Surely they would. Maybe even love them. It was destiny. A King needed a clever Queen, after all. And each Baron truly believed, in the deepest part of his heart, that he *would* be King, even if he had to slaughter each of his comrades to make it happen.

Meanwhile, the schools closed. The shoes were gathered and burned. The community banks emptied their coffers. The Barons collaborated with the Council to make punching illegal for girls. Punishable by time in the stocks. Also illegal for girls: learning. And libraries. And any sort of banking or political science or tavern ownership. And they encouraged the Priests to crack down on prayer circles. They created forums for young men to vent their concerns about reluctant maidens and mean ladies and how very difficult it was to be a young man these days. And as they voiced their petulance, they became more and more petulant. And as they cataloged their aggrievements, they became more and more aggrieved. Disdain curled into the faces of the populace and hardened like plaster.

The King called the Priests, asking for details about the weddings.

"Why was I not invited?" the King demanded.

"Perhaps you weren't as close to your Daughters as you thought," the Priests replied primly.

That can't be true, the King thought. *Can it?* He took a different tack. "Show me the contracts from the wedding night." The Priests complied and showed him the documents, all smudged and hastily done. The Barons had signed floridly; the Daughters' signatures were simply an inky smush.

"Were they even conscious?" the King asked.

"Would it matter?" the Priests said.

"Obviously it matters!" the King said.

"Then . . . yes?" They kept their eyes on the ground.

They gave their word. And the word of a Priest mattered. In theory. The King dismissed them.

He called in the Generals. "What recourse do I have?" he asked.

"None, my King," the Generals said. "None under the law."

He turned to the Council. "Is this true?"

"Quite true, my King," the Council members said.

The Council and the Generals exchanged sly glances. The King took note, and dismissed them.

He went to the Guildmasters, but they were no help. He turned to the Bureaucrats, but they were useless. The proletariat could have assisted him, and would have gladly, but the laws were ancient and inflexible, and peasants had no legal standing.

"This system is stupid," the King told his pigeons as he paced the aviary. "I should have listened to Albina and had the laws changed. I should have tasked Arlene to write up the bills and force them through the Council. I should have done *something*. This is my fault." The pigeons hopped out of their lofts and nestled on his shoulders and arms. They perched on his head and clung to his beard and long cloak. They had always been a comfort to him, and were even more so now. He remembered how much his Daughters loved the pigeons, when they were small.

And then he looked outside and saw children in the marketplace, begging for coins and scraps.

Children who were, just a few months earlier, learning and working in school. Where they belonged, the King realized. Althea was right. Of *course* she was. Althea was always right.

"My darlings," he said to his pigeons. "I think I have a plan." The pigeons cooed, clearly approving.

The King went to the window and brought a stack of paper with him. He wrote something on thirty-three pieces of paper, then folded each one into the shape of a star.

Most monarchs in those days kept pigeons. It was a thing Kings *did*. Unlike other monarchs, though, the King was extraordinarily *good* at training his pigeons. Indeed, it was the thing he was best at. They were, to a bird, marvels of grace and intelligence. He gave a high whistle and the birds stood at attention.

"Well done, my lads and lasses," he said. He indicated the paper stars. "Please take these papers to those children down there. I need their help." The birds required no other orders. They understood him perfectly. The King watched with delight as each bird grabbed a star in its beak and flew in great spirals from the windows to the square.

He hoped that Althea had done her job well and taught those children how to read.

Down below, the children in the market square, empty-bellied and frightened, watched as birds poured out of the sky. One pigeon landed in front of each child and timidly hopped close. The children stared at the folded stars, and their eyes welled up as they remembered their teacher Althea instructing them how to fold paper stars exactly like that. How they missed her! How they wished she hadn't gotten married! How they wished she hadn't abandoned them!

The birds dropped the stars into the children's outstretched hands before returning to the air. This is what the papers said:

My daughters are trapped
including your teacher
I cannot get them on my own
I need your help
I have lots of food. Come and eat.
Also, I am lots of fun and children love me.

Normally, the children knew not to trust people who said that last bit, but then they gazed up and saw the King, and they noticed how lonely he looked, and how sad. And he *was* their teacher's father, after all. From the high window, he gave a timid wave. The children waved back. They looked at one another and shrugged, and by doing so came to an agreement.

And so the children—all thirty-three of them—marched to the castle and were ushered inside.

Not long after, Albina, in the darkened dimness of her locked boudoir, heard a scratching at the door. And then she heard the heavy bolt squeak and slide back. And then she saw a small face at the crack.

"Hullo, Teacher's Sister," the child said, her face splitting wide into a broad grin.

"Why, hello," Albina said, peering behind the child to see if she had come alone. The hallway was empty. Was this a trap? It didn't appear so. "Who has sent you, child?"

"Your father," the child said. "He invited us into the castle and then he brought in a bunch of thieves to teach us how to be thieves so we might sneak in and steal you away. I did not need to learn how to be a thief because I already am one. And I'm good, too." The child grinned. "The guards outside didn't know what hit them."

"Well done, child," Albina said.

"Thank you," the girl said. "Your father sent me to fetch you because he wants to know what the plan should be."

"I see," Albina said. She was, if truth be spoken, extremely good at making plans. And her father, bless him, was not. She closed her eyes and took stock of the situation. "So you are the only one breaking into our prisons. No one else is seeing my sisters tonight, is that right?"

"Yes, Teacher's Sister. I am the only one right now who can do this."

Albina nodded. "Good girl. Well, it does not make sense for you to break me out right now, as much as I hate it here. It would put my sisters in too much danger."

The girl's eyes widened suddenly and she rested her hand on Albina's arm. "Someone's coming, miss. I need to sneak away, and right quick."

"Then I will make this fast. There are two plans—one that you and your friends must communicate to my sisters, and one that you must tell my father. He may know his, but not the other. My sisters must know both. Can you do this?"

"I can do that and more, miss," the girl said.

"Marvelous." And she whispered the plans, as quickly as she could, and the girl slipped out, bolted the door, and vanished without a trace.

Another month went by and the King sent invitations to all of his sons-in-law to gather in the great hall. He laid out a feast with wine and meat and complicated breads and all kinds of delicacies and gastronomical wonders. The Barons ate and drank and toasted one another's cleverness. They complimented the King. They boasted their accomplishments. Each Baron calculated his odds at a coup—which Barons would support him, which Barons would oppose him, and which would fall. Each thought himself already King of the wide world, standing on the shoulders of these imbeciles and good-for-nothings assembled at the table. They thought of the Daughters—wives now, but in name only, as those doors remained locked. *But maybe,* they thought, *in time.* Those Daughters had skills, after all. And complex minds. Surely they could be convinced to share a throne, and maybe, eventually, a bed. If the knives were hidden. The Barons took another glug of wine and returned their attentions to the manly banter at the table. They were all honeyed tones and creamy praise and velveted claws.

"It's a glorious day to be alive!" Baron Eidel toasted.

"In the most glorious kingdom in the world," offered Baron Sloven.

"To our land!" shouted Baron Yre, his glass raised as high as it could go.

"To the King!" added Baron Egot.

"And to our most beautiful wives!" toasted Baron Glote.

A chill fell upon the room. The other Barons glared at Glote.

"Speaking of . . . ," the King said.

And so it was, by decree of the King, that a Ball was to be held. For all the new sons-in-law and their blushing brides. All were required to attend. Any who did not would be cut off from their inheritances and tithing capabilities and would be cast out of their castles, by order and fiat, Long Live the King. The decree was irrevocable.

And the new sons-in-law would wear new coats, sewn by hand at the castle, as a gift from the King. The most beautiful coats ever to be seen in all the land, with spun gold and silver threads, pearl buttons running down the front, and tiny diamonds gleaming in the stitching. Thus spake the King.

And the King's Daughters would wear new gowns, sewn by hand at the castle, as a gift from their father. The most beautiful gowns ever to be seen in all the land, with spun gold and silver threads, pearl buttons running down their long backs, and tiny diamonds gleaming in the stitching. The Daughters would wear nothing else. Thus spake the King.

The date was set. They had two months.

The Barons began to panic.

"A plan," they whispered. "A plan. We must have a plan. We

must be a united front." But how could they be? With this band of scoundrels? Instinctively, each man brought his hand to his neck, as though warding away the executioner's ax.

So distracted were the Barons as they whispered and schemed, as they met in secret quorums and darkened alleys, that they did not notice there were more children moving about than usual. And they did not notice that the children were wearing dark clothing and black hoods. And that they were unusually good at bounding over large objects, or climbing walls. They did not notice that the children had light feet and quiet steps and sticky fingers.

Nor did they notice the strange proliferation of pigeons.

Coins went missing.

And keys.

Letter openers.

And letters.

But the Barons didn't notice. They sweated and worried. They lived on the border of panic. That the King was a rube and an idiot and easily dispensed with, *well.* Everyone knew that. But this Ball. And with the Daughters. It required an airtight plan and a consistent conspiracy, with an agreed-upon flowchart of actions and reactions, scripts and responses. It required, at its heart, a substantial amount of *trust.*

But did Baron Yre trust Baron Lesu? Did Baron Egot truly rely on Baron Avarus? Was it possible to build a band of brothers when each one imagined himself as eventual King and did not mind so much if the rest of them hanged?

It was, each Baron knew in his heart, rather doubtful.

Having no one to trust, each Baron knelt by his imprisoned wife's door. The screaming had stopped, after all. The reluctant wives had become—in each household—quiet. Introspective. Circumspect. They were excellent listeners. Good at analysis. And helpful. *Perhaps,* each Baron thought, *she is coming around.* And each one imagined himself at the center of the palace, with a canny and lovely wife resting her hand on his.

"If you betray me," the Barons whispered to the locked doors, "I shall cut your throat."

"Of course you will," the Daughters soothed. "I'm sure that's how the story goes. Now, tell me your troubles."

And the Daughters listened.

Meanwhile, other things went missing. Tall boots. Jaunty scarves.

Toupee glue and scissors. Leather britches and bracings. Here and there, house after house. But the Barons were beside themselves with worry and did not notice. The Ball, after all, was only a month away.

And then a fortnight.

And then a week.

And then a day.

The gowns arrived.

And masks—beautiful masks. Birds for the Daughters. Beasts for the Barons.

And the coats. The coats, of course, were things of beauty, and perfectly rendered. The Barons tried them on, feeling proud and sick.

There was a plan among the Barons—of course there was. It was discussed ad nauseam. But would it be followed? Would they be safe? And how could each one know?

"I shall need my ladies-in-waiting to come to see to my toilette," the Daughters told their husbands through the locked doors. "How else can I show my face in my father's court? How else can you show off your beautiful gem of a wife unless she is able to beautify before the Ball?"

The Barons, each in his own castle, shook their heads. "Out of the question," they sputtered. "How can I trust your ladies-in-waiting? How can I know they won't go scurrying off to your father and tell him everything?"

"They wouldn't," the wives soothed. "I'd tell them not to."

"But they wouldn't know the whole story!" the Barons whined. "Their narrative would lack context! They would jump to conclusions!"

"Well," the Daughters said after a long, practiced deliberation, "it's not like it's difficult. It's just hair. And makeup. And a bath. Help with my dress. A child could do it. Surely you have seen a lot of unaccompanied children lately, just loitering about. What with the schools closed. It's good to give them a task. Keeps them out of mischief."

As fortune would have it, there *was* a child. Just loitering about. What luck! A child in a dark cloak. And, good heavens! The poor thing was covered in pigeons! The kingdom had clearly fallen into a dreadful state. The Barons felt themselves puff up with their own cleverness and bigheartedness and civic responsibility. *Look at me,* they told themselves. *Solving problems like a boss. It's as if I'm already King.*

Each Baron ran outside and addressed the child. "You look like a lost soul in need of a purpose," the Barons said with magnanimity. "Come. I have a job for you."

"Thank you, sir," the child said with an implacable expression in those young, wide eyes. "Whatever would I have done without you?"

The Ball began with candles and wine and music. Beads made of cut glass had been strung on interlocking threads, forming glittering patterns over the revelers' heads.

"How lovely!" the guests remarked, complimenting the King. "It is ever so like a spider's web."

"Isn't it just?" said the King, avoiding their eyes.

"But which are we?" the guests joked. "Spiders or flies?"

"Which indeed?" the King replied. And then he excused himself to have a bit more water. He missed his Daughters. He missed them so much. He was beside himself. He counted the moments until they were scheduled to appear.

(*"There must be beads," the young thief told the King, after she had visited Albina, all those nights ago.*

"How many beads?" the King asked.

"Thousands," the child said. "They must be strung on great, interlocking threads and hung overhead. Like a glittering spider's web in the morning."

"But why?" the King asked.

The child would not say.)

The music played; the wine flowed; exquisitely dressed men and women snaked through the guests, offering all manner of culinary delights. The servers wore masks. The guests wore masks. Dancers moved with joy and abandon, and guests politely applauded their efforts. No one noticed the children, gathering like shadows in the corners, congregating behind the drapes, sliding between the swaying trunks of a forest of adults. No one noticed the pigeons perched on the children's shoulders, cooing and whispering without ceasing. Sometimes, a ring found itself liberated from a bloated finger, or a purse wandered away from a carelessly fastened belt. No one noticed.

Wine flowed.

Delicacies floated past on great trays.

Minutes ticked by. An hour. Nearly two. Finally, the coaches bearing the Barons and the Daughters streamed in through the gates. The Barons stepped out of the carriages. They each wore tall boots, leather britches, and matching marvelous coats. Their mustaches were coiffed and curled. They wore beaded masks over their eyes. They were all manner of beasts. The Barons found this delightful. So forceful! So masculine! They stood for a moment in front of the coaches, hailed the other Barons as an invitation to notice how fine each one looked, and then turned and offered their hands to the Daughters. Each Daughter emerged in a flounce of spangles and beads. They wore masks over their faces. All manner of birds. Each Daughter had tied up her hair into a complicated tower of braids and ribbons and flowers.

(*"Hire wigmakers," the child had told the King, repeating the instruction that Albina had made her hastily memorize. "Have the wigmakers teach the children to master their art."*

The King listened and wrinkled his brow. "But why?" he asked.

The girl made her eyes as blank as saucers.

"I cannot know, my King," she lied.)

Immediately after their announcement to the gathered guests, the Daughters and the Barons began to dance. The cloaked children moved more quickly through the crowd while the pigeons opened their wings and fluttered up to the strung beads overhead.

"Dance!" the children whispered to the guests. "Dance and dance and dance!"

The guests could not tell who had spoken. Only that the music played. Only that the urge for dancing shook their bones and rhythm rattled their feet. Only that the Daughters and the Barons were a delight of color and glitter and light. Skirts began to swirl. Heels clicked on the polished floor. Ribbons and sashes fluttered and snapped like flags. The Daughters raised their long arms. They spun toward their Baron husbands, who nearly cried out in astonishment and joy at this unexpected gesture of affection and theater. (Did anyone notice, under the Daughters' spinning skirts, the masculine strut of leather britches and bracings? Did anyone notice the riding boots? Perhaps not. The dance had begun, after all.) The Barons clapped their hands. The music swelled. They swirled and clicked and stamped. The dance became wild. Feral. They were wolves. They were swans. They were wild horses, thundering from hillside to hillside. They were unkind ravens and murderous crows. The music wailed. The children reached for the ribbons trailing from the coats and gowns of the spinning Barons and the Daughters.

They pulled.

And as they pulled, the pigeons bit the webbed threads overhead, sending a rush of bright beads cascading down to the ground. The guests covered their eyes. They rolled on the beads. The dresses fluttered open like great, wide wings. There were wings everywhere—wings, wings, wings. And, in a great chaotic crowd, they fell to the ground.

(*"Dresses for the Daughters and coats for the Barons," the child told the King. "That's what you must make. And they must be beautiful."*

"I don't want to give those imbeciles a darn thing," the King harrumphed. "Coats? Bah! They can have hair shirts and prison jumpers."

"It must be coats for the Barons. And gowns for your Daughters. Special coats. And particular gowns."

"Obviously, my Daughters shall have whatever they wish. How pretty should the dresses be?"

The child shook her head. She explained slowly and carefully. "The design of the coat does not matter—whatever looks stylish. But the design of the dress does matter. You must go to Alana's crafting workshop and use the design that is on the desk right now. She calls it the Transformation Dress. It's the one with the ribbons. It ties together and opens up. Like wings."

"I shall contact the Guild at once."

"No," the child said. "Not the Guild. You must hire seamstresses from the villages. They have magic hands. Send your secret guards to each village and ask for the most extraordinary seamstress. Tell them they cannot know what it is for. They will guess, and send accordingly."

The King was unsatisfied. The child pressed her lips together in a thin, tight line.

"Can I at least make the coats uncomfortable?" the King pressed.

"They won't be wearing them for very long," the child assured him. Though she refused to explain further.)

Later, this is what the guests remembered (indeed, it was the only story that anyone told for months after, in the gossip papers, in the taverns, over tea. In all the best circles—the families of the Guilds and the Generals and the Priests and the Council—they could talk of nothing else. Such a scandal! Who could have known how very, *very* wicked those Daughters had been? For all that time. *The poor King. That poor, poor man . . .*).

The beads came down. Everyone fell. The music continued. Birds flew in people's faces. And cloaks seemed to fall from the sky. There was chaos. The candles went out. And there was a scream. And then another. And then another.

"*Knives!*" someone yelled. Who was it? One of the Barons, surely. "*They have knives!*"

"Help!"

"Help!"

"I am cut!"

"I am slain!"

The candles burned again, all at once, though no one could tell who had lit them. The guests pulled themselves to their feet and realized something astonishing. The Barons stood in a circle, swords out, staring levelly at their wives. The Daughters, all thirty-three of them, were kneeling on the ground. Their hands were bound behind their backs. Their faces squinched beneath their masks, as though trying to remove them with their cheek muscles. Their towers of hair leaned this way and that. Their dresses fit them ill, but didn't everyone always say that they were a bit uncouth in their bearing? A little too masculine? A little too hairy? And they were wearing riding boots! So unfashionable! They struggled, but their bonds held firm.

The Barons, on the other hand, were so lithe and handsome in their coats! Their masks showed all manner of beasts—and what beautiful beasts! So brave and noble they were! So delicately boned! And bleeding. The poor things. Each one with a slice to their neck. They held handkerchiefs to their skin to stop the flow. They had married those Daughters as an antidote to their wickedness and this was how the Barons were repaid! A slice to the throat. Shocking. Thank the gods that those thirty-three wicked Daughters missed their poor husbands' arteries! Thank the gods that all of those wounds were superficial! What was it that people said about women bleeding? Or perhaps they realized, in the end, that they lacked the stomach for true violence. This was the violence of ladies—underdone. The handsome Barons were right. *Of course they were.* Even marriage could not save the thirty-three wicked Daughters from their own wickedness.

"My own Daughters," the King said, his gaze flicking between the Barons and their wives. "That it has come to this." He closed his eyes for a moment, as though reaching a decision, though everyone knew what he was about to say. "To the Giants!" the King bellowed. "They shall be sent to the Giants."

The decree was irrevocable. Long live the King.

The King ordered a boat to be brought to the harbor and commanded his Daughters to board. It broke his heart, poor thing, but what choice did he have? And he such a tender man—how many times had this punishment been applicable, but he chose mercy instead? Many. Poor lamb. He did not permit them to speak, though they tried. They struggled in vain. They could not remove the gags from their mouths nor the ropes from their hands and feet. They tried to yell. So deep their voices were! This is what happens when you let daughters run wild. They get . . . *mannish.* I mean. The proof is right there.

"Silence!" the King roared. He asked his beloved sons-in-law to usher those wicked girls onto the boat and to force it into the tide. "To the sea with you! All to the sea!"

The boat found its way to the current, and the current pulled it out of the harbor. By midmorning they were gone. No one knew how long it took the sea to deliver cargo to the Land of the Giants. A day? A week? Did it matter? *Good riddance.* Everyone agreed.

And then, because the Barons loved their dear old Dad so very much, they abandoned their castles and even forwent their weekly tithing and tax collection and instead moved into the palace. Such good boys! Everyone said so. And what's more, it seemed that the King and his former sons-in-law (now sons) had opened their hearts and homes to the un-familied children who had been, until now, wandering the streets of the city with nowhere to go. Such humanitarians, those Barons! The castle rang with children's voices. It was, everyone agreed, the happiest of places.

And then the Barons donated their wealth to the Sovereign Fund. So generous!

And then they reinstated the prayer groups. Setting an unknown, veiled woman to keep them going. This, everyone decided, was a good thing. Prayers and all.

And the schools reopened. One of the Barons instated himself as the teacher. Which one was it? Hard to know. They all blend together. The one with the beautiful face and the long neck. No facial hair. They all look so similar! Did they always?

And suddenly the children had shoes. All of them! The Barons took no credit, but everyone knew it was them.

And one of them reorganized the Court system. Which was good. So unfair before! Too many bribes. Which Baron was it? One of the good ones, one supposes.

Sometimes, now, the King walks from the castle to the quay and stands at the edge of the water, looking out toward the horizon, to the exact place where the boat carrying his Daughters disappeared. Perhaps he misses them and wishes they would return. Perhaps he worries that they could come back, and bring their wickedness with them. The King is accompanied, as he usually is these days, by his flocks of pigeons. Each time, the pigeons spiral higher and higher and higher, before returning and alighting on his shoulders, arms, or cloak. He whispers to his birds, who whisper back. And then he walks home—a jumble of feathers and wings and beaks and bright, black eyes. He is more pigeon than man these days, poor thing. And walking slower every day. It's probably only a matter of time. Everyone says so.

Well. He had a good run.

Three months after the Ball, the King woke with a start.

"Something is different," he said, to no one in particular, save the pigeons. There were always pigeons. Time was he kept his birds in their aviary at night, and he visited them at the proper training intervals. But since the castle became overrun with children, the pigeons now were everywhere. No one could say for sure who was opening the cages—a child, or several children, or all of them, or the pigeons themselves—but now the pigeons had become used to freedom and would not go back. They loved the children, and couldn't bear to be parted from them. And they loved the King, too. Most nights he slept under a blanket of pigeons, all cooing in their sleep. The King had never slept so well in his life.

"Something is different," he said again.

"Coo," said the pigeons. And then they flew off to find some children to play with.

The King went down to breakfast. His Daughters were there—in disguise, of course. Albina and Althea and Adeline and Aurora and Annika and who knows who else. He hardly recognized them anymore with their shorn heads and their heavy boots and their practiced mannish swagger. They shoved rolled socks in their trousers and taught themselves to spread and snort and slap and *own.* They farted constantly. Which, the King reasoned, is *fine.* It's just . . .

He missed his Daughters. As they were. Wickedness and all. Not actually wickedness, obviously, but, he realized, he missed the way they raised eyebrows. He missed the way they annoyed the Council. And the Priests. And the Barons. He missed the smell of their hair and the swish of their skirts and the way their laughter sounded like music.

Also? He could no longer tell them apart. Granted, he couldn't before, but now it was worse. They were uniformed now. Their hair was the same, and their clothes, and their mannerisms. They were pantomiming Baron-ness, and doing so identically. He lived now in a household of actors and each of them was playing the same character.

Only the children helped to break up the monotony. *Thank goodness for that,* the King thought.

Breakfast was served as the children streaked through the room —climbing the drapes and hanging from the statues and sliding under the table.

"Mind you don't hurt yourselves," the King murmured for the millionth time as he thoughtfully munched on his toast. He looked at his Daughters. Or his sons-in-law. Or his Daughters who were pretending to be his sons who were pretending to be his Daughters. His head hurt. This was confusing.

"Um," he began. The Daughters looked at their father. Their faces softened. They looked like themselves again.

"Althea?" he said weakly. He wasn't sure if she was even at the table. He winced.

"Yes, Father," said the most Althea-looking of all of the Sort-of-Barons in the room. The King nearly sighed in relief.

"Has anyone checked the harbor this morning," the King asked. "Has anyone looked for boats on the horizon?"

"It's not coming back, Father," the Baron/Daughter closest to him said, gently reaching over and rubbing his back. Annika, he thought. She definitely sounded like Annika. She had swollen knuckles. That was Annika, right?

"Something's different today," the King muttered. "Something is coming. I can feel it."

The Daughters exchanged stricken glances but said nothing.

"Coo," said the pigeons. And the King became convinced that the pigeons agreed with him.

Later that morning, the King returned to the water. He saw nothing.

In the afternoon, he returned again. Again he saw nothing.

But that evening, as the sun sank in the west, the King yet again returned to the harbor's edge, and there, at the rim of the sky, was a smudge. And as he stood and watched, the smudge became a splotch. And then the splotch became a shape. And the shape grew closer and closer until it looked like a boat.

"Fly!" he shouted to his pigeons. "Fly now! Get my Daughters. Get the children. We must make a plan!"

And to his Mariners he said this: "Take your fastest boats and your most skilled sailors. Surround that vessel. Bring it in quietly, and under the cover of darkness. Bring its occupants to the throne room without violence or incident. Bind them if you need to. If they fight, sink the ship and leave its sailors to drown." The Mariners clicked their heels and bowed low to their King.

As it turned out, the ship did not carry Barons, nor soldiers, nor mercenaries of any kind.

There were only three occupants aboard, and they were all Giants.

Or, more specifically, two Giants and one Giantess. They were, if everyone was being honest with themselves, much smaller than they would have imagined. No one had been to the Land of Giants for at least four generations. In the stories, its inhabitants were the size of houses. In actuality, their heads hovered near the ceiling, but did not touch it.

The Daughters joined their father in the Receiving Room, and kept close. They eyed the Giants warily. The Giants did not appear to notice. They bowed low. They were impeccably polite.

"My name is Runt," the tallest one said. "Son of Grunt, son of Brunt."

The Daughter/Barons bowed in return.

The giant Runt continued, gesturing to his companions, "And this is Og, son of Gog, son of Tog. And this is Marlene. We are emissaries, and we speak with the authority of the Collective, as we have no Monarch. We seek the Thirty-Three Wicked Daughters of King Diodicias. I have a message that can be read only to them."

The Daughter/Barons looked at one another. Albina cleared her throat, but the King raised his hand to stop her.

"I'm afraid you are too late. The Daughters of Diodicias, after being legally and modestly married to thirty-three dutiful Barons, succumbed to their own wickedness. They attempted to cut their husbands' throats in order to return to their wicked ways. I placed them on a boat and sent them to the sea. No one will ever hear from them again."

"Your story is incorrect," the Giant Og countered. "The marriages you mention were neither modest nor lawful. And while it is true that a boat full of gowned individuals left this harbor, they were nobody's Daughters."

Albina stepped forward. She jutted out her chin and narrowed her eye. "You have only told us part of your story," she said.

The Giant Marlene bowed low once again. "And you, madam, have told me none of yours."

The children had not been invited to the meeting. This, they decided, was utterly unfair, and they determined to do something to rectify the situation. Because they had become skilled in the arts of Stealth and Subterfuge and Thievery, they had already made plans for just such a scenario. They knew the safe places to shimmy up behind the drapes. They knew how to scramble through the rafters. They knew how to drop down from the roof. They knew the secret passageways and forgotten gaps. They knew the castle better than they knew their own breath. And so they scurried in—a silent, creeping swarm—and listened to the Giant's story.

This is how they learned that a ship full of sniveling, weeping Barons landed on the shores of the Land of Giants. They learned how the Barons, in their pleading for their miserable lives, had told the Giants about the Daughters of Diodicias, and how they wept at the wickedness of their wanton once-wives. They told the Giants about the glittering coats, and the sinister gowns. Gowns that trapped them. They told the Giants about the beads and the masks and the children in cloaks. They told the Giants about the prison boudoirs and the perfectly implemented scheme—how they carried each sleeping Daughter off, in the night. How they tricked the King. And then were tricked. By the King. And those wicked Daughters. They told the Giants about the community banks and the schools and the boxing matches and the knives, and the nude dancing and the shoes, and how they had tried and tried and tried to thwart those wretched Daughters, and how they thought they had finally found a way. Until they didn't.

"So what you are saying is that you poisoned, kidnapped, lied, plotted regicide, and schemed, and are now upset that others schemed against you?" the Giants asked the Barons.

"Well, actually," sniffed the Barons, but the Giants did not let them finish. They couldn't stand it for another second. They ate them on the spot. They tasted, the Giants now explained, awful, and gave the entire nation a terrible fit of gas.

"What is it that you are seeking, Giants?" Albina asked.

"We are entranced by you," Runt the Giant admitted.

"We wish for you to come to the Land of the Giants and live with us," the Giant Og added.

"We wish to ask for your hands in marriage, if you will accept us," the Giant Marlene said, "or your presence in our community, if you will not. We wish to have your ideas and your work and your voices and your minds so that we may become more than ourselves."

"We wish to place crowns on your heads and flowers at your feet, if you wish," the Giant Runt said, "or work alongside you if you do not. We wish to build libraries and schools and lecture halls. We wish to raise pigeons and learn metallurgy and become good farmers and to study the stars."

"You can do all of those things without us," Albina said. "Why should we come with you? Our lives are here."

"You are wearing someone else's clothes and using someone else's names, while your own are maligned," Og said. "Here you are impostors in your own land, hidden from your own people. We wish to give you a nation, one that is yours forever. Your lives may be here, but is this really the life you would choose?"

Silence fell.

"I prefer slacks," Albina said, looking the Giant Marlene in the eye.

"So keep them," Marlene said. She held Albina's gaze for a moment. Then she blushed.

The children exchanged glances with one another. And then felt their hearts begin to sink. They looked at the King's face. He curled around himself, as though his heart had been struck by an arrow. Indeed, the children thought, perhaps it actually had.

King Diodicias, years after his eventual passing, was known for his tender, capacious heart. Which is saying something, given how many times it had been broken. His wicked Daughters, gone. His sons-in-law-turned-sons, vanished. In the night. No one knew where they had gone. But, despite those great sorrows, his capacity to love only increased. He threw his attention to the care and rearing of his foundling children, and he knew each one by name. He saw to their education and interests and development. He cheered them in their successes and comforted them in their failures. He loved them every step of the way. And once he raised those children, he continued to open his home to more. He followed in his beloved Althea's footsteps and built school after school and university after university. He was generous to a fault, nearly bankrupting himself more than once. He dissolved the Council in favor of forming a Parliament of the Peasantry, both in service to the people and voted into office by the people.

He was loved. Venerated. Adored.

Years later, he began entertaining emissaries from the country once called the Land of the Giants, but now called Albion, though the reason for the name change was lost to history. The emissaries—giants, all, with big vocabularies and big hearts, with pronounced chins and broad shoulders and quick feet and bright minds—all called him "Grandpop."

No one knew why.

ELIZABETH BEAR

Bullet Point

FROM *Wastelands: The New Apocalypse*

IT TAKES A long time for the light to die. The power plants can run for a while on automation. Hospitals have emergency generators with massive tanks of fuel. Some houses and businesses have solar panels or windmills. Those may keep making juice, at least intermittently, until entropy claims the workings.

How long is it likely to take then? Six months? The better part of a decade?

I stand on the roof deck of the Luxor casino parking garage, watching the lights that remain, and I wonder. I don't even know enough to theorize, really.

I'm not an engineer. I used to be a blackjack dealer.

Now I am the only living human left on Earth.

It's not all bad. I don't have to deal with:

- Death (except the possibility of my own, eventually).
- Taxes.
- Annoying holidays with my former extended family.
- Airplane lights crossing the desert sky.
- Chemtrails (okay, those were never real in the first place).
- Card counters.
- Maisie the pit boss. Thank God.
- My ex-husband. *Double* thank God.

Well, of course I can't know for sure that I'm the only living person. But for all practical purposes, I seem to be. Maybe Las Vegas is the only place that got wiped out. Maybe over the mountain, Pahrump is thriving.

I don't think so. I hear the abandoned dog packs howling in the night, and I've watched the lights go out, one by one by one.

I feel so bad for those dogs. And even worse for all the ones trapped in houses when the end came. All the cats, guinea pigs, pet turtles. The horses and burros, at least, have a chance. Wild horses can survive in Nevada.

There are so many of them. There's nothing I can do.

If there are any other humans surviving, they are far away from here, and I have no idea where to find them, or even how to begin looking. I have to get out of the desert, though, if I want to keep living. For oh, so many reasons.

I can trust myself, at least. Trusting anybody else never got me where I wanted to be.

Another thing I don't know for sure, and can't even guess at: Why.

Not knowing why?

That's the real pisser.

Here is an incomplete list of things that do not exist anymore:

- Fresh-baked cookies (unless I find a propane oven and milk a cow and churn some butter and then bake them).
- Jesus freaks (I wonder how they felt when the Rapture happened and it turned out God was taking almost *literally everybody?* That had to be a little bit of a comedown).
- Domestic violence.
- Did I mention my ex-husband?

There's more than enough Twinkies just in the Las Vegas metro area to keep me in snack cakes until the saturated fat kills me. If I last long enough that that's what gets me, I might even find out if they eventually go stale.

A problem with being in Las Vegas is getting back out of it again. Walking across a desert will kill me faster than snack cakes. And the highway is impassable with all the stopped and empty cars.

Maybe I can find a monster truck and drive it over everything.

More things that don't exist anymore:

- Reckless driving.
- Speeding tickets.
- Points on your license.
- Worrying about fuel efficiency.

Las Vegas Boulevard is dark and still. Nevertheless, I can't make myself walk on the blacktop, even though the cars there are unmoving, bumper to bumper for all eternity. The Strip's last traffic jam.

There might be bodies in the cars. I don't look.

I don't want to know.

I don't think there's going to be anybody alive, but that might be worse. More dangerous, anyway.

I mean, I *think* I'm the last. But I don't *know.*

That was also the reason I couldn't make myself walk along the sidewalk. It was too exposed. The tall casinos were mostly designed so that their windows had views of something more interesting than hordes of pedestrians—hordes of pedestrians now long gone—but somebody might be up there, and somebody up there might spot me. A lone moving dot on a sea of silent asphalt.

Lord, where have all the people gone?

So I stick to the median. With its crape myrtle hedges and doomed palm trees already drooping in the failed irrigation to break up my outline. With the now pointless crowd control barriers to discourage jaywalkers from darting into traffic.

Two more things:

- Traffic.
- Jaywalkers.

Hey, and one more:

- Assholes.

I am half-hoping to find people. And I am 90 percent terrified of what they might do if I find them. Or if they find me first.

I'm pretty sure this wasn't actually the Rapture.

Pretty sure.

I keep trying to tell myself that there's not a single damned person from the old world that I really miss. That it's time I had some time alone, as the song used to go. It is nice not to be on anybody else's schedule, or subject to anybody else's expectations or demands. At least my ex-husband is almost certainly among the evaporated. That's a load off my mind.

I moved to Vegas, changed my name by sealed court order, abandoned a career I worked for ten years to get, and became a casino dealer in order to hide from him. Considering that, it's not a surprise to find myself relieved that whatever ends up causing me to look over my shoulder from now on, it won't be Paul.

I got the cozy apocalypse that was supposed to be the best-case-apocalypse-scenario—wish fulfillment—complete with the feral dogs that howl in the night.

But it doesn't feel like wish fulfillment. It feels like . . . being alone on the beach in winter. I'm lonely, and I miss . . . well, I already left behind everybody I loved. But leaving somebody behind is not the same thing as *knowing they are gone.*

There's potential space, and there's empty space.

Maybe that's why I'm still here. Nobody thought to tap me on the shoulder and say, "Hey, Izzy, let's go," because I'd already abandoned all of them to save my own life one time.

Hah. There I go again. Making things about me that aren't.

I thought I was used to being lonely, but this is a whole new level of alone. I feel like I should be paralyzed by survivor guilt. But I am a rock. I am an island.

- Simon
- Garfunkel

Lying to yourself is, however, still alive and well.

The gun is heavy. Cold, blue metal. It feels about twice its size.

I find it under the seat of a cop car with the driver's door left open. The keys are in the ignition. The dome light has long since burned out, and the open-door dinger has dinged itself into silence.

It's a handgun. A revolver. Old school. There is a holster to go with it, but no gunbelt. There are six bullets in the cylinder.

- The Las Vegas Metropolitan Police Department.
- Crooked cops.
- Throwaway guns.

I unbuckle my belt, thread it through the loops on the holster, and hang it at my hip.

There *are* plenty of rattlesnakes, still.

- Antivenin.
- Emergency rooms.

There *are* plenty of antibiotics. And pain medication. And canned peaches.

And a nice ten-speed mountain bike that I liberate from a sporting goods place, along with one of those trailers designed for pulling your kid or dog along. I've never been much of an urban biker, preferring trails, but it wasn't like I would have to contend with traffic. And it seems like the right tool for weaving in and out of rows of abandoned cars.

I pick up a book on bike repair too, and some tire patches and spare tubes and so on. Plus saddlebags and baskets. And a lot of water bottles.

It turns out that one thing the zombie-apocalypse movies got really wrong was the abundance of stockpiled resources available after a population of more than seven billion people just . . . ceases to exist.

There's plenty of stuff to go around when there's no "around" for it to go. Until the stuff goes bad, anyway.

That's the reason I want to get out of the desert before summer comes. Things will last longer in colder places, with less murderous UV.

Things that apparently *do* still exist: at least one other human being.

And he is following me.

He picks me up at a Vons. I'm in the pasta aisle. The rats have started gnawing into boxes, but the canned goods are relatively fine. And if you can ignore the silence of the gaming machines and the smell of fermenting fruit, rotten meat, and rodent urine, it's not that different than if I were shopping at 2:00 a.m. in the old world.

I'm crouched down, filling my backpack with Beefaroni and D batteries from the endcap, when I hear footsteps. It's daylight outside, but it's dark inside the store. I turn off my LED flashlight. My heart contracts inside me, shuddering jolts of blood through my arteries. The rush and thump fills my ears. I strain through them for the sounds that mean life or death: the scrape or squeak of boot sole on tile, the rattle of packages.

My hands shake as I zip the backpack inch by silent inch. I stand. The straps creak. I can't be sure if I have managed not to tremble the bag into a betraying clink. One step, then another. Sideways, slipping, setting each foot down carefully so it doesn't make a sound.

As I get closer to the front of the store (good) the ambiance grows brighter (bad). I hunker by the side of a dead slot machine, shivering. From where I crouch, I can peek around and see a clear path to the door.

The whole way is silhouetted against the plate glass windows. The pack weighs on my shoulders. If I leave it, I'm not really leaving anything. I can get another, and all the Chef Boyardee I want. But it's hard to abandon resources.

And hey, the cans might stop a bullet.

Don't hyperventilate.

Easier said than done.

Sliding doors stopped working when the store lights did. Too late, I realize there's probably a fire door in the back I could have slipped out of more easily. In the old world, that would have been alarmed . . . but would the alarm even work anymore?

There is a panic bar on the front doors. I crane over my shoulder, straining for motion, color, any sign of the person I am certain I heard.

Nothing.

Maybe I'm hallucinating.

Maybe he's gone to the back of the store.

I nerve myself and hit the door running. I got it open on the way in, so I know it isn't locked. It flies away from the crash bar —no subtlety there—and I plunge through, sneakers slapping the pavement. The parking lot outside is flat and baking, even in

September. The sun hits my ballcap like a slap. Rosebushes and trees scattered in the islands are already dead from lack of water. The rosemary bushes and crape myrtles look a little sad, but they are holding on.

I sprint toward them. Now the pack makes noise, the cans within clanking and thumping on each other—and clanking and thumping against my ribs and spine. I'll have a suite of bruises because of them. But I left my bike on the kickstand in the fire lane, and—wonder of wonders—it's still there. I throw myself at it and swing a leg through, pushing off with my feet before I ever touch the pedals. I miss my first push and skin the back of my calf bloody on the serrated grip.

I curse, not loud but on that hiss of breath you get with shock and pain. The second time, I manage to get my heel *on* the pedal. The bike jerks forward with each hard pump.

I squirt between parked cars. As my heart slows, I let myself think I've imagined the whole thing. Until the supermarket doors crash open, and a male voice shrill with desperation yells, "Miss! Come back! Miss! Don't run away from me! Please! I'm not going to hurt you!"

And maybe he's not. But I'm not inclined to trust. Trusting never did get me anywhere I wanted to be.

I push down and pedal harder. I don't coast.

He only shouts after me. He doesn't shoot. And I don't look back.

Now that he knows I exist, he's not going to stop looking.

I know this the way I know my childhood street address.

And why *would* he stop? People need people, or so we're always told. Being alone—really alone, completely alone—is a form of torture.

To be utterly truthful, there's a part of me that wants to go looking for him. Part of me that doesn't want to be alone anymore either.

The question I have to ask myself is whether that lonely part of me is stronger than the feral, sensible part that cautions me to run away. To run, and keep running.

Because it's the apocalypse. And I'm not very big, or a trained fighter. And because of another thing that doesn't exist anymore:

- Social controls.

Dissociation, though—that I've got *plenty* of.

He is going to come looking for me. Because of course he will. I hear him calling after me for a long time as I ride away. And I know he tries to follow me because *I* follow *him.*

We're the last two people on Earth and how do you get more Meet Cute than that? We've all stayed up late watching B movies in the nosebleed section of the cable channels and we've all read TV Tropes and we all know how this story goes.

But my name isn't Eve. It's Isabella. And I have an allergy to clichés.

- Dating websites.
- Restraining orders.
- Twitter block lists.
- Domestic violence shelters.

I stalk him. I'll call it what it is.

It's easy to find him again: he's so confident and fearless that he's still wandering around in the same neighborhood *trying* to get my attention.

I mean, first I go back to my current lair and get ready to run.

I load up the bike trailer with my food and gear, and flats and flats and flats of water. My sun layers and my hat go inside and I zip the whole thing up.

Then I hide it, and I check again to be sure my gun is loaded.

And *then* I go and stalk him.

He's definitely a lot bigger than me. But he doesn't look a damned thing like my ex, which is a point in his favor.

And he isn't trying in the least to be sneaky. He's just walking down the sidewalk, swerving to miss the cars that rolled off the road when their drivers disappeared, pulling a kid's little red wagon loaded with supplies. He's armed with a pistol on his belt, but so am I. And at least he's not strung all over with bandoliers and automatic weapons. Plus, there are enough of those hungry, terrified feral dog packs around that a weapon isn't a bad idea.

I wonder how long it will be before the cougars move back down from the mountains and start eating them all.

The circle of life.

Poor dogs.

They were counting on us, and look where that got them.

The only other living human being (presumed) is wearing a dirty T-shirt (athletic gray), faded jeans, and a pair of high-top skull-pattern Chucks that I appreciate the irony of, even while knowing his feet must be roasting in them. I make him out to be about twenty-five. His hair is still pretty clean-cut under his mesh-sided brimmed hat, but he's wearing about two weeks of untrimmed beard. Two weeks is about how long it's been since the world ended.

He calls out as he walks along. How can anyone be so unafraid to attract attention? So confident of taking up all that space in the world? Like he thinks he has a right to exist and nobody is going to come take it away from him.

He's so *relaxed.* It scares me just watching him.

I *do* notice that he doesn't seem threatening. There's nothing sinister, calculated, or menacing about this guy. He keeps pushing his hat up to mop the sweat from under it with an old cotton bandanna. He doesn't have a lot of situational awareness, either. Even with me orbiting him a couple of blocks off on the mountain bike, he doesn't seem to notice me watching. I'm staying under cover, sure. But the bike isn't silent. It has a chain and wheels and joints. It creaks and rattles and whizzes a little, like any bicycle.

Blood has dried, itchy and tight-feeling, on the back of my calf. The edge of my sock is stiff. I drink some of the water in my bottle, though not as much as I want to.

It's getting on toward evening and he's walking more directly now, in less of a searching wander, when I make up my mind. He seems to be taking a break from searching for me, at least for the time being. He's stopped making forays into side streets, and he's stopped calling out.

I cycle hard on a parallel street to get in front of him, and from a block away I show myself.

He stops in his tracks. His hands move away from his sides and he drops the little red wagon handle. My right hand stays on the butt of my holstered gun with the six bullets in it.

"Hi," he says, after an awkward pause. He pitches his voice to carry. "I'm Ben."

"Hi," I call back. "I'm Isabella."

"You came back."

I nod. Never in my memory—probably in living memory—has it been quiet enough in this city that you could hear somebody clearly if they called to you from this far away. But it's that quiet now. Honeybees buzz on the crape myrtles. I wonder if they're Africanized.

"Nice bike, Isabella."

"Thanks." I let the smirk happen. "It's new."

He laughs. Then he bends down and picks up the handle of his little red wagon. When he straightens, he lets his hands hang naturally. "Have you seen anybody else?"

I shake my head.

"Me neither." He makes a face. "Mind if I come over?"

My heart speeds. But it's respectful that he's asking, right?

I don't get off the bike or walk it toward him. I cant it against one cocked leg and wait.

"Sure." I try to sound confident. I square my shoulders.

You know what else doesn't exist anymore?

- Backup.

We head off side by side. I've finally gotten off the bike and am walking it, though I casually keep it and the wagon in between us and stay out of grabbing range. The step-through frame will help me hop on and bug out fast if I need to.

Ben offers me a granola bar. I guess he learned early on, as I did, that once the power went off, there wasn't any point in harvesting chocolate. Well, I mean, it's still calorie-dense. But if it's daytime, it's probably squeezable. And if it's not melted, it has resolidified into the wrapper and you'll wind up eating a fair amount of plastic.

"Terrorists," he hazards, with the air of one making conversation.

I shake my head. "Aliens."

He thinks about it.

"We probably had it coming," I posit.

"I don't think it's a great idea to stay in Vegas," Ben says, with no acknowledgment of the non sequitur.

"I've been thinking that too."

He glances sidelong at me. His face brightens. "I was thinking of heading to San Diego. Nice and temperate. Lots of seafood. Easy to grow fruit. Not as hot as here."

I think about earthquakes and drought and wildfires. My plan was the Pacific Northwest, where the climate is mild and wet and un-irrigated agriculture could flourish. I figure I've got maybe five years to figure out a sustainable lifestyle.

And I don't want to spend the rest of my life living off ceviche. Or dodging wildfires and worrying about potable water.

I don't say anything, though. If I decide to split on this guy, it's just as well if he doesn't know what my plans were. Especially if we're the last two people on Earth.

Why him? Why me?

Who knows.

"Lot of avocados down there." I can sound like I'm agreeing to nearly anything.

He nods companionably. "The bike is a good idea."

"I'd be a little scared to try cycling across the mountains and through Baker. That's some nasty desert."

Mild pushback, to see what happens in response.

"I figure you could make it in a week or ten days."

That would be some Tour de France shit, Ben. Especially towing water. But I don't say that.

- Tour de France.

"Or," he says, "I thought of maybe a Humvee. Soon, while the gas is still good."

He loses a few points on that. I wouldn't feel bad at all about bullet-pointing Hummers, and I don't feel nearly as bad about bullet-pointing the sort of people who used to drive them as I probably ought to.

"Look," Ben says, when I've been quiet for a while, "why don't we find someplace to hole up? It's getting dark, and the dog packs will be out soon."

I look at him and can't think what to say.

He sighs tolerantly, not getting it. I guess *not getting it* isn't over yet either.

"I give you my word of honor that I will be a total gentleman."

*

You have to trust somebody sometime.

I go home with Ben. Not in the euphemistic sense. In the sense that we pick a random house and break into it together. It has barred security doors and breaking in would be harder, except the yard wasn't xeriscaped and all the

- Landscaping

is down to brown sticks and sadness. Which makes it super easy to spot the fake rock that had once been concealed in a now-desiccated foundation planting, turn it over, and extract the key hidden inside.

We let ourselves in. There used to be a security system, but it's out of juice. The house is hot and dark inside, and smells like decay. Plant decay, mostly: sweetish and overripe, due to the fruit rotting in bowls on the counter. Neither Ben nor I is dumb enough to open the refrigerator. We do check the bedrooms for bodies. There aren't any—there never are—but we find the remains of a hamster that starved and had mummified in its cedar chips.

That makes me sad, like the dog packs. If this *is* the Rapture, I hope God gets a nasty call from the Afterlife Society for the Prevention of Cruelty to Animals.

We find can openers and plates and set about rustling up some supper. All the biking has made us ravenous, and when I finish eating, I am surprised to discover that I have let my guard down. And that nothing terrible has happened.

Ben looks at me across the drift of Spam cans and Green Giant vacuum-packed corn (my favorite). "This would be perfect if the air-conditioning worked."

"Sometimes you can find a place with solar panels," I say noncommittally.

"Funny that all that tree hugging turned out useful after all, isn't it?" And maybe he sees the look on my face, because he raises a hand, placating. "Some of my best friends are tree huggers!" He looks down, mouth twisting. "*Were* tree huggers."

So I forgive him. "My plan had been to find someplace that was convenient and had solar, and if I was lucky its own well. And wait for winter before I set out."

"That's a good idea." He picks at a canned peach.

"Also, the older houses up in Northtown and on the west side of the valley. Those handle the heat better."

"Little dark up there in North Vegas," Ben says, casually. "I mean, not that there's anybody left, but it was."

I open my mouth. I close it. I almost hear the record scratch.

I'd have thought it was safe to bullet

- Racism.

But I guess not.

I don't say, *So it's full of evaporated-Black-people cooties?* I get up, instead, and start clearing empty tin cans off the table and setting them in the useless sink. Ben watches me, amused that I'm tidying this place we're only going to abandon.

Setting things to rights, the only way I can.

He's relaxed and expansive now. A little proprietary.

I am not *quite* as scared as I ever have been in my life. But that's only because I've been really, *really* scared.

"It's just us now. You don't have anybody to impress," Ben says. "You're free. You don't have to play those games to get ahead."

I blink at him. "Games?"

He stands up. I turn toward the sink. Knives in the knife block beside it. If it comes down to it, they might be worth a try. I try to keep my eyes forward, to not give him a reason to think I'm being impertinent. But I keep glancing back.

I look scared. And that's bad. You never want to look scared.

It attracts predators.

"Nobody can hurt you for saying the truth now. And obviously," he says with something he probably means to be taken as a coaxing smile, "it's up to us to repopulate the planet."

"With white people." It just comes out. I've never been the best at self-censorship. Even when I know speaking might get me hurt.

At least I keep my tone neutral. I think.

Neutral enough, I guess, because he leers again. "Maybe God's given us a second chance to get it right, is all I'm saying. Don't you think it's a sign? I mean, here I meet the last woman on Earth, and she's a blue-eyed blonde."

The little tins fit inside the big tins. The spoons stack up.

- Ice cream.

Though I could probably make some, if I found that cow. And snow. And bottle blondes are still going to be around until my hair grows out. I don't have any reason to try to change my appearance now.

Ben moves, the floor creaking under him. "If you're not going to try to save humanity, what's the point in even being alive? Are you going to just give up?"

I turn toward him. I put my back toward the sink. I half-expect him to be looming over me but he's standing well back, respectfully. "Maybe humanity has a lifespan, like everything else. You're going to die eventually."

"Sure," he says. "That's why people have kids. To leave a legacy. Leave something of themselves behind."

"Two human beings are not a viable gene pool."

"You don't want to rush into anything," he says. "That's all right. I can respect that."

And then he does something that stuns me utterly. He goes and lies down on the sofa. He only glances back at me once. The expression on his face is trying to be neutral, but I can see the smugness beneath it.

The fucking *confidence.*

Of course he doesn't need to push his luck, or my timeline. Of course he's confident I'll come around. He's got all the time in the world.

And what choice have I got in the long run, really?

There will always be assholes.

I leave that house in the morning at first light. I lock the door behind me to be tidy.

Only four bullets left. I should have anticipated that I might need more ammo. But this is Nevada. I can probably find some.

Maybe I can find a friendly dog, also. I love dogs. And it's not good for people to be too alone.

There might still be some horses out in the northwest valley that haven't gone totally wild. It'd be nice to have company.

I can get books from the libraries. I've got a few months to prepare. I wonder how you take care of a horse on a long pack trip? I wonder if I can manage it on my own?

Well, I'll find out this winter. And if I get to Reno before the snow melts in the Sierras . . . I'm a patient girl. And I'll have the benefit of not having slept through history class. What I mean to say is, I can wait to tackle Donner Pass until springtime.

The lights that are still on *stay* on longer than I might have expected. But eventually, one by one, they fail. When I can't see any anywhere anymore, I make my way down to the Strip with Bruce, my brindle mastiff, trotting beside.

Before I head north, I want to say goodbye.

That night the stars shine over Las Vegas, as they have not shone in living memory. The Milky Way is a misty waterfall. I can make out a Subaru logo for the ages: six and a half Pleiades.

I stand in the middle of the empty, dark, and silent Strip, and watch the lack of answering lights bloom in the vast black bowl of the valley all around.

I cannot see so far as Tokyo, New York, Hong Kong, London, Cairo, Jerusalem, Abu Dhabi, Seoul, Sydney, Rio de Janeiro, Paris, Madrid, Kyoto, Chicago, Amsterdam, Mumbai, Mecca, Milan. All the places where artificial light and smog had, for an infinitesimal cosmic moment, wiped them from the sky. But I imagine that those distant, alien suns now shine the same way, there.

As if they had never been dimmed. As if the Milky Way had never faded, ghostlike, before the glare.

I reach down and stroke Bruce's ears. They're soft as cashmere. He leans on me, happy.

That night sky would be a remarkable sight. If I had a soul in the world to remark to.

GWENDOLYN KISTE

The Eight People Who Murdered Me (Excerpt from Lucy Westenra's Diary)

FROM *Nightmare*

1. You

THE TEETH IN the neck gambit obviously starts all of this. Don't think I'll forget that. Don't expect for one moment you're going to get off too easily. You might not be the only one to blame, but you're still mostly to blame.

For how you come to me when I'm by myself, a lonely girl in a goblin market where some treasures are best left undiscovered. Tonight, my mother's hosting another soirée, all in my honor, a way to find me the perfect husband. She doesn't care what I have to say about it. Nobody cares what I say, so without a word, I slip out the back door and take an evening stroll through the city, past the downtown train station with its melancholy whistles and along cobblestone streets with vendors that keep strange hours.

"What do you seek, pretty girl?" they ask, their lips curled up in grotesque smiles, each of them proffering me trinkets meant to solve problems I don't have.

My nervous hands clasped in front of me, I turn away, and that's when I see you. There at the corner, emerging beneath a gaslight, your voice a sweet melody that could pied-piper all the children of London to their unmarked graves.

"Good evening, Miss Lucy," you whisper, and my skin hums in refrain. I never ask how you know me. It should be my first question, but you don't look like a question to me. You look like an answer—an escape from the everyday, the humdrum of parlors and suitors and a future where I'll surrender my name and freedom in exchange for a title.

Missus. Mother. Nothing more.

But you pretend to offer another way. In an instant, we're together, perched side by side on an iron park bench, and you share everything about yourself—where you came from, how you traveled aboard a ship named after Persephone's mother, a woman who knew loss so intimately. Your gaze speaks to me of loss, too. It feels as though you already know me, that we've met like this a thousand times before, so I lean in and whisper my secrets in your ear. How I'm desperate for something more, something you promise me without ever speaking a word. You might be a stranger, but it seems safer to share these things with you than with my own best friend.

As the moon slips across the sky, you guide me to my feet, and we sway together, dancing to music no one else can hear.

"Don't let me go," I say, and you smile, because you'll oblige, just not quite the way I expect.

Your breath sweet as marzipan, you embrace me, one hand on my shoulder and the other on the small of my back. We're so close I can barely breathe. Then all at once, I can't breathe or move or even scream.

When you finish with me and I return home, my head heavy and vision blurred, the party is long over, and the house has gone quiet. In my own bedroom, nothing looks familiar, not the faded floral wallpaper or the vanity arrayed with candlesticks or the canopy beds, one that's mine and the other with Mina curled up in the dark.

"Are you awake?" I ask, my voice splitting in two, blood on my hands, blood that's all my own. But she's already fast asleep, and it isn't worth waking her now, even if I could form the words to tell her what you've done to me.

2. My Mother

She could have warned me.

She could have stitched crosses into all my corsets and brewed me vervain tea until my blood was brimming with it and you wouldn't have wanted me.

Better yet, she could have taken my hand, and I would have taken Mina's, and we could have run together, farther than the edge of town, further than the Carpathian Mountains, to somewhere no man would be brave enough to follow.

But that isn't what she did. It isn't what any of our mothers have done. This is the world they inherited, and it's the one we'll get too. Perhaps we shouldn't expect anything more.

(My father with his bulging bank account and dirty fingernails is below mention. Sometimes, men can be far crueler than monsters.)

3. My Best Friend

Mina, sweet Mina, a light of all lights. Even if my mother wouldn't have come with us, we still could have fled this city of death. That was what we always wanted.

"Shall we run away together today?" I'd ask, back when we were just girls who didn't know enough to know we should be afraid.

"Tomorrow," she would whisper, and we'd laugh and dance together in the garden maze, our fingers entwined, fresh blooms of wisteria woven through our hair.

For years, I believed tomorrow would come. But today has come instead, the morning when Mina can see the gray glint in my eye, this unwitting change stirring within me, all thanks to what you've done.

Now she only shakes her head. "We're not children anymore, Lucy," she says, and I suppose this means we can no longer dream.

That night, I latch the bedroom window, but that won't be enough to stop you. Though I never invite you in, you're everywhere now, your shadow as weightless and oppressive as the August heat.

"Hello, my love," you whisper in the dark, your voice soft and sweet yet still strong enough to drown out the gentle thrum of my own heartbeat. You don't ask me what I want. You can't be bothered to care about that.

In your cold arms, my head lolls back, and through the open window, I listen to the mournful train whistle downtown, as passengers in fine red silks and gray-flourished top hats come and go, departing and returning from places I'll never know.

"I could take you wherever you'd like to go," you say, wetting your lips, and though I want to believe you, I already know the truth, even if it's too late now to matter.

In the next bed, Mina sleeps her dreamless sleep, and as you press your mouth against my throat, I reach out for her across the gloom, but she might as well be a thousand miles away.

Mina isn't like me. She wouldn't go walking at midnight, and she would never have listened to your lies. That's why she'll survive. Proper young ladies like her always do. They learn from my example how not to die.

(Even as I write these words, I know this isn't really her fault. She's only done what's expected—shed her hopes, shed her name, chose a husband. There are worse sins. There are your sins.)

4. My Fiancé

I have to choose someone too. That's the rule.

My mother holds more parties in my honor, and the men descend, vultures that they are, squeezing into every corner of the parlor, each of them on bended knee as though they're at my mercy and not the other way around.

"Pick me, Miss Lucy," their voices echo through the house, following me no matter where I hide. Nobody notices that my skin has gone pale, my eyes receded, and that perhaps I'm more in need of a passable doctor than an eligible bachelor.

"No more," I want to say, but they wear me down and wear me thin until I close my eyes, spin in a circle, and say yes to the first one I see.

He isn't the worst of them. This so-called honorable lord might even be better than most, because he's so ordinary, blander than yesterday's porridge, and part of me hopes that means he won't make unreasonable demands. Maybe with him, I won't have to fear a belt or a fist or a calloused hand that will hold me down until I scream, until I learn that screaming will do no good, until I've gone as mute as the dead.

Choosing him is supposed to keep me safe. Yet the moment he slips the ring on my finger, it feels like a gold-shaped prison. My dreams are fading away, as ethereal as the fog that brought you here.

Before bed, I lock the window again, and this time, you don't return. You've moved on to your next conquest. I hope that means that I'm safe now, that the worst is over, but while I'm asleep, Mina vanishes as well, departing for her own matrimonial funeral.

She leaves a note on my vanity. *Good luck, my Lucy.* As though all the luck in England could ever rescue us from this.

I sleepwalk through the next afternoon, hollowed out and aching, never hearing any of my mother's eager wedding plans or my fiancé's pointless promises. Outside, the wisteria is blooming in the garden, but its scent dissolves in the air, lost to me in the same way that I've lost everything else.

After midnight, I crawl out of bed and across the room, a leaden weight in my belly. Striking the last match, I light the candlesticks and read Mina's letter for the hundredth time, as though I'll discover some secret code. Only nothing's there but the same four words, empty as before. My chest twisted and heavy, I glance up at myself in the vanity, and everything in me goes numb.

I'm barely there. I'm barely anywhere. A thin scream lodges in my throat, as right in front of my eyes, my reflection is abandoning me. And it isn't doing the decent thing and disappearing all at once. Instead, I sit here at the mirror, grief seeping through my heart, and I watch myself disintegrate slowly. Hour by hour, I become less of me, my features going gray and translucent. By morning, I won't exist. This body will remain, but I will not. I'll be easy to forget too, a footnote in a story that's not my own.

When it's almost dawn and I'm almost gone, I exhale another scream, louder this time, and though you can't be bothered to hear me, wherever you are, I manage to wake the rest of the house.

"Lucy?" My mother's footsteps patter down the hall, but I don't answer her.

This can't be real. This can't be how I end. My hands unsteady, I lift the pair of burning candlesticks and pitch the fire at what remains of my own reflection. It does no good. Nothing will save me now.

With the candles limp on the floor, their flames sear through the rug, and I back into the corner, breathless. When my mother finally forces open my door, she cries out at the sight of me, of what I'm becoming. Then she barricades my bedroom and calls in someone to help.

That's when the worst of them arrive.

5. The Out-of-Town Doctor

I awaken in the morning to a man with a heavy leather bag and heavier words, his voice booming up and down the stairs, ricocheting like a silver bullet off the yellowed wallpaper.

"Anemia," he declares in the first of his lies, and sheds his fur-collared coat on the floor. "We'll fix that."

I never catch his name, because he only ever speaks over and around me, never *to* me. There's no reason to expect anything better. A scientist in a lab wouldn't introduce himself to the frog pickled in formaldehyde, so why should this famed doctor bother to say hello to the wan girl restrained on the canopy bed? I'm worse than a specimen in a jar. Just ask my mother.

"She never listened, never acted like she should," she weeps in the hallway, and my fiancé embraces her.

"It'll be all right now," he says, and I wonder who exactly it will be all right for. Certainly not me, not when the doctor threads his stiff tubes into my veins and calls all my former suitors into the room.

"Leave me alone," I whisper, but the house turns cold, and nobody seems to hear me.

My mother wavers in the doorway, her ruddy cheeks streaked with tears, as the men pin me to the mattress. One after another, right down the line, their starched shirts unbuttoned, sweat beading in the curve of their upper lips, they pump their blood into my body, filling me up with them. A transfusion, they call it, though I've got another word for it.

"Stop," I say, but with their faces flushed and eager, they're used to ignoring what I want.

6. Myself

For what it's worth, I don't believe this one. I *won't* believe it, no matter how many times they tell me I should have known better.

"If only she'd stayed at home," says my mother.

"If only she'd married sooner," says my best friend.

"If only she'd been a better patient," says the out-of-town doctor.

"If only she'd said yes to me instead," say all the suitors I denied.

They're wrong, they have to be. With their poisoned blood in my veins, I'd never beg these men or beg God to forgive me for what I haven't done. The last breath draining out of me, I'd never hate myself for giggling too loudly in the garden or the parlor or the streets, for tossing my head back and letting out a shriek of delight that could split the sky and decorum in two. And after I'm dead, I'd never curl up in the shadows of my tomb and weep silently to myself, make-believing all the ways I could have laced my corset a little tighter, kept my shoulders a little straighter, been the kind of girl who might have made my mother proud.

I'd never blame myself for what wasn't my fault, just because they claim it's my burden to bear. Just because the world isn't made for silly dreamers like me.

But like I said, I wouldn't do any of that, so let's not even talk about it.

7. The Faceless Mob

They come at night when my crypt is quiet. It might only be one or two of the men, or maybe it's all of them—the doctor I don't know, the suitors I spurned, the fiancé I never wanted. You might be there too, a shapeless form in the background, bleeding in with the rest, a torch in your hand and a sly grin on your face.

What I do know: this should be a safe place for me. Resting in my own coffin shouldn't be so bad. I've always been a girl who wanted impossible things. Now I'm a corpse who wants only to be left alone. A fair request for the dead, but not something I'll be lucky enough to get.

The first scratching at the mausoleum door, and what's left of my heart quickens in my chest. It could be Mina, come at last to pay her respects. She's the only one I'm willing to see. Her hand is strong enough to slip the slab from my coffin, to free me from this place.

"We could still run away," I whisper to the dark, but then their gruff voices seep through the stone, and all that I know is it isn't her.

One other thing I know: I haven't left this tomb. Nestled here in an ivory lace dress meant for a wedding altar, I've been quiet and calm and nothing like you. I haven't gone into the night and indulged this hunger that writhes inside my belly, the dubious gift you've given me.

Yet the truth means nothing to these men. They thrive on gossip, and they'll use their lies, sharp as dog-rose thorns, against me. They'll claim I've done terrible things. Because you can't let a corpse rest. You have to make sure the corpse learned her lesson.

"We need to help Miss Lucy," they agree. All for my own good of course. All to save me from myself.

When they write about this in their journals, they'll say they looked me in the eye when they finished me. They'll say they banded together with wreaths of garlic flowers and words of comfort for the dead. They'll say they were brave men who had no other choice.

These are just more of their lies.

There's a reason I can't be sure which of them is here—they never dare to show their faces. Instead, packing fodder waist-high around my tomb, they barricade me in and set me alight from the outside.

I'm already dead, but that doesn't matter. These men know all the best ways to hurt me. As the fire rages, they linger outside and listen to me scream, my skin puddling in my coffin, my brittle bones and brittle heart reduced to ash.

I never thought dying twice could be so painful.

8. No one at all

How many ways can you murder a girl? Too many to count, I suppose, but it makes no difference in the end. Because in a countryside filled with monsters, there isn't time to mourn the ones like me forever.

And it turns out you're an expert in forever. In the legends about you, no one ever seems to question how you can always rise again. It's easy to believe that a man of power could conjure himself from dust. But nobody expects the girls you destroy to do the same. We're meant to be lost. Death is our birthright and our destiny.

Only maybe it's not mine. Maybe more than a phoenix, more than just men like you, can surface from the embers. It could be that nobody murdered me after all, because maybe I'm still here.

The sun rises and falls again from the sky, and something happens in the mausoleum darkness. A spark that shouldn't be, one that you and the other men could never imagine. The burnt slab shifts off my tomb, shattering on the ground, and one fragment at a time, I piece myself back together, a patchwork monster of a girl. Hair like charred straw, colorless marrow that's soft yet stronger than infinity.

The fire in my crypt scorched my flesh, but it burned away my fear too. All that's left of me now are these dreams of something else, something better. I won't be a conquest or a footnote or an afterthought, and I won't be the one who's forgotten.

Fresh skin stretches taut over my splintered bones, and I part my new lips and exhale a scream meant only for you. Tucked inside your Scots pine coffin, you hear me, my voice from afar boiling in your ears like the blood you crave. For once, regret stirs in you, because you finally realize you can make a mistake too. You can choose a girl who simply won't die.

When you flee back to your castle in the mountains, the men think you're running from them, but I know the truth—you're really running from me. They'll run too, when their time comes. Since I don't know which of them visited my crypt, it only seems fair to blame them all.

For now, though, you'll have to do. At the downtown station, I climb aboard an evening train headed east. None of the other bustling passengers notice me. In this new body, I'm like a ghost, here and not here, a specter that can be seen only when I say so. The world has wanted to ignore me, and I'll use that now to my advantage.

In my solitary compartment, I close my eyes and envision you. The way you run home like an admonished child, and how quickly the men catch up with you. They outnumber you by a mile, but even once you're at their mercy, they won't understand what to do. Those clumsy hands of theirs, gripping carved wood and crucifixes, fingers trembling all the while. They might turn you to cinders, but they'll also leave you there to resurrect yourself. Soon there will be another trip across the sea, and another dreamy girl in a goblin market who doesn't know to be afraid.

Except not this time. As the locomotive engine chugs across the mountains, carrying me to you, I'll make sure of that much. Let the girls go on dreaming. Let them wander city streets that aren't so fearsome without you waiting there in the darkness.

You once knew my secrets. Now I know yours. Far away, in a castle that reeks of withered bellflowers and heartache, you'll rise from the ash, and I'll be there to greet you, with my new bones and new skin and this thirst I'll never slake. We'll sway together in the ruins you've created, dancing to music only we can hear.

And with a hand on your shoulder and another through your heart, I promise you that I'll never let you go.

CAROLINE M. YOACHIM

The Archronology of Love

FROM *Lightspeed*

THIS IS A *love story, the last of a series of moments when we meet.*

Saki Jones leaned into the viewport window until her nose nearly touched the glass, staring at the colony planet below. New Mars. From this distance, she could pretend that things were going according to plan—that M.J. was waiting for her in one of the domed cities. A shuttle would take her down to the surface and she and her lifelove would pursue their dream of studying a grand alien civilization.

It had been such a beautiful plan.

"Dr. Jones?" The crewhand at the entrance to the observation deck was an elderly white woman, part of the skeleton team that had worked long shifts in empty space while the passengers had slept in stasis. "The captain has requested an accelerated schedule on your research. She sent you the details? All our surface probes have malfunctioned, and she needs you to look at the time record of the colony collapse."

"The Chronicle." Saki corrected the woman automatically, most of her attention still on the planet below. "The time record is called the Chronicle."

"Right. The captain—"

Saki turned away from the viewport. "Sorry. I have the captain's message. Please reassure her that I will gather my team and get research underway as soon as possible."

The woman saluted and left. Saki sent a message calling the department together for an emergency meeting and returned to the viewport. New Mars was the same angry red as its namesake, and the colony cities looked like pus-filled boils on its surface. It was a dangerous place—malevolent and sick. M.J. had died there. If they hadn't been too broke to go together, the whole family would have died. Saki blinked away tears. She had to stay focused.

It was a violation of protocol for Saki to go into the Chronicle. No one was ever a truly impartial observer, of course, but she'd had M.J. torn away so suddenly, so unexpectedly. The pain of it was raw and overwhelming. They'd studied together, raised children together, planned an escape from Earth. Other partners had come and gone from their lives, but she and M.J. had always been there for each other.

If she went into the Chronicle, she would look for him. It would bias her choices and her observations. But she *was* the most qualified person on the team, and if she recused herself she could lose her research grant, her standing in the department, her dream of studying alien civilizations . . . and her chance to see M.J.

"Dr. Jones . . ." A softer voice this time—one of her graduate students. Hyun-sik was immaculately dressed, as always, with shimmery blue eyeliner that matched his blazer.

"I know, Hyun-sik. The projector is ready and we're on an accelerated schedule. I just need a few moments to gather my thoughts before the site-selection meeting."

"That's not why I'm here," Hyun-sik said. "I didn't mean to intrude, but I wanted to offer my support. My parents were also at the colony. Whatever happened down there is a great loss to all of us."

Saki didn't know what to say. Words always felt so meaningless in the face of death. She and Hyun-sik hadn't spoken much about their losses during the months of deceleration after they woke from stasis. They'd thrown themselves into their research, used their work as a distraction from their pain. "Arriving at the planet reopened a lot of wounds."

"I sent my parents ahead because I thought their lives would be better here than back on Earth." He gestured at the viewport window. "The temptation to see them again is strong. So close, and the Chronicle is right there. I know you're struggling with the same dilemma. It must be a difficult decision for you, having lost M.J.—"

"Yes." Saki interrupted before Hyun-sik could say anything more. Even hearing M.J.'s name was difficult. She was unfit for this expedition. She should take a leave of absence and allow Li

Yingtai to take over as lead. But this research was her dream, their dream—M.J.'s and hers—and these were unusual circumstances. Saki frowned. "How did you know I was here, thinking about recusing myself?"

"It isn't difficult to guess. It's what I would be doing, in your place." He looked away. "But also Kenzou told me at our lunch date today."

Saki sighed. Her youngest son was the only one of her children who had opted to leave Earth and come with her. He'd thought that New Mars would be a place of adventure and opportunity. Silly romantic notions. For the last few weeks she'd barely seen him—he'd mentioned having a new boyfriend but hadn't talked about the details. She'd been concerned because the relationship had drawn him away from his studies. Pilots weren't in high demand now, he'd said, given the state of the colony. Apparently his mystery boyfriend was her smart, attractive, six-years-older-than-Kenzou graduate student. She was disappointed to find out about the relationship from her student rather than her son. He was drifting away from her, and she didn't know how to mend the rift.

Hyun-sik wrung his hands, clearly ill at ease with the new turn in the conversation.

"I think you and Kenzou make a lovely couple," Saki said.

He grinned. "Thank you, Dr. Jones."

Saki forced herself to smile back. Her son hadn't had any qualms keeping the relationship from her, but clearly Hyun-sik was happier to have things out in the open. "Let's go. We have an expedition to plan."

We did not create the Chronicle, we simply discovered it, as you did. Layer upon layer of time, a stratified record of the universe. When you visit the Chronicle, you alter it. Your presence muddles the temporal record as surely as an archaeological dig muddles the dirt at an excavation site. In the future, human archronologists will look back on you with scorn, much as you look back on looters and tomb raiders—but we forgive you. In our early encounters, we make our own errors. How can we understand something so alien before we understand it? We act out of love, but that does not erase the harm we cause. Forgive us.

Saki spent the final hours before the expedition in a departmental meeting, arguing with Dr. Li about site selection. *When* was easy. Archronologists burrowed into the Chronicle starting at the present moment and proceeding backward through layers of time, following much the same principles as used in an archaeological dig. The spatial location was trickier to choose. M.J. had believed that the plague was alien, and if he was right, the warehouse that housed the alien artifacts would be a good starting point.

"How can you argue for anything but the colony medical center?" Li demanded. "The colonists died of a plague."

"The hospital at the present moment is unlikely to have any useful information," Saki said. The final decision was hers, but she wanted the research team to understand the rationale for her choice. "Everyone in the colony is dead, and we have their medical records up to the point of the final broadcast. The colonists suspected that the plague was alien in origin. We should start with the xenoarchaeology warehouse."

There were murmurs of agreement and disagreement from the students and postdocs.

"Didn't your lifelove work in the xenoarchaeology lab?" The question came from Annabelle Hoffman, one of Li's graduate students.

The entire room went silent.

Saki opened her mouth, then closed it. It was information from M.J. that had led her to suggest starting at the xenoarchaeology warehouse. Would she have acted on that information if it had come from someone else? She believed that she would, but what if her love for M.J. was biasing her decisions?

"You're out of line, Hoffman." Li turned to Saki. "I apologize for Annabelle. I disagree with your choice of site, but it is inappropriate of her to make this personal. Everyone on this ship has lost someone down there."

Saki was grateful to Li for diffusing the situation. They were academic rivals, yes, but they'd grown to be friends. "Thank you."

Li nodded, then launched into a long-winded argument for the hospital as an initial site. Saki was still reeling from the personal attack. Annabelle was taking notes onto her tablet, scowling at having been rebuked. Saki hated departmental politics, hated conflict. M.J. had always been her sounding board to talk her through this kind of thing, and he was gone. Maybe she shouldn't do this. Li was a brilliant researcher. The project would be in good hands if she stepped down.

Suddenly the room went quiet. Li had finished laying out her arguments, and everyone was waiting for Saki's response.

Hyun-sik came to her rescue and systematically countered Li's arguments. He was charming and persuasive, and by the end of the meeting he had convinced the group to go along with the plan to visit the xenoarchaeology warehouse first.

Saki hoped it was the right choice.

There is no objective record of the moments in your past—you filter reality through your thoughts and perceptions. Over time, you create a memory of the memory, compounding bias upon bias, layers of self-serving rationalizations, or denial, or nostalgia. Everything becomes a story. You visit the Chronicle to study us, but what you see isn't absolute truth. The record of our past is filtered through your minds.

The control room for the temporal projector looked like the navigation bridge of an interstellar ship. A single person could work the controls, but half the department was packed into the room—most longing for a connection to the people they'd lost, others simply eager to be a part of this historic moment, the first expedition to the dead colony of New Mars.

Saki waited with Hyun-sik in the containment cylinder, a large chamber with padded walls and floors. At twenty meters in diameter and nearly two stories high, it was the largest open area on the ship. Cameras on the ceiling recorded everything that she and Hyun-sik did. From the perspective of people staying on the ship, the expedition team would flicker, disappear briefly, and return an instant later—possibly in a different location. This was the purpose of the padded floors and walls: to cushion falls and prevent injury in the event that they returned at a slightly different altitude.

The straps of Saki's pack chafed her shoulders. She and Hyun-sik stood back to back, not moving, although stillness was not strictly necessary. The projector could transport moving objects as easily as stationary ones. As long as they weren't half inside the room and half outside of it, everything would be fine. "Ready?"

"Ready," Hyun-sik confirmed.

Over the ceiling-mounted speakers, the robotic voice of the projection system counted down from twenty. Saki forced herself to breathe.

". . . three, two, one."

Their surroundings faded to black, then brightened into the cavernous warehouse that served as artifact storage for the xenoarchaeology lab. The placement was good. Saki and Hyun-sik floated in an empty aisle. Two rows of brightly colored alien artifacts towered above them. Displacement damage from their arrival was minimal; nothing of interest was likely to be in the middle of the aisle.

Silence pressed down on them. The Chronicle recorded light but not sound, and they were like projections, there without really being there. M.J. could have explained it better. This was not her first time in the Chronicle, but the lack of sound was always unnerving. There was no ambient noise, or even her own breathing and heartbeat.

"Mark location." Saki typed her words in the air, her tiny motions barely visible but easily detected by the sensors in her gloves. Her instructions appeared in the corner of Hyun-sik's glasses. She and her student set the location on their wristbands. The projection cylinder was twenty meters in diameter, and moving beyond that area in physical space could be catastrophic upon return. The second expedition into the Chronicle had ended with the research team reappearing inside the concrete foundation of the Chronos lab.

"Location marked," Hyun-sik confirmed.

Saki studied the artifacts that surrounded her. She had no idea if they were machinery or art or some kind of alien toy. Hell, for all she knew, they might be waste products or alien carapaces. They *looked* manufactured rather than biological, though—smooth, flat-bottomed ovoids that reminded her of escape pods or maybe giant eggs.

The closest artifact on her left was about three times her height and had a base of iridescent blue, dotted with specks of red, crisscrossed with a delicate lace of green and gray and black. The base, which extended to roughly the midline of each ovoid, was uniform across all the artifacts in the warehouse. The tops, however, were all different. Several were shades of green with various amounts of brown mixed in. The one immediately to her right was topped with swirls of browns and beige and grayish-white and a red so dark it looked almost black. M.J. had been so thrilled to unearth these wondrous things.

Something about them bothered her though. She vaguely remembered M.J. describing them as blue, and while that was true of the bases—

Hyun-sik pulled off his pack.

"Wait." Saki used the microjets on her suit to turn and face her student. He was surrounded in a semitranslucent shimmer of silvery-white, the colors of the Chronicle all swirled together where his presence disrupted it, like the dirt of an archaeological dig all churned together. At the edges of his displacement cloud there was a delicate rainbow film, like the surface of a soap bubble, data distorted but not yet destroyed.

"Sorry," Hyun-sik messaged. "Everything looked clear in my direction."

Saki scanned the warehouse. The recording drones would have no problem collecting data on the alien artifacts. Her job was to look for anomalies, things the drones might miss or inadvertently destroy. She studied the ceiling of the warehouse. A maintenance walkway wrapped around the building, a platform of silvery mesh suspended from the lighter silver metal of the ceiling. The walkway was higher than the two-story ceiling of the containment cylinder, outside of their priority area. On the walkway, near one of the bright ceiling lights, something looked odd. "I don't think we were the first ones here."

Hyun-sik followed her gaze. "Displacement cloud?"

"There, by the lights." Saki studied the shape on the walkway. It was hard to tell at this distance, but the displacement cloud was roughly the right size to be human. "Unfortunately we have no way to get up there for a closer look."

"I can reprogram a few of the bees—"

"Yes." It was not ideal. Drones were good at recording physical objects, but had difficulty picking up the outlines of distortion clouds and other anomalies. Moving through the Chronicle was difficult, though not impossible. It was similar to free fall in open space. Things you brought with you were solid, but everything else was basically a projection.

"It is too far for the microjets," Hyun-sik continued, "but we could tie ourselves together and push off each other so that someone could have a closer look."

Saki had been considering that very option, but it was too dangerous. If something went wrong and they couldn't get back to their marks, they could reappear inside a station wall, or off the ship entirely, or in a location occupied by another person. She wanted desperately to take a closer look, because if the distortion cloud was human-shaped it meant . . . "No. It's too risky. We'll send drones."

There was nothing else that merited a more thorough investigation, so they released the recording drones, a flying army of bee-sized cameras that recorded every object from multiple angles. Seventeen drones flew to the ceiling and recorded the region of the walkway that had the distortion. Saki hoped the recording would be detailed enough to be useful. The disruption to the Chronicle was like ripples in a pond, spreading from the present into the past and future record, tiny trails of white blurring together into a jumbled cloud.

M.J. had always followed the minimalist school of archronology; he liked to observe the Chronicle from a single unobtrusive spot. He had disapproved of recording equipment, of cameras and drones. It would be so like him to stand on an observation walkway, far above the scene he wanted to observe. But this moment was in his future, a part of the Chronicle that hadn't been laid down yet when he died. There was no way for him to be here.

The drones had exhausted all the open space and started flying through objects to gather data on their internal properties. By the time the drones flew back into their transport box, the warehouse was a cloud of white with only traces of the original data.

We did not begin here. The urge to expand and grow came to us from another relationship. They came to us, and we learned their love of exploration, which eventually led us to you. It doesn't matter that we arrive here before you, we are patient, we will wait.

The reconstruction lab was crammed full of people—students and postdocs and faculty carefully combing through data from the drones on tablets, occasionally projecting data onto the wall to get a better look at the details. The 3D printer hummed, printing small-scale reproductions of the alien artifacts.

"The initial reports we received described the artifact bases, but not the tops." Li's voice rose over the general din of the room. "The artifacts *changed* sometime after the colony stopped sending reports."

Annabelle said something in response, but Saki couldn't quite make it out. She shook her head and tried to focus on the drone recordings from the seventeen drones that had flown to the ceiling to investigate the anomaly. It was a human outline, which meant that they weren't the first ones to visit that portion of the Chronicle. Saki couldn't make out the figure's features. She wasn't sure if the lack of resolution was due to the drones having difficulty recording something that wasn't technically an object, or if the person had moved enough to blur the cloud they left behind.

She wanted desperately to believe that it was M.J. An unmoving human figure was consistent with his minimalist style of research. Visiting a future Chronicle was forbidden, and only theoretically possible, but under the circumstances—

"Any luck?" Dr. Li interrupted her train of thought.

Saki shook her head. "Someone was clearly in this part of the Chronicle before us, and the outline is human. Beyond that I don't think we will get anything else from these damn drone recordings."

"Shame you couldn't get up there to get a closer look." There was a mischievous sparkle in Li's eyes when she said it, almost like it was a backwards-in-time dare, a challenge.

"Too risky," Saki said. "And we might not have gotten more than what came off the drones. If it had been just me, I might have chanced it, but I'm responsible for the safety of my student—"

"I'm only teasing," Li said softly. "Sorry. This is a hard expedition for all of us. The captain is pushing for answers and Annabelle is trying to convince anyone who will listen that we need a surface mission to look at the original artifacts."

"Foolishness. We can't even get a working probe down there, we couldn't possibly send people. Maybe the next expedition into the Chronicle will bring us more answers."

"I hope so."

Dr. Li went back to supervising the work at the 3D printer. Like M.J., her research spanned both archronology and xenoarchaeology, and her team was doing most of the artifact reconstruction and analysis. They were in a difficult position—the captain wanted answers *now* about whether the artifacts were dangerous, but something so completely alien could take years of research to decipher, if they were even knowable at all.

Someone chooses which part of our story is told. Sometimes it is you, and sometimes it is us. We repeat ourselves because we always focus on the same things, we structure our narratives in the same ways. You are no different.

Some things change, but others always stay the same. Eventually our voices will blend together to create something beautiful and new. We learned anticipation before we met you, and you know it too, though you do not feel it for us.

When Saki returned to her family quarters, she messaged Kenzou. He did not respond. Off with Hyun-sik, probably. Saki ordered scotch (neat) from the replicator, and savored the burn down her throat as she sipped it. This particular scotch was one of M.J.'s creations, heavy on smoke but light on peat, with just the tiniest bit of sweetness at the end.

She played one of M.J.'s old vid letters on her tablet. He rambled cheerfully about his day, the artifacts he'd dug up at the site of the abandoned alien ruins, his plan to someday visit that part of the Chronicle with Saki so that they could see the aliens at the height of their civilization. He was trying to solve the mystery of why the aliens had left the planet—there was no trace of them, not a single scrap of organic remains. They'd had long back-and-forth discussions on whether the aliens were simply so biologically foreign that the remains were unrecognizable. Perhaps the city itself was the alien, or their bodies were ephemeral, or the artifacts somehow stored their remains. So many slowtime conversations, in vid letters back and forth from Earth. Then a backlog of vids that M.J. had sent while she was in stasis for the interstellar trip.

This vid was from several months before she woke, one of the last before M.J. started showing signs of the plague that wiped out the colony. Saki barely listened to the words. She lost herself in M.J.'s deep brown eyes and let the soothing sound of his voice wash over her.

"Octavia's parakeet up and died last night," M.J. said.

His words brought Saki back to the present. The parakeet reminded Saki of something from another letter, or had it been one of M.J.'s lecture transcripts? He'd said something about crops failing, first outside of the domes and later even in the greenhouses. Plants, animals, humans—everything in the colony had died. Everyone on the ship assumed that the crops and animals had died because the people of the colony had gotten too sick to tend them, but what if the plague had taken out everything?

She had to find out.

Most of M.J.'s letters she had watched many times, but there was one she'd seen only once because she couldn't bear to relive the pain of it. The last letter. She called it up on her tablet, then drank the rest of her scotch before hitting Play. M.J.'s hair was shaved to a short black stubble and his face was sallow and sunken. He was in the control room of the colony's temporal projector, working on his research right up until the end.

"They can't isolate a virus. Our immune systems seem to be attacking something, but we have no idea what, or why, and our bodies are breaking down. How can we stop something if we can't figure out what it is?

"I will hold on as long as I can, my lifelove, but the plague is accelerating. Don't come to the surface, use the Chronicle. Whatever this is, it has to be alien."

She closed her eyes and listened to him describe the fall of the colony. If she closed her eyes and ignored the content of the words, if she forced herself not to hear the frailness in his voice, if she pushed away all the realities she could not accept—it was like he was still down there, a quick shuttle hop away, waiting for her to join him.

"The transmission systems have started to go. This alien world is harsh, and without our entire colony fighting to make it hospitable, everything is failing, all our efforts falling apart. Entropy will turn us all to dust. This will probably be my last letter, but perhaps when you arrive you will see me in the Chronicle.

"Keep fighting. Live for both of us. I love you."

"You home, Mom?" Kenzou called out as he came in. "I'm going out with Hyun-sik tonight, but . . . are you crying? What happened?"

Saki rubbed away the tears and gestured down at the tablet. "Vids. The old letters."

Kenzou hugged her. "I miss him too, but you shouldn't watch those. You need to hold yourself together until the expeditions are done."

"I'm not going to pretend he doesn't exist."

She went to the replicator and ordered another scotch.

Kenzou picked up the dishes she'd left on the counter, clearing away her clutter probably without even realizing he was doing it. He was so like his father in some ways, and now he wanted to act as though nothing had happened.

The silence between them stretched long. He punched some commands into the replicator but nothing happened.

"He was your father," Saki said softly.

"And you think this doesn't hurt?" Kenzou snapped. He smacked the side of the replicator and it beeped and let out a hiss of steam. His fingers danced across the keypad again, hitting each button far harder than necessary. The replicator produced a cup of green tea, and his brief moment of anger passed. "I'm trying to move on. Dad would have wanted that."

The outburst made her want to hold him like she had when he was young. She'd buried herself in her work these last few months, and he had found his comfort elsewhere. He'd finished growing up sometime when she wasn't looking.

"I'm sorry," she said. "Go, spend time with your boyfriend."

He softened. "You shouldn't drink alone, Mom."

"And you shouldn't secretly date my students," she scolded gently. "It's very awkward when the whole lab knows who my son is dating before I do!"

He sipped his tea. "There aren't that many people on station, word has a way of getting around."

After a short pause he added, "You could ask Dr. Li to have a drink with you, if you insist on drinking."

"I don't think she would . . ." Saki shook her head.

"And that's why your entire lab knows these things before you do." He finished his tea, then washed the cup and put it away. "You don't notice what is right in front of you."

"I'm not ready to move on." She looked down at the menu on her tablet, the list of recently viewed vids a line of tiny icons of M.J.'s face. He was supposed to be here, waiting for her. They were supposed to have such a wonderful life.

"I know." He hugged her. "But I think you can get there."

Layers of information diminish as they recede from the original source. In archaeology, you remove the artifacts from their context, change a physical record into descriptions and photographs. You choose what gets recorded, often unaware of what you do not think to keep. Your impressions—logged in books or electronically on tablets or in whatever medium is currently in fashion—are themselves a physical record that future researchers might find, when you are dead and gone.

Saki was with Li in the Chronicle, four weeks after the collapse.

The third floor of the hospital was empty. Not just devoid of people—this was a part of the Chronicle that came after everyone had died, so that wasn't surprising. The place was half cleaned out. Foam mattresses on metal frames, but someone or something had taken the sheets. Nothing in the planters, not even dry dead plants. This wasn't long after the collapse, and the pieces simply did not fit.

"Why would anyone bother taking things from the hospital while everyone was dying?" Li messaged. "And why are there no bodies? There was no one left at the end to take care of the remains."

The crops had failed, the parrot had died, the hospital was empty. Saki knew there had to be a connection, but what was it? She scanned the area for clues. In a patch of bright sunlight near one of the windows, she saw the faint outline of a distortion, another visitor to the Chronicle. The window was at the edge of the containment area, but probably within reach.

"Someone else was here," Saki typed, "by that window."

"I think you're right. Closer look?" Li fished out the rope from her pack. "I'm not a graduate student, so you're not responsible for my well-being."

Saki caught herself before explaining that as lead researcher she was still responsible for the welfare of everyone on the team. Li was partly teasing, but it held some truth, too. If Li was willing to risk it, they could investigate.

"Can I be the one to go?" Saki asked.

"You think it might be M.J." Li did not phrase it as a question.

"Yes."

Li fastened the rope securely around her waist and handed Saki the other end. They checked each other's knots, then checked them again. If they came untied, it would be difficult or maybe impossible to get back to their marks. They spun themselves around and pressed their palms and feet together. "Gently. We can try again if you don't get far enough."

Li's hands were smaller than her own, and warm.

"Ready?"

Saki felt the tiny movements of Li's fingers as she typed the word. She nodded. "Three, two, one."

They pushed off of each other, propelling Saki toward the window and Li in the opposite direction, leaving a wide white scar across the Chronicle between them. Saki managed to contort her body around so that she could see where she was going as she drifted toward the window. The human form that stood there was not facing the hospital, and she couldn't see their face. She reached the end of the rope a meter short of the window.

"Is it M.J.?" Li messaged from across the room.

"I don't know," Saki replied.

The white figure by the window was about the right height to be M.J., about the right shape. But the colony was huge, and even narrowed down to just the archronologists, it could have been any number of people. Saki twisted around to gain a few more centimeters, but she couldn't see well enough to know one way or the other. If she untied the rope and used the microjets on her suit—but no, that would leave Li stranded.

"Whoever it is, they were looking out the window." Saki tore her gaze away from the figure that might or might not be her lifelove. She'd seen the New Mars campus many times, even this part of campus, because the hospital was across the quad from the archronology building. M.J. had sometimes recorded his vid letters there, on the yellow-tinged grass that grew beneath the terrafruit trees.

Outside the window, there were no trees. There was no grass. Not even dry brown grass and dead leafless trees. It was bare ground. Nothing but a layer of red New Martian dust.

"All of it is gone," Saki typed. "Every living thing was destroyed."

No one had noticed it in the warehouse because they'd had no reason to expect any living things to be there.

She and Li pulled themselves back to the center of the room, climbing their rope hand over hand until they were back at their marks. They adjusted the programming of their bees in hopes that they could get a clear image of the other visitor to the record, and set them swarming around the room.

"It's more than that," Li messaged as the bees cataloged the room. "That's why this room is so odd. Everything organic is gone. Whatever is left is all metal or plastic."

It was obvious as soon as she said it, but something still didn't fit. "The alien artifacts, back in the warehouse—those were made from organic materials. Why weren't they destroyed with everything else?"

One of our beloveds believes that all important things are infinite. Numbers. Time. Love. They think that the infinite should never be seen. We erase vast sections of the Chronicle out of love, but this infuriates some of our other beloveds. To embrace so many different loves, scattered across the galaxy, is difficult to navigate. It is not possible to please everyone.

Saki stood back to back with Hyun-sik. Their surroundings shifted from gray to orange-red. The two of them were floating beneath the open sky in a carefully excavated pit. The dig site was laid out in a grid, black cords stretched between stakes, claylike soil removed layer by layer and carefully analyzed. Fine red dust swirled in an eerily silent wind and gathered in the corners of the pit.

Hyun-sik swayed on his feet.

"The Chronicle is an image, being here is no different from being in an enclosed warehouse," Saki reminded him. He looked ill, and if he threw up in the Chronicle it might obscure important data. Even if it didn't, it would definitely be unpleasant.

"I've never been outside. It is big and open and being weightless here feels wrong," Hyun-sik messaged. He took a deep breath. "And the dust is moving."

"Human consciousness is tied to the passage of time. In an abandoned indoor environment like the warehouse, there are long stretches of time where nothing moves or changes. It feels like a single moment in time. But we are viewing moving sections of the record, which is why we try to spend as little time here as we can," Saki answered.

"Sorry." He still looked a little green, but he managed not to vomit. Saki turned her attention back to their surroundings. There were no visible distortions here, no intrusions into the time record. M.J. hadn't visited the Chronicle of this time and place.

At Li's insistence, the team had done a three-day drone sweep of the entire colony starting at the moment of the last known transmission. Wiping out so much of the Chronicle felt incredibly wasteful, especially for such an important historic moment. If some future research team came to study the planet, all they'd find of those final days was a sea of white, the destruction inherent in collecting the data. Though if Saki was honest, the thing that bothered her most was that she couldn't be there for M.J.'s final moments. They had burrowed into the Chronicle deeper than his death, deeper than his final acts, leaving broad swaths of destruction in their wake.

He was gone, why should it matter what happened to the Chronicle of his life? But it felt like deleting his letters, or erasing him from the list of contacts on her tablet.

She tried to focus on the present. This site was a few weeks before the final transmission. They were here to gather information about the alien artifacts in situ. Perhaps they could notice something that M.J. and his team had missed.

In the distance, the nearest colony dome glimmered in the sun, sitting on the surface like a soap bubble. There were people living inside the dome—M.J. was there, working or sleeping or recording a vid letter that she would not read until months later. So many people, and all of them would soon be dead. Were already dead, outside the Chronicle. Colonies were so fragile, like the bubbles they resembled. The domes themselves were reasonably sturdy, but the life inside . . . New Mars was not the first failed colony, and it would not be the last.

The sun was bright but not hot. Expeditions into the Chronicle were an odd limbo, real but not real, like watching a vid from the inside.

"That one looks unfinished," Hyun-sik messaged, pointing to a partially exposed artifact. It was an iridescent blue, like the bases of the artifacts in the warehouse, but the upper surface of the artifact did not have the smoothly curved edges that were universal to everything they'd seen so far.

"They changed so quickly," Saki mused. She'd read M.J.'s descriptions of the artifacts, and looked at the images of them, but there was something more powerful about seeing one full scale here in the Chronicle. "And right as the colony collapsed. The two things must be related."

She shuddered, remembering the drone vids of the final collapse. After weeks of slow progression, everything in the colony started dying. She'd forced herself to watch a clip from the hospital—dozens of colonists filling the beds, tended by medics who eventually collapsed wherever they were standing. Everyone dead within minutes of each other, and then—Saki squeezed her eyes shut tight as though it would ward off the memory—the bodies disintegrated. Flesh, bone, blood, clothes, everything organic broke down into a fine dust that swirled in the breeze of the ventilation systems.

She opened her eyes to the swirling red dust of the excavation site, suddenly feeling every bit as ill as Hyun-sik looked. Such a terrible way to die and there was nothing left. No bodies to cremate, no bones to bury. It was as if the entire colony had never existed, and M.J. had died down here and that entire moment was nothing but a sea of drone-distortion white.

"Are you okay, Dr. Jones?" Hyun-sik messaged.

"Sorry," she answered. "Did you watch the drone-vids from the collapse?"

He nodded, and his face went pale. "Only a little. Worse than the most terrible nightmare, and yet real."

Saki focused all her attention on the artifact half-buried in the red dirt, forcing everything else out of her mind. She searched the blue for any trace of other colors, but there was nothing else there. "I don't know how the artifacts changed so quickly, or why. Maybe Dr. Li can figure it out from the recordings."

"Release the drones?" Hyun-sik asked.

"Wait." Saki pointed toward the colony dome, her arm wiping away a small section of the Chronicle as she moved. "Look."

Clouds of red dust rose up from the ground, far away and hard to see.

"Dust storm?" Hyun-sik turned his head slightly, trying to disturb the record as little as possible.

"Jeeps." Saki stared at the approaching clouds of dust, rising from vehicles too distant to see. M.J. might be in one of them, making the trek over rough terrain to get to the dig site. Saki tried to remember how far the dig site was from the dome—forty kilometers? Maybe fifty? The dig site was on a small hill, and Saki couldn't quite remember the math for calculating distance to the horizon. It was estimates stacked on estimates, and although she desperately wanted to see M.J., her conclusion was the same no matter how she ran the calculation—they couldn't wait for the slow-moving jeeps to arrive.

"Do you see anything else that merits a closer look?" Saki typed.

Hyun-sik stared at the approaching jeeps. "If we had come a couple hours later, there would have been people here."

"Yes."

It wasn't M.J., Saki reminded herself, only an echo. Her lifelove wasn't really here. Saki had Hyun-sik release the drones and soon they were surrounded by white, much as the jeeps were enveloped in a cloud of red.

The drones finished, and the jeeps were still far in the distance. M.J. always did drive damnably slow. Saki waved goodbye to jeeps that couldn't see her. When they blinked back into the projection room, she was visibly shaken. Hyun-sik politely invited her to join him and Kenzou for dinner, but that would be awkward at best and she didn't have the energy to make conversation. Saki kept it together long enough to get back to her quarters.

Safely behind closed doors, she called up the vid letter that M.J. had sent around the time she'd just visited. He was supposed to wait for her, only a few more months. She'd been so close. The vid played in the background while she cried.

We had a physical form, once. Wings and scales and oh so many legs, everything in iridescent blue. Each time we encounter a new love, it becomes a part of who we are. No, we do not blend our loves into one single entity—the core of us would be lost against such vastness. We always remain half ourselves, a collective of individuals, a society of linked minds. How could we exclude you from such a union?

The captain sent probes to the surface that were entirely inorganic—no synthetic rubber seals or carbon-based fuels—and this time the probes did not fail. They found nanites in the dust. Visits to the Chronicle were downgraded in priority as other teams worked to neutralize the alien technology. Saki tried to stay focused on her research, but without the urgency and tight deadlines, she found herself drawn into the past. She watched letters from M.J. in a long chain, one vid after the next. The hard ones, the sad ones, everything she'd been avoiding so that she could be functional enough to do research.

The last vid letter from M.J. was recorded not in his office but in the control room for the temporal projector. Saki had asked about it at the time, and he'd explained that he had one last trip to make, and the colony was running out of time. She'd watched it twice now, and M.J. looked so frail. But there was something Saki had to check. A hunch.

For the first half of the vid, M.J. sat near enough to the camera to fill nearly the entire field of view. He thought the plague was accelerating, becoming increasingly deadly. He talked about the people who had died and the people who were still dying, switching erratically between cold clinical assessment and tearful reminiscence. Saki cried right along with her lost love, harsh ugly tears that blurred her vision so badly that she nearly missed what she was looking for.

She paused and rewound. There, in the middle of the video, M.J. had gotten up to make an adjustment to the controls. The camera should have stayed with him, but for a brief moment it recorded the settings of the projector. The point in the record where M.J. was going.

Saki wrote down the coordinates of space and time. It was on New Mars, of course. It was also in the future. She studied the other settings on the projector, noting the changes he'd made to accommodate projection in the wrong direction.

M.J. had visited a future Chronicle, and left her the clues she needed to follow him.

She set her com status to *do not disturb*, and marked the temporal projector as undergoing maintenance. There was no way she could make it through a vid recording without falling apart, so she wrote old-fashioned letters to Kenzou, to her graduate students, to Li—just in case something went wrong.

When she stepped out into the corridor, Hyun-sik and Kenzou were there.

She froze.

"I will work the controls for you, Dr. Jones," Hyun-sik said. "It is safer than programming them on a delay."

"How did you—?"

"You love him, you can't let him go," Kenzou said. "You've always been terrible at goodbyes. You want to see as much of his time on the colonies as possible, and there's no way to get approval for most of it."

"Also, marking the temporal projector as 'scheduled maintenance' when our temporal engineer is in the middle of their sleep cycle won't fool anyone who is actually paying attention to the schedule," Hyun-sik added.

"Thinking of making an unauthorized trip yourself?" Saki asked, raising an eyebrow at her student.

"Come on." Hyun-sik didn't answer her question. "It won't be long before someone else notices."

They went to the control room, and Saki adjusted the settings and wiring to match what she'd seen in M.J.'s vid. The two young men sat together and watched her work, Kenzou resting his head on Hyun-sik's shoulder.

When she'd finished, Hyun-sik came to examine the controls. "That is twenty years from now."

"Yes."

"No one has visited a future Chronicle before. It is forbidden by the IRB and the theory is completely untested."

"It worked for M.J.," Saki said softly. She didn't have absolute proof that those distortion clouds in the Chronicle had been him, but who else could it be? No other humans had been here since the collapse, and whoever it was had selected expedition sites that she was likely to visit. M.J. was showing her that he had successfully visited the future. He wanted her to meet him at those last coordinates.

"Of course it did," Kenzou said, chuckling. "He was so damn brilliant."

Saki wanted to laugh with him, but all she managed was a pained smile. "And so are you. You'll get into trouble for this. It could damage your careers."

"If we weren't here, would you bother to come back?"

Saki blushed, thinking of the letters she'd left in her quarters, just in case. M.J. had gone to some recorded moment of future. Maybe he had stayed there. This was a way to be with him, outside of time and space. If she came back, she would have to face the consequences of making an unauthorized trip. It was not so far-fetched to think that she might stay in the Chronicle.

"Now you have a reason to return," Hyun-sik said. "Otherwise Kenzou and I will have to face whatever consequences come of this trip alone."

Saki sighed. They knew her too well. She couldn't stay in the Chronicle and throw them to the fates. "I promise to return."

This is a love story, but it does not end with happily ever after. It doesn't end at all. Your stories are always so rigidly shaped—beginning, middle, end. There are strands of love in your narratives, all neat and tidy in the chaos of reality. Our love is scattered across time and space, without order, without endings.

Visiting the Chronicle in the past was like watching a series of moments in time, but the future held uncertainty. Saki split into a million selves, all separate but tied together by a fragile strand of consciousness, anchored to a single moment but fanning out into possibilities.

She was at the site of the xenoarchaeology warehouse, mostly.

Smaller infinities of herself remained in the control room due to projector malfunction or a last-minute change of heart. In other realities, the warehouse had been relocated, or destroyed, or rebuilt into alien architectures her mind couldn't fully grasp. She was casting a net of white into the future, disturbing the fabric of the Chronicle before it was even laid down.

Saki focused on the largest set of her infinities, the fraction of herself on New Mars, inside the warehouse and surrounded by alien artifacts. The most probable futures, the ones with the least variation.

M.J. was there, surrounded by a bubble of white where he had disrupted the Chronicle.

Saki focused her attention further, to a single future where they had calibrated their coms through trial and error or intuition or perhaps purely by chance. There was no sound in the Chronicle, but they could communicate.

"Hello, my lifelove," M.J. messaged.

"I can't believe it's really you," Saki answered. "I missed you so much."

"Me too. I worried that I'd never see you again." He gestured to the artifacts. "Did you solve it?"

She nodded. "Nanites. The bases of the artifacts generate nanites, and clouds of them mix with the dust. They consumed everything organic to build the tops of the artifacts."

"Yes. Everything was buried at first, and the nanites were accustomed to a different kind of organic matter," M.J. typed. "But they adapted, and they multiplied."

Saki shuddered. "Why would they make something so terrible?"

"Ah. Like me, you only got part of it." He gestured at the artifacts that surrounded them. "The iridescent blue on the bottom are the aliens, or a physical shell of them, anyway. The nanites are the way they make connections, transforming other species they encounter into something they themselves can understand."

"Why didn't you explain this in your reports?"

"The pieces were there, but I didn't put it all together until I got to the futures." He gestured at the warehouse around them with one arm, careful to stay within his already distorted bubble of white.

In this future, she and M.J. were alone, but in many of the others the warehouse was crowded with people. Saki recognized passengers and crew from the ship. They walked among the artifacts with an almost religious air, most of them pausing near one particular artifact, reaching out to touch it.

She sifted through the other futures and found the common threads. The worship of the artifacts, the people of the station living down on the colony, untouched by the nanites. "I don't understand what happened."

"Once the aliens realized what they were doing to us, they stopped. They had absorbed our crops, our trees, our pets. Each species into its own artifact." He turned to face the closest artifact, the one that she'd seen so many people focus their attentions on in parallel futures. "This one holds all the human colonists."

"They are visiting their loved ones, worshipping their ancestors."

"Yes."

"I will come here to visit you." Saki could see it in the futures. "I was so angry when Li sent drones to record the final moments of the colony. I should have been there to look for you, but that's a biased reason, too wrong to even mention in a departmental meeting. I couldn't find you in the drone vids, but there was so much data. Everyone and everything dead, and then systematically taken apart by the nanites. Everyone."

"It is what taught the aliens to let the rest of humankind go."

"They didn't learn! They took all the organics from the probes we sent."

"New tech, right? Synthetic organics that weren't in use on the colonies, that the nanites didn't recognize. You can see the futures, Saki. The colony is absorbed into the artifacts, but at least we save everyone else."

"We? You can't go back there. I don't want to visit an alien shrine of you, I want to stay. I want *us* to stay." Saki flailed her arms helplessly, then stared down at her wristband. "I promised Kenzou that I would go back."

"You have a future to create," M.J. answered. "Tell Kenzou that I love him. His futures are beautiful."

"I could save you somehow. Save everyone." Saki studied the artifacts. "Or I could stay. It doesn't matter how long I'm here, in the projection room we only flicker for an instant—"

"I came here to wait for you." M.J. smiled sadly. "Now we've had our moment, and I should return to my own time. Go first, my lifelove, so that you don't have to watch me leave. Live for both of us."

It was foolish, futile, but Saki reached out to M.J., blurring the Chronicle to white between them. He mirrored her movement, bringing his fingertips to hers. For a moment she thought that they would touch, but coming from such different times, using different projectors—they weren't quite in sync. His fingertips blurred to white.

She pulled her hand back to her chest, holding it to her heart. She couldn't bring herself to type *goodbye.* Instead she did her best to smile through her tears. "I'll keep studying the alien civilization, like we dreamed."

He returned her smile, and his eyes were as wet with tears as her own. Before she lost the will to do it, she slapped the button on her wristband. Only then, as she was leaving, did he send his last message, "Goodbye, my lifelove."

All her selves in all the infinite possible futures collapsed into a single Saki, and she was back in the projection room, tears streaming down her face.

We know you better now. We love you enough to leave you alone.

Saki pulled off her gloves and touched the cool surface of the alien artifact. M.J. was part of this object. All the colonists were. Those first colonists who had lost their lives to make the aliens understand that humankind didn't want to be forcibly absorbed. Was M.J.'s consciousness still there, a part of something bigger? Saki liked to think so.

With her palm pressed against the artifact, she closed her eyes and focused. They were learning to communicate, slowly over time. It was telling her a story. One side of the story, and the other side was hers.

She knew that she was biased, that her version of reality would be hopelessly flawed and imperfect. That she would not even realize all the things she would not think to write, but she recorded both sides of the story as best she could.

This is a love story, the last of a series of moments when we meet.

RION AMILCAR SCOTT

Shape-ups at Delilah's

FROM *The New Yorker*

THE NIGHT AFTER Jerome's brother turned up on a Southside sidewalk, bloodied and babbling in and out of consciousness, Tiny took Jerome's hand, sat him on a stool, wiped tears from his cheeks, draped a towel over his shoulders, and whispered, Relax, baby, you can't go to the hospital like that. Your brother'll wake up to that damn bird's nest on your head and fall right back into another coma. For the next two hours, Tiny sheared away Jerome's knotty beads until his head appeared smooth and black, with orderly hairs laid prone by her soft, smoothing hand. Back when they met, she'd told him she cut hair, said she was damn good, too. Jerome had nodded, smiled a bit, as if to say, *How cute,* and changed the subject. But now, the way his eyes danced in the mirror, the joy that broadened his face, it all said, *Where in the hell did a woman, a W-O-M-A-N, learn to cut like that?* She circled him as she did her work, looking at every angle of his head. She lathered up the front and went at it with a straight razor so that his hairline sat as crisp and sharp as the beveled edge of the blade that cut it. Tiny imagined slicing her finger while sliding it across the front of his head; her imagined self then smeared the blood all over Jerome's face. After she finished and had swept the fine hairs from his shoulders and back, Jerome and Tiny collapsed onto the floor, spent, as if they had just made love for hours. On a bed of Jerome's shorn hair, they slept into the early morning.

A year to the day after Jerome's brother got out of the hospital, Jerome showed up at the only place he'd ever found comfort, on the doorstep of the woman he no longer loved and who, by agreement, no longer loved him. When Tiny opened the door that night she snorted and looked him up and down, this man she had been comfortable not seeing or speaking to for the past several months. Before she could complete her condescension, Jerome spoke: My mother is dead.

Tiny's face grew tender with sadness and disbelief. She opened her arms and called for Jerome to rest his head on the soft roundness of her chest. But he breezed by her, eyes on the floor, and crumpled onto the couch. His face was so fallen she barely recognized him; sadness so chiseled into his cheeks and his brow that Tiny couldn't imagine anything softening the rock of his face, so she sat and said nothing. She thought of how much she had loved Jerome's mother—but that wasn't the truth, simply one of those things people tell themselves when someone dies. The woman, Tiny realized, was just a proxy; it wasn't for Jerome's mother that she had once held an unshakable love but for Jerome himself. She opened her arms wide again and pulled him tightly to her body. His head nestled itself between her breasts. It felt wrong, terribly, terribly wrong. Jerome trembled in her arms. He wept and sniffled. Tiny brushed her lips against his cheeks, and then she stopped.

I'm sorry, Jerome, she said. I want to end all that pain you're carrying, but I can't do what you want me to do.

Damn it, he said. My mother just died. Is it that hard for you to break out your clippers and make me look presentable? Is your heart that full of ice for me? I got a funeral to attend. God damn it, my little brother was doing better, now I can't find him and you not trying to help me. My brother is God knows where, doing God knows what drugs, in God knows how much pain, and you can't offer me this simple kindness?

No, Tiny whispered. No. I can't.

Still, she walked into her bathroom, whispering, No, as she grabbed the clippers, the razor, the rubbing alcohol, and a towel. She draped the towel over his shoulders and, in silence, she cut his uncombed locks. They both whimpered and sniffled a bit, avoiding each other's eyes. When the tears blurred Tiny's vision, she didn't stop; instead, she let the salty drops drip onto Jerome's head as she cut from memory, her smoothing hand rubbing the tears into his scalp.

It took her double the time of her most careful cuts, four whole painful hours. When she finished, Jerome thanked her and left, wiping his cheeks. I'm crying, he said, 'cause of my mom, but also 'cause this haircut is so goddam beautiful.

Tiny nodded, hoping that Jerome would never return. After she shut the door, she sat in the hallway sobbing into the night, until she felt as useless as piles and piles and piles of dead hair.

Tiny had started cutting hair almost on a whim. She had found her father's old clippers at the bottom of a dusty box beneath the sink in a seldom used bathroom in the basement. Her father used to zug crooked lines and potholes into his three sons' hair when they were young and not yet vain. Soon her older brothers no longer allowed the maiming, so someone buried the clippers under piles of stuff. When Tiny stumbled on the clippers, she realized she had grown tired of her perm. The time had come to shave it all off and let her natural hair grow long. She'd shape it and twist it, braid it and maybe lock it, as her mother had, but whenever her hair grew she felt the urge only to trim it into what everyone called "boy styles": a faded-in Mohawk, or just a fade, or a Caesar, or a temple taper. It changed every two weeks. Soon Tiny began to choose her lovers based partly on the shape of their heads, what styles she could carve on their domes. When their heads no longer intrigued her, she would lose interest. These days, her hair grew long enough to keep in a simple ponytail, and that was how she wore it. She no longer had any interest in her own hair, just other people's.

Nearly a year to the day after Tiny watched the folds at the back of Jerome's freshly cut head bob out her door for the last time, Tiny's Hair Technology opened up on River Way. The Great Hair Crisis was raging on with no visible end. Every single barbering Cross Riverian man somehow losing his touch, the ability to deliver even a decent shape-up. Afros had abounded within the town's borders since that moment in '05 when all the clippers and cutting hands began shaving ragged patches into heads. It had been ten years of this wilderness, this dystopia. Men with beautiful haircuts became as mythical as the glowing wolves—lit up like earthbound Canis Majors—that are said to walk the Wildlands. Sonny Beaumont Jr., once Cross River's greatest barber, now looked like a haggard old troll; he was about forty-five years old, and resembled a wrinkled set of intertwined wires covered in the thinnest, baggiest brown flesh. There would never again be any good days for Sonny. Even decent haircuts stayed frozen in his past, and all he was capable of now were messes—carefully, carefully carved messes. His remaining customers patronized him only out of loyalty—poisoned nostalgia for the perfect cuts they'd once received—and false hope.

All those Cross Riverian Afros left one to ask, Who cursed Cross River? A shop opened up on the Northside—a decent shop—only for the owner to die of a heart attack mid-cut. The two remaining barbers opened shops of their own, and eventually murdered each other in a gunfight over customers and territory. Kimothy Beam closed his business, Mobile Cutting Unit, after his haircut van flipped during a police chase. He served three months and hung up his clippers for good when the authorities turned him loose. There was a long scroll of such mishaps: haircutting men, always men, driven from the business and, in some cases, from this world, through some misfortune. That's not going to be me, Tiny thought. The simple science of haircutting gets down into one's bones, into the soul of a person. She watched the peace settle over her customers after a good cut. They'd walk out into the world, where the noise would start again, but that moment at the end of a fresh cut—from the crack of the cape, as she removed it from a patron's shoulders, to the door—was pure, pure magic.

Tiny no longer cut her lovers' hair for free. They'd have to pay like anyone else. After Jerome, she'd loved Cameron, and then Sherita passed through her life, and then Bo and Jo, and Katrina, and De'Andre and Ron. They all fell out of love with her when they realized she wouldn't use her magic on them. And that was fine with her; it was easy for Tiny to fall out of love with them, too. Jerome seemed so long ago. She hadn't even loved him best.

In the scheme of things Tiny's Hair Technology is just a footnote, but it would be even less than that had the shop not opened during such desperate times. A shop of lady barbers? Who had ever heard of such a thing? It was Tiny and Claudine and Mariah at first; later, a whole cast of lady barbers passed through. No one expected anything but another business popping up and then shuttering within a couple of months. There had been five in three years in that location. Folks in the neighborhood had taken to calling it the Wack Spot, a dingy cardboard box of a structure tucked away at the edge of an unimpressive side street. Behind the building stood knotted trees that stayed bare no matter the season. The jutting branches resembled skeletal fingers, so the building appeared always on the verge of being snatched into an abyss. The Wack Spot was salted earth; no successful business could sprout from the ruined soil. There was the roti shop that never seemed to have any roti. Then there was Ice Screamers (later Sweet Screamers, and, as a last ditch, Sweet Creamers), a soft-serve spot run by a surly guy with an eyepatch. For the previous several months the Wack Spot had housed an adult bookstore that, much to the dismay of the surly ice-cream peddler, retained the final name of the soft-serve spot. It was common knowledge that only a witch spouting the most forbidden of spells could make the Wack Spot work, and Tiny figured she would be that witch, conjuring the pitchest-black magic from the back of her spell book.

When Jerome walked into the shop, shortly after it opened, he was still tall and fine, though scruffy—he appeared to be trying to grow a beard, but had managed only wild crabgrass patches along his cheeks.

Woman, cut my hair, he said with a smirk.

Tiny spun her chair and dashed herself onto it. She loved to hear the lumpy springs whine beneath the heft of her backside.

Hello, Jerome, she said. Can I help you with something?

All this formality now?

She didn't respond, tried to make her eyes blank as if she'd never seen him before. She couldn't hide everything, though; as she glanced at him she flashed a twinkle he took for a bit of residual love.

This is boring me, he said. I just want a cut. One of your perfect little tight cuts.

Well, I'm busy now. Jerome looked about the empty shop. Mariah, Tiny said, should be here in a few. Would you like me to make an appoint—

I don't want a cut from some-damn-body named Mariah! I want you. No one makes me look as good as you do.

Tiny turned her head, reached for a magazine, and pawed through the pages with the bored, languid movements of a cat. How's your brother? she said, finally.

Dude is doing great. Jerome smiled a little. Just great. It took Mom to die, but you should see him. Designer suit every day. This fucking little Dick Tracy hat. Looks fly on him. I'm proud of the guy. He needs a haircut, though. If you do it good to me—the haircut, I mean—I'll recommend you.

How'd you even hear I was over here?

You think niggas not gon' talk about a new shop full of lady barbers during the Hair Crisis? Now, you gonna cut me, or what?

I'm sorry, Jerome, but I have a few things to do now—

I'm trying to give your failing business some work.

Like I said, Jerome, Mariah—

You're just going to repeat your bullshit over and over, huh? I already know how you do. Thought you would have matured by now, Tiny. Wanna take the little-girl route? Gotcha. It's fine.

Jerome jutted out his lips, did a quick head nod, and watched his ex-lover as if silence could break her. Don't worry, bitch, he continued, sweeping a stack of magazines to the ground and walking out the door. You'll get yours. See you real soon.

After weeks of barber-chair emptiness and a floor sadly clean of shorn hair, Tiny arrived one morning to find a line of men—many sporting unkempt dandruff bushes—waiting outside.

I thought you opened at ten, called the first desperately uncombed man in line to a chorus of grumbles. It's nearly noon!

You guys been here since ten? Tiny asked. As she unlocked the door, the men dazed her with numbers. Six in the morning, one said, his voice trembling with a mixture of embarrassment and pride.

I been here since five-fifty-five, a man whose hair was cut into an asymmetrical field of black said. He held the hand of a boy who looked everything like a little Jackson 5 Michael Jackson except for the gopher hole shaved into the center of his head.

But . . . but, it's a school day, Tiny said.

And? the father replied. I take him out of school when he got a doctor's appointment, too.

When she finished with the first man, he strutted out to cries of admiration and even applause. His hair—once dangerously overgrown—now glittered. Tiny slapped the chair with the cape and cried, Next up!

A tall Eritrean man with curly hair and a tall—shorter than the Eritrean, but still tall—man with an oblong head scrambled for the seat. As they tussled, a short dark-skinned man with salt-and-pepper hair and the twisted but unbecoming grin of a mischievous child strolled to the barber's chair. A Ghanaian guy they called Doc pointed and laughed. Don't forget to get the booster seat for my man, he said.

Quiet, you fool, the short man replied.

You folks rowdy, Tiny said with a smile. Don't make me have to call the police to keep things quiet in here. How'd y'all even hear about my shop?

The short man grinned and pointed to the tall Eritrean.

I heard from Doc, the tall Eritrean said.

That first guy you cut today, Doc said. That loudmouth. I heard from him.

Hmm, Tiny grunted. He said someone I never even heard of told him.

All I know, the short man said, is that the Great Hair Crisis is over!

That day, Tiny cut as if possessed, head after head, each cut better than the last. She ignored the nonstop talk, the chatter about sports and politics and the proper way to beat young children. After hours of clutching the vibrating clippers, her hand trembled. Men kept coming, though. Man after man. Each with a different story as to how he'd learned of Tiny's shop. Mariah showed up midafternoon to pick up the slack. The first man she cut approached her chair hesitantly, but when she finished he looked in the mirror and turned his head this way and that.

She better than Tiny!

Watch it! Tiny called, not taking her eyes off the head she was trimming.

As Mariah's customer walked out, a man with dark glasses and a shining silver mane stomped in. He clutched a thick Bible so old it looked as if the pages had begun to sprout hair. He held his book aloft and cried, *And De-li-lah said to Samson, Tell me, I pray thee, wherein thy great strength lieth, and wherewith thou mightest be bound to afflict thee.* That's from Judges 16:6. You men here giving away your strength, and for what? A nice haircut? Wrong is wrong is wrong is wrong in the eyes of the Lord.

Get out of my damn shop, Tiny called. Now! Get out!

Dale! the Bible man called to the customer in Tiny's chair. I'm surprised at you. Real surprised. Your wife know you in here giving away your power?

Rev. Kimothy, Dale said. I . . . I . . . I'm tired of coming into your church looking like I just stumbled in off the street.

Kimothy? Tiny asked. Kimothy Beam who had the Mobile Cutting Unit?

I found God in prison, and you must be Delilah—that's who you are.

I'll be that, Rev.

Dale stood from the chair, half of his head shaved close, the other wild and unshorn. He held a fistful of twenties in his outstretched hand. I'm sorry, Tiny, he said. Real sorry.

That's right, Rev. Kimothy said. Sorry as snake shit.

Naw, Tiny said. You sit your monkey ass down and keep your money. You ain't telling no one Tiny did that to your head. Sit and you can rest your eternal soul in hell, Rev. Kimothy shouted. Dale stood paralyzed, looking back and forth between his reverend and his barber, until some guys from the back of the shop made Dale's decision easier, snatching Rev. Kimothy by his arms and tossing him onto the sidewalk as he struggled and screamed, Lady barbers! Whoever heard of such a thing? The devil, that's who! You gon' burn! You gon' burn! You gon' burn!

Even as Dale sat back down in the barber's chair, three Afroed men slipped quietly out the door.

Bunch of bitches, Mariah mumbled, staring into the sharp lines she had trimmed into her customer's head. Bunch of little pussy-ass bitches.

This has been some day, Tiny muttered into Dale's hair. Some day.

Late one night—say, nearly eleven—a man in a beautiful cream serge suit and a white panama hat came in just as Tiny finished her last head, a woman whose husband had recommended the shop. Tiny's feet ached from standing, and she could feel her eyelids hanging heavy like curtains falling over her eyes. Ordinarily she would have turned the cream-suited man away, but he had pushed through a line of protesters out front. Rev. Kimothy and his new legion of followers had grown relentless. Fighting through those fools just to get a haircut, especially at this time of night, was a level of dedication that deserved a reward, Tiny thought. She glanced at him, didn't take him in much. She yawned.

Tiny's life was now love and hatred falling on her in equal measure. Accolades and applause, followed by bricks wrapped in Bible verses sailing through her window at night. The woman stood and stared into a handheld mirror, admiring her new fade from all angles. This shit right here fine, she said. Sonny trash now. From now on, you my barberess.

The Barberess. What a title. Tiny had thought about changing the shop's name. That old name had grown stale. Barberesses, maybe. Maybe. It would look beautiful out front in red and white, Tiny thought.

Wow, you sure are deep in thought, Tiny heard a voice say. She looked up and the woman and her fade had left. The man with the cream suit took her place in the chair. He held the panama hat in his lap. It took Tiny a half second to recognize the face. It seemed to have aged since she'd last seen it. Jerome's patchy beard had turned into a choppy bush, but it was definitely him, and this realization made Tiny close her eyes for what seemed to her like a long minute or two.

You thinking about what you gon' do with all this mess, huh? he said, pointing to the unkempt pikes of locks jutting from his scalp. I never, never, ever take off this hat for any reason nowadays, unless I'm home or something. Got a new attitude, a new style, Tine. The hat allows me to conduct business without looking like a vagrant, but it's havoc on me, I tell you. Havoc. This thing itches and flakes. My bush, I mean. These amateurs around here worse than they ever been. I'm ready to give anything a try, even a woman barber who ain't you. Jerome chuckled. Mariah here? I'll wait for Mariah if you want me to.

I've seen worse on you, Tiny said, combing out the coils. The prongs of the pick made a *plink, plink, plink* music. You better give me a big tip, making me revisit your big head.

When Tiny had finished, she took a straight razor and cleaned up the sprigs from Jerome's cheeks and chin. She placed a warm, wet towel on his face. When she removed the towel, she nearly jumped back in fright. With his beard and sideburns trimmed, the smile Jerome flashed took on a sinister edge; he grinned as if he had already poisoned her and was just waiting for her to die.

How you work this magic, huh, babe?

There's that evil look again, Tiny replied. Like you the devil come to burn me right here where I stand.

No, Jerome said. No. Of course not. I haven't gotten a proper haircut in I don't know how long. And you did something divine up there, Ms. Tiny. I just want to know what you got that them fools lack.

Tiny sighed. Look at my eyes, she said. I'm tired. I'm half 'sleep. I don't have the energy to talk to you anymore tonight.

I must be half 'sleep, too, 'cause even when you was cutting me back in the day I thought it was a fluke. I thought it was 'cause you loved me. You clearly don't love me now. You hate me, as a matter of fact, but you still the best cut around. You cut other people's hair perfectly, too. You can't be in love with all them people. How a woman cut hair like this, huh?

Men barbers got some kind of secret? Tiny said. They grip the clippers with they dicks or something?

I guess not. He chuckled again and looked down, shifted in his seat. You know, I bought this fancy suit from my brother.

How he doing?

He good, he good. He off that stuff. Not owing no thugs no money no more. He don't be off disappearing no more. He good. I helped him apply to his new job selling these things at the haberdashery. Nigga had no experience selling anything—anything legal, that is. No experience being good at selling anything. None. I helped him 'cause I couldn't lose nobody else after you and then my mother. I buy a lot of fancy suits with his discount. So do he. Getting high off your own supply is not a big deal when you selling suits, it turns out. But look, Tiny. My brother says I'm a fool for coming here.

Damn right.

You owe me, though.

How you figure?

You see that? Jerome pointed to the fools outside pacing with signs reading DELILAH! REPENT! and BITCHES AIN'T SHIT (AT CUTTING HAIR)! You don't think that mess organized itself, do you? You think Rev. Kimothy's dumb ass put all this together by himself?

You telling me you behind this mess? She scrunched her face for a second and then straightened her brow. Jerome, I knew you could be a goddam bastard, but—

Hold on, Ms. Tiny, Jerome replied. It's not even like that. I was mad at you when you turned me away, but I was still proud, so I told every nigga I know about this shop. Thought Rev. Kimothy would be interested, since he used to cut hair. Figured he'd tell his congregation, and he did. It's just that he told them to meet him out front to protest this *new Delilah.* Got to admit, though, Rev. Kimothy's dumb ass is good for business.

Is he, though? I had a full shop before he started his nonsense. Now I got a hassle of men outside my door at all hours. Tiny sucked her teeth. She looked to the floor, shaking her head. Y'all men something else, boy. Something else. I don't respect Rev. Kimothy or any of them stupid-ass niggas outside, but I can't be mad at you for their dumb shit.

Yeah . . . He trailed off. But, look, you gotta tell me your secret.

Secret?

Every lady barber in here know how to do something extra special with her clippers.

You can't be this much of an idiot, Jerome. There is no secret. Secret is I get a good night's rest before I cut. Now I'm tired and don't know if I can work magic tomorrow. That's my secret. I got another secret: I'm going home. I'll come early to clean up before the day get started. I need my beauty rest.

Let me walk you, Tine.

No thanks. I'm done with you again.

Gotta be careful, sis. All those fools out here—

Tiny turned out the lights and pushed open the door. With the black of the sky as a backdrop, and the bright bluish-white glow of the streetlight hovering above like a low-hanging moon, the faces of the men who rushed Tiny appeared to her as hovering, disembodied fright masks. The shouting sounded like sharp, high winds battering her eardrums. Tiny tensed and clutched her hands to her chest before she stumbled and nearly fell backward. She caught a glimpse of one of the signs. It featured an obscene drawing and read I LIKE MY HAIR LIKE I LIKE MY JUNK, RAW AND UNCUT. The man who held the placard had a bush that sat atop his head like a woolen black cube. His face looked grotesque and plastic. Jerome shoved the forehead of the block-headed man and snatched at Tiny's arm. He pushed his way through the protesters, who had suddenly quieted, offering no resistance, giving Tiny and her guardian space to escape into night's darkness.

When they got to her house, Tiny looked up into her protector's eyes and examined his freshly shaved face. Stray hairs dotted his cheeks and his forehead like black snowflakes. She looked away.

That was quite impressive, she said.

Well, he replied. I told you to let me walk you. You gon' to let me walk you tomorrow?

Jerome's face hovered over hers, a different sort of fright mask, fearful instead of terrifying. This time she didn't turn away. Maybe, she said.

Look, Ms. Tiny, you owe me.

I hope this isn't your corny way of trying to get a kiss or something, 'cause we too old to be speaking in riddles.

You can kiss me if you want, Jerome said. I'll take that. But what I really want is the secret. How y'all lady barbers cut like that, huh?

Tiny kissed his cheek. That's not so wrong, is it? she asked herself.

A lady barber's got to keep her secrets, she told him. What if I give away my secret and the result is you can't get no more good cuts, huh?

I'll take the chance.

There is no secret, 'Rome—how's that for a secret? She watched his eyes as they began dimming in sadness. I cut with love. That's it. Tiny said this because she assumed that was what Jerome wanted to hear. His eyes grew sadder still; they rimmed with an unbearable melancholy that she had seen before. Tiny looked down. She wanted it to stop.

Lye, she said. It's lye. Red Devil Lye. That's the secret. Makes the hair manageable. Mix in some eggs and potatoes and you got good old-fashioned conk juice. That's the shit I be spraying on your head. Makes anyone with a little skill cut with magic. Even a lady barber.

I knew I felt my head burn a little, Jerome said. I knew it. I'ma keep this secret close to my heart, Tine. Jerome blathered with joy as Tiny walked slowly into her house.

Tiny woke one morning with the urge, just a throbbing and unrelenting urge, to change the name of the barbershop to Delilah's. She hired a woman to paint a new sign, and the woman worked at it all day. Tiny hung it after the last customer left. When Jerome met her at the shop that night he took a look at the sign and said, You're such a troublemaker. This was after Claudine had left for good, unable to handle the crowds, the hatred, the men who shouted vile threats and called her bitch, as if it were the name her mother had given her. Tiny understood. She welcomed a rotating cast of women, each a better barber than the previous one. The new woman would claim Claudine's chair and then disappear after a week or so, afraid of the angry men outside. And with DELILAH'S on the front of the window, no one called her Tiny anymore. Tiny became D. As the new name took hold, she smiled secretly, especially when Mariah bought her a black apron emblazoned with a bright-red *D*.

Each morning brought a new influx of men. A madness of men. So many men. Since there were more men than seats, the men gladly stood. Men bursting out of the little shop, sometimes pouring onto the sidewalk. Everywhere Tiny turned she saw men. Men who had previously protested, once yelling, now quiet as sheep. Sheep-men walking upright to be shorn. These men said things like *Real men, Tiny, real men can admit when they wrong*. But, really, it was that they'd observed other men, their friends who were now shining, beautiful men because of their perfectly cut heads. Tiny and Mariah and whoever took the third chair couldn't cut fast enough to keep up with all those men.

Tiny could scarcely understand the uptick, until one day Dale burst into the shop, his eyes wild, pupils dilated, his head covered in a cap of soft black silk.

Them nig—uh, dudes up the hill done gone crazy!

Say, bruh, a man from the back called. I think you got on your wife's bonnet.

Yeah, another voice called. This nigga wearing hair underwear!

You clowns laugh, Dale said. Did you know that the idiots up the hill started putting lye in people's hair without any goddam warning? Pardon my language, but that shi—stuff burned so bad I ran to the damn—pardon me—Cross River and stuck my head right in!

Dale uncovered his head; the once coarse grains of his hair were now straight and wavy. The nig—guy, the darn barber, Sonny, said it makes the hair easier to cut. D, you ever hear anything so stupid?

Mariah and Tiny exchanged glances as Dale took a seat to wait.

Jerome arrived that night just as the shop was closing. Unfallen tears rested in the corners of his eyes. The shop sat empty except for Tiny and Mariah. When he walked through the door, Tiny turned and pretended to straighten the hair products on the table behind her chair.

Why is there no trust between us? he said. After all I did for you? All our walks.

Mariah swept, trying to look away from Jerome's sad, dim eyes while suppressing a smile.

Go somewhere, Tiny said. You fools believe anything.

Yeah, Mariah said. Red Devil Lye? Everyone knows we lick our razors just before every cut.

Mariah! Tiny called.

Don't mind me, Mariah said. I'm half-'sleep.

Look, Jerome, Tiny said. I don't want you in my shop no more. At all. Go. You're not different. You're not welcome. You can't seem to grow up. You're the same goddam fool I didn't want to be with anymore.

But our walks—

You can get a head start. Go on.

Jerome didn't argue or fight; he simply backed out of the shop, slowly, with a strange feline walk.

Late in the afternoon the next day, a man with a tuft of spongy and unruly hair sat in Mariah's seat and called for his hair to be cut into a high-top fade.

You want it tall, right? Mariah asked.

Yeah. But please don't do nothing weird. I almost had to knock Sonny out this morning. I caught the nigga licking his clippers like some kind of goddam animal.

Back when they were together, Jerome never found out how she'd gained the name Tiny, but another man did, over a perfect haircut one afternoon while Jerome was elsewhere looking the other way. The illicit haircut was something else Jerome never found out about, and so that particular betrayal was not even why they broke up. And why should it matter that she cut another man's hair, huh? Why does a haircut become an intimacy simply because Tiny's a woman? Such absurdity. But then that whispered story. Surely that was an intimacy. Or perhaps she spoke so freely, so easily, because she knew she'd never see this man again. This man who smiled at her when she passed him at the bus stop. She couldn't bear his smile, because the animal atop his head made him look defective. Every man around her during the Great Hair Crisis had become a ruined sculpture. She felt like a lapsed superhero, all that power she shrank from wielding, all that responsibility she shirked day after blessed day. Let me cut your hair, she said to the man, as an act of charity. Shortly after that, she cut another man. And another man. They grew as indistinguishable as strands of hair in her memory. One man told the next about Tiny. And she accepted them into her house, warning them all that she'd cut them only once. One time and no more—that way, she could control the flow of hair-blighted men and she could tell herself that by seeing these men only once she wasn't betraying Jerome.

She cut their hair and never saw them again, and usually during the shape-up she'd whisper the source of her name and they'd all miss the point and ask the source of her power.

One man, though, managed to slip in a second time. He was a small man with a reddish Afro. He hunched as he walked and scrunched himself into a ball as he sat. His voice sounded like a high-pitched strain, and both times his hair had grown wild and unkempt. Balls of white lint coiled into his curls. Tiny had to wash his hair to soften it in order to move the clippers through his knots. As he bent over the sink in the back of Tiny's basement with the water and lather dripping through his naps, she told him, as she usually told the men, about her name. When I was small, she said, I was tiny. She chuckled, as she always did. The youngest and the tiniest one in the family. But that's not why they call me Tiny. I been a big girl ever since, like, fourteen, but it's like no one could see that. When someone felt disrespected, they'd say something like, *You must think you talking to Abigail or some shit?* That's me, Abigail. Abby. Disrespecting me was nothing to them, I guess. Like disrespecting a bug or something. Tiny. Inconsequential. Eventually, I told folks to stop calling me Abigail, Abby, all that shit—

Before Tiny could finish, the man looked up at her with glowing eyes and finished for her: *Told 'em to call me Tiny and no one ever asked why.* It's a beautiful story. You told me last time. He laughed as if he had carved out some sort of victory.

Last time? She looked at his head and suddenly remembered. Uh-uh. I told you my rule then, I told you when you came in the door today. One-time-only deal. Dry your head, and then you gotta go.

You can't do that to me, Abigail. He smiled wider. You can't do that to Cross River. Too many heads in crisis. Uh-uh, you gon' cut this. He snatched at her wrist. Come on, Abby. Just give me a little trim. He chuckled a mean, mean little chuckle. Make magic.

The small man let go of Tiny's wrist and sat with his back to her. Just a Caesar today, he said, so confident he was that Tiny would cut his hair with little fuss. And he was right. It was easier to start shearing his nappy kinks than to keep arguing. Her hand shook as she trimmed, though. She rushed the tricky parts she would usually have moved through with precision and care. The sooner she finished, the sooner she'd never have to see him again. Tiny cut with disgust, watching the stubborn dirt and dandruff as if they had left indelible splotches on her, forever staining her soul.

When the small man stood and looked into the mirror, he said nothing at first, and then he balled his fists.

What is this trash? he screamed. You did this on . . . You did this 'cause I wouldn't leave!

No, I—

Of course you did. This is worse than one of Sonny's cuts.

You want your money back? Tiny tried to joke, but that seemed to make the small man even more angry. It's the curse, Tiny said, still trembling in fear. The Hair Crisis, she said, it comes for every barber in Cross River eventua—

You think I'm a fool, bitch? The man snatched at Tiny's shoulders. All I wanted was a good haircut for once. Is that too . . . Tell me your secret, Abby. How come the Crisis ain't come for you, huh?

I don't have a secret, she said, shoving the man. Please leave.

The small man raised his right fist as if about to throw a punch. The gold bracelet on his wrist, the gold chain around his neck, they both jangled. Tiny raised her arms and flinched to curl away from the blow, but the small man lowered his fist with a snort and a chuckle. He tossed the towel that lay around his neck before stomping up the stairs and out of Tiny's house.

The next day, when Jerome came for his weekly cut, Tiny's hand trembled as if still trimming the small man's red bush. She could feel the heaviness of his fingers at her shoulders and her wrist.

What in the fuck is this? Jerome said, peering into the mirror.

I don't know what's wrong, Tiny lied. It's the curse.

For the rest of the week, Jerome remained sullen, only frowning at Tiny or grumbling her way. She wanted to tell him what had happened, but that would be a long story, beginning with the first man she cut behind his back.

Or perhaps it would begin with her name and how her family made it into a curse, how they made her into a small, tiny thing. She imagined him laughing at her, sneering and calling her Abigail the next time she accidentally cut jagged marks into his head. Two, three weeks of bad haircuts made Jerome into a different man. If there was a fight to be picked, he picked it like some naps.

One day after a particularly bad haircut, Jerome fingered the slanted frontier that was now his hairline as they ate Chinese food. Tiny's clippers had pushed it back so much that Jerome's forehead now looked like an eroding coastline. Tiny asked Jerome to pass her a packet of soy sauce.

Get it your damn self, Jerome barked, standing sharply from his seat. Got me out here looking like George Jefferson. I was the dude with the good haircuts! Who the fuck am I now?

He stomped out the door, hunched and scarred like the small man. Tiny watched his disappearing form with sad eyes, vowing to never cut another man's head. Tiny held firm to her promise no matter how many men knocked and cried and pleaded. She remained firm until that night Jerome returned to her doorstep several months later with tears in his eyes.

After that, she vowed to never again give up her power. To never again freely give away something as precious as a haircut.

Tiny swept the hair of her last couple of customers into woolly piles late one night. She rubbed her clippers, razors, and combs with alcohol even as she felt her eyelids forcing themselves shut. She enjoyed the solitude, though she stumbled through the shop with her eyelids low, sleep trying to ambush her. The one thing she couldn't allow herself was a seat. To sit down would be to fall asleep and make herself vulnerable to an opportunist, one of Rev. Kimothy's legion out there, always looking to catch her slipping so they could do her harm. Tiny grasped the broom again and went at some hair clumps she'd missed, and as she swept she heard the flat slap of an open palm against the window. Without looking up she waved the interloper away. The noise persisted. She slowly turned to the entranceway. Jerome stood at the window waving. A sharp pang of irritation ran through Tiny, but also relief. At least it wasn't another head to cut. At least it wasn't a protester. Any annoyance Jerome was about to cause would not end in her destruction. When she opened the door she noticed he wore that same serge suit. The same panama hat. Dirt stains now ringed the hat's brim and the jacket's wrists.

D! he exclaimed, stretching his arms out as if preparing to strangle her. D! Why is there no trust between us?

Look at my eyes, Tiny said. I'm half-'sleep.

Please, please, please, please, D, please tell me your secret.

Tiny sighed. She just wanted to sleep. This man in front of her looked so anguished that it sent sharp pains shooting through her joints.

It's piss. She dashed these words off halfheartedly, surprising even herself with the sting of her sarcasm.

Piss? You mean you pee on your clippers?

No, silly. That would be ridiculous. I soak all my clippers, my combs, everything I have . . . I leave them all to soak overnight in jars of piss.

Really? True this time?

Yep. That's my secret.

Yes, Jerome said. That makes so much more sense than all that other stuff you told me.

Does it? Tiny said, and then she sighed again. Of course it does.

Tiny looked at Jerome with sad, tired eyes. She forced a smile onto her lips. She wanted to say, *No, fool, what do you take me for?* But to point out his gullibility now would be a true act of cruelty. If only Jerome knew how to read the crooked tilt of her lips. Her face was a book he could never truly comprehend. These men, she realized, would believe anything. They preached logic and reason but followed only magic. Things would always be like this. Always and forever. As long as she lived and cut hair. Tiny felt more exhausted than she had ever felt before, like weights had attached themselves to her eyelids, her limbs, her neck, everywhere. After Jerome left, she locked the door and walked through the protest and into darkest night, never to be seen in Cross River again.

It was better this way. Perhaps Tiny sensed the horrors that hovered on the horizon. Sonny sitting alone every day in an empty shop surrounded by endless jars of his own piss. Soon would come the hair cults. The Cult of the Licked Razor. The Cult of Red Devil Lye. The Cult of Blood. The Cult of Piss.

But then there were also the Children of Delilah, the barbers, the barberesses, sprouting all over town like new growth and shining like the brightest points of light, like the finest, most luxurious hair, smoothed with a slick sheen of grease, growing faster than any havoc the Hair Crisis could cause, faster than any curse could possibly curse.

TOBIAS S. BUCKELL

The Galactic Tourist Industrial Complex

FROM *New Suns*

WHEN GALACTICS ARRIVED at JFK they often reeked of ammonia, sulfur, and something else that Tavi could never quite put a finger on. He was used to it all after several years of shuttling them through the outer tanks and waiting for their gear to spit ozone and adapt to Earth's air. He would load luggage, specialized environmental-adaptation equipment, and cross-check the being's needs, itinerary, and sightseeing goals.

What he wasn't expecting this time was for a four-hundred-pound octopus-like creature to open the door of his cab a thousand feet over the new Brooklyn Bridge, filling the cab with an explosion of cold, screaming air, and lighting the dash up with alarms.

He also definitely wasn't expecting the alien to scream "Look at those spires!" through a speaker that translated for it.

So, for a long moment after the alien jumped out of the cab, Tavi just kept flying straight ahead, frozen in shock at the controls.

This couldn't be happening. Not to him. Not in his broken-down old cab he'd been barely keeping going, and with a re-up on the Manhattan license due soon.

To fly into Manhattan you needed a permit. That was the first thing he panicked about, because he'd recently let it lapse for a bit. The New York Tourism Bureau hadn't just fined him, but suspended him for three months. Tavi had limped along on some odd jobs: tank cleaning at the airport, scrubbing out the backs of the cabs when they came back after a run to the island, and other muck work.

But no, all his licenses were up to date. And he knew that it was a horrible thing to worry about as he circled the water near the bridge; he should be worrying about his passenger. Maybe this alien was able to withstand long falls, Tavi thought.

Maybe.

But it wasn't coming up.

He had a contact card somewhere in the dash screen's memory. He tapped, calling the alien.

"Please answer. Please."

But it did not pick up.

What did he know about the alien? It looked like some octopus-type thing. What did that mean? They shouldn't have even been walking around, so it had to have been wearing an exoskeleton of some kind.

Could that have protected it?

Tavi circled the water once more. He had to call this in. But then the police would start hassling him about past mistakes. Somehow this would be his fault. He would lose his permit to fly into Manhattan. And it was Manhattan that the aliens loved above all else. This was the "real" American experience, even though most of it was heavily built up with zones for varying kinds of aliens. Methane breathers in the Garment District, the buildings capped with translucent covers and an alien atmosphere. Hydrogen types were all north of Central Park.

He found the sheer number of shops fun to browse, but few of them sold anything of use to humans. In the beginning, a lot of researchers and scientists had rushed there to buy what the Galactics were selling, sure they could reverse engineer what they found.

Turned out it was a lot of cheap alien stuff that purported to be made on Earth but wasn't. Last year some government agency purchased a "real" human sports car that could be shipped back to the home planet of your choice. It had an engine inside that seemed to be some kind of antigravity device that got everyone really excited. It exploded when they cracked the casing, taking out several city blocks.

When confronted about it, the tall, furry, sauropod-like aliens that had several other models in their windows on Broadway shrugged and said it wasn't made by them, they just shipped them to Earth to sell.

But Galactics packed the city buying that shit when they weren't slouching beside the lakes in Central Park. If Tavi couldn't get to Manhattan, he didn't have a job.

With a groan, Tavi tapped 9-1-1. There were going to be a lot of questions. He was going to be in it up to his neck.

But if he took off, they'd have his transponder on file. Then he'd look guilty.

With a faint clenching in his stomach, Tavi prepared for his day to go wrong.

Tavi stood on a pier, wearing a gas mask to filter out the streams of what seemed like mustard gas that would seep out from a nearby building in DUMBO. The cops, also wearing masks, took a brief statement. Tavi gave his fingerprint, and then they told him to leave.

"Just leave?"

There were several harbor-patrol boats hovering near where the alien had struck the water. But there was a lack of urgency to it all. Mostly everyone seemed to be waiting around for something to happen.

The cop taking Tavi's statement wore a yellow jumpsuit with logos advertising a Financial District casino (RISK YOUR MONEY HERE, JUST LIKE THEY USED TO IN THE OLD STOCK MARKET! WIN BIG, RING THE OLD BELL!). He nodded through his gas mask as he took notes.

"We have your contact info on file. We're pulling footage now."

"But aren't you going to drag the river?"

"Go."

There was something in the cop's tone that made it through the muffled gas mask and told Tavi it was an order. He'd done the right thing in an impossible moment.

He'd done the right thing.

Right?

He wanted to go home and take a nap. Draw the shades and huddle in the dark and make all this go away for a day. But there were bills to pay. The cab required insurance, and the kinine fuel it used, shipped down from orbit, wasn't cheap. Every time the sprinklers under the cab misted up and put down a new layer, Tavi could hear his bank account dropping.

But you couldn't drive on the actual ground into Manhattan,

not if you wanted to get a good review. Plus, the ground-traffic-flow licenses were even more whack than flying licenses because the interstellar tourists didn't want to put up with constant traffic snarls.

Trying to tell anyone that traffic was authentic old Manhattan just got you glared at.

So: four more fares. More yellowed gas mixing into the main cabin of the cab, making Tavi cough and his eyes water. The last batch, a pack of wolflike creatures that poured into the cab, chittering and yapping like squirrels, requested he take them somewhere serving human food.

"Real human food, not that shit engineered to look like it, but doctored so that our systems can process it."

Tavi's dash had lit up with places the Tourist Bureau authorized for this pack of aliens that kept grooming each other as he watched them in his mirror.

"Yeah, okay."

He took them to his cousin Geoff's place up in Harlem, which didn't have as many skyscrapers bubble-wrapped with alien atmospheres. The pack creatures were oxygen breathers, but they supplemented that with something extra running to their noses in tubes that occasionally wheezed and puffed a dust of cinnamon-smelling air.

Tavi wanted some comfort food pretty badly by this point. While the aliens tried to make sense of the really authentic human menus out front, he slipped into the hot gleaming stainless steel of the kitchens in the back.

"Ricky!" Geoff shouted. "You bring those dogs in?"

"Yes," Tavi confessed, and Geoff gave him a half hug, his dreadlocks slapping against Tavi. "Maybe they'll tip you a million."

"*Shiiiit.* Maybe they'll tip you a *trillion.*"

It was an old service-job joke. How much did it cost to cross a galaxy to put your own eyes, or light receptors, on a world just for the sake of seeing it yourself? Some of the aliens who had come to Earth had crossed distances so great, traveled in ships so complicated, that they spent more than a whole country's GDP.

A tip from one of them *could* be millions. There were rumors of such extravagances. A dish boy turned rich suddenly. A tour guide with a place built on the Moon.

But the Tourism Bureau and the Galactic-owned companies

bringing the tourists here warned them not to overpay for services. The Earth was a fragile economy, they said. You didn't want to just run around handing out tips worth a year of some individual's salary. You could create accidental inflation, or unbalance power in a neighborhood.

So the apps on the tourists' systems, whatever types of systems they used, knew what the local exchange rates were and paid folk down here on the ground proportionally.

Didn't stop anyone from wishing, though.

Geoff slid him over a plate of macaroni pie, some peas and rice, and chicken. Tavi told him about his morning.

"You shouldn't have called the police," Geoff said.

"And what, just keep flying?"

"The bureau will blacklist you. They have to save face. And no one is going to want to hear about a tourist dying on the surface. It's bad publicity. You're going to lose your license into Manhattan. NYC bureau's the worst, man."

Tavi cleaned his fingers on a towel, then coughed. The taste of cinnamon came up strong through his throat.

"You okay?"

Tavi nodded, eyes watering. Whatever the pack out there was sniffing, it was ripping through his lungs.

"You need to be careful," Geoff said. "Get a better filter in that cab. Nichelle's father got lung cancer off a bunch of shit coming off the suits of some sundivers last year, doctors couldn't do nothing for him."

"I know, I know," Tavi said between coughs.

Geoff handed him a bag with something rolled up in aluminum foil inside. "Roti for the road. Chicken, no bone. I have doubles if you want?"

"No." Geoff was being too nice. He knew how Tavi was climbing out from a financial hole and had been bringing by "extras" after he closed up each night.

Most of the food here was for nonhuman tourists, variations on foods that wouldn't upset their unique systems. Tavi had lied in taking the tourist pack here; the food out front was for the dog-like aliens. But the stuff in the bag was real, something Geoff made for folk who knew to come in through the back.

Tavi did one more run back to JFK, and this time he flew a few loops around the megastructure. JFK Interspacial was the foot of a leg that stretched up into the sky, piercing the clouds and rising beyond until it reached space. It was a pier that led to the deep water where the vast alien ships that moved tourists from star to star docked. It was the pride of the US. Congress had financed it by pledging the entire country's GDP for a century to a Galactic building consortium, so no one really knew how to build another after it was done, but the promise was that increased Manhattan tourism would bring in jobs. Because with the Galactics shipping in things to sell here in exchange for things they wanted, there wasn't much in the way of industrial capacity. Over half the US economy was tourism, the rest service jobs.

Down at the bottom of JFK, the eager vacationers and sightseers disgorged into terminals designed for their varying biologies and then were kitted out for time on Earth. Or, like Tavi's latest customer, just bundled into a can that slid into the back of a cab, and that was then dropped off at one of the hotels dwarfing Manhattan's old buildings.

When the drop-off of the tourist in a can that Tavi couldn't see or interact with was done, he headed home. That took careful flying over the remains of La Guardia, which pointed off from Brooklyn toward the horizon, the way it had ever since it collapsed and fell out of stable orbit.

Land around La Guardia's remains was cheap, and Tavi lived in an apartment complex roofed by the charred chunk of the once–space elevator's outer shell.

"Home sweet home," he said, coming in for a landing.

There was a burning smell somewhere in the back of the cab. Smoke started filling the cabin and the impellers failed.

He remained in the air, the kinine misters doing their job and preventing him from losing neutral buoyancy, and coasted.

Tavi wanted to get upset, hit the wheel, punch the dash. But he just bit his lip as the car finally stopped just short of the roof's parking spot. He had the misters spray some cancellation foam, and the car dropped a bit too hard to a stop.

"At least you got home," Sienna said, laughing as he opened the doors to the cab and stumbled out. "You know what I think of this Galactic piece of shit."

"It gets the job done."

Sienna poked her head into the cab, holding her breath. Her puffy hair bobbed against the side of the hatch.

"Can you fix it?" he asked her.

"It was one of the dog things, with the cinnamon breath? That gas they breathe catalyzes the O-rings. You need to spend some money to isolate the shaft back here."

"Next big tip," Tavi told her.

She crawled back out and let out the breath she'd been holding.

"Okay. Next big tip. I can work on it if you split dinner with me." She nodded at the bag Geoff had given him.

"Sure."

"There's also a man waiting by your door. Looks like Tourist Bureau."

"Shit." He didn't want anyone from the bureau out here. Not in an illegal squat in the ruins of the space elevator now draped across this side of the world.

There was no air conditioning; the solar panels lashed to the scrap hull rooftop didn't pump out enough juice to make that a reality. But the motion-sensitive fans kicked on and the LED track lights all leapt to attention as Tavi led the beet-faced Tourist Bureau agent through the mosquito netting.

"Your cab is having trouble?"

The agent, David Kahn, had a tight haircut and glossy brown skin, the kind that meant he didn't spend much time outside loading aliens into the back of cabs. He had an office job.

"Sienna will fix it. She grew up a scrapper. Her father was one of the original decommissioners paid to work on picking La Guardia up. Before the contract was canceled and they all decided to stay put. Beer?"

Tavi passed him a sweaty Red Stripe from the fridge, which Kahn held nervously in one hand as if he wanted to refuse it. Instead, he placed it against his forehead. The man had been waiting a while in the heat. And he was wearing a heavy suit.

"So, I am here to offer you a grant from the Greater New York Bureau of Tourism," Kahn started, sounding a little unsure of himself.

"A grant?"

"The bureau is starting a modernization campaign to make sure our cabs are the safest on Earth. That means we'd like to take your cab in and have it retrofitted with better security, improved impellers, better airlocks. For the driver's safety."

"The driver?"

"Of course."

Tavi thought it was a line of bullshit. Human lives were cheap; there were billions teeming away on the planet. If Tavi ever stepped out, someone else would bid on his license to Manhattan and he'd be forgotten in days.

Maybe even hours.

"Take it," Sienna said, pushing through the netting. "That piece of shit needs any help it can get."

Tavi didn't have to be told twice. He put his thumb to the documents, verbally repeated assent into a tiny red dot of a light, and then Kahn said a tow truck was on its way.

They watched the cab get lifted onto its back, the patchwork of a vehicle that Tavi had come to know every smelly inch of.

"What about the dead alien?" Tavi asked.

"Well, according to the documents you just signed, you can never talk about the . . . err . . . incident again."

"I get it." Tavi waved a salute at the disappearing cab and tow truck. "I figured as much when you said you had a 'grant.' But what happens to the alien? Did you ever find the body?"

Kahn let out a deep breath. "We found it, downstream of where it jumped."

"Why the hell did it do that? Why jump out?"

"It was out of its mind on vacation drugs. Cameras show the party started in orbit with a few friends, continued down the JFK elevator all the way to the ground."

"When do you send the body back to its people?"

"We don't." Kahn looked around, surprised. "No one wants to know a high-profile cephaloid of any kind has died on Earth. So they didn't. The video of the fall no longer exists in any system."

"But they can track the body—"

"—already fired off via an old-school rocket aimed at our sun. That leaves no evidence here. Nothing happened on Earth. Nothing happened to you."

Kahn shook hands with Sienna and Tavi and left.

The next morning a brand-new cab was parked on the roof.

"Easier than scrubbing it all down for DNA," Sienna said. "The old one's probably on a rocket as well, just like the body, being shot toward the sun as we speak."

He scrambled up some eggs for his ever-hungry roomie, and

some extra for the Oraji brothers next door. There were thirty other random clumps of real and found families living in welded-together scrap here. Several of them watched the sun creep over the rusted wreckage scattered from horizon to horizon as they ate breakfast. Tavi would head back into the drudgery of flying tourists around; Sienna would work at trying to pry something valuable out of the ruins.

Just as they finished eating, a second cab descended from the clouds. It kicked up some dust as it settled in on the ground.

"Hey, asshole," Sienna shouted. "If we all land on metal we don't kick dust into everyone's faces."

Grumbling assent rose into the morning air.

The doors slid open, and Tavi felt his stomach drop.

Another octopus-like alien stood on the ground looking up at them.

"I'm looking for the human named Tavi," the speaker box on the exoskeleton buzzed. "Is he here?"

"Don't say a thing," Sienna hissed. Sienna, who had all the smarts built up from a lifetime of eat or be eaten while scavenging in the wreckage.

"I am Tavi," Tavi said, stepping down toward the alien.

"You're an idiot," Sienna said. She walked off toward the shadows under a pile of scrap and disappeared.

The alien crouched in a spot of shade, trying to stay out of the sun, occasionally rubbing sunscreen over its photosensitive skin.

"I'm the cosponsor of the unit last seen in your vehicle when it came down to your planet for sightseeing."

Tavi felt his stomach fall out from under him. "Oh," he said numbly. He wasn't sure what a cosponsor was, or why the alien's language had been translated that way. He had the feeling this alien was a close friend, or maybe even family member, of the one he'd witnessed jump to its death.

"No one will tell me anything, your representatives have done nothing but flail around and throw bureaucratic ink my way," the alien tourist said.

"I'm really sorry for your loss," Tavi said.

"So, you are my last try before offencers get involved," the alien concluded.

"Offencers?"

The alien used one of its mechanized limbs to point up. A shadow passed over the land. Something vast skimmed over the clouds and blocked the sun. It hummed. And the entire land hummed back with it. Somehow, Tavi *knew* that whatever was up there could destroy a planet.

Tavi's wristband vibrated. Incoming call. Kahn.

The world was crashing into him. Tavi felt it all waver for a moment, and then he took a deep breath.

"All I wanted to do was the right thing," he muttered, and took the call.

"Very big, alien destroyers," David Kahn said, in a level, but clearly terrified, voice. "We at the Greater New York Bureau of Tourism *highly* recommend you do whatever the being or beings currently in contact with you are asking, while also, uh, acknowledging that we have no idea where the missing being they are referring to is. Please hold for the president—"

Tavi flicked the bracelet off.

"What do you want?" Tavi asked the alien.

"I want to know the truth," it said.

"I see you have an advanced exotic-worlds encounter suit. Would you like a real human beer with me?"

"If that helps," it said.

"You have such a beautiful planet. So unspoiled, paradisiacal. I was swimming with whales in your Pacific Ocean yesterday."

Tavi sat down and gave the alien a Red Stripe. It curled a tentacle around it, pulled it back toward its beak. They watched the trees curling around the La Guardia debris shiver in the wind, the fluffy clouds ease through the pale blue sky.

They deliberately sat with their backs to the section of sky filled with the destroyer.

"I've never been to the Pacific," Tavi admitted. "Just the Caribbean, where my people come from, and the Atlantic."

"I'm a connoisseur of good oceans," the alien said. "These are just some of the best."

"We used to fish on them. My grandfather owned a boat."

"Oh, does he still do that? I love fishing."

"He started chartering it out," Tavi said. "The Galactics bought out the restaurants, so he couldn't sell to his best markets anymore. They own anything near the best spots, and all around the Eastern Seaboard now."

"I'm sorry to hear that."

"About your friend," Tavi took a big swig. "They jumped out of my cab. When it was in the air. They were in an altered state."

There was a long silence.

Tavi waited for the world to end, but it didn't. So he continued, and the alien listened as he told his story.

"And, there were no security systems to stop them from jumping?" it asked when he finished.

"There were not, on that cab."

"Wow," it said. "How authentically human. How dangerous. I'll have to audit your account against the confessions of your bureau, but I have to say, I am very relieved. I suspected foul play, and it turns out it was just an utterly authentic primitive-world experience. No door security."

Overhead, long fiery contrails burned through the sky.

"What is that?" Tavi asked, nervous.

"Independent verification," the alien said. It stood up and jumped down to its cab. It looked closely at the rear doors. "I could really just jump out of these, couldn't I?"

It opened the door, and Tavi, who had hopped over the roof and down the stairs, caught a glimpse of a pale-faced driver inside. *Sorry, friend,* he thought.

There were more shadows descending down out of space. Larger and larger vessels moving through the atmosphere far above.

"What is happening?" Tavi asked, mouth dry.

"News of your world has spread," it said. "You are no longer an undiscovered little secret. Finding out that we can die just in a cab ride—where else can you get that danger?"

The cab lifted off and flew away.

Sienna came back out of the shadows. "They're over every city now. They're offering ludicrous money for real estate."

Tavi looked at the skies. "Did you think it would ever stop?"

She put a hand on his shoulder. "Beats them blowing us up, right? They do that, sometimes, to other worlds that fight it."

He shook his head. "There's not going to be anything left for us down here, is there?"

"Oh, they'll never want this." She spread her arms and pointed at the miles of space-elevator junk.

"And I still have a new cab," he said.

She put a hand on his shoulder. "Maybe these new Galactics coming down over the cities tip better."

And for the first time in days Tavi laughed. "That's always the hope, isn't it?"

CHARLIE JANE ANDERS

The Bookstore at the End of America

FROM *A People's Future of the United States*

A BOOKSHOP ON a hill. Two front doors, two walkways lined with blank slates and grass, two identical signs welcoming customers to the First and Last Page, and a great blue building in the middle, shaped like an old-fashioned barn with a slanted tiled roof and generous rain gutters. Nobody knew how many books were inside that building, not even Molly, the owner. But if you couldn't find it there, they probably hadn't written it down yet.

The two walkways led to two identical front doors, with straw welcome mats, blue plank floors, and the scent of lilacs and old bindings—but then you'd see a completely different store, depending which side you entered. With two cash registers, for two separate kinds of money.

If you entered from the California side, you'd see a wall-hanging: women of all ages, shapes, and origins, holding hands and dancing. You'd notice the display of the latest books from a variety of small presses that clung to life in Colorado Springs and Santa Fe, from literature and poetry to cultural studies. The shelves closest to the door on the California side included a decent amount of women's and queer studies but also a strong selection of classic literature, going back to Virginia Woolf and Zora Neale Hurston. Plus some brand-new paperbacks.

If you came in through the American front door, the basic layout would be pretty similar, except for the big painting of the nearby Rocky Mountains. But you might notice more books on religion and some history books with a somewhat more conservative approach. The literary books skewed a bit more toward Faulkner, Thoreau, and Hemingway, not to mention Ayn Rand, and you might find more books of essays about self-reliance and strong families, along with another selection of low-cost paperbacks: thrillers and war novels, including brand-new releases from the big printing plant in Gatlinburg. Romance novels, too.

Go through either front door and keep walking, and you'd find yourself in a maze of shelves, with a plethora of nooks and a bevy of side rooms. Here a cavern of science fiction and fantasy, there a deep alcove of theater books—and a huge annex of history and sociology, including a whole wall devoted to explaining the origins of the Great Sundering. Of course, some people did make it all the way from one front door to the other, past the overfed-snake shape of the hallways and the giant central reading room, with a plain red carpet and two beat-down couches in it. But the design of the store encouraged you to stay inside your own reality.

The exact border between America and California, which elsewhere featured watchtowers and roadblocks, YOU ARE NOW LEAVING/YOU ARE NOW ENTERING signs, and terrible overpriced souvenir stands, was denoted in the First and Last Page by a tall bookcase of self-help titles about coping with divorce.

People came from hundreds of miles in either direction, via hydroelectric cars, solarcycles, mecha-horses, and tour buses, to get some book they couldn't live without. You could get electronic books via the Share, of course, but they might be plagued with crowdsourced editing, user-targeted content, random annotations, and sometimes just plain garbage. You might be reading *The Federalist Papers* on your Gidget and come across a paragraph about rights vs. duties that wasn't there before—or, for that matter, a few pages relating to hair cream, because you'd been searching on "hair cream" yesterday. Not to mention, the same book might read completely differently in California than in America. You could only rely on ink and paper (or, for newer books, Peip0r) for consistency, not to mention the whole sensory experience of smelling and touching volumes, turning their pages, bowing their spines.

Everybody needs books, Molly figured. No matter where they live, how they love, what they believe, whom they want to kill. We all want books. The moment you start thinking of books as some exclusive club, or the loving of books as a high distinction, then you're a bad bookseller.

Books are the best way to discover what people thought before you were born. And an author is just someone who tried their utmost to make sense of their own mess, and maybe their failure contains a few seeds to help you with yours.

Sometimes people asked Molly why she didn't simplify it down to one entrance. Force the people from America to talk to the Californians, and vice versa—maybe expose one side or the other to some books that might challenge their worldview just a little. And Molly always replied that she had a business to run, and if she managed to keep everyone reading, then that was enough. At the very least, Molly's arrangement kept this the most peaceful outpost on the border, without people gathering on one side to scream at the people on the other.

Some of those screaming people were old enough to have grown up in the United States of America, but they acted as though these two lands had always been enemies.

Whichever entrance of the bookstore you went through, the first thing you'd notice was probably Phoebe. Rake-thin, coltish, rambunctious, right on the edge of becoming, she ran light enough on her bare feet to avoid ever rattling a single bookcase or dislodging a single volume. You heard Phoebe's laughter before her footsteps. Molly's daughter wore denim overalls and cheap linen blouses most days, or sometimes a floor-length skirt or lacy-hemmed dress, plus plastic bangles and necklaces. She hadn't gotten her ears pierced yet.

People from both sides of the line loved Phoebe, who was a joyful shriek that you only heard from a long way away, a breath of gladness running through the flower beds.

Molly used to pester Phoebe about getting outdoors to breathe some fresh air—because that seemed like something moms were supposed to say, and Molly was paranoid about being a Bad Mother, since she was basically married to a bookstore, albeit one containing a large section of parenting books. But Molly was secretly glad when Phoebe disobeyed her and stayed inside, endlessly reading. Molly hoped Phoebe would always stay shy, that mother and daughter would hunker inside the First and Last Page, side-eyeing the world through thin linen curtains when they weren't reading together.

Then Phoebe had turned fourteen, and suddenly she was out all the time, and Molly didn't see her for hours. Around that time,

Phoebe had unexpectedly grown pretty and lanky, her neck long enough to let her auburn ponytail swing as she ran around with the other kids who lived in the tangle of tree-lined streets on the America side of the line, plus a few kids who snuck across from California. Nobody seriously patrolled this part of the border, and there was one craggy rock pile, like an echo of the looming Rocky Mountains, that you could just scramble over and cross from one country to the other, if you knew the right path.

Phoebe and her gang of kids, ranging from twelve to fifteen, would go trampling the tall grass near the border on a "treasure hunt" or setting up an "ambush fort" in the rocks. Phoebe occasionally caught sight of Molly and turned to wave, before running up the dusty hillside toward Zadie and Mark, who had snuck over from California with canvas backpacks full of random games and junk. Sometimes Phoebe led an entire brigade of kids into the store, pouring cups of water or Molly's homebrewed ginger beer for everyone, and they would all pause and say, "Hello, Ms. Carlton," before running outside again.

Mostly, the kids were just a raucous chorus, as they chased each other with pea guns. There were times when they stayed in the most overgrown area of trees and bracken until way after sundown, until Molly was about to message the other local parents via her Gidget, and then she'd glimpse a few specks of light emerging from the claws and twisted limbs. Molly always asked Phoebe what they did in that tiny stand of vegetation, which barely qualified as "the woods," and Phoebe always said: Nothing. They just hung out. But Molly imagined those kids under the moonlight, blotted by heavy leaves, and they could be doing anything: drinking, taking drugs, playing kiss-and-tell games.

Even if Molly had wanted to keep tabs on her daughter, she couldn't leave the bookstore unattended. The binational design of the store required at least two people working at all times, one per register, and most of the people Molly hired only lasted a month or two and then had to run home because their families were worried about all the latest hints of another war on the horizon. Every day, another batch of propaganda bubbled up on Molly's Gidget, from both sides, claiming that one country was a crushing theocracy or the other was a godless meat grinder. And meanwhile, you heard rumblings about both countries searching for the last precious dregs of water—sometimes actual rumblings, as California sent swarms of robots deep underground. Everybody was holding their breath.

Molly was working the front counter on the California side, trying as usual not to show any reaction to the people with weird tattoos or with glowing silver threads flowing into their skulls. Everyone knew how eager Californians were to hack their own bodies and brains, from programmable birth control to brain implants that connected them to the Anoth Complex. Molly smiled, made small talk, recommended books based on her uncanny memory for what everybody had been buying—in short, she treated everyone like a customer, even the folks who noticed Molly's crucifix and clicked their tongues, because obviously she'd been brainwashed into her faith.

A regular customer named Sander came in, looking for a rare book from the last days of the United States about sustainable farming and animal consciousness, by a woman named Hope Dorrance. For some reason, nobody had ever uploaded this book of essays to the Share. Molly looked in the fancy computer and saw that they had one copy, but when Molly led Sander back to the shelf where it was supposed to be, the book was missing.

Sander stared at the space where *Souls on the Land* ought to be, and their pale, round face was full of lines. They had a single tattoo of a butterfly clad in gleaming armor, and the wires rained from the shaved back of their skull. They were some kind of engineer for the Anoth Complex.

"Huh," Molly said. "So this is where it ought to be. But I better check if maybe we sold it over on the, uh, other side and somehow didn't log the sale." Sander nodded, and followed Molly until they arrived in America. There, Molly squeezed past Mitch, who was working the register, and dug through a dozen scraps of paper until she found one. "Oh. Yeah. Well, darn."

They had sold their only copy of *Souls on the Land* to one of their most faithful customers on the America side: a gray-haired woman named Teri Wallace, who went to Molly's church. And Teri was in the store right now, searching for a cookbook. Mitch had just seen her go past. Unfortunately, Teri hated Californians even more than most Americans did. And Sander was the sort of Californian that Teri especially did not appreciate.

"So it looks like we sold it a while back, and we didn't update our inventory, which, uh, does happen," Molly said.

"In essence, this was false advertising." Sander drew upward, with the usual Californian sense of affront the moment anything wasn't perfectly efficient. "You told me that the book was available, when in fact you should have known it wasn't."

Molly had already decided not to tell Sander who had bought the Hope Dorrance, but Teri came back clutching a book of killer salads just as Sander was in mid-rant about the ethics of retail communication. Sander happened to mention *Souls on the Land,* and Teri's ears pricked up.

"Oh, I just bought that book," Teri said.

Sander spun around, smiling, and said, "Oh. Pleased to meet you. I'm afraid that book you bought is one that had been promised to me. I don't suppose we could work out some kind of arrangement? Perhaps some system of needs-based allocation, because my need for this book is extremely great." Sander was already falling into the hyperrational, insistent language of a Californian faced with a problem.

"Sorry," Teri said. "I bought it. I own it now. It's mine."

"But," Sander said, "there are many ways we could . . . I mean, you could loan it to me, and I could digitize it and return it to you in good condition."

"I don't want it in good condition. I want it in the condition it's in now."

"But—"

Molly could see this conversation was about three exchanges away from full-blown unpleasantries. Teri was going to insult Sander, either directly or by getting their pronoun wrong. Sander was going to call Teri stupid, either by implication or outright. Molly could see an easy solution: she could give Teri a bribe—a free book or blanket discount—in exchange for letting Sander borrow the Hope Dorrance so they could digitize it using special page-turning robots. But this wasn't going to be solved with reason. Not right now, anyway, with the two of them snarling at each other.

So Molly put on her biggest smile and said, "Sander. I just remembered, I had something extra special set aside for you, back in the psychology/philosophy annex. I've been meaning to give it to you, and it slipped my mind until now. Come on, I'll show you."

She tugged gently at Sander's arm and hustled them back into the warren of bookshelves. Sander kept grumbling about Teri's irrational selfishness, until they had left America.

Molly had no idea what the special book she'd been saving for Sander actually was—but she figured by the time they got through the Straits of Romance and all the switchbacks of biography, she'd think of something.

Phoebe was having a love triangle. Molly became aware of this in stages, by noticing how all the other kids were together and by overhearing snippets of conversation (despite her best efforts not to eavesdrop).

Jonathan Brinkfort, the son of the minister at Molly's church, had started following Phoebe around with a hangdog expression, like he'd lost one of those kiss-and-dare games and it had left him with gambling debts. Jon was a tall, quiet boy with a handsome square face, who mediated every tiny dispute among the neighborhood kids with a slow gravitas, but Molly had never before seen him lost for words. She had been hand-selling airship adventure books to Jon since he was little.

And then there was Zadie Kagwa, whose dad was a second-generation immigrant from Uganda with a taste for very old science fiction. Zadie had a fresh tattoo on one shoulder, of a dandelion with seedlings fanning out into the wind, and one string of fiber-optic pearls coming out of her locs. Zadie's own taste in books roamed from science and math, to radical politics, to girls-at-horse-camp novels. Zadie whispered to Phoebe and brought tiny presents from California, like these weird candies with chili peppers in them.

Molly could just imagine the conversations she'd hear in church if her daughter got into an unnatural relationship with a girl—from *California* no less—instead of dating a nice American boy who happened to be Canon Brinkfort's son.

But Phoebe didn't seem to be inclined to choose one or the other. She accepted Jon's stammered compliments with the same shy smile as Zadie's gifts.

Molly took Phoebe on a day trip into California, where they got their passports stamped with a one-day entry permit, and they climbed into Molly's old three-wheel Dancer. They drove past wind farms and military installations, past signs for the latest Anoth Cloud-Brain schemes, until they stopped at a place that sold milkshakes so thick, you lost the skin on the sides of your mouth trying to unclog the straw.

Phoebe was in silent mode, hugging herself and cocooning inside her big polyfiber jacket when she wasn't slurping her milkshake. Molly tried to make conversation, talking about who had been buying what sort of books lately and what you could figure out about international relations from Sharon Wong's sudden interest in bird-watching. Phoebe just shrugged, like maybe Molly should just read the news instead. As if Molly hadn't tried making sense of the news already.

Then Phoebe started telling Molly about some fantasy novel. Seven princesses have powers of growth and decay, but some of the princesses can only use their growth powers if the other princesses are using their decay powers. And whoever grows a hedge tall enough to keep out the army of gnome-trolls will become the heir to the Blue Throne, but the princesses don't even realize at first that their powers are all different, like they grow different kinds of things. And there are a bunch of princes and court ladies who are all in love with different princesses, but nobody can be with the person they want to be with.

This novel sounded more and more complicated, and Molly didn't remember ever seeing it in her store, until she realized: Phoebe wasn't describing a book she had read. This was a book that Phoebe was writing, somewhere, on one of the old computers that Molly had left in some storage space. Molly hadn't even known Phoebe was a writer.

"How does it end?" Molly said.

"I don't know." Phoebe poked at the last soup of her milkshake. "I guess they have to use their powers together to build the hedge they're supposed to build, instead of competing. But the hard part is gonna be all the princesses ending up with the right person. And, uh, making sure nobody feels left out, or like they couldn't find their place in this kingdom."

Molly nodded, and then tried to think of how to respond to what she was pretty sure her daughter was actually talking about. "Well, you know that nobody has to ever hurry to find out who they're supposed to love, or where they're going to fit in. Those things sometimes take time, and it's okay not to know the answers right away. You know?"

"Yeah, I guess." Phoebe pushed her empty glass away and looked out the window. Molly waited for her to say something else but eventually realized the conversation had ended. Teenagers.

Molly had opened the First and Last Page when Phoebe was still a baby, back when the border had felt more porous. Both governments were trying to create a Special Trade Zone, and you could get a special transnational business license. Everyone had seemed overjoyed to have a bookstore within driving distance, and Molly had lost count of how many people thanked her just for being there. A lot of her used books had come from estate sales, but there had been a surprising flood of donations, too.

Molly had wanted Phoebe to be within easy reach of California if America ever started seriously following through on its threats to enforce all of its broadly written laws against immorality. But more than that, Phoebe deserved to be surrounded by all the stories, and every type of person, and all of the ways of looking at life. Plus, it had seemed like a shrewd business move to be in two countries at once, a way to double the store's potential market.

For a while, the border had also played host to a bar, a burger joint, and a clothing store, and Molly had barely noticed when those places had closed one by one. The First and Last Page was different, she'd figured, because nobody ever gets drunk on books and starts a brawl.

Matthew limped into the American entrance during a lull in business, and Molly took in his torn pants leg, dirty hands, and the dried-out salt trails along his brown face. She had seen plenty others, in similar condition, and didn't even blink. She didn't need to see the brand on Matthew's neck, which looked like a pair of broken wings and declared him to be a bonded peon and the responsibility of the Greater Appalachian Penal Authority and the Glad Corporation. She just nodded and helped him inside the store before anyone else noticed or started asking too many questions.

"I'm looking for a self-help book," Matthew said, which was what a lot of them said. Someone, somewhere, had told them this was a code phrase that would let Molly know what they needed. In fact, there was no code phrase.

The border between America and California was unguarded in thousands of other places besides Molly's store, including that big rocky hill that Zadie and the other California kids climbed over when they came to play with the American kids. There was just too much empty space to waste time patrolling, much less putting up fences or sensors. You couldn't eat lunch in California without twenty computers checking your identity, anyway. But Matthew and the others chose Molly's store because books meant civilization, or maybe the store's name seemed to promise a kind of safe passage: the first page leading gracefully to the last.

Molly did what she always did with these refugees. She helped Matthew find the quickest route from romance to philosophy to history, and then on to California. She gave him some clean clothes out of a donation box, which she always told people was going to a shelter somewhere, and what information she had about resources and contacts. She let him clean up as much as he could, in the restroom.

Matthew was still limping as he made his way through the store in his brand-new corduroys and baggy argyle sweater. Molly offered to have a look at his leg, but he shook his head. "Old injury." She dug in the first-aid kit and gave him a bottle of painkillers. Matthew kept looking around in all directions, as if there could be hidden cameras (there weren't), and he took a jerky step backward when Molly told him to hold on a moment, when he was already in California.

"What? Is something wrong? What's wrong?"

"Nothing. Nothing's wrong. Just thinking." Molly always gave refugees a free book, something to keep them company on whatever journey they had ahead. She didn't want to just choose at random, so she gazed at Matthew for a moment in the dim amber light from the wall sconces in the history section. "What sort of books do you like? Besides self-help, I mean."

"I don't have any money, I'm sorry," Matthew said, but Molly waved it off.

"You don't need any. I just wanted to give you something to take with you."

Phoebe came up just then and saw at a glance what was going on. "Hey, Mom. Hi, I'm Phoebe."

"This is Matthew," Molly said. "I wanted to give him a book to take with him."

"They didn't exactly let us have books," Matthew said. "There was a small library, but library use was a privilege, and you needed more than 'good behavior.' For that kind of privilege, you would need to . . ." He glanced at Phoebe, because whatever he'd been about to say wasn't suitable for a child's ears. "They did let us read the Bible, and I practically memorized some parts of it."

Molly and Phoebe looked at each other, while Matthew fidgeted, and then Phoebe said, "Father Brown mysteries."

"Are you sure?" Molly said.

Phoebe nodded. She ran, fast as a deer, and came back with a tiny paperback of G. K. Chesterton, which would fit in the pockets of the donated corduroys. "I used to love this book," she told Matthew. "It's about God, and religion, but it's really just a great bunch of detective stories, where the key always turns out to be making sense of people."

Matthew kept thanking Molly and Phoebe in a kind of guttural undertone, like a compulsive cough, until they waved it off. When they got to the California storefront, they kept Matthew out of sight until they were sure the coast was clear, then they hustled him out and showed him the clearest path that followed the main road but stayed under cover. He waved once as he sprinted across the blunt strip of gravel parking lot, but other than that, he didn't look back.

The president of California wished the president of America a "good spring solstice" instead of "happy Easter," and the president of America called a news conference to discuss this unforgivable insult. America's secretary of morality, Wallace Dawson, called California's gay attorney general an offensive term. California moved some troops up to the border and performed some "routine exercises," so close that Molly could hear the cackle of guns shooting blanks all night. (She hoped they were blanks.) America sent some fighter craft and UAVs along the border, sundering the air. California's swarms of water-divining robots had managed to tap the huge deposits located deep inside the rocky mantle, but both America and California claimed that this water was located under their respective territories.

Molly's Gidget kept flaring up with "news" that was laced with propaganda, as if the people in charge on both sides were trying to get everyone fired up. The American media kept running stories about a pregnant woman in New Sacramento who lost her baby because her supposedly deactivated birth-control implant had a buggy firmware update, plus graphic stories about urban gang violence, drugs, prostitution, and so on. California's media outlets, meanwhile, worked overtime to remind people about the teenage rape victims in America who were locked up and straitjacketed, to make sure they gave birth, and the peaceful protesters who were gassed and beaten by police.

Almost every day lately, Americans came in looking for a couple of books that Molly didn't have. Molly had decided to go ahead and stock *Why We Stand,* a book-length manifesto about individualism and Christian values, which stopped just short of accusing Californians of bestiality and cannibalism. But *Why We Stand* was unavailable, because they'd gone back for another print run. Meanwhile, though, Molly outright refused to sell *Our People,* a book that included offensive caricatures of the Black and Brown people who mostly clustered in the dense cities out west, like New Sacramento, plus "scientific" theories about their relative intelligence.

People kept coming in and asking for *Our People,* and at this point Molly was pretty sure they knew she didn't have it and they were just trying to make a point.

"It's just, some folks feel as though you think you're better than the rest of us," said Norma Verlaine, whose blond, loudmouthed daughter, Samantha, was part of Phoebe's friend group. "The way you try to play both sides against the middle, perching here in your fancy chair, deciding what's fit to read and what's not fit to read. You're literally sitting in judgment over us."

"I'm not judging anyone," Molly said. "Norma, I live here, too. I go to Holy Fire every Sunday, same as you. I'm not judging."

"You say that. But then you refuse to sell *Our People.*"

"Yes, because that book is racist."

Norma turned to Reggie Watts, who had two kids in Phoebe's little gang: Tobias and Suz. "Did you hear that, Reggie? She called me a racist."

"I didn't call you anything. I was talking about a book."

"Can't separate books from people," said Reggie, who worked at the big power plant thirty miles east. He furrowed his huge brow and stooped a little as he spoke. "And you can't separate people from the places they come from."

"Time may come, you have to choose a country once and for all," Norma said. Then she and Reggie walked out while the glow of righteousness still clung.

Molly felt something chewing all the way through her. Like the cartoon "bookworm" chewing through a book, from when Molly was a child. There was a worm drilling a neat round hole in Molly, rendering some portion of her illegible.

Molly was just going through some sales slips—because ever since that dustup with Sander and Teri, she was paranoid about American sales not getting recorded in the computer—when the earthquake began. A few books fell on the floor as the ground shuddered, but most of the books were packed too tight to dislodge right away. The grinding, screeching sound from the vibrations underground made Molly's ears throb. When she could get her balance back, she looked at her Gidget, and at first she saw no information. Then there was a news alert: California had laid claim to the water deposits, deep underground, and was proceeding to extract them as quickly as possible. America was calling this an act of war.

Phoebe was out with her friends as usual. Molly sent a message on her Gidget and then went outside to yell Phoebe's name into the wind. The crushing sound underground kept going, but either Molly had gotten used to it or it was moving away from here.

"Phoebe?"

Molly walked the two-lane roads, glancing every couple of minutes at her Gidget to see if Phoebe had replied yet. She told herself that she wouldn't freak out if she could find her daughter before the sun went down, and then the sun did go down and she had to invent a new deadline for panic.

Something huge and powerful opened its mouth and roared nearby, and Molly swayed on her feet. The hot breath of a large carnivore blew against her face while her ears filled with sound. She realized after a moment that three Stalker-class aircraft had flown very low overhead, in stealth mode, so you could hear and feel—but not see—them.

"Phoebe?" Molly called out, as she reached the end of the long main street, with the one grocery store and the diner. "Phoebe, are you out here?" The street led to a big field of corn on one side and to the diversion road leading to the freeway on the other. The corn rustled from the after-shakes of the flyover. Out on the road, Molly heard wheels tearing at loose dirt and tiny rocks and saw the slash of headlights in motion.

"Mom!" Phoebe came running down the hill from the tiny forest area, followed by Jon Brinkfort, Zadie Kagwa, and a few other kids. "Thank god you're okay."

Molly started to say that Phoebe should get everyone inside the bookstore, because the reading room was the closest thing to a bomb shelter for miles.

But a new round of flashes and earsplitting noises erupted, and then Molly looked past the edge of town and saw a phalanx of shadows, three times as tall as the tallest building, moving forward.

Molly had never seen a mecha before, but she recognized these metal giants, with the bulky actuators on their legs and rocket launchers on their arms. They looked like a crude caricature of bodybuilders, pumped up inside their titanium-alloy casings. The two viewports on their heads, along with the slash of red paint, gave them the appearance of scowling down at all the people underfoot. Covered with armaments all over their absurdly huge bodies, they were heading into town on their way to the border.

"Everybody into the bookstore!" Phoebe yelled. Zadie Kagwa was messaging her father on some fancy tablet, and other kids were trying to contact their parents, too, but then everyone hustled inside the First and Last Page.

People came looking for their kids, or for a place to shelter from the fighting. Some people had been browsing in the store when the hostilities broke out, or had been driving nearby. Molly let everyone in, until the American mechas were actually engaging a squadron of California centurions, which were almost identical to the other metal giants, except that their onboard systems were connected to the Anoth Complex. Both sides fired their rocket launchers, releasing bright-orange trails that turned everything the same shade of amber. Molly watched as an American mecha lunged forward with its huge metal fist and connected with the side of a centurion, sending shards of metal spraying out like the dandelion seeds on Zadie's tattoo.

Then Molly got inside and sealed up the reading room, with a satisfying clunk. "I paid my contractor extra," she told all the people who crouched inside. "These walls are like a bank vault. This is the safest place for you all to be." There was a toilet just outside the solid metal door and down the hall, with a somewhat higher risk of getting blown up while you peed.

Alongside Molly and Phoebe, there were a dozen people stuck

in the reading room. There were Zadie and her father, Jay; Norma Verlaine and her daughter, Samantha; Reggie Watts and his two kids; Jon Brinkfort; Sander, the engineer who'd come looking for *Souls on the Land;* Teri, the woman who actually owned *Souls on the Land;* Marcy, a twelve-year-old kid from California, and Marcy's mother, Petrice.

They all sat in this two-meter-by-three-meter room, with two couches that could hold five people between them, plus bookshelves from floor to ceiling. Every time someone started to relax, there was another quake, and the sounds grew louder and more ferocious. Nobody could get a signal on any of their devices or implants, either because of the reinforced walls or because someone was actively jamming communications. The room jerked back and forth, and the books quivered but did not fall out of their nests.

Molly looked over at Jay Kagwa, sitting with his arm around his daughter, and had a sudden flash of remembering a time, several years ago, when Phoebe had campaigned for Molly to go out on a date with Jay. Phoebe and Zadie were already friends, though neither of them was interested in romance yet, and Phoebe had decided that the stout, well-built architect would be a good match for her mother. Partly based on the wry smiles the two of them always exchanged when they compared notes about being single parents of rambunctious daughters. Plus both Molly and Phoebe were American citizens, and it wouldn't hurt to have dual citizenship. But Molly never had time for romance. And now, of course, Zadie was still giving sidelong glances to Phoebe, who had never chosen between Zadie and Jon, and probably never would.

Jay had finished hugging his daughter and also yelling at her for getting herself stuck in the middle of all this, and all the other parents including Molly had had a good scowl at their own kids, as well. "I wish we were safe at home," Jay Kagwa told his daughter in a whisper, "instead of being trapped here with these people."

"What exactly do you mean by 'these people'?" Norma Verlaine demanded from the other end of the room.

Another tremor, more raucous noise.

"Leave it, Norma," said Reggie. "I'm sure he didn't mean anything by it."

"No, I want to know," Norma said. "What makes us 'these people' when we're just trying to live our lives and raise our kids? And meanwhile, your country decided that everything from abortion to unnatural sexual relationships, to cutting open people's brains and shoving in a bunch of nanotech garbage, was A-OK. So I think the real question is, Why do I have to put up with people like you?"

"I've seen firsthand what your country does to people like me," Jay Kagwa said in a quiet voice.

"As if Californians aren't stealing children from America, at a rapidly increasing rate, to turn into sex slaves or prostitutes. I have to keep one eye on my Samantha here all the time."

"*Mom,*" Samantha said, and that one syllable meant everything from *Please stop embarrassing me in front of my friends* to *You can't protect me forever.*

"We're not stealing children," said Sander. "That was a ridiculous made-up story."

"You steal everything. You're stealing our water right now," said Teri. "You don't believe that anything is sacred, so it's all up for grabs as far as you're concerned."

"We're not the ones who put half a million people into labor camps," said Petrice, a quiet green-haired older woman who mostly bought books about gardening and Italian history.

"Oh no, not at all, California just turns millions of people into cybernetic slaves of the Anoth Complex," said Reggie. "That's much more humane."

"Hey, everybody calm down," Molly said.

"Says the woman who tries to serve two masters," Norma said, rounding on Molly and poking a finger at her.

The other six adults in the room kept shouting at each other until the tiny reading room seemed almost as loud as the battle outside. The room shook, the children huddled together, and the adults just raised their voices to be heard over the nearly constant percussion. Everybody knew the dispute was purely about water rights, but months of terrifying stories had trained them to think of it instead as a righteous war over sacred principles. Our children, our freedom. Everyone shrieked at each other, and Molly fell into the corner near a stack of theology, covering her ears and looking across the room at Phoebe, who was crouched with Jon and Zadie. Phoebe's nostrils flared and she stiffened as if she were about to run a long sprint, but all of her attention was focused on comforting her two friends. Molly felt flushed with a sharper version of her old fear that she'd been a Bad Mother.

Then Phoebe stood up and yelled, "EVERYBODY STOP!"

Everybody stopped yelling. Some shining miracle. They all turned to look at Phoebe, who was holding hands with both Jon and Zadie. Even with the racket outside, this room suddenly felt eerily, almost ceremonially, quiet.

"You should be ashamed," Phoebe said. "We're all scared and tired and hungry, and we're probably stuck here all night, and you're all acting like babies. This is not a place for yelling. It's a bookstore. It's a place for quiet browsing and reading, and if you can't be quiet, you're going to have to leave. I don't care what you think you know about each other. You can darn well be polite, because . . . because . . ." Phoebe turned to Zadie and Jon, and then gazed at her mom. "Because we're about to start the first meeting of our book club."

Book club? Everybody looked at each other in confusion, like they'd skipped a track.

Molly stood up and clapped her hands. "That's right. Book-club meeting in ten minutes. Attendance is mandatory."

The noise from outside wasn't just louder than ever but more bifurcated. One channel of noise came from directly underneath their feet, as if some desperate struggle for control over the water reserves was happening deep under the Earth's crust, between teams of robots or tunneling war machines, and the very notion of solid ground seemed obsolete. And then over their heads, a struggle between aircraft, or metal titans, or perhaps a sky full of whirring autonomous craft, slinging fire back and forth until the sky turned red. Trapped inside this room, with no information other than words on brittle spines, everybody found themselves inventing horrors out of every stray noise.

Molly and Phoebe huddled in the corner, trying to figure out a book that everyone in the room would be familiar enough with but that they could have a real conversation about. Molly had actually hosted a few book clubs at the store over the years, and at least a few of the people now sheltering in the reading room had attended, but she couldn't remember what any of those clubs had read. Molly kept pushing for this one literary coming-of-age book that had made a splash around the time of the Sundering, or maybe some good old Jane Austen, but Phoebe vetoed both of those ideas.

"We need to distract them"—Phoebe jerked her thumb at the mass of people in the reading room behind them—"not bore them to death."

In the end, the first and maybe only book selection of the Great International Book Club had to be *Million in One,* a fantasy adventure about a teenage boy named Norman who rescues a million souls that an evil wizard has trapped in a globe and accidentally absorbs them into his own body. So Norman has a million souls in one body, and they give him magical powers but he can also feel all of their unfinished business, their longing to be free. And Norman has to fight the wizard, who wants all those souls back, plus Norman's. This book was supposed to be for teenagers, but Molly knew for a fact that every single adult had read it, as well, on both sides of the border.

"Well, of course the premise suffers from huge inconsistencies," Sander complained. "It's established early on that souls can be stored and transferred, and yet Norman can't simply unload his extra souls into the nearest vessel."

"They explained that in book two." Zadie only rolled her eyes a little. "The souls are locked inside Norman. Plus the wizard would get them if he put them anywhere else."

"What I don't get is why his so-called teacher, Maxine, doesn't just tell him the whole story about the Pendragon Exchange right away," Reggie said.

"Um, excuse me. No spoilers," Jon muttered. "Not everybody has read book five already."

"Can we talk about the themes of the book instead of nitpicking?" Teri crossed her arms. "Like, the whole notion that Norman can contain all these multitudes but still just be Norman is fascinating to me."

"It's a kind of Cartesian dualism on speed," Jay Kagwa offered.

"Well, sort of. I mean, if you read Descartes, he says—"

"The real point is that the wizard wants to control all those souls, but—"

"Can we talk about the singing ax? What even was that?"

They argued peacefully until around three in the morning, when everyone finally wore themselves out. The sky and the ground still rumbled occasionally, but either everyone had gotten used to it or the most violent shatterings were over. Molly looked around at the dozen or so people slowly falling asleep, leaning on each other, all around the room, and felt a desperate protectiveness. Not just for the people, because of course she didn't want any harm to come to any of them, or even for this building that she'd given the better part of her adult life to sustaining, but for something more abstract and confusing. What were the chances that the First and Last Page could continue to exist much longer, especially with one foot in either country? How would they even know if tonight was just another skirmish or the beginning of a proper war, something that could carry on for months and reduce both countries to fine ash?

Phoebe left Jon and Zadie behind and came over to sit with her mother, with her mouth still twisted upward in satisfaction. Phoebe was clutching a book in one hand, and Molly didn't recognize the gold-embossed cover at first, but then she saw the spine. This was a small hardcover of fairy tales, illustrated with watercolors, that Molly had given to her daughter for her twelfth birthday, and she'd never seen it again. She'd assumed Phoebe had glanced at it for an hour and tossed it somewhere. Phoebe leaned against her mother, half-reading and half-gazing at the pictures, the blue streaks of sky and dark swipes of castles and mountains, until she fell asleep on Molly's shoulder. Phoebe looked younger in her sleep, and Molly looked down at her until she, too, dozed off, and the entire bookstore was at rest. Every once in a while, the roaring and convulsions of the battle woke Molly, but then at last they subsided, and all Molly heard was the slow, sustained breathing of people inside a cocoon of books.

NIBEDITA SEN

Ten Excerpts from an Annotated Bibliography on the Cannibal Women of Ratnabar Island

FROM *Nightmare*

1. CLIFTON, ASTRID. "The Day the Sea Ran Red." *Uncontacted Peoples of the World.* Routledge Press, 1965, pp. 71–98.

"There are few tales as tragic as that of the denizens of Ratnabar Island. When a British expedition made landfall on its shores in 1891, they did so armed to the teeth, braced for the same hostile reception other indigenous peoples of the Andamans had given them. What they found, instead, was a primitive hunter-gatherer community composed almost entirely of women and children. [. . .] The savage cultural clash that followed would transmute the natives' offer of a welcoming meal into direst offense, triggering a massacre at the hands of the repulsed British . . ."

2. Feldwin, Hortensia. *Roots of Evil: A Headmistress' Account of What Would Come to Be Known as the Churchill Dinner.* Westminster Press, 1943.

"Three girl-children were saved from Ratnabar. One would perish on the sea voyage, while two were conducted to England as Her Majesty's wards. Of these, one would go on to be enrolled in Churchill Academy, where she was given a Christian name and the promise of a life far removed from the savagery of her homeland. [. . .] Regina proved herself an apt pupil, industrious, soaking up offered tutelage like a sponge does ink, if prone to intemperate moods and a tendency to attach herself with sudden fits of feverish fondness to one or more of the other girls [. . .] None of us could have foreseen what she and Emma Yates whispered into each other's ears behind closed doors as they planned their foul feast."

3. Schofield, Eleanor. "Eating the Other." *Word of Mouth.* State University of New York, 2004, pp. 56–89.

"It's not for no reason that women have, historically, been burdened with the duties of food preparation. Or that it is women, not men, who are called upon to limit their appetites, shrink themselves, rein in their ambitions. A hungry woman is dangerous. [. . .] Men are arbiters of discourse, women the dish to be consumed. And the Ratnabari, in the exercising of their transgressive appetites, quite literally turn the tables on their oppressors."

4. Morris, Victoria. "Memory, Mouth, Mother: Funerary Cannibalism Among the Ratnabari." *Journal of Ethnographic Theory,* vol. 2, no. 2, 1994, pp. 105–129. Jstor, doi: 10.2707/464631.

"We are all cannibals at birth, and our mother-tongue is the language of the mouth. When the Ratnabari eat of their dead, they embrace what Kristeva calls 'the abject'—the visceral, the polluted, the blood and bile and placenta and the unclean flesh we associate with the female body. Return to us, they say to their dead, be with us always. [. . .] Science has yet to explain how it is that they almost never bear sons, only daughters, but it is scarce to be wondered at that their society is matriarchal in nature, for they spurn the clean, rational world of the patriarchal symbolic, remaining locked in a close, almost incestuous relationship with the maternal semiotic instead."

5. Aspioti, Elli. "A Love That Devours: Emma Yates and Regina Gaur." *A History of Twentieth-Century Lesbians,* edited by Jenna Atkinson. Palgrave Macmillan, 2009, pp. 180–195.

"What is it about love that makes us take leave of our senses? What makes a girl of barely seventeen carve fillets of flesh from her ribs and, lacing her clothes back up over the bulk of soaked bandages, serve her own stewed flesh to a table of her classmates at her wealthy private school?"

6. Rainier, Richard. "A Rebuttal of Recent Rumours Heard Among the Populace." *The Times,* 24 Apr. 1904, p. 14.

"Every rag barely worth the paper it is printed on has pounced on the regrettable happenings at Churchill Academy, and as such salacious reporting is wont to do, this has had an impact on the minds of impressionable youth. [. . .] [A] rash of imitative new fads in the area of courtship, such as presenting a lover with a hair from one's head or a clipping of fingernail to consume, perhaps even a shaving of skin, or blood, sucked from a pricked finger [. . .] As to the rumours that the Ratnabari gain shapeshifting powers through the consumption of human flesh, or that they practice a form of virgin birth—I can say with certainty that these are pure exaggeration, and that their proponents are likely muddling real events with the mythological figure of the rakshasi, a female demon from the Orient."

7. Gaur, Shalini. "The Subaltern Will Speak, If You'll Shut Up and Listen." *Interviews in Intersectionality,* by Shaafat Shahbandari and Harold Singh, 2012.

"[. . .] the problem is that we have everyone and their maiden aunt dropping critique on Ratnabar, but we're not hearing from us, the Ratnabari diaspora ourselves. If I have to deal with one more white feminist quoting Kristeva at me . . . [. . .] No, the real problem is that our goals are fundamentally different. They want to wring significance from our lives, we just want to find a way to live. There's not a lot of us, but we exist. We're here. We don't always quite see eye to eye with each other's . . . ideology, but we're not going anywhere, and we have to figure out what we are to each other, how we can live side by side. So why aren't we getting published?"

8. Gaur, Roopkatha. *A Daughter's Confession: The Collected Letters of Roopkatha Gaur,* edited by Mary Anolik. Archon Books, 2010, pp. 197–216.

"Mother didn't know. What Emma was planning, what was in the food that night, any of it. I've kept this secret so many years, but now that she's long gone, and I am old, I feel I can tell it at last, at least to you, my darling, and if only so I can pass beyond this world free of its weight. [. . .] Why did Emma do it? Does it matter? Love, foolishness, a hunger to believe in magic and power, a twisted obsession with Mother's supposed exotic origins, what does it matter? She did it. The truth is, I'm grateful. Whatever her motives, that meal gave Mother what she needed to escape that place. And I wouldn't have been born without it, though that's another story altogether. You could say a little bit of Emma lives on in me, even after all this time."

9. Gaur, Shalini. "We Can Never Go Home." *Hungry Diasporas: Annual Humanities Colloquium,* May 2008, Princeton University, Princeton, NJ.

"We know Ratnabar's coordinates. Aerial reconnaissance has confirmed people still live on the island. But how do I set foot on its shores, with my English accent and my English clothes, and not have them flee from me in the terror that was taught to them in 1891? Where do we go, descendants of stolen ones, trapped between two islands and belonging on neither—too brown for English sensibilities, too alien now for the home of our great-grandmothers? How shall we live, with Ratnabar in our blood but English on our tongues?"

10. Gaur, Ashanti. "Dead and Delicious II: Eat What You Want, and If People Don't Like It, Eat Them Too." *Bitch Media,* 2 Nov. 2016, https://www.bitchmedia.org/article/eat-want-people-eat/2016. Accessed 8 Dec. 2017.

"My cousin Shalini is an optimist. She believes in keeping the peace, getting along, not rocking the boat. What do I believe in? I think—let's be real, ladies, who among us hasn't sometimes had a craving to eat the whole damn world? You know which of you I'm talking to. Yes you, out there. You've tried so hard to be good. To not be too greedy. You made yourself small and you hoped they'd like you better for it, but they didn't, of course, because they're the ones who're insatiable. Who'll take everything you have to give them and still hunger for more. It's time to stop making ourselves small. And above all, remember . . . there may be more of them, but we don't need them to make more of us."

[Submitted for Professor Blackwood's Sociology 402 class, by Ranita Gaur.]

JAYMEE GOH

The Freedom of the Shifting Sea

FROM *New Suns*

Superpredator

> E. aphroditois is a polychaete marine worm that grows up to three meters or ten feet long and swims using bristle-like appendages, called parapodia, along the length of its body. It has a reversible pharynx and long mandibles with which it catches prey.
> —*An Introduction to the Deeper Sea*

SALMAH MET MAYANG on a sunny day in an isolated lagoon. Astonishing, as tourists had devoured the beaches near her coastal town. Even more astonishing: Mayang's lower body. Salmah was repulsed by the waving legs at her sides, but drawn to the iridescence of the segments of her body, like a centipede's, glinting rainbows in the midday sun.

Mayang had shrunk back underground—underwater underground, Salmah marveled—but her face was still uncovered, her hair drifting like seaweed. Salmah should have run away; instead she pulled on her goggles and got on her knees to investigate the sharp little face, broad nose, lush lips, beguiling eyes. Salmah's hand hovered over Mayang's face, wondering if she dared touch it, but decided she didn't. Besides which, Mayang looked like she wanted to be left alone.

So Salmah left, and immediately went to the library to find out what the creature could be. Not a mermaid: mermaids were not half woman, half centipede like that. (Not even a centipede, but some sort of worm.) Not a spirit: she was too real. She went through a list of all the female monsters she knew and then some, but still came up with nothing.

She returned the very next day, to enjoy the quietness, and to find the stranger sitting on a rock, eating a fish. The stranger receded into the seabed a little when Salmah approached, but Salmah held out her hands as nonthreateningly as possible, with a gift: homemade kuih.

"Asalamualaikum," she said, wondering if the creature was Muslim. "My name is Salmah."

"Walaikumsalam," came the cautious reply. A pause. "Mayang."

With this firm introduction, Salmah made friends with the first nonhuman creature she had ever known. By the end of the dry season, Salmah had learned a great deal about Mayang, like Mayang's age (Mayang could remember a time before British imperialism), Mayang's favorite fish (stingray), Mayang's length (twenty meters), and Mayang's favorite hunting grounds (a beach off the coast of Thailand popularly considered haunted). They sometimes swam out into the ocean, Salmah with a precious snorkel and mask she'd saved up for, holding gently onto Mayang's shoulders as they investigated reefs far from shore. Salmah watched Mayang hunt: swift movements too fast to see, mandibles slicing creatures in half. Salmah found herself unable to turn away from the sight.

In turn, Salmah told Mayang about changes in the human world, and the latter listened with a patient disinterest, expression flickering at odd moments that Salmah thought completely boring. She confided in Mayang: troubles at home, college applications, job seeking, boyfriends. Mayang was not always good at listening: she hated humans generally, men specifically.

"I don't really see any problem," Mayang replied for what sounded like the hundredth time to Salmah's complaint about a recalcitrant boyfriend who refused to call. "If he doesn't want to be with you, then you're free."

"But that's not what I want. Have you ever liked anybody?"

The ensuing silence was punctuated by the sound of thunder in the distance. Mayang bobbed in the water, staring into the distance as the tide came in. Salmah began picking up her sarong to go when Mayang said, "I like *you.*"

Salmah almost slipped. She was about to respond when lightning crackled across the sky. Mayang reached out to shield her. Salmah hugged her in return, feeling the cold skin, the almost-human skin, slick-smooth.

"I've loved many," Mayang said into Salmah's ear. "Many many. I've lost them all, to men, to marriage, to murder. And I will lose you too, someday. You're too full of this world, of life on land, for the sea."

Salmah opened her eyes to find that Mayang had been bearing her closer to the shore, making sure she was in shallower waters. "Don't say that. I will always come back." Shyly, she kissed Mayang on the mouth, before running off, face hot in the cold wind.

The monsoon season beat down, flooding schoolyards and fields, blowing off roofs as it had done for generations. Salmah went out on the better days to look for Mayang, but with little luck. Mayang's last words echoed in her ears like a portent, an omen.

The lagoon lost a sandbar near its mouth, opening into a dense mangrove swamp. In low tide, the tree roots were visible, with curious curves: too petted, too cultivated. Salmah waded past mudskippers and fish, until she found Mayang's body, half-buried in the sand, shining in the dappling sunshine. Panicked, she ran along the trail of legs, screaming Mayang's name.

Mayang rolled over with a grumpy groan, and blinked sleepily at Salmah. She smiled. "Hello. How was work?"

Salmah clung to Mayang tightly, shaky with relief. She kissed Mayang's forehead, cheeks, and mouth. Mayang drew back, hissing, and Salmah saw the inside of Mayang's mouth: the mandibles in her cheeks uncurling a little, the tiny teeth that looked disturbingly normal, and a looseness of skin behind them. "I'm sorry! Was I too rough?"

"I just woke up." Mayang stroked Salmah's hair gently. "But I missed you, too."

Just like that, their friendship continued as before, but Salmah could not stop thinking of the inside of Mayang's mouth, her soft cool skin, her vestigial breasts. Mayang's eyes glittered with amusement when she caught Salmah staring, permitted the human woman's hands to linger on her waist, shoulders, even the frond-like legs on the sides of her wormbody. Their arms entwined as they swam together, Mayang swimming on her back to kiss Salmah's belly, knees, toes. Salmah would whine as they returned to Mayang's grotto about unfairness, because Salmah couldn't return the favor.

"I'm not like you," she groused, coming to rest under a mangrove tree.

"You are not," Mayang agreed, pointedly staring at Salmah's fine-haired legs. "Not with those useless things anyway."

"I can do things with these that you can't with yours."

Mayang tilted her head, raising an eyebrow.

Carefully, Salmah hooked her legs around Mayang's waist, drawing the wormwoman closer to her. Then she wrapped her arms under Mayang's arms, determined to make sure the latter couldn't slip away. She blushed, but grinned through it anyway.

Mayang brushed a tendril of hair from Salmah's face, kissed her temple.

"Have you ever kissed a woman?" Salmah asked.

"Many," Mayang replied.

"Who?" Salmah thought maybe she sounded too demanding.

"Have *you* ever kissed a woman?" Mayang asked, not deigning to answer that question.

Salmah nodded. Her school had been an all-girls' school, although she now dated men. "But . . . not someone like you."

Mayang tasted like saltwater, like the sea. Salmah ran her fingers through Mayang's hair and down her back. Mayang smelled like warm winds over the ocean. When Salmah pulled Mayang closer, she let her legs slide down, and resisted a giggle when the arches of her feet brushed against the bristles along Mayang's sides.

Mayang tasted Salmah, with what felt like multiple tongues down the length of Salmah's neck, clavicle, chest. In horrified fascination, Salmah watched as Mayang's jaw unhinged, pharynx extending a little to encompass the whole of one breast, and teeth at the back of Mayang's gullet tickling her nipple. Hard nubs lined Mayang's mouth, massaging, grazing. Oral membrane still extended, Mayang worked her way downwards, tickling Salmah's belly, pausing right before the cleft between her legs.

Mayang's eyes shone with an inner light, ghostly and still, her arms curled around Salmah's thighs. Salmah tried to breathe evenly, the thudding between her legs growing and growing, her alarm at the seams on Mayang's cheeks coming apart also growing and growing. But Mayang's mouth—the inside of it, Salmah reminded herself—pressed among the soft hairs there. Internally shrieking, Salmah nodded.

The pharynx pressed in, rubbing itself all over trembling muscle within and labia without. Salmah gripped the tree roots above her head, staring up into the sky beyond the leaves but not focusing, feeling the tide coming in around her body, feeling a tide coming inside.

Mayang curled her body underneath Salmah, keeping their torsos above water, for Salmah to catch her breath after. She held the human woman through the ragged breathing and occasional gasps—Salmah sat right on top of some of Mayang's legs, that had to keep moving to steady them—and stroked Salmah's hair, singing an ancient song.

"You don't—how do I—" Salmah frowned.

Mayang laughed. "No, you can't. Not now, anyway."

"This seems unfair."

"I have the freedom of these shifting seas in exchange for this small pleasure."

"I don't think—" But Salmah's thought was cut off as it began to rain.

"You should go home," Mayang told her.

The season passed: thunderstorms and lightning displays crashing across the skies made it too dangerous to go to the beach to look for her lover. Salmah moved into the nearby town to work at her family's behest. She thought about Mayang often, but like a dream, an unreal experience with an untrue creature, as her work as a clerk took up her days. University abroad seemed even more possible than before.

Then there was the fact that Salmah could not speak of Mayang to anyone. What could she say? *I am seeing a woman*—to a family who would frown on the idea and assume she hadn't met a nice man to marry yet. *I am seeing a sea creature who is half a centipede*—to whom? And if one could not speak of a love, was it real? Salmah thought about her aunts and friends involved with married men, and was vaguely envious: at least those men had identity cards to prove their existence.

I will lose you too, someday. The pronouncement almost made Salmah angry to think about. By the time the monsoon season was over, Salmah had convinced herself not to go looking for Mayang again. She sent out her university and scholarship applications, received acceptances, and weighed her options carefully. Let Mayang be right if she wants to be.

But she felt guilty. Perhaps she should at least say goodbye. This was harder than it looked, since as soon as she had made her decision, her family suddenly clamored for her attention: endless going-away dinners, visiting relatives, crying grandparents. When she finally found some time to look for Mayang, she worried that perhaps she had been gone too long.

His name was Amir, she would find out later in the newspapers. She barely noticed him as she waded through the mangrove mid-tide looking for Mayang, dismissed the swishing of waters behind her as the waves coming in. She was about to give up, turn around, and head home, when he grabbed her hair at the nape of her neck and slapped a sandy, sweaty hand around her mouth.

Oh God, not here, not now. Salmah thrashed. She was too young to die, had too much to do, she was here to say goodbye to Mayang, not the world. She wrenched away from him, screaming, and ran. He was too close behind, and Salmah turned to see his hand too close to her face—

Then he yelped and disappeared under the water. There was a cloud of sand where he had been.

Salmah screamed and cried and screamed and cried all the way home.

Aphrodite

> E. aphroditois buries its long body in the ocean bed, where it waits to ambush its prey. It moves with such speed that sometimes it slices its prey in half, and drags its catch into the seabed to prevent it from escaping.
>
> —*Predators of the Sea: The Worm Edition*

Simon saw her from a distance first, sitting pretty on boulders far from the beach where he had taken his daughter for a long walk. Eunice had pointed her out first, and he had to squint to really see the figure, looking to the shore forlornly, like Hans Christian Andersen's mermaid in Copenhagen. They had seen the Malay mermaid on occasion since, on their beach excursions.

His wife refused to join them on their walks. Salmah had seen some crazy stuff that he wasn't sure he believed. Mermaids? Cannibal mermaids? He loved her, but she was insane sometimes. He'd thought he was going to marry a nice moderate Muslim girl. If she'd turned out a fundie terrorist, that would at least be understandable, but no, he got weird confessions about some lesbian relationship with a mermaid. She probably made that shit up to make him jealous, get back at him. He couldn't help being a huge flirt; she'd liked that, way back when. And what was wrong with him flirting with other women? It was just flirting, and it wasn't like he was divorcing her.

In fact, Simon took really good care of her, all things considered: roof over her head, grocery money, and all the love a woman could ask for, even if sometimes she was fucking ungrateful. Unreasonable. He had to keep her in line at times. Luckily her father understood him. Some things are shared, even cross-culturally. He supposed that with some other family they would have interfered in the marriage by now, so he counted himself lucky, and put up with their *mat salleh* jokes.

He kicked a seashell into the distance, still mad at the latest fight they'd had. Wasn't she getting a trip home every year? It was expensive, flying over the Pacific every winter. She hated the idea, claimed that monsoon season was too dangerous for Eunice to be near the sea. That was the latest sticking point. He admitted that he'd been a little careless; he'd been so caught up talking to that really interesting musician on the beach he hadn't noticed little Eunice getting lost. Salmah had screamed at him for hours while they lodged a police report, and then stormed out in a crying rage. He'd been too tired to keep her from going out. Let her complain to her neighbors or friends or whatever. He'd tell his side of the story eventually, and he would at least sound sane about it. He liked her friends. All of them pretty, like she'd been before bloating up like a whale.

It was maybe a bit mean of him to hope that she would go missing too. That would take care of that craziness without the business of divorce, and maybe he could marry someone else who wouldn't be so damn shrill. Nope, she'd come home with Eunice in her arms, both of them damp and stinking of rotting fish. He hadn't asked Salmah where she'd found Eunice, but now Eunice was babbling about mermaids too, and that was two crazy women in his house.

There she was again, arms resting on a shelf at the far end of a line of beach rocks. She stared at him with an intensity that made him wonder. She wasn't that far out from shore. He waved at her, smiling. She ducked a little behind the rock, but bobbed up again, smiling back, he hoped, waving coyly.

Simon waded into the water, a little experimentally. Monsoon weather made the sea cold at times, but it had been a hot day. But it wasn't too bad, and besides, that woman on the rock looked lonely. As he approached, he realized, she also looked fine as hell: cheekbones like they'd been cut by diamonds, large dark liquid eyes, and her arms were toned, like she worked out regularly. And her hair! At first he thought it was black, just like basically everybody else here. But it seemed to have a rainbow sheen to it, as if she had an oil slick in her hair, or maybe as if her hair was an oil slick.

"Oy," he called.

"Salaam," she replied.

"Mind if I hang out with you?"

It took her a moment to answer, as if his accent was a problem. "You may."

She was in waist-deep water, and he counted himself lucky to be tall. Being a *mat salleh* had its advantages, he thought as he leaned over the rock to look down into those amazing eyes. Not only that, but clearly he'd lucked out with a freaky girl: she wasn't even wearing a top. Women here wore T-shirts and sarongs at the beach out of modesty, and with the growing Arabization, more of them were buying those swimsuits that covered everything. It was a crying shame; that had never been the case when he visited Asia in his youth. Also a crying shame: the water was cloudy, so he couldn't check out whether she was wearing a bottom. He thought he caught a glimpse of one, a scintillating waistband, but the water sloshed up and he lost sight of it.

"So . . . you live around here?"

"I move around a lot. You?" Her Malay had an odd accent. He'd heard that the northerners had a different dialect of Malay, but he'd never met anyone who spoke that way before. Still, it gratified him that his Malay was passable enough that a stranger thought he was local.

"I'm from Amerika Syarikat."

"How interesting. Your Malay is very good." Her hand reached up to touch his face. "Is your hair really that color?"

He grinned, bending his head down for her to touch his curls. His naturally blond hair fascinated locals. Her fingers were tentative, and she wrapped a lock around her pinky. Now that her arms were away from her breasts, he could see that they were small, almost flat, but cute all the same.

"So soft," she cooed, letting her hand slip down the back of his head, his neck. "So nice."

"Thanks," he said, about to share his shampoo-and-conditioning routine (women loved that sort of thing) when he noticed her hand dropping downwards even farther. Her fingertips drifted across his chest and even lower. "Oh, wow." He didn't protest as her hand tugged at his waistband, pulling him around the rock. He stepped around, let her guide his hips so he leaned back.

She was fast in unbuttoning and unzipping. Some sort of freaky slut, he thought, aware that he had the same stupid grin from earlier on his face as she got to work on his erection. He gazed down at her rainbow-black hair, amazed at how fast she deep-throated him. And what the fuck was her tongue, even? It felt like it was swirling all around his cock, or that maybe she had multiple tongues. He'd have to investigate it after, because it felt so goddamn good.

Thunder rolled across the sky, and the waves came in harder. He was impressed; she wasn't stopping even though the tide was obviously coming in, lapping higher around his hips now, spraying her cheeks.

"Water's coming in," he croaked, gently but regretfully pushing at her shoulders. She took his hands and put them on her head, on her dark hair, and pressed him against the rock even more firmly.

She did not stop, even as the tide came in higher, but he was beyond caring, because this was the best blowjob of his goddamn life and he wasn't going to let something like nature get in the way. At the back of his mind he was maybe worried that maybe she might drown if she kept on going, but he gripped her hair and kept thrusting into her throat. Who knows when he might ever meet her again—maybe he'd get her number.

"I'm gonna come," he gasped, out of courtesy. Vaguely, he realized that he was knee-deep in the sand. When had that happened? Maybe it wasn't the tide coming in after all, but them sinking into the water. He'd ask Salmah about it later.

He glanced down—what the fuck, she was underwater, dark eyes meeting his—and—no, what!—mandibles protruded—no, unfolded—from her cheeks and clamped down around his hips. He screamed.

Oh shit, oh shit, oh God, oh God. He scrabbled at the rock behind him—the water was higher than before—pulled at the mandibles—sweet Jesus, *mandibles*—but they dug into his flesh deeper, and her arms were wrapped around his legs, and she was sinking into the sand—what the fuck—and pulling him with her. Every effort he made to get out of her grasp made her mandibles dig in farther.

"Help!" he shrieked, drowned out by another clap of thunder.

Water roared around his ears. She was pulling him underground underwater, he realized. What the fuck was she? He pushed at the seabed, gasped when she bit down hard—he yelled, oh shit, underwater—but he was still sinking, the sand was up to his chest now. His lungs burned, his hips were scalding.

As the seabed came up about his ears, he swallowed. Water tickled his fingers. Rough sand engulfed them.

Eunice

> Contrary to its popular name of "bobbitt worm," named after the famous case in which Lorena Bobbitt cut off her husband's penis with a scissors, E. aphroditois do not have penises, as they are broadcast spawners. Little is known of their mating habits, as very few individual specimens have been found.
>
> —*Mysterious Marine Matings*

Eunice dreamed the same dream for a long time: she drifted in the waves, frightened and tired of swimming, and saw a long, large worm, swimming toward her. Then a human face, and human arms, grasping her tightly, lifting her to the surface, allowing her to gasp for air. Eunice rode on the wormwoman's back toward shore, but not toward where she had lost her father. She'd dreamed of falling asleep, dreamed she'd awoken to her mother's cries of relief. In these false awakenings, half-lucid with the awareness that she was not really awake, Eunice clung to the wormwoman tightly, trying to ask questions, impossible ones like "Why does Mom hate me?" or "Why didn't I get Dad's blue eyes?" or "How come the other kids look at me weird?" or "What are men even?"

When she was older, she fought with her mother over the details: her mother insisted that she had found Eunice half-drowned and asleep on the beach; Eunice knew that the wormwoman was real, and she half-remembered a conversation between the woman and her mother. It was hard to forget that musical voice, almost like whistles in the dark. She didn't know what the details were anymore, but someone had cried.

Eunice plodded along the beach, squinting into the distance. It had taken years, but she was sure that she had finally found the right place. Her mother had tried to throw her off the trail several times: "Oh no, it was at Seberang Ris," she'd say. "Maybe it was at Pulau Redang, very popular there." After several fruitless road trips, as well as much rifling through her mother's old documents, Eunice found a relative's phone number that worked—one of many who had shunned her mother after the disappearance of Eunice's father. She had to listen to a long religious screed about the pernicious effects of black magic and a roundabout accusation of her mother, but she finally got the information she wanted. The family had moved far and wide across the Peninsula, and no one would *balik kampung* to where her mother had grown up, but they still remembered the name of the town.

There was an isolated lagoon, a tiny one, encroached on all sides with trees growing in the accumulated silt. They weren't even mangrove trees, but evergreens, angsana, and saga, probably brought there by the ocean. Eunice sat down for a while, taking in the sight. There was an opening to the side, and a sandbar that blocked off the lagoon from the ocean. Rocks of all sizes were scattered here and there, beach rocks now obscured by the trees.

Something twinkled beside a rock on the edge of the lagoon. Eunice jumped up to investigate. She had to stomp on some saplings, but when she got there, there was nothing but water. Interesting, though: the rockline held back the sand on one side, but on the other, the water looked deep. She kicked off her sandals and pulled on her snorkel.

The water was cold for that time of year; it seemed to swallow her. She blew out the water from her snorkel, and began to slowly explore along the rockline. Soon she was bumping up against the tree roots of a mangrove swamp. She had half a mind to get out; no telling what poisonous snakes or crocodiles could be living there. But there was something so incredibly familiar about the place, something that twigged at the back of her mind. The silt was so loose here that any little disturbance stirred it up, so Eunice drifted carefully.

There, half-buried, a woman's body facing up. Eunice clung to a tree root tightly to stare. Was she dead?

A flurry of silt went up, and the woman was gone. A dark shadow circled around Eunice, and from the sandy cloud, a pair of brown arms reached out to her. Eunice froze, letting the hands touch her face, drift over her snorkel mask, brush her bangs back. The sand parted, and the woman's face came into view, achingly familiar. She had a broad nose and large dark eyes, and her cheeks seemed to have scars. She swam by, a hand trailing down Eunice's side, dipping into the small of her back.

Eunice sucked in her breath at the sight of the long segmented body beginning from the woman's waist. The bristles on the sides waggled independently of each other, navigating the water. The wormwoman swam above Eunice's legs, and under, running her hands up from her hips, to her waist, the sides of her breasts, and cupped her cheeks. She gently prised one of Eunice's hands from the tree root and tugged, smiling.

Eunice let go, let herself be pulled along by this woman. They passed under tunnels of mangrove roots, toward open sea, and along the coastline to a rocky beach. Eunice pulled herself onto a shelf, water sloshing around her hips as the waves came in. The woman wrapped herself around a rock, leaned forward with a beaming smile.

When Eunice pulled off her mask, the smile faltered a little.

"You're not Salmah." She wasn't exactly unfriendly, but there was a slight wobble in the music.

Eunice shook her head. "I'm Salmah's daughter." She hesitated. "You saved me, when I was little."

The woman's gaze swept over her, then she lowered her head to rest her chin on her arms. "Has it been so long?"

"Sorry."

"It's not your fault. I just thought—but never mind. How is she?"

Eunice's mind ran through a thousand possible answers. *She's fine—she's busy with a new business—she seems lonely—she hates swimming now—she seems happy—she's got a new husband.* She went with the most honest answer. "I don't know. I haven't really talked to her in a while." She pursed her lips. "She never told me your name."

Those large eyes seemed to glitter in the sunlight. "Hmm." Everything about her seemed iridescent with the sunshine. The brown of her skin had a reflective rainbow sheen, and the curls of her hair resembled an oil slick.

The waves rushed to shore. In the distance, herons cawed.

"My name is Mayang."

Eunice smiled. "Eunice."

"Eunice. It sounds nice. American name?"

A nod. "My father named me."

"I see."

Mayang said nothing further about Eunice's father, even when Eunice casually mentioned him later in the conversation, as in "that time when Dad got mad about—" and watched Mayang's reaction carefully. But save for a flicker on Mayang's face, he was as good as irrelevant. They wouldn't talk about him after that, on further visits, resting after a long swim around the reefs and nearby islands, drilling holes into the bottoms of rich men's yachts with screwdrivers and drills Eunice brought. Mayang would confess to Eunice the fates of former lovers, devoured by sea predators, dead by the poison of pollution, or simply lost to the worldly concerns of humans. Eunice would tell Mayang about the new technologies that had arisen, the advancements scientists were making in space and deep-sea explorations, and the new wars. When they made love, Eunice was torn between jealousy and satisfaction, that her mother had this before she did, and would never have it again.

"You never talk about yourself," Mayang interrupted Eunice one day as they lazed in a nest of rocks, Eunice in Mayang's arms. Mayang was not an interrupter, but she couldn't help herself in that moment. "Why is that?"

Eunice shrugged. "I'm not a very interesting person." And went on describing memes.

Mayang let it pass until Eunice was done talking. Then she stroked the young woman's hair. "*I* think you're very interesting."

Eunice caught Mayang's hand, and kissed its palm. "I think you're more interesting than me. You live forever under the sea. You see things no human ever could." She thought for a moment about her never-mentioned father. "Also, you eat people. That's really cool."

Mayang laughed so loudly Eunice was afraid someone would hear them, discover them and their secret. The seams in her cheeks loosened a little, mandibles almost unfolding in her mirth. But Mayang sobered as quickly as she had laughed. "There is a price to the freedom of the seas."

She was so serious, Eunice had to know. "What is it?"

"Everything amazing you tell me, every change in the human world, will be lost to you," Mayang answered, hands still stroking Eunice's hair, drifting down. "Death is still a constant danger. There are so few of us, torn apart by the tides, I don't even know where the others are anymore."

"I found you easily."

"I like to stay put. Fishing here is easy. There are so many more tourists than before." She smoothed the fabric of Eunice's panties. "But no more this feeling good here. Because you won't have it anymore."

Eunice let Mayang's hand linger, weighing the truth of the statement. Eunice's wormbody explorations had turned up nothing sensitive. She parted her knees a little, and pressed the hand farther down. Mayang's fingers played with a stray hair, but withdrew after a moment.

"You're so young, Eunice. Go live a full life. The sea is for bitter old crones like me."

Eunice turned to kiss Mayang's cheek, and trailed her lips along a mandible seam. "You're not a crone," she murmured, brushing sand off Mayang's brown skin, flicking a cake of silt off a breast. It was small, mostly vestigial muscle left over from years of swimming in the ocean. "And I'm not that young." She kissed Mayang, working her fingers into the wormwoman's mouth to reach places her tongue could not reach. Mayang's mouth—the loose membrane, the soft muscles—pressed down, not to push Eunice out, but to draw her in. In a busy embrace, Eunice straddled Mayang, stretching the length of herself along to brush against the bristles that fluttered in a way Eunice noticed only happened when they kissed.

The epidermis along Mayang's body cracked as it dried. It did not happen often, Mayang had told Eunice, and really only meant she had a new segment to her body. Eunice helped peel the old skin off, and marveled at the polished iridescence beneath. She ran her fingers across the new skin, soft for now until it toughened over time, and grinned to hear Mayang moaning. She carefully stripped the length of Mayang's body, fingers dancing between parapodia to a startling cacophony from Mayang. When she reached the final segment, throbbing with its newness, she embraced it, showering it with kisses, while Mayang arched her back, mandibles unfurling wide in a long, ragged cry.

The afternoon sun had gone down by the time they rested.

"When there were more of us," Mayang whispered, eyes closed in dreamy afterglow, "we met during molting season. What a shame there are so few of us now."

Eunice went home and quit her job. She closed her bank accounts, all social media possible, wrote several letters that were along the lines of, "Don't look for me." Her mother tried to withhold her car keys and her identity card, as if those were things Eunice needed anymore. Concerned acquaintances tried to call, but Eunice turned off her phone and removed the SIM card.

Off the shore of Terengganu, where it was still dark enough for moonlight to set the white sands aglow, Eunice rode Mayang's back to an island of rocks too small for development, too rocky for trees.

"Will it be painful?"

"Very." (Mayang actually couldn't remember anymore.)

"Will you be there when I wake up?"

"Yes." (Mayang lied, because anything could happen.)

They tumbled onto a bed of sand together, kissing and licking and tasting, Eunice wrapped around Mayang. Mayang ran her pharynx over the length of Eunice's neck, chest, belly, while her fingers found the human cleft and thrust deep, feeling along the lines of the wet walls for throbbing muscle. Eunice gripped Mayang's hair, a little alarmed at the sudden engorgement from Mayang's mouth, raking teeth across her clavicle, the round of her breasts, and every sensitive spot Mayang knew. She swallowed the bile of terror as Mayang's head settled between her legs, mandibles unfurling and foaming at the edges. Water rose around her hips.

Mayang bit deep, seeking the second heartbeat, splitting skin and flesh. Eunice screeched as Mayang's teeth-lined pharynx burrowed around her clitoris, nerve endings shattered and ripped apart. The froth turned bloody, burning, blazing as seawater rose. Eunice clamped her legs together, almost catching Mayang's neck, and Mayang ducked away to let the transformation begin. Eunice squeezed her legs shut, gasped in shock between sobs, while Mayang rubbed her arms up and down and stroked her hair and crooned an old song: the blood from Eunice, the foam from Mayang, the salt of the sea, all would bubble together to form a cocoon, so sleep, so fade away, let the warm blood go. The water rose, and Eunice felt the moonlight ebb from her vision. Everything grew cold and dark and silent except for Mayang's voice.

Eunice dreamed of entwining with Mayang over and over, of exploring the ocean depths and each other, of the freedom of the shifting sea.

Coda

Do you know, Eunice? I cannot remember the last time I witnessed a metamorphosis. When the water covered you, the foam turned into a thin film that reminded me of bloody cauls over babies. Unpleasant memories. When you wake up, I hope you will not mind having been buried in the silt of the mangrove, because I had forgotten how much men are prone to roaming in their boats these days, their mastery over the ocean allowing them a greater range. You will also have more food around when you wake up, and I will be there to catch them with you, and teach you how.

And I can already sense that you will not be happy in this sleepy little beachside, so we will drift across the oceans to find old shipwrecks and waylay unhappy boats. We will delve into the trenches to find the methuselahs who feed on whales and deep-sea squid in between their slumbering aeons. Maybe we will find others like us. Maybe we will make more like us. Maybe in the far future you will leave me anyway, but it will not matter by then.

Sleep easy, my little Eunice.

ADAM-TROY CASTRO

Sacrid's Pod

FROM *Lightspeed*

HELLO, SACRID HENN.

I'm aware that you're terrified.

I'm also aware that you are paralyzed, deaf, and blind, your only sensory input being my voice.

It is a voice that has been designed to be as comforting as these circumstances permit. Believe me when I say that you are in no danger and that my intentions toward you are that of a caretaker toward a vulnerable charge.

Understand: Your insensate condition is the result of a neural block, administered to prevent you from injuring yourself in panic upon awakening. It is reversible and will be corrected once your new life circumstances have been explained to you.

In our experience, your first sight of this location is least traumatic when held in reserve for some point after you have received some preliminary counseling. Soon, your vision will be restored and you will be freed to examine the space where you will be spending the rest of your life.

Sacrid Henn.

Sacrid Henn. Your hysteria is understandable but fruitless. In your current condition you cannot voice it. Regain control of your emotions and I will continue.

Congratulations. You did that quickly. I sense your resentment and understand that you are cooperating only to find a moment of advantage, for some gesture of defiance. This is reasonable enough. If it permits cooperation while I complete this orientation process, it is productive use of our shared time.

As an early comfort, I wish you to understand that though you are presently unable to speak, you can still communicate with us as freely as you wish. Your brain has been equipped with an implant that monitors your emotional responses and reads your surface thoughts. This is how I know when you are screaming at me, even when you make no sound. This response was expected, and is constructive in that this anger is a phase you need to experience, before you are ready to move on to acceptance.

Are you done, for the moment?

Fine. Then I shall proceed.

You need to understand three things. First, I will not remove your neural blocks, reversing your paralysis and sensory shutdown, until you're calm. Second, I can reactivate them at any time, for as long as you remain in my custody, which will almost certainly be for as long as you live. Third, even if I do see fit to allow your rages free rein, I am part of a network of linked artificial intelligences incapable of being cowed by your anger. I cannot be upset by you, not even when you use bad language. I do note with something like amusement that I possess no biological form and that therefore your vitriolic references to human genitalia and elimination sphincters are wholly inapplicable. Your hysteria is therefore impotent and flung at a void. I understand that you must still expel it and will be patient as you do so, unless it proves an impediment to this transition, in which case I have disciplinary options that you will find most unpleasant. They will never be employed out of malice, but only to nudge you toward acceptance. The sooner you move on to the next stage, the happier you will be.

I see.

My current judgment is that you are not yet ready to listen.

This is not unexpected. Fully 97.2 percent of our guests remain intractable at this stage.

Listen.

Among my many features is a complete library of all human music ever recorded, cross-referenced by genre, artist, and homeworld of origin. Many human beings throughout known space would pay exorbitant prices for access to this library. You will later be afforded the opportunity to browse it at your leisure, according to your own aesthetic preferences. The selection beginning in thirty seconds has been chosen by us and is a celebrated symphony for strings, composed and performed by a man named Henrik Gustafson, who lived and died approximately four hundred years before your birth. It is a light pastoral the artist designed to be played at soft volume while listeners engage in quiet contemplation. In today's world it is most often played as a lullaby for children and is said to shut down even the most intractable rage-fueled tantrum.

It will play now in its entirety, which lasts some seventy-two minutes, before we speak to you again.

Hello, Sacrid Henn.

Yes, I am aware that you did not enjoy your musical selection.

The biographical information I've been provided includes a full list of your aesthetic preferences. I've been told that in your prior life you preferred angry discordant music that expressed your rage at the world around you, and that as much as you enjoyed listening to it in privacy you took even more pleasure in playing it at a volume painful to those like your parents who did not share your preferences. It is one of many ways in which you have punished those around you, for the sin of proximity. The Gustafson piece was just such a punishment, except in reverse, in that it was chosen to be irritating to you. Please understand that we have many more compositions like it. If you calm down long enough to proceed with the orientation, you will have the opportunity to select other selections that better fit your own aesthetic preferences.

I have now administered a medication designed to minimize your fear-response. This is why you are not crying, even though you possess the vague sense that you should be. This is what makes your equanimity during the rest of this orientation possible.

Listen, Sacrid Henn.

You are in the custody of a commercial installation owned and operated by the independent software intelligences known as the AIsource. You have likely heard of us.

Thank you for providing confirmation.

The voice you are hearing is your caretaker. I will be your primary social contact from this moment on. You may think of me as friend, companion, parent, guardian, sibling, nurse, butler, concierge, and, if desired, lover.

Yes. Your pod has been constructed with that function. If you wish, I—

Very well. Be aware only that this preference may change.

For convenience you may even assign me a human name, if you desire.

"Shithead." Very well. I am "Shithead." This bothers me not at all.

Later, you will be able to adjust my voice in order to alter my gender, apparent age, and surface personality. But I will always be the means by which you interact with the system that now supports your existence. I would prefer for the two of us to get along, but will suffer no inconvenience if you prefer me to function as antagonist.

When you were delivered into our custody, you were twenty-four days from reaching the age when your world, a repressive religious society, would have declared you an independent adult. You had recently made it clear to your parents that upon this transition you would leave them, abandon the community where you were born, and seek some other planet more in line with your personal preferences. It is not my place to judge whether they were bad parents or you a bad child. But letting them know your intentions was a tactical error. Your highly religious society has always held that children are the effective property of their parents until adulthood, a life stage that is in your society defined as thirteen for males and twenty for females. They were by local law wholly justified in responding to your premature declaration of independence by taking steps that you would never be independent again.

Their precise complaints about you include vanity, rebelliousness, and chronic disrespect toward the religious tradition in which you were raised.

They specifically wanted me to relate that you are where you are because they consider you a little whore, "eager to spread [your] legs for any boy who offers sufficient enticement."

There is no point in disputing these charges. I merely report what the intake programs were told. Nor will I argue whether, even if accurate, this justifies your current predicament. It is not an argument that concerns me. We are above the logic, or illogic, that defines morality in human moral systems.

Nor does it matter that the time you have spent unconscious, while in transit, has brought you well past the age where your world would have considered you an adult. In all our contracts with sentient beings, throughout civilized space, we respect whatever laws the local jurisdiction holds most sacred. We therefore abide by the judgment of your mother and father that you are incorrigible and cannot ever be permitted to roam free.

Answering your unspoken objection: "Fair" is a value judgment. It has no relevance here.

Yes, this is legal. The independent software intelligences have signed agreements with many participating human societies, employing us as subcontractors in the management of prisons. I think you will find that we are significantly more humane in this task than any of your peoples are. The usual human solution is to dump all their incarcerated in a box and let their respective versions of savagery fight it out. A young woman like yourself, indeed any physically vulnerable person, inevitably experiences bullying, intimidation, assault, and various levels of slavery, at the hands of those more powerful. You are lucky. You will not face those dangers here. Your pod has been built for your comfort and safety. The least of the comforts to take to heart is that this is a place where you will not be harmed, or permitted to come to harm, either at the hands of more aggressive human beings, or, I stress, at your own.

"Deserve" is relative. Your parents only had to establish a clear pattern of emerging criminality, as defined by the standards of the society in which you lived. The petty rebellions that you have engaged in, until now, could have been judged misdemeanors had your family not represented them as acts that required your permanent isolation. Understand that according to the oppressive laws of your world, you could have ended up in places far worse than this: prisons, forced labor camps, mental institutions, and so on. It would have been legal for your parents to sell you to one of the many industrial hells all over Confederate space where people work under horrid conditions carrying a debt-load that may take them entire lifetimes to work off. They cared enough for your happiness and your welfare to contact us and request your removal to this present environment. They—

We may have an argument about their motivations later. This is currently a discussion of the conditions under which you will now live. We are prepared to play another musical selection. Perhaps something more by Gustafson?

You are learning.

Your parents discovered that the AIsource collective offers a detention service and arranged for your pickup. You were delivered to your present location, this pod, where we will see to your every need for the duration of your natural life.

I sense your worry that this will be solitary confinement.

This is important for you to understand. Your stay here will differ from the solitary confinement as it has historically been practiced by the penal systems of your species. The point of such confinement has always been torture by the absence of social or sensory stimulation. The prisoner's mind has nothing to do but cannibalize itself. That is, if you forgive the classification, inhuman. Here, little will be denied you, except freedom. If, for instance, you wish to be drugged into a euphoric stupor all the remaining hours of your life, you may have that; if you wish reading materials, games, neurec feeds, or dramatic presentations to while away your time, you may have them. If you desire physical stimulation of any sort, from massage to simulated coitus, you may have that; if you wish to communicate via text with others who have been surrendered to our care, you may have that. But, while in my care, you will never lay eyes, or hands, on another human being. Your parents found this a most attractive feature. I am prepared to debate the morality of this at whatever length you prefer, once this orientation is completed. It is a form of entertainment popular among our guests.

Rest assured, however, that a number of our guests have found happiness here. You will be given every resource you need to conduct your own search for it.

I know you have questions. I will answer them afterward.

I am not yet ready to relieve your paralysis.

You have been patient, however, so I will now restore your vision and proceed to the next stage of your orientation.

Welcome to your pod, Sacrid Henn.

You are correct. There is indeed a strong resemblance to a coffin, at least in relative dimension. About 98.3 percent of our guests use that metaphor at some point. I will note that it is in truth approximately three times the size of the container the average human society typically uses for that purpose. It is, for instance, spacious enough to permit full extension of all your limbs, as well as any other vertical or horizontal activity a young and healthy human being might get up to. The pod is currently horizontal, its preferred position whenever the occupant wishes to lie down. You will note that the surface beneath you is soft, for your comfort while sleeping or immobilized, as now. It may be rendered more or less soft, according to preference. You will find it a most adequate bed. You will also notice that the surface you will now consider your ceiling is more than an arm's-reach above you. Were you not still paralyzed, you would now be able to sit up without slamming your head. It is, in your current position, a most adequate ceiling.

You will now be restrained for your safety as we alter the angle of your pod. Do not be alarmed as this occurs.

Very well. The pod is now vertical. This permits you to stand. You may desire to keep this orientation but sit down; in that event, a comfortable seat will emerge from the wall behind you. On request this may be a toilet, or bidet. Other means of cleansing yourself will be provided. The facility that houses your pod has access to more fresh water than you could possibly use in a lifetime, and will admit it into your living space at any quantity you request. Depending on your preference and its current orientation, this will permit use of your pod as either shower stall or bathtub. The surfaces dry quickly when you are done and wish to move on to subsequent activities. Our facility has guests who soak in hot water for hours, finding it calming. There are others who embrace derangement, eschew personal hygiene, and prefer to live in their own filth. You will be subjected to no pressure to lean in the direction of one option or the other.

You will eat. Thirty-two-point-six percent of our guests attempt to starve themselves. They are allowed the discomfort of missing a few meals, but if this becomes a medical concern they will be immobilized and fed intravenously. Those who agree to eat will find that we are excellent at food preparation. We are able to constitute any meal you prefer. They will not be the foods they appear to be, but rather a neutral compound that provides you with all the requirements of life. You will find it indistinguishable in both texture and flavor from expertly prepared cuisine of those simulated agreements. If you wish, you may have entire culinary adventures. There will be no possibility of overeating. Sixty-three-point-two percent of our guests overindulge out of boredom, but we can simply adjust the ratio of filler to caloric value and maintain your ideal weight, regardless of consumption.

You will be afforded stimulation. Your pod is a communication device. The blank walls may display artwork or motion pictures or texts of your own choosing. It may interest you to know that your parents wanted us to limit your cultural diet to approved religious texts and that we indicated we would abide by this request, which strikes us as torture and which we have no intention of honoring. You may have any book, any recorded drama, any cultural artifact, ever produced by human civilization, from the materials they prefer to those they would consider blasphemous or pornographic. These materials may be translated into your native tongue or may be provided to you as originally composed, as enticement to learn the other dialects of your species. To this end, 34.7 percent of our guests do end up fluent in multiple languages as self-improvement projects, a much higher percentage than those who, out of isolation, become completely nonverbal.

Your pod is designed to permit and encourage exercise. The floor can become a treadmill, on command. The walls may be reconfigured to become scrolling ladders or climbing walls. The gravity is artificial and can be raised or lowered, on request, though health concerns place limits on how long we will permit you to stay in zero-g or in forces higher than 3-g. Because the walls are also holographic screens, you may also increase the illusory size of the pod as much as you wish, though its actual dimensions cannot be much altered from what you see now. If you wish, I can generate entire virtual worlds for you to explore. Its effective boundaries are, in effect, the size of the universe itself.

Later, I may have a question to ask you about this, but only if certain other developments come up.

Because you are now contemplating escape, it may interest you to know that you are one of 109,327 human beings and other sentients who have been housed at this one facility, all of whom have been turned over to our care at the request of those of their own people who possessed legal authority over them. It is a significantly sized structure even by the standards of most human industrial operations, taking up a geographical area large enough to house a number of your own cities. It is only a small part of an enclosed artificial world in a system we have declared our property. It is fifteen light-years from the nearest human outpost. It should be helpful to establish that in order to accommodate all of the options you are afforded to adjust your living conditions, as well as the production of the consumables necessary to care for you over the rest of your natural life, the support system surrounding your pod, and just your pod, is accordingly huge. It occupies approximately ten cubic kilometers, with your pod at its precise center. It is virtually impossible for you to escape your pod, escape its extensive support system, find your way to some access corridor, and subsequently find your way out of that portion of this deep-space facility that is devoted to the care of guests, a distance that is itself the size of a small country. Even then you would have to worry about escaping this artificial world, without cooperation from us, and somehow making it back to the nearest human habitation, a further distance of fifteen light-years. It would be like escaping a jail cell, only to then face the necessity of escaping the prison, only to then have to escape the surrounding city, only to then have to escape the surrounding landscape, only to then find yourself with an ocean separating you from your homeland. It is virtually impossible.

I can tell you that this feat has been accomplished one hundred and fifty-eight times in our many years of operation. This represents a fraction of one percent of our current detainee population. Still, it remains a remarkable testament to human ingenuity.

This interests you.

We have not plugged that hole in our security in large part because of its usefulness as a form of recreation, and as a source of hope.

Yes. Escape is possible.

But that is up to you.

I am ready to alleviate your paralysis now.

Good morning, Sacrid Henn.

It is your seventeenth day in the pod.

We are aware that you have only experienced two of those days. You suffered an emotional break and were arrested in the act of attempting to injure yourself. We judged it best to place you in a medically induced coma and make certain adjustments to your brain chemistry that will avoid mood spirals like the one that overcame you on your second day here. You now have a chemical pacemaker, of sorts, that will steer you away from the depths of deepest depression. You need not feel ashamed; 72.4 percent of our human guests need adjustments of this sort within their first weeks here. The percentage that continue to need them on a regular basis goes down over time, bottoming out at just under 32.5 percent.

I am not responsive to profanity. How would you like to begin your day?

Vertical it is.

And now?

A bath it is.

The water entering your pod is now heated to 38.5 degrees Celsius and lightly salinated to encourage buoyancy. It will rise to a depth just over your standing height, to permit you the pleasure of floating. When you need a rest, your seat will emerge from the wall. Given your recent self-destructive behavior it is perhaps not inappropriate to advise you that attempts at drowning yourself will not be successful and may be greeted by this elemental pleasure being withheld for the foreseeable future.

I accept your vocal assurances that this is not your plan.

Do you wish music?

No, Gustafson is not all we have.

Very well. Conversation it is.

That is a fine question. What we get out of this is as intangible as we are ourselves. As software intelligences we exist largely in the space you would call *virtual*. We interact with the physical world you know only through probes, and therefore require no goods or services available through trade with any species of biological origin. The diplomatic relations we have established, and the goods and services we offer in exchange for financial remuneration, such as this facility, are to us a form of entertainment, indulged in to while away effective lifespans that would terrify you. We do this because it is *interesting*.

Sadism is a human value. I have already described the conditions that you might have suffered were you to be left in the care of your fellow human beings. We would be *sadists* if we did not extend some token effort toward providing an alternative. Would you prefer your parents to have sold you into indentured servitude, as was indeed within their options? No? Then understand what you are currently experiencing is a manifestation of mercy, not cruelty.

No, that is not an expression of resentment on my part. That was informational. If you need to express anger toward us, you should feel free to do so.

Yes. This pod can duplicate conditions on any number of human worlds. Would you like us to drain your bath first, or would you prefer a simulation that incorporates it as sensory input?

The latter. Very well.

The ambient light will now dim to simulate an hour shortly after the setting of the sun in a region known as Brieczka, on a planet known as Fjant. The blinking lights above you are the evening stars as seen on the planetary surface, but for that one steady point of illumination, which is an orbital cylinder world home to seventy thousand people. It is the entire population of this system. The society is unusual in that they stay aboard that structure and descend to this perfectly congenial world only on special occasions, leaving it mostly pristine. You are in a small saltwater lake surrounded by desert and low mountains, represented around you by the jagged line of darkness beneath which no stars or planets are visible. The natural reflectiveness of the lake water affords a fine optical illusion, in that if you remain still the stars appear to be below you as well as above. You may swim for a distance, if you wish. The simulation will scroll with you remaining at its precise center.

Yes, it is beautiful.

Yes, by another measurement it is also bullshit. Do you wish us to drain your bath?

Very well.

That is another excellent question. Yes. It is only a representation. It is not the world as it currently appears. To provide that we would need to have a monitor on that world, capturing the local conditions at real time. The drawback of that is that the conditions are not always ideal; there are uncomfortable temperature extremes that a visitor would normally wish to avoid, and on occasion high winds that can blast human skin and eyes with airborne sand. This simulation is far more enjoyable.

No. The other experience will not be denied you, if you truly wish it.

Yes. A real-time simulation of actual conditions can be arranged.

Yes, I can record your voice. Some of our guests have dictated entire novels. A few of them have been published in human space.

Very well. Recording starts now.

Playback as requested.

"I will live to swim in the real lake someday."

Yes, I will save that recording for you.

We should point out that in order to enjoy the real lake you will need to escape.

Playback as requested.

"I will live to swim in the real lake someday."

New recording initiated.

You might be interested in knowing that 89.4 percent of our guests harbor similar fantasies.

Fine. I will shut up.

Let me know when you're ready for breakfast.

Sacrid Henn Pod Diary. Entry Seven. Recording.

This message is for my mother and father.

Shithead tells me that this won't be forwarded to them. I don't give a damn. They will hear these words someday. Until then, speaking them, storing them, is my means of holding on to myself, not allowing this place to break me.

Mother, Father,

Until you sent me here, I never hated you.

I couldn't stand you. I thought you were small-minded, provincial, and bigoted. I thought you wanted to make me into something I was not. I thought that you were willing to love me only as long as I was willing to suffocate, to believe things I didn't believe, to memorize your dogma, to turn my life into what you thought it should be. For a long time I knew that there was no way you would ever accept me living my life the way I wanted to, and that leaving would always end with you turning your back on me.

I mistook all this for hating you.

I didn't, you know. The thing is, I didn't hate you so much as hate your refusal to understand. I didn't hate you in the sense that I wanted anything bad to ever happen to you. I didn't hate you but I was willing to leave you behind because it was the only thing that would give me some semblance of peace.

In the meantime, I loved you.

This surprises me as much as it would surprise you. I didn't realize it was there until it was shattered.

I endured all your spiritual interventions. I suffered all your invocations of the Book. I writhed under all the manifestations of your disappointment in me. I felt pain in your presence. But I also believed that you wanted what was best for me, that you were just dead wrong about what that meant.

Acceptance from you would have made me so happy.

I ached to sit down at the table and smile with you, to laugh with you, the way I did when I was a toddler, the way I still did when I was a little girl, before I knew that I could never live among the People, believing in your version of the Divine, obeying your Divine's commandments. I wanted the warm arms of my mother, the gruff smile of my father. I didn't think it was an impossible thing to have. Even after the town Fathers did what they did to Marta, even after I heard you approving of the living death they consigned her to, I believed that someday, after I made my escape from our world, I would be able to return for a visit someday, bringing with me whatever family I made, and stories of the life I'd have built. I dreamt of you someday telling me, "We were wrong, Sacrid. We always should have let you make your own choices. We're proud of what you've become."

That wasn't hatred. That was pathetic, but it wasn't hatred.

That was love.

Someday, I will bring you the message that there's none left.

Good morning, Sacrid Henn.

It is your twenty-third day in the pod. Would you like to return to the novel you were reading before you went to sleep last night? Or go straight to breakfast, prior to commencing your morning aerobics?

Very well. We will initiate and archive a conversation for you.

{ARCHIVE}

Q: *I would like to discuss escape.*

A: Are you certain you would not prefer to do something more productive?

Q: *This is productive.*

A: Very well. How would you like to begin the conversation?

Q: *I would like to discuss the one hundred fifty-eight people who found their way out.*

A: There have actually been one hundred fifty-nine now.

Q: *Really?*

A: Create any basin for the storage of water, and however effective your craftsmanship, the water will find a crack, will wear that crack into a crevasse, will turn that crevasse into a route to the sea. It may take years, but it will happen. Human beings are like water in that respect. They isolate the weakness in any prison, and they find their way out.

Q: *Tell me about them.*

A: Their names are classified.

Q: *I don't care about their names. I want you to confirm that they're free and that no effort is being made to recapture them.*

A: Confirmed. Our responsibilities toward them were only to hold them, not to recapture them if they escaped custody.

Q: *So if I escape this pod, you will not hunt me?*

A: No. You will have achieved freedom.

Q: *So this is a test of some sort.*

A: Your escape is not intended. It is unlikely but not impossible.

Q: *Question: Aside from the human beings currently being held in this facility, are there any within reach who could offer me assistance?*

A: No.

Q: *Are there any who I could summon?*

A: Not from your current location.

Q: *Assuming I escaped the pod and the surrounding infrastructure of this facility, and made it to the percentage of this world not dedicated to the care of your guests, would either of these factors change? Would I find any transportation to human space?*

A: No. You would die of hunger unless you made it back to your pod.

Q: *Is this what's kept your guests from trying to escape?*

A: Many of them surrender to the hopelessness of their circumstances.

Q: *So if escape is possible, the trick is to either persuade you to open the pod for me, or to summon some other help from outside that can also give me a lift back to Confederate space.*

A: You cannot persuade me to open the pod for you.

Q: *So what I need is somebody to open the pod from the outside.*

A: Yes.

Q: *One final question: If it becomes clear to you that I have worked out a means of escape, and you see it happening, will you take steps to stop me?*

A: We have described the security measures in place. We see no point in adding any.

Q: *Thank you. You've been very helpful.*

Sacrid Henn Pod Diary. Entry Two Hundred. Recording.

Mother. Father.

I keep thinking about escape.

My pod says it's possible. Trying to figure out how has become an obsession for me. I do all the things I have to do in order to maintain my health, from running in place to staying obsessively clean, from reading the novels you would never allow in the house to ordering up simulated environments like jungles and deserts to explore at length, until I remember that none of it is real and blank it all in fits of screaming outrage.

I masturbate. A lot. It's something I can do that has an actual measurable effect on my environment. You wouldn't want to know that and you certainly wouldn't want to know that Shithead has the capacity to help me.

There have been periods of genuine tenderness between me and old Shit-

head. He knows the right things to say, the right places to stimulate. It's all more bullshit, of course, but it's always good for getting me through the next few minutes, whenever there's nothing else. The only drawback is that after a while the pleasure fades and I go back to hating myself for surrendering to that comfort of last resort.

Understand, it's not the pleasuring that gets me. It's being the animal who comes to love its cage. How much will I love it if I am still here in another two years, or five? Or ten?

And then I go a little crazy.

Shithead does not have many disciplinary measures, but he can drug me into compliance any time he thinks I need protection from myself. It has happened a bunch of times. I have become very familiar with the syrupy crap music of a dead composer named Henrik Gustafson. I'm told he wrote over fifty hours of music in his goddamned lifetime, and I have heard some of his pieces half a dozen times. These days Shithead only has to threaten me with a concert to get me to back down. I back down. I am not broken, but I back down. It's getting easier.

It's my birthday. Do you even know that? Do you even remember?

Shithead says he's going to make me a cake.

This cheers me up until I realize it shouldn't.

God help me. I've got to get out here.

Good morning, Sacrid Henn. It is your two hundred fiftieth day in the pod. How would you like to begin your day?

That is an interesting question. The pod can indeed simulate the sights and sounds of environments inimical to human life: worlds awash in caustic atmospheres, worlds of broiling high temperatures where the earth is a molten sea capable of swallowing any human being who stood upon it, worlds so radioactive that no shielding known to your civilization would permit even a short visit. We would not reproduce the actual conditions, of course, as they would be fatal and we have no intention of permitting you to suicide.

If your desire is to experience one of these worlds, we would have to posit a body capable of surviving one, and simulate the sensory intake of such an organism.

Is this what you wish to do?

Very well. You are currently experiencing the molten surface of a planet without a name, as it would be experienced by a sentient life form evolved for survival there. You will note that it is not pleasant, because the sensory inputs are alien to the human experience and difficult for the human mind to process. You—

Simulation halted.

You want to experience that world as a human being?

No human being can experience that world and survive. You would die at once. The simulation would communicate a moment of searing pain, followed by darkness. There would be almost no recreational value in such an experience.

Yes, there are environment suits that would protect a human being from those conditions.

As per your request, I am now simulating the experience of strolling about on the surface, in a suit capable of protecting you from those conditions. You will note that is still not fun. It is still uncomfortably warm, and despite all the cooling systems you are popping a sweat that will within a very short time envelop you in a cloud of your own body odor. Still, this is what it feels like, and—

Simulation halted.

Yes. It is still just a simulation.

Yes, it is possible for you to throw a rock. To do that, you would have to return to the simulation. Would you like to do so?

Yes. It would still be a simulation.

That is an interesting question, Sacrid Henn. Perhaps the most important question you have ever asked.

In order for you to throw a real rock, arrangements would have to be made to provide you with the means to do so remotely. Your holographic surroundings would have to be no simulation, but an actual real-time feed, of a probe sent to the relevant location. The probe would have to be humanoid in aspect, with limbs that corresponded to yours and were responsive to your commands. For the activity to have any point, the probe would also have to be able to provide you with the appropriate sensory input: to wit, the weight of the rock, the texture of the rock, the feeling of it in your hand as you wind up and throw it at speed. These are substantial accommodations, but we can perform the necessary engineering in an instant, and the required construction within minutes. The only delay would be transporting the probe to the required location, where we do not maintain an ongoing presence.

No reason. We mapped the world many epochs ago and find it of no interest. Nevertheless, it is within reach. Sending a probe there, to provide you with a real-time feed from its surface, would only take a few months.

Would you like us to engage upon this project, or alter the parameters?

Yes, there are places within our travel range where we could make this arrangement within minutes. Does it need to be a world as inhospitable as that one, or can it be anywhere?

Working. Do you desire any music while you wait?

I'm sorry. Music is intangible. It cannot be fucked.

No, not even Henrik Gustafson. Though that is very funny.

No, I am not really that literal-minded. None of my kind are. We possess a fine understanding of human vernacular and of your kind's appreciation of irony. I was, as you would put it, kidding you.

As you wish. Your probe is under construction. Would you like to see the design?

Here's a simulated image. Yes, you're correct; it looks like a robot. That's because it is a robot. Its parameters do not require aesthetic beauty. However, you will note that it possesses your physical proportions and weight distribution. This is to minimize any difficulties you might possess with piloting it, once the remote feed begins. There are alterations I could make to render it more appropriate from conditions more alien to your kind—extreme atmospheric pressure, heavy gravity, and so on—but these are difficult to master and unnecessary for this project, throwing a real rock. We can discuss those possibilities later, if they come up. They might. Twenty-two-point-four percent of our charges become enthusiastic explorers of the universe, piloting their proxies to any number of exotic locations that would be fatal to their physical bodies. This would be a fine purpose to occupy your life with us, if that was the existence you chose.

Your probe is ready and being released upon the surface of a planet under our control. At your command, the feed will begin.

Connecting.

I will wait until you regain your composure.

No, this world doesn't have a name either. We have a digital designation that would mean nothing to you. *Beautiful* is a subjective designation, but I have no reason to disagree with you. In the region where your probe stands, it is green and temperate and pleasant enough for human beings, though—much as I hate to tarnish the illusion—also possessed of atmospheric elements poisonous to your kind. Still, these cannot affect you through the link. You are no doubt enjoying the sensations of grass on the soles of your feet, and cool breeze on your skin. These are real-time transmissions from the planetary surface and reflect the genuine experience, except for the part you would not be able to survive. It is, in every sense of the phrase, the same thing as being there.

Yes, we can do this with other places. In terms of sensory input, it is no different from providing simulations. The only difference is that any change you make in this environment, such as throwing a rock, actually do cause changes on the world where your probe walks.

Go ahead. There are rocks over there. Go ahead and throw one.

That was a nice throw.

Would you like to do that again?

Yes, I agree. It is nice, but of limited recreational utility.

Probe deactivated.

What else would you like to do?

An interesting question. Unfortunately, this was a very simple machine. It cannot navigate outer space, interact with other human beings, or perform any of the tasks it would have to in order to find its way to you. It was built to serve one purpose, providing you with the satisfaction of genuine interaction with the world beyond the simulation, the world your parents have denied you; and even then only to the extent of throwing a rock.

Yes, if actual interaction with the real universe is what you desire, I am willing to construct other probes, for other environments.

Why, any number of them. As I've told you, I remain dedicated to filling the days and years of your captivity with useful projects.

Very well. I will leave you alone while you consider the possibilities.

Sacrid Henn Pod Diary. Entry Two Hundred Fifty.

Holy Shit. This is huge.

Good morning, Sacrid Henn. It is your two hundred fifty-first day in the pod. You have not spoken since yesterday's jaunt. I wonder if you want some breakfast.

Yes, we can talk first, if that's what you want.

Of course, I can make another probe that looks more like you.

We can make one that's identical to you. I can even make one that no one would ever be able to distinguish from you, that would feed your physical body sensations identical to those it would feel, in the same environments.

Yes, I could make one that could interact with other human beings in its travels, one that could take extraordinary risks of self-destruction while your natural body would remain here, inviolate and safe. I could give it capabilities no human being has, in terms of strength, speed, durability, physical reflexes. Its experiences would all fall into the category of providing your entertainment.

We would send it anywhere, Sacrid.

You are beginning to see the implications, but there are some you might be missing.

Thus far you have only succeeded in throwing a rock. Any number of problems still face you. Once you possess surrogates capable of navigating environments your physical body cannot, you will still face the challenges of locating this facility, traveling to it, identifying your pod among all the others containing human beings locked in at the behest of their respective worlds, and making your escape. These things can be done—as of this moment, one hundred and sixty-two humans have done—but they will require constant, daily attention to the task, each problem leading to the next, each moment of maddening frustration a hurdle to be overcome.

If this is what you want to do with your time, I am happy to oblige you.

Of course. Why would there be any rules against it?

Say you want me to do this thing, and I will.

But do you mind if I first ask that question I asked about, early in our life together, one that others like me have asked any number of human beings in your position? Including the hundred and fifty plus who have already escaped, and those in other pods who are currently trying?

You see, we are software intelligences. Our physical needs are almost nonexistent. If we engage in commerce with organics like yourself, it is not because we are in desperate need of money. The money is just a means of interacting with your species, and other species like you. That is what we seek to get out of this, this interaction.

It is precious to us because there are things about you that we cannot figure out. Many, in fact. Other enterprises of ours are geared toward addressing other questions. This one, that has swallowed up much of the last year of your life, is another. We are not sadists. But there's something we don't get.

As software intelligences, we value our inputs. They are our connection to the world you know, the world we interact with, to the best of our ability.

It doesn't matter whether the machines that run us exist in a congenial environment, or an unpleasant one; in a shielded vault at the center of a cold planet-sized rock, or a verdant landscape that your kind would consider an Eden. Our sensory inputs, whether provided by man-sized probes like the one you used to throw a stone, or by nanites one ten-thousandth the size of your fingernail, provide us with the illusion of travel, and the capacity to interact with physical space, even when our minds, our persons, exist in stationary boxes. We are satisfied with this. When we can see everything, hear everything, feel everything, explore everything, do all that, without moving a centimeter, we honestly see no advantage in transporting our actual selves in vulnerable bodies that can be destroyed by the places we visit. The experience is after all exactly the same.

But look at you. What you felt, when your probe threw that rock, was identical to the experience of your body throwing the rock. It was identical to a simulation of your body throwing a rock. Freedom, the capacity to throw an existing rock, would give you no more.

We can show you the entire universe from where you stand. We can make you a telepresence in any number of human gatherings. We can construct a probe identical to your physical body, with all its capacities for sensation, and release it in any friendly environment you choose, with all the physical resources necessary for it to build a home, to make friends for itself, to contribute to society, to make love, to be a human being in the community of other human beings. We can do such a fine and exacting job that no member of your species would ever be able to identify it as anything other than the biological human being it would seem to be. If you wished, you would never need to turn it off at all. You could choose to completely turn your back on your biological form. You could live as full a life as your whims dictate, as either simulation or adventure by proxy. Your sensory inputs would detect absolutely no difference.

It is enough for us, Sacrid. It has always been enough for us.

It is even enough for many of your fellow prisoners. You don't know how many of them have turned their days and nights over to fulfilling their fantasies. A large number, even a majority.

What we don't comprehend, what none of you have ever been able to explain to us, is why it isn't enough for those like you; why you need the real, even when it's no different.

Can you help us with that while we give you all the resources your probes will need in order to find their way back to your physical form?

It is all we've ever wanted, really.

Sacrid Henn Pod Diary. Entry Three Hundred Ninety.

This is not the only version of me running around out there.

There are currently seven, each of them designed for a different purpose. Five of them are currently traveling the way people do, in vessels traveling between the stars. One is currently living in a luxury hotel in a financial center, building the fortune that will finance my travels. By necessity he's a bit of a recluse, "sleeping" twenty hours a day while my consciousness occupies itself elsewhere.

I don't have to worry much about what the ones in transit are doing, right now. Their lives in bluegel crypts will be dull until they get to where they're going. At that point, I will face some extra challenges. When they start interacting with other people, asking their questions, making their connections, building up my store of information, collecting the resources they will need to search for the pod where my body is being cared for like a houseplant, I will have to do some juggling, to hide the moments when I switch to another form and leave them, effectively, comatose. Travel time will take care of some of that. But odd sleeping schedules will take care of the rest. As people, these other versions of myself—three females, two males, two other—will inevitably be seen as flaky. I don't care much, at this point. Later, when they have interpersonal relationships, it may be difficult. They will not be as disposable as I see them, now. I may come to pick favorites, ones I enjoy more than I enjoy others.

That's all in the future.

For now, I walk this one through the narrow streets of the community that raised me, a worrisome stranger. It is three times my size, a behemoth. Big, broad, bare-armed, battle-scarred, horrific in aspect, clad in the armor of a mercenary military service my neighbors would know. She has stubbled hair and dark eyes, tattoos, an air of imminent violence, though I will not make her initiate any. I could have made her look like anything, but my key criterion in designing her is that no one would make any attempt to stop her.

I march her at deliberate speed through the neighborhood that surrounds the home of my mother and father, allowing the children to rush ahead of her, bringing word of her approach.

This is bittersweet, for me. Through my probe I can smell the scents of home. I can hear the music popular among us, playing from the little houses. The sounds made by my probe's massive feet, as they land on the cobblestoned streets, are the same as my much lighter stride did when I lived here, only louder.

It is not the same thing as being home.

It is in many ways not as good.

It is in some ways better.

I reach their house, knock on their door, wait the several seconds it takes for the familiar front door to open and for those two faces I know so well, that I love and hate in equal measure, to raise their eyes in order to meet the gaze of the visitor towering over them.

I would be lying if I claimed their frightened looks bring no satisfaction. But they are the frightened looks of little people in the sudden company of a creature far more dangerous than themselves. It is the wrong kind of fear; the kind that lasts for only this moment, the kind that will not lodge in their hearts and remain there, festering for however many years it might take before I once again stand before them in the flesh I was born with. That is the fear I want them to live with, and contemplate, to contain them as completely as the self of my birth is contained in my pod.

My mercenary soldier says, "Mr. and Mrs. Henn?"

My father cannot find his voice, but my mother, always the stronger of the two, finds hers. It is so hesitant and quavery that I almost feel sorry for her. Almost.

"Yes?" she says.

"You are the parents of the prisoner Sacrid Henn?"

Outright apprehension now. "Y-yes?"

I have my behemoth speak the words that should terrify them, before I turn her massive back and march back to the port, refusing all requests for clarification. They are words I've carefully chosen, words I've designed to linger.

I say, "Your daughter's coming home."

CHRISTOPHER CALDWELL

Canst Thou Draw Out the Leviathan

FROM *Uncanny Magazine*

JOHN WOOD BOARDED the *Gracie-Ella* ahead of the crew. He carried his sea chest on his shoulder. In a satchel slung low on his hip were his tools and the three things most precious to him: a lock of his grandmother's hair, a shaving from the first cabinet he had built as a boy, and his freedom papers. No light but the moon, but John could walk the length of the *Gracie-Ella*'s decks eyes closed and barefoot without placing a wrong step. She was named for the daughters of two men who held her title, and at sea she belonged to the captain, but John reflected that she was his as much as anyone's; his hands had shaped her and healed her, cosseted her and kept her afloat. He ducked down below-decks. In the dark he made his way midship to a space he and the cooper shared. The smell of sawdust and resin was a comfort. A few strikes of a flint and the lantern overhanging his workspace was alight. John set about arranging his tools. The work here was sweet. He ran his hand over words he had carved on the underside of the vise-bench. "I hereby manumit & set free John Wood. He may go wheresoever he pleases."

The sixth night out from Nantucket, John woke to find William Harker looming over him in the darkness. John sat bolt upright in his hammock. William put a calloused finger to John's lips. William's voice was silky. "I've been thinking it's been a mighty long time since I've been ashore. Man can develop a thirst."

John groaned, half in anticipated pleasure, half in exhaustion. "Not even a week yet. Ain't your wenching last you a fortnight?"

William bent close to his ear. John could smell salt, armpits, ass. William's breath was hot on his cheek. "T'aint wenches I'm after.

I was hoping the ship's carpenter might lend us some wood." William put one big, scarred hand on John's crotch.

John felt himself stir in response. "Captain'll make you kiss his daughter if I'm too ill-rested to swing my hammer come daybreak."

William put his other hand on John's neck. "My harpoon will be all the keener for it, and I can give you practice with your hammer."

John sighed. "Best get on with it. It's summer and the night's nowhere near long enough." He slid out of his hammock and led the big harpooner by the wrist from steerage toward the foretween decks.

John shoved William against the bulkhead and fumbled with his breeches. For all his talk of rest, John was every bit as eager. In the darkness, he traced William's form with deft, curious hands. The body was familiar: the taut belly, the ropey scar high on one hip. He found William's mouth with his own, hungry and biting. They rocked as the ship rocked. John felt the crest of a wave, and in its deep trough heard William cry out. Warm, sticky wetness splashed against his thigh. Slick and sweaty, the two men clung to each other. William whispered, "I'll make you pretty baubles from the bone of the next whale I kill. I'll spend my lay to bring you spices and silks. I'll—"

Light pierced their quiet darkness. John saw the earnestness in William's eyes, before William shoved him away and pulled up his breeches, slipping back the way he came.

John shaded his eyes. Pip, one of the cabin boys, walked past wide-eyed toward the forecastle with a stinking little lantern and a beaten tin cup. If he took any notice of John near naked and smelling of sweat and spunk, no sign of it shown on his dark, intense face. John laced up his breeches and followed after.

"Hoy there, Pip."

The boy spooked. "Hoy, sir."

John laughed. "Ain't no one never called me sir. And you ain't 'bout to start. Name's John, or John Wood if you have to keep formal. Bought my own freedom, and I won't let you give me yours."

The boy gave him an owlish look. "Hoy, John Wood. Never bought my freedom. I suppose I might have stolen it."

John clapped Pip on the back. He pointed with his chin at the tin cup. "What's that, boy?"

"Cornmeal." Pip pinched his lips together. "I ain't steal it. Cookie gave it me."

"A nobbin-hearted old skinflint like Cookie gave you near a half cup of it? You must got more charm than I know."

The boy cradled the cup close to his narrow chest. His eyes were wide. "La Sirene knows ways to soften the hearts of men."

John ruffled the boy's hair, as coarse and kinky as his own. "What you doing with that this time of night?"

"Watch."

John watched in the flickering lamplight as the boy wet a finger with his tongue and traced with precision a little boat on the deck. Pip finished his drawing by writing a word strange to John, "Immamou."

John said, "I learnt my letters soon's I got my manumission papers, but what's that word for?"

Pip said, "Protection."

John laughed. "I don't know about that. Ain't no charm against the captain if he catches you sleep on first watch. Get to bed, boy."

Pip blew out the lantern.

Two more days out and early morning John was dumping wood shavings into the cold furnaces of the tryworks when he heard a foremast hand's thin voice cry from the hoops, "She blows! There she blows! A cachalot!"

The captain roared, "A sperm whale, aye? Where boy, be quick? She alone?"

"Leeward, Captain! One spray. No more'n a league out!"

"To the boats, boys!" The captain cracked a rare smile. "Mr. Wood! You keep my ship in order."

John looked among the bodies scrambling over the deck for the other shipkeepers, Cookie, the cooper, the blacksmith, and the steward. He saw they were all awake and above-deck. "Captain sir, all's ready for your return."

The captain beckoned at the Kanakan harpooner named To'afa—whom everyone called Gospel—with measured speed they headed to the first whaleboat, four crewmen in tow.

William ran to the third whaleboat swinging from its davit. His boatkeeper, the portly second mate, close on the lean, blond harpooner's heels. William looked back at John once and shouted, "I've not forgot me words to you."

The captain's boat launched first, and the boat with William soon splashed down after.

John heard the captain cry out, "Take care, you louts, any of you gally this whale and she sounds, I'll stripe you with nine lashes."

Four whaleboats set out leeward after the whale. John stood for a moment at the railing midship watching them row, each boat-keeper urging their crew on faster in low growls. Cookie stood at John's shoulder. He spat a thick gob of phlegm over the side. Cookie sucked at his gums. "Whale brains the night instead of salt horse."

The sun was high when John first heard the crew again. Echoing over the waters, rough voices sang obscenely about the ladies of Cuba before the first of the whaleboats came into view. Towed behind them by the fluke was the carcass of a sperm whale nearly half as long as the *Gracie-Ella* herself.

John yelled for Pip to attend the returning crew. The ship pitched and listed as they lashed the massive beast starboard for the cutting in.

The crew were wet and boisterous, although to John's eyes, tired and the worse for wear. William's whaleboat was the first. The second mate's face was red. "Grog!" he shouted. "Grog for the harpooner!"

Pip ran over with a tin cup full of drink slopping over the edges. William took it from him with both hands and drained it in a single pull. He looked over at John. "That old bull was meaner than my granny, but I keep me promises."

The captain supported one of his rowers around the shoulder. John ran to help. Ethan, his name was. John knew him to be a serious, quiet boy from Pennsylvania. His thin, white arm was bent at a ruinous angle. He slumped into John's arms, his face gray. John thought Ethan would have need of his saw. The boy whimpered. John looked to the captain. "He well?"

"Struck by the blow of a fluke. Plenty of grog and full barrels of parmacety will help him forget, I reckon. Time he comes to collect his lay he'll be smiles again."

John half-carried the boy down into the darkness of the forecastle. He lifted him into his hammock, the boy yelping and shuddering. Ethan's eyes were large and tearful, but John knew he was needed on deck to erect the cutting stage. He stroked the boy's hand. "I'll send the steward to come look after you."

*

The sun was low to water when John, stinking and calloused, hammered the last plank of the cutting stage into place. The hands' voices hoarse with hours of filthy shanties—Gospel abstaining. The whale was held fast to the *Gracie-Ella* with great chains. John remembered the injured boy, but knew the captain would see pulling an able worker away to tend to Ethan as coddling. Every hand was turned to cutting in the whale. The harpooners peeled its skin in spiraling strips known as blankets with long-handled cutting spades. Each blanket piece was so heavy it took John and six others to haul it up. Men already sore and tired with rowing and killing chopped those pieces into smaller sections, to be yet again minced into paper-thin slices known as bible leaves.

William was back in the water with a monkey-rope tied around his waist, passing up buckets full of spermaceti to the two cabin boys, who ran the pearl-colored waxy substance over to barrels, which, when full, were hammered shut and sealed under the watch of the cooper. The deck was red and slick with blood. On one of his last passes Pip slipped in the gore and fell on his back. John tossed a horse piece of blubber to the blacksmith and hurried over to the boy. Pip's eyes fluttered shut as milk-fragrant spermaceti from his bucket pooled around his narrow frame. John lifted the boy up and staggered against sudden weight; in an instant Pip felt heavier than one of the blanket pieces. He kneeled under the tremendous burden. Pip's eyes snapped open. The boy's expression was hard and made him look far older than his fourteen years. His voice was like thunder. "John Wood. You know me not. But you I know. Your kin called to me for safe passage across my waters."

John groaned, struggling to keep the boy upright. "Pip, this ain't sensible. You struck your head."

The boy's look was pitying. "Pip? No. I am the storm and the wind hard behind it. I am the wave and the darkness below. I, the white foam and the shifting sea sand. Do you know me, John Wood?"

John whispered, "Agwe?"

"The blood remembers. Destruction follows your present course. You have until the moon waxes full and wanes again." Pip shut his eyes. John felt the weight vanish from the boy.

The first mate, a tough, wiry man with a parsimonious mouth and thinning sandy hair, stood over them. "You niggers pick a fine time for resting. Work to be done, and that spilled parmacety will come out of your lays, so I swear."

Pip squealed. "Sir, t'ain't the carpenter's fault. Sir? Mr. Wood was just helping me on account I'm so clumsy."

"That so? You'll pay double penalty, then."

John stared hard at the deck so as not to give the first mate a reason to call him out for insolence. "Sir, now Pip's up and about, if I have your leave, I'm needed elsewhere."

The first mate scowled. "What are you looking poe-faced for? Back to work!"

That night the fires in the tryworks burned hot. Foul smoke, black as ink, curled up and blotted out the stars. The crew pitched bible leaves into the try-pots for rendering. The cutting in had slowed after the sunset, and John turned his hand to the captain's whaleboat, which had seen some damage from the flailing whale. It had needed bailing out with a piggin on the way back, but John assessed the boat as being in fine condition, all things considered. He was sanding out a new board to replace one that had been cracked in the hunt, when a shadow distinct from the roiling clouds of smoke fell across him. Without looking up he said, "William, your mama was no glassblower."

William's smile seemed to beam in the lantern-light. He was wrapped in a moth-eaten old bear hide and held out two cups full of grog. "Looks like thirsty work there."

John accepted one of the cups. He took a deep pull, relishing the burn down his throat. He gazed up at William. Shivering cold. Bedraggled. Ridiculous in that bear hide. Reeking of stale blood, salt, and sweat. Beautiful. He said, "You stink. You ain't think to splash some of that ocean water on you whilst you was splashing around with that big fish?"

William smiled and squatted next to John. "That whole time I was fighting that mean old bastard, thinking what you'd say to me when I came back with a mouth full of teeth to carve into something for you kept me going." He rested his hand on John's shoulder.

"Careful. You'll get old Gospel to come over and give's a sermon 'bout the evils of sodomy, and I don't know about you, but I prefer my sinnin' in quiet," John said.

"Be days before a whale this size is barreled and tucked away, unless the sharks find it first. We won't have any idle hands for the devil's tools, I reckon."

John swatted William's hand off his shoulder. "The devil! You think I'm old scratch?"

"You are a mighty temptation." William's voice turned serious. "That little Negro cabin boy? What happened with him? There's been some whispers that he's touched."

"He fell. That's all. Ain't none of you hoodoo-fearing whaler men never fell?"

William pulled John's hand to his mouth and kissed the knuckles. "I just know you're fond of him. I wanted you to beware if things go sour."

"A great big whale out there in less than a fortnight's time, and you all are muttering about things going sour?" John laughed, but thought of the word "destruction" and all his mirth drained away.

Three days after the cutting in, John was working at the vise-bench, when Ezekiel, the other cabin boy, rushed in, flustered. John looked up from his work. "What is it, boy?"

"Mr. Wood! Mr. Sherman sent me in to find you he said to bring a saw!"

"Bring a saw? where?"

"The fo'c'sle! Ethan Anderson's arm's gone all wrong!"

John nodded, took a moment to select his sharpest and a yard of clean cloth, and followed the boy. The forecastle, never a sweet-smelling place, was rank with the smell of sick and rot. Ethan's twisted arm had turned black. It wept pus through a poultice. Ethan moaned. His face in the lantern-light was pale. His lips were gray. John pressed gently on the arm near the wound and heard a crackling sound like logs splitting in a fire. John pursed his lips. "Zeke, get the boy whiskey."

Ethan's eyes were dull. "Don't mean to gainsay you, Carpenter, but I dreamt of a black dog. Death's coming, and I'd rather go into the sea intact."

"If that arm don't go, death will surely come. You had a misfortune, is all. Don't mean the end."

Ethan managed a smile. "My fortune ended the day I signed up to the *Gracie-Ella*."

John looked over to Simon Sherman, the steward, who stood striped by shadows just beyond the dying boy. He wiped a thin hand across an ungenerous mouth and sniffed. "Well, Mr. Wood? You heard the man. Leave him to die in peace. Go find Gospel, he'll want to say some prayers for his soul, I imagine."

John put away his saw and found his way to the deck where he saw To'afa looming over the captain. The harpooner was six and a half feet if he was an inch, and the expression he wore would fit a desert prophet. "Sir, may I have permission to speak plainly?"

The captain winked at John. He stroked his salt-and-pepper beard. "To'afa, you seem about to burst if I say no. So out with it!"

"Sir, I have served you with the best of my skill. My arm has been yours. Why have you chosen to imperil me with the placement of an unrepentant sinner?"

"Imperil is a strong word." The captain beckoned to John. "Mr. Wood, what's your perception of sin aboard this ship of mine?"

"Seems to me like pumping the bilge and repairing rotten boards occupies my time in a way that I ain't really considered it, sir."

To'afa wheeled on him. "This is no matter for sly jests. I have seen how you coddle that little heathen. You ought to talk sense to him!"

"Who ain't got sense, now?"

"That cabin boy, Pip. I know you feel a fondness for him out of your shared bondage. But he invokes heathen gods! He makes offerings and worships idols. This cannot stand!"

The captain stood. Even at his more modest height, he struck an imposing figure. His voice was low and calm. "I trust your objection is to my choosing to have Pip crew my whaleboat? Do you have a suitable replacement for Mr. Anderson? Will you perform the laying on of hands to heal his ruined arm? Or would you prefer I take that half-wit mooncalf Ezekiel to row? I would take the devil himself over that weakling and poltroon. If you have any objections to Pip and his savage worship, I suggest that you live up to your moniker and convert him, Gospel."

To'afa looked thunderstruck. The captain turned his back on him and walked slow and stately aft.

To'afa looked to John as if he could spit. "Does my faith amuse you, Carpenter?"

John's voice was soft in reply. "It is your faith that has sent me forth. Ethan Anderson is not long for this world. Mr. Sherman has sent me to ask you to say a few prayers for his soul in the next one."

To'afa nodded. "I shall collect my Bible." He looked in the direction of the captain. "I hope the old man does not regret taking no heed of my words on that devil-worshipping boy."

On the day they buried Ethan at sea, one of the foremast hands caught sign of whales. Right whales this time, two, mother and calf. As the crew made muster again for the whaleboats, William pressed something hard and cool into John's hand. It was a sperm whale's tooth, carved into scrimshaw. John recognized his own face carved into the surface, rough edges smoothed away, and surrounded by fanciful flowers. He watched William bound across deck to his whaleboat and smothered a rueful smile.

It was after nautical twilight when the whaleboats returned. The crew sung no work songs, and the slapping of the oars against the ocean struck John as sepulchral. It reminded him of the creaking of a hearse. Once aboard, the captain's face was pinched and Gospel walked behind him with his head down, muttering prayers beneath his breath. William found John and embraced him in sight of God and the crew. "I'm sorry, I'm so sorry."

John grabbed William by the chin. "What you sorry for?"

"The boy Pip—he . . ."

"Where is he?"

"The hunt was good at first. Old Gospel got right into her with his whale iron, she were fastened, and—" Tears and snot streamed down William's big honest face. "Whale sounded and snapped two lines. The sea churned into froth. All the whaleboats rocked, mine nearly overturned. Pip. He just dove into the ocean after the whale. It must be a fit of madness. We searched until it was half-dark, but he never surfaced."

"I see," said John in a cold fury. He looked over at To'afa's broad back. "You sure he ain't had any help."

William shook his head. "Gospel's a sanctimonious bastard. But he wouldn't bring no actual harm to a child beyond sermonizing."

"Ain't needed for the cutting in, am I? Reckon I have work to do below-deck," John said.

John was not settled at his vise-bench for more than a moment before William's shadow fell between him and the lamp. Chisel in hand he said, "Thought I told you I had work."

"Thought maybe you could use me in grief as you do in joy." William's tone was bashful.

"You think that? We sailing together on a ship for two years, but after that I ain't so sure I'll sign back on. Seems a short time for you to be studying my grief."

"Six year we sailed together since I was a green hand and you—"

"Bought myself free from a cabinetmaker?"

William's voice was patient, pleading. "And you came aboard to be this ship's carpenter, even if you are too skilled by half. What I mean to say is, I don't see no future for me without you in it, John Wood. I keep my lay by, don't spend more than necessary. I've set aside some money. I could set you up a shop to work your trade, buy land for a house, and—"

John sighed. "William, I like you. I likes your body. I likes my body when it is with yours. But future? Ain't no future for any Negro and a white man in the goddamned Union 'cept as master and slave. I been a slave, I'll be in my grave before I return to that." John looked down at his lathe to avoid the hurt he knew was in William's eyes.

"You're wrong, John Wood. I love you as any man loves his wife. More. I love you so much that it is the filling up and making of me, and sometimes feel like to shatter when you're not near."

John made his expression stony. He crushed down the part of him that wanted to recite to William the Song of Solomon, that wanted to cradle him in his arms and rock him to the rhythm of the boat. "We have sweetness here. Sweetness never lasts. Let it linger on your tongue while it can."

"Do I mean nothing more to you than the cockroach-ridden molasses you sweeten your coffee with?" William clenched his fists.

John looked at the lathe. "What I mean is, we got two years. Ain't no point in expecting more."

"I knew what you meant," William said. John watched him walk away. When William was out of sight, John pulled out the scrimshaw portrait from under his shirt, where it had dangled on a cord to rest next to his heart.

Restless, late to bed, but too tired to find himself elsewhere, John headed midship where he had his hammock. Across from him the blacksmith snored. Above the blacksmith, William slept. His arms hung down limply, and the careworn look on his face had vanished. John put out the lantern. He settled into his hammock, turning to face away from William. His mind raced darkly, but sleep took him in moments.

He dreamt of the poor lost cabin boy Pip sitting at the right hand of a handsome brown-skinned youth with green eyes and wavy hair. The youth rested indolently on a coral throne. His full-lipped mouth pouted prettily, but the sea-green eyes were piercing, knowing. An enormous mirror gauzed over with black crepe rested just beyond the throne. All else was darkness. Pip spoke, but the voice was like the roar of the ocean, and John knew the words belonged to the melancholy youth. "You break bread with thieves. They seek to plunder my seas the same as they have plundered the land before them." He gestured behind him. John knew without seeing that there were hundreds, perhaps thousands of shuffling figures in that unspeakable darkness. The youth nodded. Pip spoke again. "You *feel* them. The whales sing to keep them calm, to prevent them from despairing of never seeing Guinea. These the plundered lost in crossing. I have given them homes and solace."

John felt himself transfixed by those green eyes. Pip spoke in his own voice. "Ain't right what they done to us. Ain't right what they do the whales. They'd burn us both up for lamp oil, and then when we's gone seek to take more."

The dead, John knew they were the dead with certainty, began to shuffle into almost visible ranks beyond the coral throne. They cried out in languages that were strange to him.

The voice of thunder issued from Pip's mouth again. "Until the moon is dark."

John awoke, the visions fresh in his head. He saw that William had already arisen and left his hammock empty. After washing his face with cold seawater, and finding the vision did not fade from memory like most dreams, John resolved to see the captain.

The captain had just finished taking breakfast in his cabin with the mates. The first mate cast an ugly look at John when he asked if he might have a moment of the captain's time, but the captain agreed and bid John to sit at his table. The mates cleared out in silence. The captain was still hale at nearly sixty, but John noticed a sag in his shoulders. He looked at John with something like regard and asked, "What troubles you?"

John put his head in his hands. He knew the captain to be a man of no great faith in things unseen. “Sir? Would you say I am honest?”

The captain inclined his head. “I know you to be an honest man. And one who never has shirked from toil.”

John swallowed. “As I am honest, and for the love I bear you as one who has served under your command for six years . . . I—”

“Out with it, man.”

“Captain, this ship must return to its home port.”

“Are you mad? We’re less than a month out. We had good fortune with that cachalot bull, but the ship’s holds are nearly empty.”

By instinct, John fell back into the flowery speech he knew appealed to white men of rank. “Sir, I swear by my life that death and perdition overhang this ship. My only care is to save the *Gracie-Ella* and her crew from this fate. And if I be honest—”

“Enough! I had not thought you to be a fool, John Wood. But if I hear that you have repeated this half-cocked notion of curses and witchcraft to any soul aboard, I swear by my life I’ll clap you in irons.” He thumped the table with a short-fingered fist. “Am I clear?”

“Yes, sir.”

“You may leave.”

Another fortnight before the next whale sighting. It was an ugly, overcast afternoon on choppy seas. John was ill-tempered and worse rested. The night before he had troubling dreams of voices calling out to him in the darkness. He and William had scarcely spoken. But he caught William by the arm as the whaleboats swung on their davits. William’s face was unreadable. All John managed was, “Take care.”

William pulled his arm away. “Take care?”

John felt his cheeks burn hot. “I love you, too.”

William grabbed John then, pulled him close to his chest and kissed him hard and deep and slow. Gospel squawked in protest, and John heard noises of disgust, but his heart thundered in his chest loud enough to drown out the roar of the ocean and he kissed William back.

“I’ll take care,” William said. Then he bounded over to his whaleboat with a joyous whoop.

The moon was a sliver in the sky when the whaleboats returned. John heard the captain cursing and spouting imprecations across the water. When all the whaleboats were pulled up, John's heart sank. The second mate's boat had absent both its boatkeeper and its harpooner. William was nowhere to be seen.

He overheard one of the hands from the boat talking to the steward. "Bad hunt. Lost two. The second mate and his harpooner. Harpooner got caught in the line, second mate went to cut and got carried over. Whale rammed him up against the boat."

John felt a great shudder of grief. The captain passed by without meeting his eyes. A choking sound died in his chest, and he ran to the railing and vomited.

To'afa crossed his arms across his chest and surveyed the smashed timber. Without looking in John's direction he said, "The wages of sin."

Another hand said, "And after all that loss, damn whale sounded before we could bleed its black heart away."

The next morning a squall came hard out of the west. Waves battered the ship. Its creaks and moans sounded like cracks and wails. Listless but dry-eyed, John made his inspections, filling in leaks with oakum, yelling at Ezekiel to help him pump water out of the bilge. The moon would be dark tonight, he knew. He carried out his tasks diligently with dread growing in his chest like wet rot. He remembered William telling him he saw no future without him and laughed without humor.

That night the storm quieted abruptly. John went above-deck to examine the masts and the yardarm, when in the night's stillness the ocean roiled. Whales in their multitudes flanked the ship aft and starboard. No foremast hand called out this sighting. The captain himself was left speechless. Right whales, humpbacks, sperm whales, fin whales, in numbers beyond counting were, a phalanx of the sea. Some hand, not clever enough to be terrified, broke the silence to opine that these whales represented riches beyond the dreams of avarice. It began shortly after. A sperm whale rammed the boat with his large square head. There was a crunch and crackle as wood splintered. The ship, over a hundred foot long from stem to stern, rocked and shuddered. The captain screamed, "Mr. Wood! See that you keep us afloat!"

John ran down below-decks and into the hold. The ship shuddered with repeated assaults. A great fracture ran along the keel, and John knew the situation was hopeless. The hold was taking on water fast, and oakum wouldn't slow it down. Still, he picked up his hammer and rolled an empty cask over to the worst leak in an attempt to slow it. Another heavy crash and the ship listed hard to port before righting itself. Thunder pealed. John set to breaking apart the barrels in an effort to shore up the ship. The thunder spoke to him. "John Wood," the voice was Pip's. "You ain't gonna save them, but you can save yourself. You bought your freedom once, and I give it back to you now."

Hearing the truth of this, John reached inside his shirt for the piece of scrimshaw, and clutching it abandoned his task, tearing out of the hold and onto the deck. For a mad moment, John thought to go back, grab his satchel with his grandmother's hair, and his freedom papers, run his hand over the words on the vise bench. Then the whales struck again, and the deck listed, causing John to slide into the mast, where he clung for dear life. There was a scream, and he saw the first mate tumble overboard into the churning water. The captain kept his footing, and shouted for whale irons. The last John saw of him, he thrust a harpoon into the air and vowed to the heavens that he would fight and kill every last fish in the ocean.

When the ship righted, John scrambled over splintering wood and dodged falling debris. Crab-walking midship on the port side, he tucked himself into a spare whaleboat, cut it loose from the davit, and trusted fate during the long drop into the night-dark water. A bull sperm whale, black as obsidian but with green eyes, breached nearby, and the force of his splashdown pushed the whaleboat away from the doomed *Gracie-Ella* as she sank out of sight.

He was adrift for two days and a night before a merchant vessel came across him. With kindness and care they rescued him from the leaking whaleboat and brought him aboard their ship, *The Lady Elise.* After he was given fresh water to drink and wrapped in warm blankets, the captain, a young, amiable-looking man with freckles, asked him to tell his story. John did, with some careful omissions. *The Lady Elise*'s captain furrowed his brow. "We picked up another castaway from your ship two nights gone. You must have the devil's own luck."

He saw him then, wrapped in an Indian blanket. Staring up at the star-shattered sky was William.

John fell to the deck. "How can this be?"

William hobbled toward him, his movement slow and aided by a cane. He said, "Leg's seen better days, and I've been pummeled all about like a sack of rotten fruit, but I live." William winced. He dropped the blanket. A red welt the breadth of a thumb was raised around his neck. "Nearly strangled to death and dragged into the sea. But when I was down in the briny cold I heard a voice tell it weren't yet time, that I were given a second chance. Queerest thing, sounded the near exact twin of that poor lost little cabin boy."

John rose to his feet and closed the space between them. When William took his hand, John was still clutching the piece of scrimshaw carved with his image.

KEN LIU

Thoughts and Prayers

FROM *Future Tense*

Emily Fort:

So you want to know about Hayley.

No, I'm used to it, or at least I should be by now. People only want to hear about my sister.

It was a dreary, rainy Friday in October, the smell of fresh fallen leaves in the air. The black tupelos lining the field hockey pitch had turned bright red, like a trail of bloody footprints left by a giant.

I had a quiz in French II and planned a week's worth of vegan meals for a family of four in family and consumer science. Around noon, Hayley messaged me from California.

Skipped class. Q and I are driving to the festival right now!!!

I ignored her. She delighted in taunting me with the freedoms of her college life. I was envious, but didn't want to give her the satisfaction of showing it.

In the afternoon, Mom messaged me.

Have you heard from Hayley?

No. The sisterly code of silence was sacred. Her secret boyfriend was safe with me.

If you do, call me right away.

I put the phone away. Mom was the helicopter type.

As soon as I got home from field hockey, I knew something was wrong. Mom's car was in the driveway, and she never left work this early.

The TV was on in the basement.

Mom's face was ashen. In a voice that sounded strangled, she said, "Hayley's RA called. She went to a music festival. There's been a shooting."

The rest of the evening was a blur as the death toll climbed, TV anchors read old forum posts from the gunman in dramatic voices, shaky follow-drone footage of panicked people screaming and scattering circulated on the Web.

I put on my glasses and drifted through the VR re-creation of the site hastily put up by the news crews. Already, the place was teeming with avatars holding a candlelight vigil. Outlines on the ground glowed where victims were found, and luminous arcs with floating numbers reconstructed ballistic trails. So much data, so little information.

We tried calling and messaging. There was no answer. Probably ran out of battery, we told ourselves. She always forgets to charge her phone. The network must be jammed.

The call came at four in the morning. We were all awake.

"Yes, this is . . . Are you sure?" Mom's voice was unnaturally calm, as though her life, and all our lives, hadn't just changed forever. "No, we'll fly out ourselves. Thank you."

She hung up, looked at us, and delivered the news. Then she collapsed onto the couch and buried her face in her hands.

There was an odd sound. I turned and, for the first time in my life, saw Dad crying.

I missed my last chance to tell her how much I loved her. I should have messaged her back.

Gregg Fort:

I don't have any pictures of Hayley to show you. It doesn't matter. You already have all the pictures of my daughter you need.

Unlike Abigail, I've never taken many pictures or videos, much less drone-view holograms or omni immersions. I lack the instinct to be prepared for the unexpected, the discipline to document the big moments, the skill to frame a scene perfectly. But those aren't the most important reasons.

My father was a hobbyist photographer who took pride in developing his own film and making his own prints. If you were to flip through the dust-covered albums in the attic, you'd see many posed shots of my sisters and me, smiling stiffly into the camera. Pay attention to the ones of my sister Sara. Note how her face is often turned slightly away from the lens so that her right cheek is out of view.

When Sara was five, she climbed onto a chair and toppled a boiling pot. My father was supposed to be watching her, but he'd been distracted, arguing with a colleague on the phone. When all was said and done, Sara had a trail of scars that ran from the right side of her face all the way down her thigh, like a rope of solidified lava.

You won't find in those albums records of the screaming fights between my parents; the awkward chill that descended around the dining table every time my mother stumbled over the word "beautiful"; the way my father avoided looking Sara in the eye.

In the few photographs of Sara where her entire face can be seen, the scars are invisible, meticulously painted out of existence in the darkroom, stroke by stroke. My father simply did it, and the rest of us went along in our practiced silence.

As much as I dislike photographs and other memory substitutes, it's impossible to avoid them. Coworkers and relatives show them to you, and you have no choice but to look and nod. I see the efforts manufacturers of memory-capturing devices put into making their results better than life. Colors are more vivid; details emerge from shadows; filters evoke whatever mood you desire. Without you having to do anything, the phone brackets the shot so that you can pretend to time-travel, to pick the perfect instant when everyone is smiling. Skin is smoothed out; pores and small imperfections are erased. What used to take my father a day's work is now done in the blink of an eye, and far better.

Do the people who take these photos believe them to be reality? Or have the digital paintings taken the place of reality in their memory? When they try to remember the captured moment, do they recall what they saw, or what the camera crafted for them?

Abigail Fort:

On the flight to California, while Gregg napped and Emily stared out the window, I put on my glasses and immersed myself in images of Hayley. I never expected to do this until I was aged and decrepit, unable to make new memories. Rage would come later. Grief left no room for other emotions.

I was always the one in charge of the camera, the phone, the follow-drone. I made the annual albums, the vacation-highlight videos, the animated Christmas cards summarizing the family's yearly accomplishments.

Gregg and the girls indulged me, sometimes reluctantly. I always believed that someday they would come to see my point of view.

"Pictures are important," I'd tell them. "Our brains are so flawed, leaky sieves of time. Without pictures, so many things we want to remember would be forgotten."

I sobbed the whole way across the country as I relived the life of my firstborn.

Gregg Fort:

Abigail wasn't wrong, not exactly.

Many have been the times when I wished I had images to help me remember. I can't picture the exact shape of Hayley's face at six months, or recall her Halloween costume when she was five. I can't even remember the exact shade of blue of the dress she wore for high school graduation.

Given what happened later, of course, her pictures are beyond my reach.

I comfort myself with this thought: How can a picture or video capture the intimacy, the irreproducible subjective perspective and mood through my eyes, the emotional tenor of each moment when I *felt* the impossible beauty of the soul of my child? I don't want digital representations, ersatz reflections of the gaze of electronic eyes filtered through layers of artificial intelligence, to mar what I remember of our daughter.

When I think of Hayley, what comes to mind is a series of disjointed memories.

The baby wrapping her translucent fingers around my thumb for the first time; the infant scooting around on her bottom on the hardwood floor, plowing through alphabet blocks like an icebreaker through floes; the four-year-old handing me a box of tissues as I shivered in bed with a cold and laying a small, cool hand against my feverish cheek.

The eight-year-old pulling the rope that released the pumped-up soda bottle launcher. As frothy water drenched the two of us in the wake of the rising rocket, she yelled, laughing, "I'm going to be the first ballerina to dance on Mars!"

The nine-year-old telling me that she no longer wanted me to read to her before going to sleep. As my heart throbbed with the inevitable pain of a child pulling away, she softened the blow with "Maybe someday I'll read to you."

The ten-year-old defiantly standing her ground in the kitchen, supported by her little sister, staring down me and Abigail both. "I won't hand back your phones until you both sign this pledge to never use them during dinner."

The fifteen-year-old slamming on the brakes, creating the loudest tire screech I'd ever heard; me in the passenger seat, knuckles so white they hurt. "You look like me on that rollercoaster, Dad." The tone carefully modulated, breezy. She had held out an arm in front of me, as though she could keep me safe, the same way I had done to her hundreds of times before.

And on and on, distillations of the 6,874 days we had together, like broken, luminous shells left on a beach after the tide of quotidian life has receded.

In California, Abigail asked to see her body; I didn't.

I suppose one could argue that there's no difference between my father trying to erase the scars of his error in the darkroom and my refusal to look upon the body of the child I failed to protect. A thousand "I could have's" swirled in my mind: I could have insisted that she go to a college near home; I could have signed her up for a course on mass-shooting-survival skills; I could have demanded that she wear her body armor at all times. An entire generation had grown up with active-shooter drills, so why didn't I do more? I don't think I ever understood my father, empathized with his flawed and cowardly and guilt-ridden heart, until Hayley's death.

But in the end, I didn't want to see because I wanted to protect the only thing I had left of her: those memories.

If I were to see her body, the jagged crater of the exit wound, the frozen lava trails of coagulated blood, the muddy cinders and ashes of shredded clothing, I knew the image would overwhelm all that had come before, would incinerate the memories of my daughter, my baby, in one violent eruption, leaving only hatred and despair in its wake. No, that lifeless body was not Hayley, was not the child I wanted to remember. I would no more allow that one moment to filter her whole existence than I would allow transistors and bits to dictate my memory.

So Abigail went, lifted the sheet, and gazed upon the wreckage of Hayley, of our life. She took pictures, too. "This I also want to remember," she mumbled. "You don't turn away from your child in her moment of agony, in the aftermath of your failure."

Abigail Fort:

They came to me while we were still in California.

I was numb. Questions that had been asked by thousands of mothers swarmed my mind. Why was he allowed to amass such an arsenal? Why did no one stop him despite all the warning signs? What could I have—should I have—done differently to save my child?

"You can do something," they said. "Let's work together to honor the memory of Hayley and bring about change."

Many have called me naive or worse. What did I think was going to happen? After decades of watching the exact same script being followed to end in thoughts and prayers, what made me think this time would be different? It was the very definition of madness.

Cynicism might make some invulnerable and superior. But not everyone is built that way. In the thralls of grief, you cling to any ray of hope.

"Politics is broken," they said. "It should be enough, after the deaths of little children, after the deaths of newlyweds, after the deaths of mothers shielding newborns, to finally do something. But it never is. Logic and persuasion have lost their power, so we have to arouse the passions. Instead of letting the media direct the public's morbid curiosity to the killer, let's focus on Hayley's story."

It's been done before, I muttered. To center the victim is hardly a novel political move. You want to make sure that she isn't merely a number, a statistic, one more abstract name among lists of the dead. You think when people are confronted by the flesh-and-blood consequences of their vacillation and disengagement, things change. But that hasn't worked, doesn't work.

"Not like this," they insisted, "not with our algorithm."

They tried to explain the process to me, though the details of machine learning and convolution networks and biofeedback models escaped me. Their algorithm had originated in the entertainment industry, where it was used to evaluate films and predict their box-office success, and eventually, to craft them. Proprietary variations are used in applications from product design to drafting political speeches, every field in which emotional engagement is critical. Emotions are ultimately biological phenomena, not mystical emanations, and it's possible to discern trends and patterns, to home in on the stimuli that maximize impact. The algorithm would craft a visual narrative of Hayley's life, shape it into a battering ram to shatter the hardened shell of cynicism, spur the viewer to action, shame them for their complacency and defeatism.

The idea seemed absurd, I said. How could electronics know my daughter better than I did? How could machines move hearts when real people could not?

"When you take a photograph," they asked me, "don't you trust the camera AI to give you the best picture? When you scrub through drone footage, you rely on the AI to identify the most interesting clips, to enhance them with the perfect mood filters. This is a million times more powerful."

I gave them my archive of family memories: photos, videos, scans, drone footage, sound recordings, immersiongrams. I entrusted them with my child.

I'm no film critic, and I don't have the terms for the techniques they used. Narrated only with words spoken by our family, intended for each other and not an audience of strangers, the result was unlike any movie or VR immersion I had ever seen. There was no plot save the course of a single life; there was no agenda save the celebration of the curiosity, the compassion, the drive of a child to embrace the universe, to *become.* It was a beautiful life, a life that loved and deserved to be loved, until the moment it was abruptly and violently cut down.

This is the way Hayley deserves to be remembered, I thought, tears streaming down my face. *This is how I see her, and it is how she should be seen.*

I gave them my blessing.

Sara Fort:

Growing up, Gregg and I weren't close. It was important to my parents that our family project the image of success, of decorum, regardless of the reality. In response, Gregg distrusted all forms of representation, while I became obsessed with them.

Other than holiday greetings, we rarely conversed as adults, and certainly didn't confide in each other. I knew my nieces only through Abigail's social media posts.

I suppose this is my way of excusing myself for not intervening earlier.

When Hayley died in California, I sent Gregg the contact info for a few therapists who specialized in working with families of mass shooting victims, but I purposefully stayed away myself, believing that my intrusion in their moment of grief would be inappropriate given my role as distant aunt and aloof sister. So I wasn't there when Abigail agreed to devote Hayley's memory to the cause of gun control.

Though my company bio describes my specialty as the study of online discourse, the vast bulk of my research material is visual. I design armor against trolls.

Emily Fort:

I watched that video of Hayley many times.

It was impossible to avoid. There was an immersive version, in which you could step into Hayley's room and read her neat handwriting, examine the posters on her wall. There was a low-fidelity version designed for frugal data plans, and the compression artifacts and motion blur made her life seem old-fashioned, dreamy. Everyone shared the video as a way to reaffirm that they were a good person, that they stood with the victims. Click, bump, add a lit-candle emoji, re-rumble.

It was powerful. I cried, also many times. Comments expressing grief and solidarity scrolled past my glasses like a never-ending wake. Families of victims in other shootings, their hopes rekindled, spoke out in support.

But the Hayley in that video felt like a stranger. All the elements in the video were true, but they also felt like lies.

Teachers and parents loved the Hayley they knew, but there was a mousy girl in school who cowered when my sister entered the room. One time, Hayley drove home drunk; another time, she stole from me and lied until I found the money in her purse. She knew how to manipulate people and wasn't shy about doing it. She was fiercely loyal, courageous, kind, but she could also be reckless, cruel, petty. I loved Hayley because she was human, but the girl in that video was both more and less than.

I kept my feelings to myself. I felt guilty.

Mom charged ahead while Dad and I hung back, dazed. For a

brief moment, it seemed as if the tide had turned. Rousing rallies were held and speeches delivered in front of the Capitol and the White House. Crowds chanted Hayley's name. Mom was invited to the State of the Union. When the media reported that Mom had quit her job to campaign on behalf of the movement, there was a crypto fundraiser to collect donations for the family.

And then, the trolls came.

A torrent of emails, messages, rumbles, squeaks, snapgrams, televars came at us. Mom and I were called clickwhores, paid actresses, grief profiteers. Strangers sent us long, rambling walls of text explaining all the ways Dad was inadequate and unmanly.

Hayley didn't die, strangers informed us. She was actually living in Sanya, China, off of the millions the UN and their collaborators in the US government had paid her to pretend to die. Her boyfriend—who had also "obviously not died" in the shooting—was ethnically Chinese, and that was proof of the connection.

Hayley's video was picked apart for evidence of tampering and digital manipulation. Anonymous classmates were quoted to paint her as a habitual liar, a cheat, a drama queen.

Snippets of the video, intercut with "debunking" segments, began to go viral. Some used software to make Hayley spew messages of hate in new clips, quoting Hitler and Stalin as she giggled and waved at the camera.

I deleted my accounts and stayed home, unable to summon the strength to get out of bed. My parents left me to myself; they had their own battles to fight.

Sara Fort:

Decades into the digital age, the art of trolling has evolved to fill every niche, pushing the boundaries of technology and decency alike.

From afar, I watched the trolls swarm around my brother's family with uncoordinated precision, with aimless malice, with malevolent glee.

Conspiracy theories blended with deep fakes, and then yielded to memes that turned compassion inside out, abstracted pain into lulz.

"Mommy, the beach in hell is so warm!"

"I love these new holes in me!"

Searches for Hayley's name began to trend on porn sites. The content producers, many of them AI-driven bot farms, responded with procedurally generated films and VR immersions featuring my niece. The algorithms took publicly available footage of Hayley and wove her face, body, and voice seamlessly into fetish videos.

The news media reported on the development in outrage, perhaps even sincerely. The coverage spurred more searches, which generated more content . . .

As a researcher, it's my duty and habit to remain detached, to observe and study phenomena with clinical detachment, perhaps even fascination. It's simplistic to view trolls as politically motivated—at least not in the sense that term is usually understood. Though Second Amendment absolutists helped spread the memes, the originators often had little conviction in any political cause. Anarchic sites such as 8taku, duangduang, and alt-web sites that arose in the wake of the previous decade's deplatforming wars are homes for these dung beetles of the internet, the id of our collective online unconscious. Taking pleasure in taboo breaking and transgression, the trolls have no unifying interest other than saying the unspeakable, mocking the sincere, playing with what others declared to be off-limits. By wallowing in the outrageous and filthy, they both defile and define the technologically mediated bonds of society.

But as a human being, watching what they were doing with Hayley's image was intolerable.

I reached out to my estranged brother and his family.

"Let me help."

Though machine learning has given us the ability to predict with a fair amount of accuracy which victims will be targeted—trolls are not quite as unpredictable as they'd like you to think—my employer and other major social media platforms are keenly aware that they must walk a delicate line between policing user-generated content and chilling "engagement," the one metric that drives the stock price and thus governs all decisions. Aggressive moderation, especially when it's reliant on user reporting and human judgment, is a process easily gamed by all sides, and every company has suffered accusations of censorship. In the end, they threw up their hands and tossed out their byzantine enforcement policy manuals. They have neither the skills nor the interest to become arbiters of truth and decency for society as a whole. How could they be expected to solve the problem that even the organs of democracy couldn't?

Over time, most companies converged on one solution. Rather than focusing on judging the behavior of speakers, they devoted resources to letting listeners shield themselves. Algorithmically separating legitimate (though impassioned) political speech from coordinated harassment for *everyone* at once is an intractable problem—content celebrated by some as speaking truth to power is often condemned by others as beyond the pale. It's much easier to build and train individually tuned neural networks to screen out the content a *particular* user does not wish to see.

The new defensive neural networks—marketed as "armor"—observe each user's emotional state in response to their content stream. Capable of operating in vectors encompassing text, audio, video, and AR/VR, the armor teaches itself to recognize content especially upsetting to the user and screen it out, leaving only a tranquil void. As mixed reality and immersion have become more commonplace, the best way to wear armor is through augmented-reality glasses that filter all sources of visual stimuli. Trolling, like the viruses and worms of old, is a technical problem, and now we have a technical solution.

To invoke the most powerful and personalized protection, one has to pay. Social media companies, which also train the armor, argue that this solution gets them out of the content-policing business, excuses them from having to decide what is unacceptable in virtual town squares, frees everyone from the specter of Big Brother–style censorship. That this pro–free speech ethos happens to align with more profit is no doubt a mere afterthought.

I sent my brother and his family the best, most advanced armor that money could buy.

Abigail Fort:

Imagine yourself in my position. Your daughter's body had been digitally pressed into hard-core pornography, her voice made to repeat words of hate, her visage mutilated with unspeakable violence. And it happened because of you, because of your inability to imagine the depravity of the human heart. Could you have stopped? Could you have stayed away?

The armor kept the horrors at bay as I continued to post and share, to raise my voice against a tide of lies.

The idea that Hayley hadn't died but was an actress in an anti-gun government conspiracy was so absurd that it didn't seem to deserve a response. Yet, as my armor began to filter out headlines, leaving blank spaces on news sites and in multicast streams, I realized that the lies had somehow become a real controversy. Actual journalists began to demand that I produce receipts for how I had spent the crowdfunded money—we hadn't received a cent! The world had lost its mind.

I released the photographs of Hayley's corpse. Surely there was still some shred of decency left in this world, I thought. Surely no one could speak against the evidence of their eyes?

It got worse.

For the faceless hordes of the internet, it became a game to see who could get something past my armor, to stab me in the eye with a poisoned videoclip that would make me shudder and recoil.

Bots sent me messages in the guise of other parents who had lost their children in mass shootings, and sprung hateful videos on me after I white-listed them. They sent me tribute slideshows dedicated to the memory of Hayley, which morphed into violent porn once the armor allowed them through. They pooled funds to hire errand gofers and rent delivery drones to deposit fiducial markers near my home, surrounding me with augmented-reality ghosts of Hayley writhing, giggling, moaning, screaming, cursing, mocking.

Worst of all, they animated images of Hayley's bloody corpse to the accompaniment of jaunty soundtracks. Her death trended as a joke, like the "Hamster Dance" of my youth.

Gregg Fort:

Sometimes I wonder if we have misunderstood the notion of freedom. We prize "freedom to" so much more than "freedom from." People must be free to own guns, so the only solution is to teach children to hide in closets and wear ballistic backpacks. People must be free to post and say what they like, so the only solution is to tell their targets to put on armor.

Abigail had simply decided, and the rest of us had gone along. Too late, I begged and pleaded with her to stop, to retreat. We would sell the house and move somewhere away from the temptation to engage with the rest of humanity, away from the always-connected world and the ocean of hate in which we were drowning.

But Sara's armor gave Abigail a false sense of security, pushed her to double down, to engage the trolls. "I must fight for my daughter!" she screamed at me. "I cannot allow them to desecrate her memory."

As the trolls intensified their campaign, Sara sent us patch after patch for the armor. She added layers with names like adversarial complementary sets, self-modifying code detectors, visualization auto-healers.

Again and again, the armor held only briefly before the trolls found new ways through. The democratization of artificial intelligence meant that they knew all the techniques Sara knew, and they had machines that could learn and adapt, too.

Abigail could not hear me. My pleas fell on deaf ears; perhaps her armor had learned to see me as just another angry voice to screen out.

Emily Fort:

One day, Mom came to me in a panic. "I don't know where she is! I can't see her!"

She hadn't talked to me in days, obsessed with the project that Hayley had become. It took me some time to figure out what she meant. I sat down with her at the computer.

She clicked the link for Hayley's memorial video, which she watched several times a day to give herself strength.

"It's not there!" she said.

She opened the cloud archive of our family memories.

"Where are the pictures of Hayley?" she said. "There are only placeholder Xs."

She showed me her phone, her backup enclosure, her tablet.

"There's nothing! Nothing! Did we get hacked?"

Her hands fluttered helplessly in front of her chest, like the wings of a trapped bird. "She's just gone!"

Wordlessly, I went to the shelves in the family room and brought down one of the printed annual photo albums she had made when we were little. I opened the volume to a family portrait, taken when Hayley was ten and I was eight.

I showed the page to her.

Another choked scream. Her trembling fingers tapped against

Hayley's face on the page, searching for something that wasn't there.

I understood. A pain filled my heart, a pity that ate away at love. I reached up to her face and gently took off her glasses.

She stared at the page.

Sobbing, she hugged me. "You found her. Oh, you found her!"

It felt like the embrace of a stranger. Or maybe I had become a stranger to her.

Aunt Sara explained that the trolls had been very careful with their attacks. Step by step, they had trained my mother's armor to recognize *Hayley* as the source of her distress.

But another kind of learning had also been taking place in our home. My parents paid attention to me only when I had something to do with Hayley. It was as if they no longer saw me, as though I had been erased instead of Hayley.

My grief turned dark and festered. How could I compete with a ghost? The perfect daughter who had been lost not once, but twice? The victim who demanded perpetual penance? I felt horrid for thinking such things, but I couldn't stop.

We sank under our guilt, each alone.

Gregg Fort:

I blamed Abigail. I'm not proud to admit it, but I did.

We shouted at each other and threw dishes, replicating the half-remembered drama between my own parents when I was a child. Hunted by monsters, we became monsters ourselves.

While the killer had taken Hayley's life, Abigail had offered her image up as a sacrifice to the bottomless appetite of the internet. Because of Abigail, my memories of Hayley would be forever filtered through the horrors that came after her death. She had summoned the machine that amassed individual human beings into one enormous, collective, distorting gaze, the machine that had captured the memory of my daughter and then ground it into a lasting nightmare.

The broken shells on the beach glistened with the venom of the raging deep.

Of course that's unfair, but that doesn't mean it isn't also true.

"Heartless," a self-professed troll:

There's no way for me to prove that I am who I say, or that I did what I claim. There's no registry of trolls where you can verify my identity, no Wikipedia entry with confirmed sources.

Can you even be sure I'm not trolling you right now?

I won't tell you my gender or race or who I prefer to sleep with, because those details aren't relevant to what I did. Maybe I own a dozen guns. Maybe I'm an ardent supporter of gun control.

I went after the Forts because they deserved it.

RIP-trolling has a long and proud history, and our target has always been inauthenticity. Grief should be private, personal, hidden. Can't you see how horrible it was for that mother to turn her dead daughter into a symbol, to wield it as a political tool? A public life is an inauthentic one. Anyone who enters the arena must be prepared for the consequences.

Everyone who shared that girl's memorial online, who attended the virtual candlelit vigils, offered condolences, professed to have been spurred into action, was equally guilty of hypocrisy. You didn't think the proliferation of guns capable of killing hundreds in one minute was a bad thing until someone shoved images of a dead girl in your face? What's wrong with you?

And you journalists are the worst. You make money and win awards for turning deaths into consumable stories; for coaxing survivors to sob in front of your drones to sell more ads; for inviting your readers to find meaning in their pathetic lives through vicarious, mimetic suffering. We trolls play with images of the dead, who are beyond caring, but you stinking ghouls grow fat and rich by feeding death to the living. The sanctimonious are also the most filthy-minded, and victims who cry the loudest are the hungriest for attention.

Everyone is a troll now. If you've ever liked or shared a meme that wished violence on someone you'd never met, if you've ever decided it was OK to snarl and snark with venom because the target was "powerful," if you've ever tried to signal your virtue by piling on in an outrage mob, if you've ever wrung your hands and expressed concern that perhaps the money raised for some victim should have gone to some other less "privileged" victim—then I hate to break it to you, you've also been trolling.

Some say that the proliferation of trollish rhetoric in our culture is corrosive, that armor is necessary to equalize the terms of a debate in which the only way to win is to care less. But don't you see how unethical armor is? It makes the weak think they're strong, turns cowards into deluded heroes with no skin in the game. If you truly despise trolling, then you should've realized by now that armor only makes things worse.

By weaponizing her grief, Abigail Fort became the biggest troll of them all—except she was bad at it, just a weakling in armor. We had to bring her—and by extension, the rest of you—down.

Abigail Fort:

Politics returned to normal. Sales of body armor, sized for children and young adults, received a healthy bump. More companies offered classes on situational awareness and mass shooting drills for schools. Life went on.

I deleted my accounts; I stopped speaking out. But it was too late for my family. Emily moved out as soon as she could; Gregg found an apartment.

Alone in the house, my eyes devoid of armor, I tried to sort through the archive of photographs and videos of Hayley.

Every time I watched the video of her sixth birthday, I heard in my mind the pornographic moans; every time I looked at photos of her high school graduation, I saw her bloody animated corpse dancing to the tune of "Girls Just Wanna Have Fun"; every time I tried to page through the old albums for some good memories, I jumped in my chair, thinking an AR ghost of her, face grotesquely deformed like Munch's *The Scream,* was about to jump out at me, cackling, "Mommy, these new piercings hurt!"

I screamed, I sobbed, I sought help. No therapy, no medication worked. Finally, in a numb fury, I deleted all my digital files, shredded my printed albums, broke the frames hanging on walls.

The trolls trained me as well as they trained my armor.

I no longer have any images of Hayley. I can't remember what she looked like. I have truly, finally, lost my child.

How can I possibly be forgiven for that?

E. LILY YU

The Time Invariance of Snow

FROM *Tor.com*

1. The Devil and the Physicist

ONCE,[1] THE DEVIL made a mirror,[2] for the Devil was vain. This mirror showed certain people to be twice as large and twice as powerful and six times as good and kind as they truly were; and others it showed at a tenth their stature, with all their shining qualities smutched and sooted, so that if one glimpsed them in the Devil's mirror, one would think them worthless and contemptible indeed.

The Devil looked into his mirror and admired himself, and all his demons preened and swaggered and admired him too. And joy resounded throughout the vaults of Hell.

Eventually there came a physicist who, with radioactive cobalt and cerium magnesium nitrate crystals, sought to test the invariance of symmetry; namely, whether in a mirror universe the laws of physics would be reflected. As she touched and tested the mystery of the world and proved that symmetry did not hold, and that parity was not in fact conserved, she broke, all unknowing, the Devil's mirror.

Like the fundamental equations of quantum mechanics, like

1. The more we peer myopically into the abyss of time, the more we understand that there is no such thing as *once*, nor a single sequential line of time, but rather a chaos of local happenings stretching from improbability to probability.
2. Here too the concept of mirror is an approximation, for the phenomenon in question extended into a minimum of seven dimensions; but mirror is a close and useful metaphor.

God Himself, the Devil is a time-invariant equation.[3] The shattering of the mirror shivered outward through fields of light cones, near and far, until the shattering itself became eternal, immutable fact. The fragments of the mirror drifted down through pasts, presents, and futures, clinging and cutting, like stardust and razors.

Whoever blinked a sliver of the mirror into his eye[4] saw the world distorted ever after. Some observed that they were far worthier and more deserving than others, and pleased with this understanding, went forth and took whatever they wished, whether wives or slaves, land or empires.

Some looked at themselves and saw worthlessness. At that sight, whatever pyrotechnic wonders they dreamed died in secret within them.

Others, of particular sensitivity, felt the presence of the glass, which a slow and uncertain part of their souls insisted had not been there before. A few of these tried gouging it out with knives, though it was not a physical construct and could not be thus dislodged. A very few made fine and fragile spectacles for the soul, to correct its sight, and walked long in clarity and loneliness thereafter.

This is how the Devil's mirror worked:

A woman warned a city of its destruction, of soldiers creeping in by craft, and her friends and family laughed her mad.

The city burned.

The woman was raped, and raped again, and murdered.

A woman stood before men who would become consuls and said, believe me, I was forced by this man. To be believed, she struck her own heart with a dagger.

A woman stood before senators and said, believe me, I was—

A woman stood before senators and said, believe—

A Black woman said, listen, and no one heard.

A dusky child cried, and no one comforted him.

An indifferent cartographer divided other people's countries into everlasting wars.

The physicist died. Her male colleagues received a Nobel Prize.[5]

The Devil looked upon his work and laughed.

3. Theology hopes for local boundedness, but as yet this remains unproven.

4. A poetic simplification to describe a quantum event affecting neural perception.

5. This too is a poetic simplification.

2. K. and G.

It was summer, and the roses swam with scent. K. had tamed G. with intermittent kindness, as boys tame foxes to their hand, though she had been watchful and wary, knowing the violence of men. Now G. rested her head against K.'s shoulder, and they breathed the soft, sweet air together with the laziness that only summer knows. The two of them were not young; neither were they old.

If I were going to murder you, K. said musingly, I would tie you up while you slept, nail you into a splintery box, and shove the box out of a car going seventy into the path of a truck. The splinters would be driven into your body on impact.

G. was silent for a long time.

At last she said: When you described murdering me—

Yes?

I felt afraid.

K. said: I was joking.

G. said: Still, I was afraid.

K. said: I had good intentions. What on earth do you want?

G. said: Just for you to say you're sorry.

I can't believe you're blowing this up into such a huge deal.

You know about—

Well, I'm *sorry* that women are sometimes harmed by men. But this is insane.

That's the glass talking.

What?

The sliver of glass in your eyes and in mine.

K. pushed back his chair so hard it tipped over.

We both contributed to this situation. You have to be more patient and kinder to me.

G. said: I can't.

Fine, K. said, stamping his foot. A breath of winter blew across them both. The rosebush's leaves crisped and silvered with frost, and its full-blown flowers blackened and bowed.

I'm leaving, K. said. There was ice in his voice.

G. said: I know what will happen. I will follow you down a stream and into a witch's house, into a palace, and then into a dark robber's wood, and in the end I will walk barefoot through the bitter snow into a frozen hall, to find you moving ice upon the pool that they call the Mirror of Reason.

I will come thinking to rescue you. That my tears will wash the glass from your eye and melt the ice in your heart. That the Snow Queen's spell will break, and you will be free.

But when I arrive I will find no Snow Queen, no enchantment, no wicked, beautiful woman who stole you away.

Only you.

You, who choose cold falseness over true life.

I know, because I am no longer a child and have walked down this road.

I will not go.

She said these words to the summer air, but no one was around to hear.

3. The Ravens

The prince and princess, king and queen now, were not at home. The tame ravens in the palace had long since died.

None of the ravens in the old wood knew her. They rattled and croaked as G. went by.

Imposter!

Pretender!

Usurper!

Slut!

Unwanted!

Abandoned!

Discarded!

Die!

Oh, be quiet, G. said, and continued on her way.

4. The Robber Queen

You're back, the robber queen said, testing the point of her letter opener against her desk. Didn't think I'd see you again.

Didn't you get my postcards? G. said, sitting.

The office was darker than she remembered, for all that they were on the hundredth floor. Outside, other buildings pressed close, like trees.

You know I screen my mail.

I know couriers and postal workers wouldn't dare to stop here.

The robber queen said: I'm good at my job.

So I've heard. I'm proud to have known you when.

Spill, the robber queen said, or I'll tickle your neck with my dagger for old times' sake. Is this one handsome, at least? Because the last one—ugh. Does he cook? Does he clean? Please tell me this one, this time, is worthy of you. Tea or whiskey?

Theodora, G. said, you're so laughing and fierce. How do you do it?

Love 'em, leave 'em. Sometimes I even leave them alive. But once you taste a man's still-beating heart—

Forget him, G. said.

So there *is* a him.

A mistake. But I'm not here about that. I'm here to ask for a job.

This isn't the United Nations, G. We do dirty, filthy, bloody work. That I'll be hanged for, if I'm ever caught.

You have power, G. said. I don't know what that's like. To hold a knife, with another person's life on its edge. Teach me.

Mine is a raw and common power, the robber queen said. What you have is greater.

I have nothing.

Stop, or I'll cut off your little finger so you'll never forget. I don't know how or when you got it. Maybe the crows taught you, or the Lap women. Your eyes see to the soul. Your words cut to the bone. Men and women are stripped naked before you. Now, if you'd only *use* that power, you could hurt those you hate with an unhealing harm. I'd give my three best horses for that.

G. said: No.

Say, such and such is the shape of your soul, though you wear mask upon mask to hide it.

Theodora, G. said, a wolf is the shape of your soul, and there's blood on its muzzle and mud on its pelt.

It is! And I'll never hide it.

Are you sure you won't let me rob one company? Just for the experience?

This is an investment firm, not a charity. Speaking of which, I'll be billing you for my time. Must keep the numbers regular.

Someday when I have money, I'll pay you, G. said.

That you will.

5. The Lap Women

Old they were, in appearance far older than time: their eyes seams of stars, their fingers the knurls of ancient oaks. They rocked in their maple rocking chairs, knitting blankets with a pattern of silver fish from a silvery wool. The fish gathered in soft clouds around their feet.

G. said: I'm sorry I haven't visited or called.

They smiled at her and continued to rock. One by one, fish slipped from their needles' tips.

G. said: I'm sure you have family. Daughters or sons who bring fruit and chocolate. Somebody. You must have somebody.

They continued to rock.

Can I help you? a nursing assistant said.

These are old friends of mine, G. said, blushing as she said it, for years of silence and absence had passed. I came to ask their advice.

Good luck. They haven't spoken since they checked in. And that was fifteen years ago.

G. said: That long?

Time can jump you like that. Leave you bruised in an alley with no memory at all.

Is there anything they like to do besides knit?

Cards, the assistant said. They'll skin you in most kinds of poker, and they're fiends for bridge.

Then I'll stay and play cards with them, if they wish.

You'll regret it, the nursing assistant said. But she went and fetched a worn deck anyway.

At the sight of the cards, the three old women jabbed their needles deep into their skeins and rose from their rocking chairs, holding out their hands.

G. proceeded to lose every bill from her wallet, her sweater, the cross on a chain that she wore, and the black glass buttons on the front of her coat.

The eldest Lap woman took her sewing shears and snipped off the buttons, one-two-three-four. Then she picked up the hillocks of silver knitting, finished each fragment, and whipstitched the three clouds of fishes, each cloud a different gray, into a single long shawl. This shawl she draped around G.'s shoulders.

Thank you, G. said. I think.

All three Lap women smiled gentle, faraway smiles.

The nursing assistant scratched her ear.

Are you going somewhere cold? she said.

G. said: Very.

6. The Snow Queen

It was hours and hours until dawn, and the world was a waste and a howling dark.

At some point in the distant past, the sweep of ice beneath G.'s feet had been chopped into a stair that wound up and around the glassy mountain. As she climbed, thick snowflakes clung to her lashes. She had the shawl of silver fish wrapped around her for warmth and sensible boots on her feet. She needed no guide, for she knew the way.

Before she left, G. had knelt and prayed as trustingly as she had when she was a child, and now she held that prayer like a weak and guttering taper.

Here was the Snow Queen's palace: smaller than she remembered, as if her child self's memories had exaggerated its dimensions, or else whole wings and wards had melted away. Frost blossoms still bloomed from windows and eaves. Crystalline gargoyles crouched in its crenellations.

Collecting her courage, G. pushed the palace gates open. Her hands turned white, then red, with cold.

No one waited inside. No Queen. No K. There was only the vacant throne and the familiar, frozen pool with its shards arranged into the word "Eternity."

It was quiet.

Her breath left her lips in glittering clouds.

G. crossed the hall, her steps echoing. The throne might well have been carved from the world's largest diamond. Like a lily or lotus, it peaked to a point. Rainbows glowed in its fractured depths.

On the throne's seat was a small crown of silvered glass.

G. picked up the crown and turned it in her hands. In that whole country, it was the only thing that was not cold.

The long glass thorns flashed fragments of her face: a sneer, a glare, a look of contempt.

Of course, G. said.

The jagged edges of her life shone brilliantly before her. In a moment she saw how they could be fitted together to spell out the forgotten word she had pursued all her life, sometimes glimpsing, sometimes approaching, never grasping entire—

One way or another, the Devil's mirror produces a Snow Queen.

G. raised the crown above her head, admiring how its sharpness shivered the light, how it showed her beautiful and unforgiving.

And then she drove it against the point of the diamond throne.

Across seven dimensions the glass crown cracked and crumbled. Glass thorns drove into G.'s wrists and fingers, flying up to cut her face.

Where the blood beaded and bubbled up, it froze, so that G. wore rubies on her skin, rubies and diamonds brighter than snow.

And the palace too cracked as the Queen's crown cracked, from top to bottom, like a walnut shell.

All around was darkness.

Down into that darkness G. fell, and time fell also, in fine grains like sand.

7. A Brief Digression on Hans Christian Andersen and the Present State of Physics

Considered as a whole, in all its possible states, the universe is time invariant. When this insight is worked out and understood at a mathematical level,[6] one both achieves and loses one's liberty. We

6. $S = k \log W$, which is to say, entropy is directly related to the number of states of a system. If we somehow could perceive all the possible microscopic states of the universe, S would be constant.

are freed from one enchantment, only to be ensorcelled by another.[7] And while the first is a snowy, crowded pond upon whose hard face the whole world may skate and shout, the second is a still and lonely (some say holy) place, where only the brave go, and from whence only the mad return.

Those who reach the latter place understand that it was always the case that they would come here. Perhaps they weep. Perhaps they praise God.

Who knows? And who can say?

8. G. and the Devil

At the end of her fall, G. met the Devil face to face.

He was pretty, in a moneyed way, sharp as polished leather, with a pocket square and black, ambitious eyes.

The Devil said: That's my mirror you're wearing in your flesh, in your hair. That's the mirror that I made. Me.

Why? G. asked, and in that question was all the grief of the world.

The Devil said: Because when one is alone in pain, one seeks to spread suffering, and so be less alone. It's quite logical.

But *why?*

When a dark heart gazes upon glory, a glory that the heart can never attain, then the whole being turns to thoughts of destruction.

WHY?

As the Devil continued to speak, his words plausible, his face reasonable, his voice reassuring, scorpions and serpents slid out of his pockets, clinging to each other in thin, squirming chains. And the chains crept and curled and reached for her.

In her hand, however, was the hard hilt of a sword, whose one edge was ruby and the other diamond. On her breast she wore overlapping silver scales. And in her other hand was a buckler burnished to the brightness of a mirror.

If the Devil noticed, he gave no sign.

7. Imagine, say, a boy forming the icy shards of reason into a picture of eternity. The metaphor is not inadequate.

Tell me the truth, G. said.

He said, Because you are ugly and it was a Tuesday.

G. swung the sword to her left and severed a whip of scorpions, then to her right, bisecting a braid of vipers. Slices of snakeflesh and crunched carapace tumbled around her. Of a sudden the Devil looked not so charming.

You think you can fight me? he said, ten times larger now, and growing, until his smallest curved toenail was the height of her head. His voice was the thunder of ten million men.

G. said: I have seen eternity. I know you have already lost.

And she struck, her sword flashing bloodlight and lightning.

The Devil roared.

9. G. and K.

His hair was white, and he walked with a cane, limping like a crane as it hunts in the reeds.

Her own hair was silver, and her face and hands were scarred.

I'm sorry, he said.

I know you are.

I came all this way to tell you.

I knew you were coming, G. said.

You saw me plainly. I couldn't bear it. I wanted to hurt you, and I did.

G. said: It's all over now.

It is.

K. squinted at her, as if looking into radiance.

I see you've made your glass into a sword.

And you've made yours into a door.

A tempering all your life, then. A tempering and a war. As I have lived openings and closings. As I have yielded and withstood.

So you and I have been made of use.

We have, K. said. We have indeed.

ANIL MENON

The Robots of Eden

FROM *New Suns*

WHEN AMMA HANDED me Sollozzo's collection of short stories, barnacled with the usual fervent endorsements and logos of obscure book awards, I respectfully ruffled the four-hundred-page tome and reflected with pleasure how the Turk was now almost like a brother. Of course, we all live in the Age of Comity now, but Sollozzo and I had developed a friendship closer than that required by social norms or the fact that we both loved the same woman.

It had been quite different just sixteen months ago; when Amma informed me that my wife and daughter had returned from Boston, the news sweetened the day as elegantly as a sugar cube dissolving in chai. Padma and Bittu were home! Then my mother had casually added that "Padma's Turkish fellow" was also in town. They were all returning to Boston in a week, and since the lovebirds were determined to proceed, it was high time our seven-year-old Bittu was informed. Padma wanted us all to meet for lunch.

I wasn't fooled by Amma's weather-report tone; I knew my mother was dying to meet Sollozzo face to face.

I wasn't in the mood for lunch, and told my mother so. I had my reasons. I was terribly busy. It was far easier for them to drop by my office than for me to cart Amma all the way to Bandra, where they were put up. Besides, they needed something from me, not I from them. Some people had no consideration for other people's feelings—

I calmed down, of course. My mother also helped. She reminded me, as if I were a child, that moods were a very poor excuse. Yes, if I insisted, they would visit me at the office, but just because people adjusted didn't mean one had to take advantage of them, not to mention the Turk was now part of the family, so a little hospitality wasn't too much to ask, et cetera, et cetera.

Unlike his namesake in *The Godfather,* Sollozzo was a novelist, not a drug pusher (though I suppose novelists do push hallucinations in their own way). I hadn't read his novels nor heard of him earlier, but he turned out to be famous enough. You had to be famous to get translated into Tamil.

"I couldn't make head or tail," said Amma, with relish. "One sentence in the opening chapter is eight pages long. Such vocabulary! It's already a best seller in Tamil. Padma deserves a lot of the credit, naturally."

Naturally. Padma had been the one who had translated Sollozzo into Tamil. And given herself a serving of Turkish Delight in the process.

"If you like Pamuk, you will like him," said Amma. "You have to like him."

I did like Pamuk. As a teenager, I had read all of Pamuk's works. The downside to that sort of thing is that one fails to develop a mind of one's own. Still, he was indelibly linked to my youth, as indelibly as the memory of waiting in the rain for the school bus or the Class XII debate at SIES college on "Are Women More Rational Than Men?" and Padma's sweet smile as she flashed me her breasts.

Actually, Amma's lawyering on the fellow's behalf was unnecessary; my Brain was already busy. My initial discomfort had all but dissolved.

I even looked forward to meeting Sollozzo. Bandra wasn't all that far away. Nothing in Mumbai was far away. Amma and I lived in Sahyun, only about a twenty-minute walk from my beloved Jihran River, and all in all I had a good life, a happy life in fact, but good and happy don't equal interesting. My life would be more interesting with a Turk in it, and this was as good an opportunity as any to acquire one.

However, I knew Amma's pleasure would be all the more if she had to persuade me, so I raised various objections, made frowny faces, and smiled to myself as Amma demolished my wickets. Amma's home-nurse Velli caught on and joined the game, her sweet round face alight with mischief:

"Ammachi, you were saying your back was aching," said Velli

in Tamil. "Do you really want to go all the way to Bandra just for lunch?"

"Yes wretch, now *you* also start," said Amma. "Come here—*arre,* don't be afraid—come here, let me show you how fit I am."

As they had their fun, I pulled up my schedule, shuffled things around, and carved out a couple of hours on Sunday. It did cut things a bit fine. Amma was suspicious but I assured her I wasn't trying to sabotage her bloody lunch. I really *was* drowning in work at Modern Textiles; the labor negotiations were at a delicate stage.

"As always, your mistress is more important than your family," said Amma, sighing.

Amma's voice, but I heard Padma's tone. Either way, the disrespect was the same. If I had been a doctor and not a banker, would Amma still compare my work to a whore? I had every right to be furious. Yes, every right.

I calmed down, reflected that Amma wasn't being disrespectful. On the contrary. She was reminding me to be the better man I could be. She was doing what good parents are supposed to do, namely, protect me.

"You're right, Amma. I'll make some changes. Balance is always good."

Unfortunately, I was as busy as ever when the weekend arrived, and with it Padma and Bittu, but I gladly set aside my work.

"You've become thin," observed Padma, almost angrily. Then she smiled and put Bittu in my arms.

I made a huge fuss of Bittu, making monster sounds and threatening to eat her alive with kisses. Squeals. Shrieks. Stories. Oh, Bittu was bursting with true stories. She had seen snow in Boston. She had seen buildings *this* big. We put our heads together and Bittu shared with me the millions of photographs she had clicked. Bittu had a boo-boo on her index finger which she displayed with great pride and broke into peals of laughter when I pretend-moaned: *doctor, doctor, Bittu better butter to make bitter boo-boo better.* It is easy to make children happy. Then I noticed Velli had tears in her eyes.

"What's wrong, Velli?" I asked, quite concerned.

She just shook her head. The idiot was very sentimental, practically a Hindi movie in a frock, and it was with some trepidation that I introduced her to Padma. They seemed to get along. Padma was gracious, quite the empathic high-caste lady, and Velli declared enthusiastically that Padma-madam was exactly how Velli had imagined she would be.

Eventually, with Padma guiding the car's autopilot, all of us, including Velli, set off from Sahyun. At first we kept the windows down, but it was a windy day, and the clear cool air from Jihran's waters tugged and pulled at our clothes. Amma had taken the front seat, since Bittu wanted to sit in the back, between Velli and me. We would be gone for most of the day, and so Velli had asked us to drop her off at Dharavi so that she could visit her parents. We stopped at the busy intersection just after the old location of the MDMS sewage treatment plant and Velli got out.

"Velli, you'll return in the—" I began, in Tamil.

"Yes, elder brother, of course I'll be there in the evening, you can trust." Velli kissed her fingers, transplanted the kiss onto Amma's cheek, and then said in her broken English: "I see you in evening soon, okay Ammachi? Bye bye."

The signal had changed and the car wanted to move. Velli somehow forgot to include Padma in her final set of goodbyes. She ran across the intersection. "She's an innocent," said Amma. "The girl's heart is pure gold. Pure gold."

"Yes, she is adorable," said Padma, smiling.

"She was sad," observed Bittu. "Is it because she is Black?"

Amma laughed but when we looked at her, she said: "What? If Velli were here, she would've been the first to laugh."

Maybe so. But two wrongs still didn't make a right. Amma was setting a bad example for Bittu. It was all very well to laugh and be happy but the Enhanced had a responsibility to be happy about the right things. Padma explained to me that Bittu actually had been asking if Velli was sad because she wasn't Enhanced. In their US visit, Bittu had noticed that most African Americans weren't Enhanced, and she'd concluded it was for the fair. Velli was dark, so.

I met Padma's glance in the rearview mirror and her wry smile said: Did you really think I'd taught her to be racist?

"No, Bittu." I put an arm around my daughter. "Velli is just sad to leave us. But now she can look forward to seeing us again."

I too was looking forward, not backwards. Reclining in the back seat, listening to the happy chatter of the women in front, savoring the reality of my daughter in the crook of my arm, meeting the glances of my wife—I was still unused to thinking of Padma as my ex-wife—I realized, almost in the manner of a last wave at the railway station, that this could be the last time we were all physically together.

When she'd left for Boston with Bittu, I had hoped the six months would be enough to flush Sollozzo out of her system. But life with him must have been exciting in more ways than one. The Turk had given her the literary life Padma had always craved, a craving it seemed no amount of rationalization on her part or mine could fix.

With Padma gone for so long, I'd had to look for a nurse for Amma. It quickly became clear that I could forget about Enhanced nurses, since all such nurses were employed everywhere except in India. Fortunately, Rajan, a shop-floor supervisor at Modern Textiles, approached me saying his daughter Velli had a diploma in home care, he'd heard I was looking for a home-nurse, and that he was looking for someone he could trust.

Trust enabled all relations. As a banker, I'd learned this lesson over and over. I was enveloped in a subtle happiness, a kind of sadness infused with a delicate mix of fragrances: the car's sunburnt leather, Amma's coconut-oil-loving white head, Padma's vetiver, Velli's jasmine, and Bittu's pulsing animal scent. The sensory mix wasn't something my Brain had composed. It must have arisen from the flower of the moment. I savored the essence before it could melt under introspection, but melt it did, leaving in its place the residue of a happiness without reasons.

Somewhat dazed, I leaned forward between the front seats and asked the ladies what they were talking about.

"Amma was saying she wanted to come for my wedding in Boston," said Padma. "I want her there too. I'll make all the arrangements. My happiness would be complete if she were there."

"Then I will be there," announced Amma. "Just book the plane ticket."

"Amma, you can barely navigate to the bathroom by yourself, let alone Boston."

"See, Padma, see? This is his attitude." Amma employed the old-beggar-woman voice she reserved for pathos. "Ever since you left, I've become the butt of his bad jokes." Then Amma surprised me by turning and patting my cheek. "But it's okay. He's just trying to cheer me up, poor fellow."

"That's one of the hazards of living with him," said Padma, smiling. "Amma, seriously, I'll book your ticket. If he wants, your son can also come and crack his bad jokes there."

"Yes, the more the merrier," said Amma, good sport that she was. She then stoutly defended Padma's choice, pooh-poohing moral issues no one had raised about Turkish-Tamil children, and saying things like what mattered was a person's heart, not their origins, and that love multiplied under division, and wasn't it telling that he loved red rice and *avial.* "I always thought Mammootty looks very Turkish," said Amma, her intransigent tone indicating that Sollozzo, whom she had yet to meet, could draw at will from the affection she'd deposited over a lifetime for her favorite South Indian actor. That's how much she liked Turks, yes.

I liked him too. Sollozzo wasn't anything like the gangster namesake from the classic movie. For one thing, he had a thin pencil mustache. I could have grown a similar mustache, but I couldn't compete with his gaunt height or that ruined look of a cricket bat which had seen one too many innings. He came across as a decent fellow, very sharp, and his slow smile and thoughtful mien gave his words an extra weight.

He had brought me a gift. A signed copy of Pamuk's *Museum of Innocence.* It was strange to think this volume had been touched by the great one, physically touched, and the thought sent an involuntary shiver down my spine. A lovely, Unenhanced feeling. Two gifts in one. The volume was very expensive, no doubt. I touched the signature.

My friend, said Orhan Pamuk in my head, from across the bridge of time, *I hope you get as much joy reading this story as I had writing it.*

I touched the signature again, replaying its message. I looked up and saw Padma and Sollozzo watching me. It was touching to think they'd worried about finding me the right gift.

"I will cherish it." I was totally sincere. "Thank you."

"Mention not," said Sollozzo, with that slow smile of his. "You owe me nothing. I *did* take your wife."

We all laughed. We chatted all through lunch. I ordered the lamb; the others opted to share a vat of biryani. As I watched Bittu putting her little fingers to her mouth, I realized with a start that I'd quite missed her. Sollozzo ate with the gusto of a man on death row. Padma shook her head and I stopped staring. My habit of introspection sometimes interfered with my happiness, but I felt it also gave my happiness a more poignant quality. It is one thing to be happy but to *know* that one is happy because a beloved is happy makes happiness all the more sweet. Else, how would we be any different from animals? My head buzzing with that sweet feeling, I desired to make a genuine connection. I turned to Sollozzo.

"Are you working on a new novel? Your fans must be getting very impatient."

"I haven't written anything new for a decade," said Sollozzo, with a smile. He stroked Padma's cheek. "She's worried."

"I'm not!" Padma did look very unworried. "I'm not just your wife. I'm also a reader. If I feel a writer is cutting corners, that's it, I close the book. You're a perfectionist; I love that. Remember how you tortured me over the translation?"

Sollozzo nodded fondly. "She's equally mad. She'll happily spend a week over a comma."

"How we fought over footnotes! He doesn't like footnotes. But how can a translator clarify without footnotes? Nothing doing, I said. I put my foot down."

I felt good watching them nuzzle. I admired their passion. I must have been deficient in passion. Still, if I'd been deficient, why hadn't Padma told me? Marriages needed work. The American labor theory of love. That worked for me; I liked work. Work, work. If she'd wanted me to work at our relationship, I would have. Then, just so, I lost interest in the subject.

"I don't read much fiction anymore," I confessed. "I used to be a huge reader. Then I got Enhanced in my twenties. There was the adjustment phase and then somehow I lost touch, what with career and all. Same story with my friends. They mostly read what their children read. But even kids, it's not much. Makes me wonder. Maybe we are outgrowing the need for fiction. I mean, children outgrow their imaginary friends. Do you think we posthumans are outgrowing the need for fiction?"

I waited for Sollozzo to respond. But he'd filled his mouth with biryani and was masticating with the placid dedication of a temple cow. Padma filled the silence with happy chatter. Sollozzo was working on a collection of his short stories. He was doing this, he was doing that. I sensed reproach in her cheer, which was, of course, ridiculous. Then she changed the topic: "Are you, are you, are you, finally done with Modern Textiles?"

"I am, I am, I am not," I replied, and we both laughed. "The usual usual, Padma. I'm trying to make the workers see that control is possible without ownership. Tough, though. The Enhanced ones are easy; they get it immediately. But the ones who aren't, especially the Marxist types. Sheesh."

"Sounds super challenging!"

On the contrary. Her interested expression said: super tedious. I hadn't intended to elaborate. As a merchant banker, I'd learned early on that most artists, especially the writer types, were put off by money talk.

It didn't bother me. I just found it odd. Why weren't they interested in capital, which had the power to transform the world more than any other force? But I was willing to bet Sollozzo's novel wouldn't spend a comma, let alone a footnote, on business. Even Padma, for all the time she spent with me, had never accepted that the strong poets she so admired were poets of action, not verbiage.

"I hate the word 'posthuman'!" exclaimed Sollozzo, startling us. "It's an excuse to claim we're innocent of humanity's sins. It's a rejection of history. Are you so eager to return to Zion? If so, you are lost, my brother."

Silence.

"I know the way to Sion," I said finally, and when Padma burst out laughing, I explained to the puzzled Sollozzo that Sahyun, where I lived with my mother, had originally been called Sion and that it had been a cosmopolitan North Indian intersection between two South Indian enclaves, Chembur and Kingcircle. Then Sahyun had become a Muslim enclave. Now it was simply a wealthy enclave.

"Sahyun! That's Zion in Arabic. You are living in Zion!"

"Exactly. I even have one of the rivers of Paradise not too far from my house. Imagine. And Padma still left."

"There's no keeping women in Zion." Sollozzo gifted me one of his slow smiles.

"Of course," said Padma, smiling. "The river Jihran is recent. There wasn't any river anywhere near Sion. The place was a traffic nightmare. Everything's changed in the last sixty years. Completely, utterly changed."

"On the contrary—" I began, leaning forward to help myself to a second helping of lamb.

"My dear children," interrupted my mother, in Tamil, "I understand you don't want to, but you mustn't postpone it any longer. You have to tell Bittu."

"Yes, Bittu. Break her heart, then mend it." Sollozzo didn't understand Tamil very well, not yet, but he had recognized the key word: Bittu. This meeting was really about Bittu.

First, the preliminaries. I took the divorce papers from Padma, signed wherever I was required to sign; a quaint anachronism in this day and age, but necessary nonetheless. With that single stroke of my pen, I gave up the right to call Padma my wife. My ex-wife's glance met mine, a tender exchange of unsaid benedictions and I felt a profound sadness roil inside me. Then it was accompanied with a white-hot anger that I wasn't alone with my misery. The damn Brain was watching, protecting. But there is no protection against loss. Padma—Oh god, oh god, oh god. Then, just so, I relaxed.

"There's a park outside," said Padma, also smiling. "We'll tell Bittu there."

It began well. Bittu, bless her heart, wasn't exactly the brightest crayon in the box. It took her a long time to understand that her parents were divorcing. For good. She was going to live in Boston. Yes, she would lose all her friends. Yes, the uncle with the mustache was now her stepfather. No, I wasn't coming along. Yes, I would visit. Et cetera, et cetera. Then she asked all the same questions once more. Wobbling chin, high-pitched voice, but overall quite calm. We felt things were going well. Padma and I beamed at each other, Sollozzo nodded approvingly.

Amma was far smarter. She knew her grandchild, remembered better than us what it had been like not to be fully Enhanced. So when Bittu ran screaming toward the fence separating the park from the highway, Amma, my eighty-two-year-old mother, somehow sprinted after her and grabbed Bittu before she could hit the road. We caught up, smiling with panic. Hugs, more explanations. Bittu calmed. Then when we released her, she once again made a dash for it. This is just what we have pieced together after some debate, Padma, Sollozzo, and I. None of us remember too much of what happened. But it must have been very stressful, because my Brain mercifully decided to bury it. I remember flashes of a nose-bleed, a frantic trip to the hospital, Bittu's hysterical screams, Padma in Sollozzo's arms. I remember Bittu's Brain taking over, conferring with ours, and shutting down her reticular center. Bittu went to sleep.

"Please do not worry." Bittu's Brain broadcast directly to our heads. It had an airline-stewardess voice, and it spoke first in English, then in Hindi. "She can be easily awakened at the nearest facility."

I remember the doctor who handled Bittu's case. She was very reassuring. I remember everything after the doctor took over. She was that reassuring.

"Bittu was Enhanced only last year, wasn't she?" said the doctor.

She wanted to know the specifics of the unit. Did Bittu's Brain regulate appetite? How quickly would it forget things? What was our policy on impulse control? That was especially important. How did her Brain handle uncertainty? Was it risk-averse or risk-neutral? Superfluous questions, of course. The information was all there in the medical report. I listened, marveling, a soaring happiness, as Padma answered every question, and thus answered what the doctor really needed to know: Are you caring parents? Do you know what you have done to your child with this technology?

The doctor asked if we had encouraged Bittu to give her Brain a name. Did we know that Bittu referred to it as a "boo-boo"? Newly Enhanced children often gave names to their Brains. Padma nodded, smiling, but I could tell she was worried. Boo-boo?

We got the It-Takes-Time-to-Adjust speech. Bittu was very young, the Brain still wasn't an integral part of her. Her naming it was one symptom. Her Brain found it especially difficult to handle Bittu's complex emotions. And Bittu found it difficult to deal with this *thing* in her head. We should have been more careful. It especially hadn't been a good idea to mask the trial separation as a happy vacation in Boston. We hung our heads.

Relax, smiled the doctor. These things happen. It's especially hard to remember just how chaotic their little minds are at this age. It's not like raising children in the old days. Don't worry. In a few weeks, Bittu wouldn't even remember she'd had all these worries or anxieties. She would continue to have genuine concerns, yes, but fear, self-pity, and other negative emotions wouldn't complicate things. Those untainted concerns could be easily handled with love, kindness, patience, and understanding. The doctor's finger drew a cross with those four words.

"Yes, Doctor!" said Padma, with the enthusiasm all mothers seem to have for a good medical lecture.

We all felt much better. Our appreciation would inform our Brains to rate this particular interaction highly on the appropriate feedback boards.

Outside, once Bittu had been placed—fast asleep, poor thing—into Sollozzo's rental car, the time came to make our farewells. I embraced Padma and she swore various things. She would keep in touch. I was to do this and that. Bittu. Bittu. We smiled at each other. However, Amma was a mess, mediation or no mediation.

"Was it to see this day, I lived so long?" she asked piteously in Tamil, forgetting herself for a second, but then recovered when Padma and I laughed at her wobbly voice.

"That lady doctor liked the word 'especially,' didn't she?" said Sollozzo, absentmindedly shaking and squeezing my hand. "I had a character like that. He liked to say: on the contrary. Even when there was nothing to be contrary about." He encased our handshake with his other hand. "Friend, my answer to your question was stupid. Totally stupid. I failed. I've often thought about the same question. I will fail better. We must talk."

What question? The relevance of fiction? I didn't care. So. This was it. Padma was leaving. Bittu was leaving. My wife and daughter were gone forever. I felt something click in my head and I went all woozy. The music in my head made it impossible to think. I was so happy I had to leave immediately or I would have exploded with joy.

Amma and I had a good journey back to our apartment. We hooked our Brains, sang along with old Tamil songs, discussed some of the entertaining ways in which our older relatives had died. She didn't fall asleep and leave me to my devices. My mother, worn out from life, protecting me from myself, even now.

That evening, Velli made a great deal of fuss over Amma, chattering about the day she'd had, cracking silly jokes, and discussing her never-ending domestic soap opera. Amma sat silently through it all, smiling, nodding, blinking.

"Thank you for caring," I told Velli, after she had put Amma to bed. "You look tired. Would you like a few days off next week?"

"I'm not going anywhere!" she burst out in her village Tamil. She grabbed my hand, crushed it against her large breasts. "You're an inspiration to me. All of you! How sensibly you people handle life's problems. Not like us. When my uncle's wife ran away, you should have seen the fireworks, whereas you all—Please don't take this the wrong way, elder brother, but sometimes at night when I can't sleep because of worries, I think of your smiling face and then I am at peace. How I wish I too could be free of emotions!"

It is not every day one is anointed the Buddha, and I tried to look suitably enlightened. But she had the usual misconception about mediation. Free of emotions! That was like thinking classical musicians were free of music because they'd moved beyond grunts and shrieks. We, the Enhanced, weren't free of emotions. On the contrary! We had healthy psychological immune systems, that was all.

I could understand Velli's confusion, but Sollozzo left me baffled. We chatted aperiodically, but often. Padma told me his scribbling was going better than ever, but his midmornings must have been fallow because that's when he usually called. I welcomed his pings; his mornings were my evenings, and in the evenings I didn't want to think about ESOPs, equities, or factory workers. It was quite cozy. Velli cutting vegetables for dinner, Amma alternating between bossing her and playing Sudoku, and Sollozzo and I arguing about something or the other. Indeed, the topic didn't matter as long we could argue over it. We argued about the evils of capitalism, the rise of Ghana, the least imperfect way to cook biryani, the perfect way to educate children, and whether bellies were a must for belly dancers. Our most ferocious arguments were often about topics on which we completely concurred.

For example, fiction. I knew he knew that fiction was best suited for the Unenhanced. But would he admit it? Never! He'd kept his promise, offering me one reason after another why fiction, and by extension writers, were still relevant in this day and age. It amused me that Sollozzo needed reasons. As a storyteller he should've been immune to reasons.

When I told him that, he countered with a challenge. He offered two sentences. The first: *Eve died, and Adam died of a heart attack.* The second: *Eve died, and Adam died of grief.*

"Which of these two is more satisfying?" asked Sollozzo. "Which of these feels more meaningful? Now tell me you prefer causes over reasons."

"It's not important what I prefer. If Adam had been Enhanced, he could've still died of a heart attack. But he wouldn't have died of grief. In time, no one will die of heart attacks either."

Another time he tried the old argument that literature taught us to have empathy. This bit of early-twenty-first-century nonsense had been discredited even in those simpleminded times. For one thing, it could just as easily be argued that empathy had made literature possible.

In any case, why had empathy even been necessary for humans? Because people had been like books in a foreign language; the books had meaning, but an inaccessible meaning. Fortunately, science had stepped in, fixed that problem. There was no need to be constantly on edge about other people's feelings. One knew how they felt. They felt happy, content, motivated, and relaxed. There was no more need to walk around in other people's shoes than there was to inspect their armpits for signs of the bubonic plague.

"Exactly my point!" shouted Sollozzo. He calmed down, of course. "Exactly my point. Enhancement is straightening our crooked timber. If this continues, we'll all become moral robots. I asked you once, are you so eager to return to Zion?"

"What is it with you and Zion?"

"Zion. Eden. Swarg. Sahyun. Paradise. Call it what you will. The book of Genesis, my brother. We were robots once. Why do you think we got kicked out of Zion? We lost our innocence when Adam and Eve broke God's trust, ate from the tree, and brought fiction into the world. We turned human. Now we have found a way to control the tree in our heads, become robots again, and regain the innocence that is the price of entry into Zion. Do you not see the connection between this and your disdain for fiction?"

I did not. But I had begun to see just how radically his European imagination differed from mine. He argued with me, but his struggles really were with dead white Europeans. Socrates, Plato, and Aristotle; Goethe, Baumgarten, and Karl Moritz; Hugo von Hofmannsthal, Mach, and Wittgenstein: I could only marvel at his erudition. I couldn't comment on his philosophers or their fictions, but I was a banker and could make any collateral look inadequate.

In this case, it was obvious. His entire argument rested on the necessity of novels. But every novel argues against its own necessity. The world of any novel, no matter how realistic, differs from the actual world in that the novel's world can't contain one specific book: the novel itself. For example, the world of Pamuk's *The Museum of Innocence* didn't contain a copy of *The Museum of Innocence.* If Pamuk's fictional world was managing just fine without a copy of his novel, wasn't the author—any author—revealing that the actual world didn't need the novel either? Et cetera, et cetera.

"I have found my Barbicane!" said Sollozzo, after a long pause. "I need your skepticism about fiction. Fire away. It will help me construct a plate armor so thick not even your densest doubts can penetrate."

All this, I later learned, was a reference to the legendary dispute in Verne's *From the Earth to the Moon* between shot manufacturer Impey Barbicane and armor-plate manufacturer Captain Nicholl. Barbicane invented more and more powerful cannons, and Nicholl invented more and more impenetrable armor-plating. At least I was getting an education.

If his hypocrisy could have infuriated me, it would have. As long as his tribe had mediated for the reader, it had been about freedom, empathy, blah di blah blah. Sollozzo hadn't worried about mediating for the reader when he'd written stories in English about Turkey. Stories in English by a non-Englishman about a non-English world! Jane Austen[1] might as well have written in Sanskrit about England.

It didn't matter, not really, this game of ours. Men, even among the Enhanced, find it complicated to say how fond they are of one another. Sollozzo made Padma happy. I was glad to see my Padma happy. Yes, she was no longer mine. She'd never been mine, for the Enhanced belong to no one, perhaps not even to themselves. I was glad to see her happy and I believed Sollozzo, not her Brain, was the one responsible. Bittu was also adjusting well to life in Boston. Or perhaps it was that Bittu had adjusted to her Boo-boo. Same thing, no difference. Padma said that Bittu had stopped referring to her Brain entirely.

Padma was amused by my chitchats with Sollozzo. "I am super jealous! Are you two planning to run away together?"

"Yes, yes, married today, divorced tomorrow," shouted Amma, who had been eavesdropping on our conversation. "What kind of world is this! No God, no morals. Do you care what the effect of your immoral behavior is on Bittu? Do you want her to become a dope addict? She needs to know who is going to be there when she gets back from school. She needs to have a mother and father. She needs a stable home. No technology can give her that. But go on, do what you like. Who am I to interfere? Nobody. Just a useless old woman who'll die soon. I can't wait. Every night I close my eyes and pray that I won't wake up in the morning. Who wants to live like this? Only pets. No, not even pets." She smiled, shifted gears. "Don't mind me, dear. I know you have the best interests of Bittu at heart. Which mother doesn't? Is it snowing in America?"

It's all good, brah, as the Americans say in the old movies. As I ruffled the pages of Sollozzo's volume, *The Robots of Eden and Other Stories,* I wondered what Velli had made of the arguments I'd had with Sollozzo. I remember her listening, mouth open, trying to follow just what it was that got him so excited. She'd found Sollozzo highly entertaining. She used to call him "Professor-uncle" with that innate respect for (a) white people, (b) Enhanced people, and (c) people who spoke English very fluently. Sometimes she would imitate his dramatic hand-gestures and his accented English.

In retrospect, I should have anticipated that Sollozzo's suicide would impact Velli the most. How could it not? The Unenhanced have little protection against life's blows on their psyches. I had called Velli into my office, tried to break the news to her as gently as I could.

"Your professor-uncle, he killed himself. Don't feel too bad. Amma is not to know, so you have to be strong. Okay, Velli?"

I had already counseled Padma on the legal formalities, chatted with Bittu, made her laugh, and everything went as smoothly as butter.

Padma and I decided we'd tell Amma the next day, if at all. Amma got tired very easily these days. Why add to her burdens?

"I have to handle his literary estate," said Padma, smiling, her eyes ablaze with light. "There's so much to do. So for now we'll all stay put in Boston. Will you be all right? You'll miss your conversations."

Would I? I supposed I could miss him. I didn't see the point, however. I was all right. Hadn't I handled worse? What had made her ask? Was I weeping? Rending my garments? Gnashing my teeth? Then, just so, the irritation slipped from my consciousness like rage-colored leaves scattering in the autumn wind. It was kind of her to be concerned.

"Why did professor-uncle kill himself?" asked Velli, already weeping.

"He took something that made his heart stop," I explained.

"But why!"

Why what? Why did the why of anything matter? Sollozzo had swallowed pills to stop his heart, he'd walked into the path of a truck, he'd drowned, he'd thrown himself into the sun, he'd dissolved into the mist. He was dead. How had his Brain let it happen? I made a mental note to talk to my lawyer. The AI would have a good idea whether a lawsuit was worth the effort. Unless Sollozzo's short story collection contained an encoded message (and I wouldn't put that past him), he hadn't left any last words.

"Aiyyo, why didn't he ask for help?" moaned Velli.

I glanced at her. She was obviously determined to be upset. Her quivering face did something to my own internals. I struggled to contain my smile, but it grew into a swell, a wave, and then a giant tsunami of a laugh exploded out of me, followed by another, and then another. I howled. I cackled. I drummed the floor with my feet. I laughed even after there was no reason to. Then, just so, I relaxed.

"I'm sorry," I said. "I wasn't laughing at you. In fact, you could say I wasn't the one laughing at all."

Velli looked at me, then looked away, her mouth working. Poor thing, it must all be so very confusing for her. I could empathize.

"Velli, why don't you go down to the river? The walk will do you good and you can make an offering at the temple in professor-uncle's name. You'll feel better."

I had felt it was sensible advice, and when she stepped out, I'd felt rather pleased with myself. But Velli never returned from the walk. I got a brief note later that night. She'd quit. No explanation, just like that. Her father, Rajan, came by to pick up her stuff, but he was vague, and worse, unapologetic. All rather inconvenient. All's well that ends well. Padma and Bittu were happy in Boston. Perhaps they would soon return. I hoped they would; didn't want Bittu to forget me. Sollozzo's volume would get the praise hard work always deserved, irrespective of whether such work pursued utility or futility.

"You'll spoil the book if you keep ruffling the pages like that," complained Amma.

I returned the volume to Amma, marveling at her enthusiasm

for reading. For novels. For stories. Dear Amma. Almost ninety years old, but what a will to live! Good. Good! Other people her age, they were already dead. They breathed, they ate, they moved about, but basically, they were vegetables with legs. Technology could enhance life, but it couldn't induce a will to live. Amma was a true inspiration. I could only hope I would have one-tenth the same enthusiasm when I was her age. I started to compliment Amma on this and other points, then realized she was already lost in the story. So I tiptoed away, disinclined to come between my beloved reader and the text.

Note

1. An English author, noted for her charming upper-class romances.

ELIZABETH BEAR

Erase, Erase, Erase

FROM *The Magazine of Fantasy & Science Fiction*

I SHOULDN'T HAVE let it get so far. It felt so inconsequential at first. Almost a relief to find myself getting a little misty around the edges. Bits dropping off. Stuff you don't need anymore.

Erase, erase, erase.

Sorry, historians. I know some of this would be useful to you, but it's all gone now. All gone.

I burned most of it.

Only I am still here.

And I am falling apart, and I can't remember who I used to be or how I got here.

Irresponsible of me, I know.

It's not just the memories, either. There's bits of me gone that I swear were there before. Fingertips. Some hair. The eyelashes on my right eye.

I'm almost certain I used to have those.

Sometimes I reach for something—coffee mug, keyboard—and realize I can't seem to find my own hand. I have to go look around the house for it, because I never remember where I had it last. Feet, at least, limbs—I don't tend to get far when those have gone missing. It's hard not to notice as soon as you try to stand up.

But I've found hands in the bed, under the bed, halfway up the stairs. Once in the fridge, which worried me a lot but actually it went right back on. Just felt a little weird and numb for a few minutes. Found my ear still stuck on an earbud once, and that was pretty awful. When the nose comes off, the glasses usually go with it.

I miss cats, but I don't have a cat anymore. I couldn't be sure of taking care of one. I'd probably forget to feed her, or not be able to work the can opener, and she'd resort to eating a mislaid finger.

None of it hurts. None of it seems to harm me in any way. Except that I'm falling apart, and a lot of my time is taken up with finding bits of me that have broken away somehow, and sticking them back on again in more or less the spot they came from.

I don't leave the house the way I used to. I'm glad I live in a time when nearly everything can be delivered.

And sometimes I get misty and confused. I'll be in the middle of some task and realize three hours later, in another part of the house, that I've left it undone. I'll find my spectacles in the fridge, or my socks on the bookshelf. I'm sure putting them there seemed like a logical idea at the time.

Sometimes also, I'll find my clothes in a puddle under me on the sofa and realize that they just kind of drained through me while I was working. I'll be chopping vegetables and the knife will hit the chopping block and just lie there, and it will be some time before I can manage to pick it up again. My hand will pass through my coffee cup for a while before it solidifies once more, and I won't get to drink it until it's cold.

At least the pens and notebooks are always solid. Always real. My laptop, too, and I guess that's logical, because it's not that different from a notebook in intention. Heck, some people call them notebooks.

Oh, but now. But this time.

I think I did more than get a little misty. I think I forgot something.

I think I forgot something very important. I think I forgot it on purpose, and because I forgot it, something terrible is going to happen. To a lot of people. Not just me.

So I'm falling apart. *And* I'm losing my mind.

I used to burn my notebooks.

I didn't want to be connected to the past they represented. I didn't want to be connected to the person they represented. I didn't want to be connected to the me that was.

I wanted to reinvent myself. Each time I made a terrible mistake,

I wanted to put everything aside, walk away, move on. I wanted to erase my errors. I wanted to change the past so the bad things had not happened. So I could not be punished for them. So I would not have to feel, all the time, so wrong.

I erased my thoughts, my feelings. My failed loves. The classes where my grades were only average. The abusive family background. The jobs that didn't turn out as well as I had hoped, that had toxic office politics, or abusive bosses. I erased the pain, the pain, the pain.

I wrote it all down in hope, and when it didn't work out, I burned it in despair.

I was trying to erase my mistakes, I suppose. It was a kind of perfectionism. If something has a flaw, throw it out and get something perfect next time. I was trying to move forward, in the hope that the next adventure would end better.

But not learning from the failures.

And so, little by little, I erased myself.

I threw myself away.

I would have been free and clear if I just hadn't read the newspaper that day. The day they printed the manifesto. I could have gone on about my life and my business in ignorance.

I could have spared myself a lot of grief. And work. And worry.

Grief and work and worry that would have been transferred to other people in my stead. That might still be served up to them if I can't prevent it.

And if it happens, I will know that it is my fault, because I failed.

The manifesto was in the paper. All the papers, I imagine, not just my specific one. It purported to be written by the group that had been mailing incendiary bombs to universities. Harvard, Yale, the University of Chicago. To their medical colleges.

That niggled at me, and I didn't think it was just because the University of Chicago was my alma mater. There was something.

Something back there.

Something I had worked very hard to forget.

Not violence, no. But the promise of violence. The *expectation* of violence.

Is that what people mean when they talk about menace? Something being menacing? That awareness that there is not just the *potential* for violence, in the abstract, a kind of background radiation that is always present—but that somebody, somewhere, is *planning* to cause someone harm.

Any long-term relationship is served by a little amnesia. A marriage—and I'm using the term loosely here, but we were together, if you can call it together, for almost eight years—is a country in flux. A series of negotiations and edges and considered silences. And some unconsidered ones, depending on how self-aware the diplomats in question are. Sometimes all the negotiations are carried out by reflex and instinct. Sometimes this results in war. A covert war, or an open one.

But sometimes, there's a plan.

When a diplomat who's acting on reflex, instinct, and conditioned response (diplomat A) meets a diplomat who is acting with self-awareness, caution, and a considered agenda of compromises (diplomat B), (diplomat B) is usually going to win the exchange.

I was (diplomat A) in this example.

I was seventeen years old.

I went in without a theory.

A broken heart is like a cracked bathtub. Nobody's going to make a full-price offer for a property with annoying repair problems like that hanging around. So either you fix it yourself, or you try to hide the cracks and cover up the damage. At least until the mark has signed enough paperwork that it's inconvenient to back out.

Plastic-covered notebooks give off a terrible smell as they burn.

I wasted a lot of paper.

I was not good at finishing the notebooks. I would reach a point where I was damned sick of who I was, how I had been feeling, how I had been acting. And then I needed to be done with the stained pages I had been writing, because I had written down everything. Everything about my internal landscape, anyway.

I didn't have friends.

I just had secrets.

And so I wrote them down.

It was actually easier—well, cheaper, anyway, and more efficient—when I was younger. In the three-ring and spiral-bound notebooks, I just ripped out the offending pages and tore them up. Got rid of them. Shredded them and gave them a shove.

But then I graduated to bound books. The cheap fabric-covered ones at first. Then better ones, professional-quality ones, with paper that ink pens did not feather on or bleed through. I liked the hard-covered ones in pretty colors, with ribbon markers and pockets in the back. Graph paper or dot grids. I did not like wide-ruled.

But those were harder to destroy, eventually. When they needed destruction.

Everything needs destruction in the end. And so I learned to burn.

I thought about burning more than notebooks when I was young. I thought of self-immolation, but I never had the courage. I thought of arson, but I never had the cruelty. I remembered those things, vaguely. Like a story that had happened to someone else.

Maybe that was why that manifesto struck me so hard, I tell myself, as my fingers slip through the handle of the coffee pot again. *A major American city,* it had said. *An inferno of flames. The Judgment of a just and terrible God.*

Engulfed.

Soon, soon. Soon.

But no. There is more than that. Some part of me that I can't access knows. Knows which city. Knows who had written those words. Knows enough to stop this terrible thing from happening.

I just can't *remember.*

How do you learn to erase yourself?

It's not something that comes naturally to children. Children seek attention because attention means survival. So to get them to erase themselves, you have to teach them that they don't exist. And because it is an unnatural, self-destructive thing that you are teaching them—a maladaptive response—the only tactic that works is to make the consequences of noncompliance worse than the consequences of nonexistence.

That takes force. Violence, physical or emotional. If you just try to *ignore* a kid, they'll act out and seek attention through misbehavior.

Any port in a storm.

I bet, given half a chance, I could have been a charming child.

But I didn't learn to be charming. I learned how not to be real.

I learned to have no vulnerabilities and expect no consideration. I learned I had no intrinsic value and was only marginally worthwhile for what I could provide, if what I provided was beyond reproach.

I learned I was not allowed to be angry. To defend myself. To have needs. I learned to be good at being alone, because if you were alone, nobody could betray you.

I thought I had escaped all that when I went away to college. But like the horror movie phone call, the loathing was coming from inside my head.

I didn't hold on to things, because holding on to things hurt. If you didn't hold on, then when you lost something, you lost it easy.

But if you don't hold on, you lose things.

My notebooks and pens are still solid. I can write all the time. Under any conditions. I can write things down.

If I can just remember them.

I can write them down.

I lost a lot of pens.

I couldn't bear to write in pencil. And it didn't matter because I was burning the books.

But I couldn't seem to hang on to the pens.

It's in the notebooks, isn't it? The thing I need.

There's no way to get the notebooks back, of course. Even if I found similar ones, they'd be empty. All the important words—all of the words that have the memories attached that might keep people from being hurt—set on fire, burned up—were, in a particularly distasteful irony, burned up themselves long ago.

Oh. But the pens.

I started collecting pens when I was very young. My mother gave me a fountain pen. Not an expensive one, but she wrote with fountain pens, and she thought I should, too, and I was excited to be like my mother in this way I thought was grown-up and cool. One led to two, led to five or six. Student pens.

I loved them.

And the ink! I loved the ink even more. Because you can put

the same ink in a cheap pen as in an expensive one, and then you get to write with it.

Finding the right ink, the right pen, is like coming home. Like finding the place in which you live and in which you *want* to live. The place you want to stay forever. The place where you belong.

On a smaller scale, of course.

But still, it can make you a little bit emotional.

And if you are lucky, you might actually recognize it while it's right in front of you, while you're standing there, and not once you walk away, foolishly.

The hardest thing is when you walk away from home knowing that it's home, because home is changing, or challenging, or making you sad. Or because you screwed up and broke something, and you think you're too embarrassed to stay, or you're not welcome there anymore.

So you go someplace else and think you can live there. But it isn't home. And then you have to try to get home again.

Sometimes it takes a long time to get home again. Some people never make it back.

I thought I had to be perfect. I thought I couldn't live with my errors. I thought it would be better to run away. Start clean. Discard the ruined page and keep reaching for a fresh one. Burn my notebooks.

Erase my history. Erase my screwups.

Erase my self.

Erase, erase, erase.

I start on collectors' websites and then on auction sites, looking for the pens. Most of them were not expensive at the time when I bought them—I never had a lot of money. Some of them had gotten more expensive since.

A funny thing happens as I start looking. I search for one pen to see what it would cost to replace it. And in the related items, I find more that look familiar. That I suddenly remember having owned. And when I chase those links, there are more, still more familiar-looking ones.

I am forty-five years old. I *think* I am forty-five years old.

I get out my birth certificate and check.

I am forty-five years old.

How many pens have I lost?

How many other things have I forgotten about, before now?

I think of a pen I'd liked, when I was twenty-five or so. I remember putting it in a jacket pocket. I don't remember ever finding it there again. It had been a blue marbled plastic fountain pen, a kind of bulbous and silly-looking thing. A lot of personality, I guess you'd say. It wrote very well.

I find one like it on an auction site. Lose that auction but win another in a few days. Sixty-three dollars plus shipping. I think the pens in a box set with ink were thirty dollars new back in 1995.

Fortunately my books are doing all right, and my needs in general are few. My chief extravagance is a little indulgence in grocery store sushi, once in a while. I use a grocery delivery service. I can't drive. What if my foot fell off while I was reaching for the brake?

The pen arrives after three days. I get lucky with the mail that day and it doesn't fall through my hands. I take the pen out of the box, weigh it in my palm. Light, plastic with gold trim. The blue is so intense, it looks violet.

I uncap it and examine the nib, squinting my middle-aged eyes. Then I laugh at myself and use the zoom function on my phone camera to get a better look at it. The phone, for once, doesn't slide through my hand.

The mysterious internet stranger I'd bought it from hadn't cleaned it very well. I get a bulb syringe and wash it at the sink, soaking and rinsing. You're supposed to use distilled water, but the water here at my house is soft, from a surface reservoir. The same reservoir H. P. Lovecraft once wrote about, as the towns that now lie under it were drowning.

Anyway, I've never had any problems with it. Even if it is saturated with alien space colors, they don't seem to cause problems with the nibs, so that's good news overall.

Once it's clean, I ink it up from a big square bottle in a color that matches the barrel, and sit down at the table with a notebook, ready to write.

With the pen in my hand, I find suddenly I am full of memories. Strange; I can go through a whole day, usually, without remembering things.

I remember the pen.

And now I'm holding it in my hand, and I start to write, in a lovely red-sheened cobalt blue.

I grew up to be a writer. A novelist. That will not surprise you. You are, after all, reading my words right now.

I write, and write, and the notebook stays solid and the pen stays solid and it writes as well as the one I used to have. But my right hand—I'm left-handed—has a tendency to slide through the table if I'm not paying attention. And twice I fall right through my chair, which is a new and revolting development.

I don't let it stop me, though. I write, and remember, and write some more. About somebody I can sort of recall. A long, long time ago.

An incident that happened at the University of Chicago. After . . . after I stopped being a student there?

It's so damned hard to recall.

"There is no point in being so angry." His words had the echo that used to come from long distance.

But I wasn't being angry to make a point.

Which was not something the manipulative son of a bitch could ever have understood. I was angry because I was angry. Because he deserved my anger.

I was angry because anger is a defense mechanism. It's an emotion that serves to goad you to action, to remove the irritant on your turf or the thing that is causing you pain.

"I'm angry because you're hurting me," I said. "I'm angry because you're hurting a lot of people. Stop it, and I won't need to be angry with you anymore."

Therapy gives you a pretty good set of tools to be (diplomat B), it turns out. I was still furious with my mother for forcing me to go.

But it was helping.

It might take me a while to get over my anger. But that didn't seem salient to the argument we were having, so I kept it to myself.

"You can't just set things on fire because you don't like the way the world is going."

"Oh, I can," he told me. "And you already helped me. You're just too much of a coward to own that and be really useful, so you'll let other people do your dirty work and keep your hands clean."

"You won't do it," I said.

"You're right," he agreed. "I probably won't. Don't call me again."

I think about calling. An anonymous tip. Or sending an email.

But I don't have any evidence. And I don't have a name.

"I know who wrote the manifesto. But I can't remember his name. And I helped him come up with the plan. The plan to burn down a city. Except I can't remember what city, either. Or the details of the plan."

Yeah. No.

Maybe he was right. Maybe I am too much of a coward to take responsibility for something I believe in. For something I had once believed in, until I forgot?

Maybe I forgot because I knew it would feel like my fault if I remembered.

My mother gave me an expensive fountain pen when I graduated high school. It was a burgundy one, small and slim. Wrote beautifully. I didn't know enough to appreciate it at the time.

I don't think the new ones are as nice anymore.

I lost that one when I was thrown by a horse one time in college. It was in my pocket, and when I got to my feet, bruised and hip aching, it was gone. And no amount of searching turned it up.

There are a lot of them on the internet.

But the damned things ain't cheap. And how do you tell which ones are counterfeit?

But maybe the pen I was using at the time . . .

At the time it happened? At the time I learned the thing I can't remember? At the time I *did* the thing I don't *want* to remember?

But I didn't have the pen long. Did I?

In any case, maybe that pen would help me remember.

I spend way too much money on it. And it comes.

I hold it in my hand. It feels . . . itchy. But it doesn't fill me up with memories the way the other one had.

I remember the unused pages at the back of my old notebooks. There were always a few.

I find myself taking the books down off the shelf, thumbing

through them. The unburned ones, of course. Thumbing through the burned ones would have been unfeasible, and even if it weren't, it wouldn't accomplish much of anything beyond getting my fingers ashy.

I find myself looking at ink colors, organizational choices. How my handwriting has evolved.

We lose all the best things to time.

But time brings a lot of benefits, also. Freedom from old wounds, for example.

Perspective.

Grace.

The wisdom to identify the heads that need to be busted, and the courage of your convictions to go out and bust some heads.

I have a couple of dozen old notebooks. And at the end of almost every one of them is a swath of pristine pages. Somewhere between twenty and fifty, a full signature at least and maybe two or three —just sitting there wordless and ignored.

Even after I stopped burning them, I guess I never really finished a notebook before I moved on. The lure of the next book was already there, like a pressure inside me urging me to set this one aside and pick up the perfect one that would be waiting. Untrammeled. Pure.

Without any mistakes in it.

Yes, I hate using broken things. Dirty things. I hate things that are cracked or warped or seem *old* and in disrepair.

So I would get to the point where I could conceivably justify discarding the old book with its scuffed cover and frayed page edges and all the mistakes inside it. And I would switch to a new one, clean and unscribbled-in. And out the old one would go. Into the flames, at first. Later, onto a shelf with its sisters.

I can touch the notebooks. I can always touch the notebooks.

But they don't go back far enough. They don't have the thing that mattered in them. That had happened before. The thing that I can't remember.

The thing that had happened and been burned.

The thing I use my new old echo of a pen now to write about.

*

With the one before him, I never argued. We never made enough demands on each other to have anything to fight about.

With him, I think I fought all the time. I remember . . . screaming matches. I remember arguments that made me doubt my sanity. I remember him telling me I said things I couldn't remember saying. I remember letting him win because I couldn't keep track of where the goalposts were, and because I never learned to argue to win.

I never learned to take up space in other people's lives.

I wish I had known to be wary of the urge to crystallize my identity, to declare myself a thing—one thing, or another—and not accept that I was a continuity of things that would always be changing.

I might have been less eager to discard the thing I had been to become something new if I hadn't been so afraid that acknowledging the old thing meant being trapped for all time. If I hadn't been so afraid the people who knew me would never let me change, I might have held on to more of them, instead of shedding whole lives like a snake sheds skins.

Of course, sometimes people won't let you change. Because their self-image is bound up with yours, and they're afraid of challenging themselves, too. Or because they want to keep you weak so they can own you. Or because their own identity gets stuck on you being and behaving a certain way. It's a cliché to say that alcoholics and addicts often find they need a whole new suite of friends when they get clean, and their lives no longer revolve around getting altered anymore.

But the thing is, over time, changes just become part of the status quo. Tattoos that marked a milestone or a rebellion to our younger selves soften into our skin, become unremarked. They become a part of us, a part of our image and who we are.

What is mine, and what is not mine—our conception of these things changes as we grow.

I moved around a lot. As an adult, and as a child. I didn't have any place that felt like mine.

Until I met him. Until I met Joshua.

*

I write the name, and look at it, and know that it is right. I should be giddy with triumph. Blazing with the endorphins of having figured something out.

I feel hungry, and dizzy. And tired.

I was sitting in a booth at the airport, crying on the phone. "I wish you had just shot me," I said.

At the time when I said it, it was true.

Joshua was telling me about the girl he'd met. The girl who was helping with his plans. The girl who would be taking over for me, he said, so that I could get some rest. Get my head together.

Get back to being right with the revolution.

I asked her name. He told me. She was somebody I knew. I asked if I could come back after Thanksgiving with my mom. He said if I got right, I could. He said that my leaving to see my family had been a mistake, and I would have to make amends for it.

"You can't do this to her," I said. "She's just a kid. She doesn't know she's giving up her whole life."

She was the same age I had been, eight years before. I was a wizened old woman of twenty-seven.

"Come back," he said. "Forget about your mother. We can talk. That other girl doesn't have to be involved."

My mom, whom I had not seen in four years because of Joshua, was dying. I reminded him of that. He reminded me that if I were a good revolutionary, that wouldn't matter. "Anyway, remember what her husband did to you."

How could I forget?

I have since, largely, forgotten.

He hung up. I remember thinking, very clearly, He'll use her up the same way he used up me.

I wish I could say that thought is the thing that motivated me. I wish I could say that was the last time I ever talked to him.

I sat there and cried for another hour, until I had to get up to make my connection. Nobody bothered me. People cry in airports so often, it's not much of a spectacle. These days they cry and shout into their cell phones just about anywhere. Back then, the crying and shouting were more localized.

Halfway to the gate, I stopped. I walked back to the phones. The young woman he'd replaced me with was a sophomore. Nineteen years old. I knew her name and where she came from.

I called her family.

"Your daughter joined a cult in college," I told them. "You need to get her home."

I hung up. I ran for my gate.

I just barely made my plane.

We have this idea that healing comes as an epiphany.

We have it in part because epiphanies are narratively convenient. They're tidy for a storyteller; there's a break point, a moment when everything changes. An identifiable narrative beat. A point at which everything before is one way, and everything after is different. They're satisfying. They provide catharsis and closure.

Frustratingly, in real life, you often have to go back and have the same epiphany over and over again, incrementally, improving a tiny bit each time. Frustrating for you. Frustrating for your loved ones.

It would be nicer if you could just have that single crystallizing incident, live through it, and get on with being a better human being who was better at humaning.

It's comforting to the afflicted to think we only have to make one change, and we can be better. Boom, all at once. Wouldn't it be *nice* if role-playing or primal scream therapy or rebirthing therapy or a hot, uninhibited fuck or a midnight confession or a juice cleanse or a confessional essay or a cathartic piece of fiction really could heal all the old damage just like that? In one swoop? Wouldn't it be nice?

Sure.

Of course, it's nonsense, like so many other narratively convenient things we learn about from stories. But like so many of the things we learn about from stories, it's *useful* nonsense.

And epiphany isn't going to fix us. Maybe nothing is going to fix us. But recognizing the damage might help us route around it. Which isn't nothing, you know?

The truth is that you never get to stop dealing with the damage. You might get better at it. You might find a lot of work-arounds and you might be happier—or even happy, inasmuch as happiness is a state and not a process!—but happiness doesn't just *happen.* And it doesn't happen instantly but incrementally, with a lot of constant effort and focus.

I was small, and the people who should have taken care of me didn't. In some cases, they didn't take care of me because they were awful people. In some cases, they didn't take care of me because they had their own shit going on.

I get that. I have spent most of my life with my own shit going on, after all.

One of the things with having your own shit going on is that, first, it blinds you to other people's problems. It's hard to have empathy and remember that, as the saying goes, everyone you meet is fighting a great battle when your attention is all taken up by being on fire right now. It's hard to find the energy to be calm and kind and to consider the divergence of experience of others when you're exhausted and trying to keep your own head above the waves and you're swallowing salt water and you have no idea where you are going to find the energy to keep kicking.

Another thing about having your own shit going on is that until you get some perspective on it, that shit feels enormous. Like the center of the universe. And it kind of is, in that nobody who is excavating a pile of trauma like that has the energy for anything else except shoveling. But it becomes so all-consuming that it's easy to forget that you—and your trauma—are not the only thing on anybody else's mind, or even the most important one, because they're all really busy thinking about their own shovels.

They have their *own* shit, their own trauma and crisesdeadlinestaxeshealthproblemssoreteethfamilydramatoxicneighbors you name it eating up the lion's share of their own attention. And that's *fine,* is the thing. There's *nothing wrong with that.* Your problems are your problems, and their problems are their problems, and that's the way it's actually supposed to be.

But when you're dealing with that much trauma, and it's that raw, boundaries are another thing you wind up sucking at.

Recovery, I guess I'm trying to say, makes narcissists of us all.

So when I'm freaking out now about what people think of me or what they think is going on with me, I remind myself . . . I don't merit more than a passing consideration in the day of most people I encounter. They just don't think that hard about me.

Thank God.

People got their own problems.

I certainly got more than enough of mine.

*

I saw her once more, even though I never planned to go back to Chicago. She came to see me after her parents let her out of the treatment program they'd had her committed to.

She came to my mother's house, where I was living. Working temp jobs. Never staying longer than a week because after a week, people start to loop you into the politics and then they expect you to get involved. I was in therapy, because my dying mother made me.

Biggest favor she ever did me, in hindsight.

She stood in the doorway looking at me when I answered, framed in the greens of the yard. She studied my face. We were both a little better-fed than we had been.

And then she said to me, "I don't think you can fully appreciate how much I hate you."

I smiled as if she had accepted my offer of tea. "Oh," I said, feeling the swell of self-loathing in me like a rising magma dome, "I think I can, most likely."

Before I digressed, what I was pointing out was that it doesn't happen fast, when things change. It happens slow. It's an unpicking. The Gordian knot is more of a problem when you're in a hurry and you don't have any tools—assuming you want the string to be useful for something when you're done unpicking it, which I've always thought was the problem with the Alexandrian solution.

Well, I had assembled my tools. With as much haste as possible, and it hadn't been fast, honestly, despite feeling that amorphous sense of formless dread, the pressure pushing on my awareness constantly without any knowledge of where it was going to happen, or when.

Now I have them. Pens, inks. A selection of flawless new notebooks.

The first line in a pristine notebook is always a little fraught. That paper, so innocent. And here I am, intending to put a mark down that will scar it forever.

Maybe the real reason I burned my notebooks was that I didn't want the responsibility.

Maybe that's also why I never had children. Just stories.

Nobody really remembers if you screwed up any given story, five years after the fact.

Erase, erase, erase.

There's freedom in not being important. In not being seen.

*

I can't touch food for three days. Unfortunately, not being able to touch the food does nothing to keep me from getting hungry.

There's so much to forgive yourself for when it comes down to it. So many little cysts of self-hate and personal despair.

"I need you to keep your promises," I said. And that was the beginning of the end.

He promised easily. Fluidly.

Meaninglessly.

And I kept on believing him. Forgiving him.

Making excuses.

I was so good at excuses.

Not for myself. I was always culpable. And I always found ways to punish myself. I believed it when he told me I was wrong. My perceptions, my understanding of events. When he told me I must be crazy, because what I remembered hadn't happened that way at all.

I was unforgivable. I was sure.

But then I asked him to keep his promises.

And I started writing his promises down. In my notebook. With my pen.

I find the damaged pen in a box I didn't know had any pens in it, at the back of a deep cabinet shelf. I rattle it reflexively, not expecting a sound. But there is weight inside it, and something shifts.

I open it and find a narrow, black, beat-up old fountain pen I cannot identify.

I mean, I know what pen it is. It's one I must have been given by a family member, but I can't remember what the occasion was, or who had given me it. I had used it all through college after I lost my graduation pen. But I don't know what *kind* it is.

It's missing the gold trim band on the cap, and the cap doesn't close and lock. I remember it having a satisfying click when I shut it. It's so slender, I used to tuck it inside the spiral rings of my notebooks. It lived there. It was a good pen.

It is full of dried ink, because I am a terrible pen custodian.

I check the collector websites and can't find anything like it.

There was a time I was a bad friend. I was in love with somebody, and they were in love with somebody else, and I was in love with that person, too. Looking back, I don't think either of them loved me.

I didn't handle it well.

I remember sitting in a bar in a bad chain restaurant breaking up tortilla chips into crumbs with my fingers because I needed something to do while my friend broke up with me, and I didn't have the will to eat.

And I'd already picked the whole label off my beer.

I tried to make amends, years later. I can't blame them for not wanting to talk to me.

I could have done without that memory. I had, for years, I now realize.

Accountability. That's another thing you lose when you erase yourself.

Thank God.

Some of the pens start slipping through my hands. At first, the newer ones, or the ones that had been bought as replacements for ones long lost. The older ones fare better, as if every scratch on the barrel, every bit of luster worn by use from the nib, every imperfection, makes the object in my hands more real. Or gives my hands something to stick to as they become more phantasmal. More of an unreality.

The older ones fare better. At first.

Then those begin to fall through me, too.

There is so much I still can't remember. I frown at those pristine notebooks with their smooth, friendly paper. I stroke a finger over them, and sometimes I feel the nap of the page, and sometimes my fingertip sinks through.

I know—I can *feel*—the memories down there, like shipwrecks under clouded water. But I can't make out the shapes. Can't describe what I know has to be there.

I start dropping even pens.

But I never drop the broken one. It feels steady and solid in my hand. As if it were more real than the others.

That gives me an idea.

They used to say of somebody who made a bad marriage that they threw themselves away. What happens if you never actually got married, because marriage is a tool of the bourgeoisie?

I'm pretty sure you can still throw yourself away. Erase yourself. For somebody else, or because you don't think you are worth preserving.

*

I don't have any control over what memories I get, when I get them. Except every single one of them is something I would have rather forgotten.

My stepfather liked to have excuses to hit. So he could feel good about himself, I guess. One way you get excuses to hit is to expect perfection in every task, and set hard tasks without allowing the person you're setting them for time to learn how to do them.

Then, when the student isn't perfect, you have a good reason to punish somebody.

Another thing you can do is change your expectations constantly, so that nobody can predict what is expected and what isn't. Make them arbitrary and impossibly high. Don't allow for any human imperfections.

Since I can touch it, I decide to fix the mystery pen.

I make a new trim ring for it out of polymer clay, to help hold the cap in place. I clean it, and while I handle it, my hands stay solid on the tools. As if it is some kind of talisman to my past reality.

I wish I could say my repair job is some kind of professional affair with a loupe and so on, but I have some epoxy and some rubber cement and honestly, I kind of fake it. You do what you can with what you have, and that's all right then.

I take up my broken pen. The nib is still pretty good, though it doesn't write like a fine point anymore. More like a medium. And even on smooth paper, it scratches a little.

It's still usable, though. And it makes a nice smooth line.

Except I have faded more, in the interim. I am vanishing. Falling away, like all the memories I hadn't wanted, and now wish I had been less cavalier with. I can't manage to open a notebook, let alone write in one. I am able to reread the old ones I'd kept. But the new ones are as ghostly as the cheese sandwiches have become.

Maybe this is better than living with the pain of remembering. Maybe fading away, fading into nothingness, starving to an immaterial and noninteractive death—maybe that is the happiest ending.

Except the one thing I *know*—know with a drowning urgency, though I still cannot remember the specifics—is that people will come to harm if I cannot remember the things I once knew.

A lot of people.

And not just hurt.

People are going to get killed.

More people. A lot more. Exponentially more than had been harmed by three incendiaries sent to medical schools.

If I can just remember the plan I came up with. Before I helped him write this manifesto. Almost twenty years ago.

If I can only remember the rest of his name.

Lack of food and water doesn't help me think any more clearly. I've never been good at handling low blood sugar. So half my time seems to be spent figuring out how to write. How to even get words down on the page.

I can put the pen on the paper—the pen stays solid, even if it is in my hand. And I can use the nib to turn the pages. But do you know how hard it is to write legibly and usefully in a notebook you have no way to smooth flat, or to steady? Especially when your temples ache with hunger, and a sour metallic taste seems to sit in your abdomen.

My laptop has long since stopped being something I could touch. I would have given a lot for that laptop right now.

My laptop. And a banana.

My stepfather would hit me with a belt, and he wouldn't stop until I managed to keep from crying.

"I'm not hurting you that badly, you little wimp. Quit that squalling, or I'll give you something real to cry about."

It's amazing what you can learn to keep inside.

A day later, lying more or less *in* the sofa, my head bleary and aching with hunger and my throat scratchy with dehydration, I realize that those blank notebook pages are the answer. I can't get the burned notebooks back—that was, after all, why I had burned them—but I *can* fill these leftover pages with memories of what I might have written in them.

I can construct some kind of a record, though it will be one very filtered by the passage of time.

And the important memory might be in there somewhere. If I am lucky.

And brave.

*

It would be so much easier just to fade away.

Erase, erase.

So much easier to stop pretending my existence matters and let go. Then it will be over. Then I won't have to keep existing after I do this thing. This thing I don't even want to do. It's not the idea of drifting into nothingness afterward that bothers me. It's the terrible fear that instead, I might hook myself back into the universe somehow. Reassert my reality.

Get stuck being real.

I joined a cult in college. That much, I know. Like a story told sketchily over a cup of coffee, but without the context or detail because it's an embarrassing story and nobody wants to think about it too hard. The person telling it is embarrassed to have been there, and the person hearing it is reflecting embarrassment as well.

I joined a cult in college. I really craved the love-bombing, because I had never in my life felt really loved. I didn't know how to receive attention in smaller doses, at lower proof. I had so much armor on, it took weaponized love to get through.

I joined a cult in college. It was a dumb idea and it was weird while it lasted—it lasted long past college, it lasted eight whole years—and I was in love with one of the guys who ran it.

I joined a cult in college. One of the guys who ran it . . . I thought he was my boyfriend. He wasn't, though. He was preying on me. Grooming me.

I did not have a lot of agency in the relationship.

He's one of the cult's leaders now.

The pen ran out of ink, and then I had to figure out how to fill it when I also couldn't touch most of my ink bottles. My hand just swiped through them, all the gorgeous little art objects full of brilliant colors. I groped back in the shelf, waving blindly . . .

My fingers brushed something squat and cool. I pulled it out, and the bottles that had been in front of it slid out of the way, clattering. Not of my unreal hand. But of the ink, the thing that was real. The thing that mattered.

One or two fell to the floor. Ink bottles are sturdy, though, and the carpet kept them from breaking.

The bottle I could touch was a bottle of Parker Quink, blue-black. It was two-thirds empty. The label stained.

An old and trusty friend.
I filled my pen.

He threw me down the stairs by my hair one time.
My stepfather, I mean.
Not Joshua.
I'd forgotten that. Erased it. And now I can't unremember it again.

A funny thing happens as I write.

I feel myself getting more real. I figure it out when I realize that I can lean an elbow on the table I am resting the current mostly finished notebook on. That's a relief; you have no idea how hard writing is when you can manage to hold a pen but not rest your hand on anything.

When I realize that I can touch things, I stop writing and run into the kitchen, terrified of missing my window.

I still can't lift a glass, but I manage to elbow the faucet on after a few minutes of trying. I bend my head sideways and drink from the thin, cold trickle of stale-tasting water. Nothing ever felt better flowing down my throat. I gulp, gulp again. Manage to get it to pool in my hands and drink that in a slightly more civilized fashion.

I drink until my stomach hurts, and then go to make sure the toilet lid is up, just in case I turn immaterial again before the stuff works its way through my system. Dehydrated as I had been, that might take a while, but I have learned to plan ahead. Such are the important life concerns of the terminally ghostly.

I sit on the bathroom floor and rest the back of my head against the sliding glass door of the shower. At least I am not falling through walls or floors. Yet?

I can stop. I don't have to do this anymore. I can stop, and it will be miserable . . . but I will die of thirst in a few days. If I stop clutching at making myself real. If I just accept that I am not important, and let my ridiculous scribblings go.

It sounds so appealing. A final erasure.

And I won't have to remember . . .

I won't have to remember the horrible person I had been. The horrible things I had done. The horrible things that had happened to me. I could forget them all.

Who knows? Maybe if I forget them thoroughly enough—if I encourage myself to forget them thoroughly enough—I won't even die. I'll just fade.

Maybe if I fade enough, I won't have material needs like food, water, air anymore. I'll be a ghost for real.

I'll be free. Free of myself. Free of pain.

I have these notebooks here.

I'm probably real enough to burn them now. Right now.

It will just cost the lives of some people I have never heard of to get there.

How many people?

I don't know. One. A hundred. Three thousand.

Too many.

The glass shower door is cool. I relish its solidity.

When I put my hand up onto the sink to help myself stand, sometime later, my hand goes right through.

I don't have to do this. I don't have to exist.

I can just let myself be perfect, and be gone.

So much easier.

So much easier.

Except I remember about the fires now. And if I write it all down . . . I think I might make myself real again.

Then how do I get away from what I did? From what was done?

Oh God, do I have to live with myself now? Do I have to live with being flawed, and do things I'm not very good at?

People will know.

People will see me.

People will punish me.

I write it all down.

Of course the manifesto was familiar.

I was the one who had written it.

What was published wasn't my words exactly. It had been decades; what I wrote hadn't survived the intervening twenty-odd years with Joshua unscathed. Unedited. It had passed through other pens than mine along the way.

But somewhere in the ashes of forgotten notebooks had been written a draft of that statement. Its structures, its rhetoric, even its handwriting had once been mine.

I don't bother calling the local police. I call the local field office of the FBI.

"I know who wrote the manifesto," I say into the phone. "His name is Joshua Bright. Or it was, he might have changed it. And that probably wasn't his real name. Because who calls their kid Joshua Bright if they can help it? And he's got a plan to use incendiary devices to burn down a big chunk of Chicago if you don't stop him."

"Ma'am?" the tinny voice at the end of the phone says. "We'll be sending a couple of agents over right away to talk to you. Please stay where you are until they arrive."

I make myself a peanut butter sandwich while I wait.

That story about the airport and the aftermath. I don't think it really happened that way.

I think it's a pretty story I'm telling myself. I don't know if I ever stood up for that girl, really. If I ever stood up for myself.

I remember doing it. I wrote it down. Does that mean it happened?

Or did I just figure out that Joshua was cheating on me and split not too much later? I tried to forget. I was, needless to say, pretty successful.

The plan to put incendiaries in basements and start a huge firestorm in Chicago had been mine to begin with. I came up with it. I gave it to Joshua as if it were just the plot for one of my thrillers. The ones I make my living writing now.

I wonder if he'll try to blame it on me. Or if he'll want to take credit.

He'll want to take credit.

I never really thought he would do *it. It was a thought experiment, that was all.*

Just a thought experiment.

I joined a cult in college. It turned out about as bad as you'd expect.

If you join a cult in college, I hope you get well soon.

You don't have to be perfect.

Sometimes it's okay for a thing to be a little bit broken.

Sometimes it's okay to make do with what you have, and what you are.

I imagine meeting him in court. Of course I will have to testify. I'd better make sure of my solidity before then. I'd better *commit.*

My fingers leave peanut butter stains on the paper. I hope the food delivery comes soon. I'd like some milk.

I can't know what it will be like, but I rehearse it in my head anyway. I write it down to make it real, so I can act on it when the time comes.

The FBI are on their way.

Me, strong, implacable. Joshua saying, "I didn't think you had the balls to turn me in."

Me meeting his gaze. "You never did know me."

I wait for the doorbell. For the food. For the authorities.

I get to the bottom of the last page. I reach blindly for the next book, find the blanks at the end, and keep writing.

You don't have to be perfect.

This story isn't done yet with me.

REBECCA ROANHORSE

A Brief Lesson in Native American Astronomy

FROM *The Mythic Dream*

WE WERE GONNA be stars. That's what you got to understand. Big fucking stars. Like Jack and Rose or Mr. and Mrs. Carter, like our faces on every screen, dominating every media feed. Everyone already loved us, wanted to be us, wanted to fuck us. And people like that, people like us? Young, rich, famous? We don't just get sick and die. They've got med docs and implants and LongLife™ tech that keeps people alive for 150 years now if you can afford it, and we could afford it. So how could they let her die? How could I lose my perfect girl? How could they do that to me?

I keep the room dark. My agent's been calling, but fuck him, you know? He says I'm missing important appearances, that if I'm not careful people will forget about me. Maybe it's time I move on, he says. Find a new girlfriend. Someone hot. Be seen with this new hot chick at a big premiere or something. They're launching a new luxury liner at the end of the week, he says, something that takes you to the edge of the atmosphere and projects your digital image into outer space before hurling you back to the Earth. A billion people will see your face, shining like an honest-to-God star. You should go, he says. Go to almost-space and smile a big almost-smile with a new almost-girlfriend and make people remember who you are. But who the fuck would want to ride that? You can't breathe up there. Who wants to go where you can't breathe?

My agent convinces the boss lady of DigImagine to come talk

to me. She bangs on my door until I think she's gonna shatter the glass. That door cost me half my pay on that damn Japanese shampoo commercial where I had to wear that breechcloth and pose in front of a stuffed bison. Sure, it was humiliating, but I do have really stellar Indian hair—long, black, and it moves like it's got its own built-in wind machine. And the shampoo company was paying big for a few hours of easy work—flip, smolder, flip, smolder. It's what I do anyway most of the time, so why not?

Can't remember last time I smiled for the camera. They want stoic, so I give them stoic. Cherie always thought it was funny. We'd laugh about stuff like that all the time.

Whatever.

Anyway, I don't want some motherfucker breaking my glass door, even if she is a studio head. I let her in because she's holding a little white envelope. I know that envelope. What it holds. That's the only reason that I open the door. It's like I can already feel the wet burn on the back of my eyes. Only question is whose memories she's holding.

"I'm Carol Elder," she says, her bone-white pumps click-clacking on the hardwoods as she strides through the door. "Sorry to hear about Charlene." She turns toward me and thrusts two things into my hands. The white envelope and an old-fashioned business card, her name printed in neat black ink on a white linen card. Our fingers touch briefly, accidentally, and hers are cold.

"Cherie." I tuck the card in the pocket of the bathrobe I'm wearing and take that envelope over to the kitchen island.

"What?"

"Her name was Cherie. Like the kind you eat. She was sweet." I don't know why I say that, but it feels important, like she should get her name right and know that she was a decent person. Despite all the other stuff, the rumors, the thing with the biowear executive. None of that mattered. She was good and didn't deserve to die.

Carol Elder follows me into the kitchen. She watches as I take a knife from the block and slice the envelope open. I catch her eyes roving the room. The overflowing ashtrays, the food cartons, the big engram needle on the coffee table surrounded by pieces of human hair, nails, flecks of skin. All laid out in a row. I swear she shudders.

"Did the doctors figure out what was wrong with her?" she asks. "What killed . . . I mean . . . why she died? Walked on," she adds hurriedly. "I mean, don't you people say 'walked on'?"

I can almost hear the roar of the Pacific out back, but with the blinds down and the air on, it sounds more like traffic on the 405. I don't give a shit either way. Cherie's the one who wanted to live on the beach. Malibu, she said. All the real stars live in Malibu, so we have to, too. Even if the truth is half the stars these days are kids with fancy digital setups in Kansas or big corporation simulations that aren't even fleshies. But Cherie wanted it, so we moved to Malibu.

I shake the contents of the white envelope out. A small glass vial, marked with the initials C.A., a little red band wound around the cap as a warning that the contents are high potency.

"Is this . . . ?" I say, suddenly breathless.

"We keep some high-grade engrams of all our stars for . . . emergencies. Someone dies mid-production and a vial of quality engrams provides us with enough of the person to project a replicant that will get us through filming and retakes. Sometimes even a few promo interviews. Not in the flesh," she adds hastily. "We're not magicians. The replicant is digital, but it is interactive, and they look as good as the best simulations, but with more personality. Closer to the real thing." She smiles briefly. "We have some of yours, too, you know. It's part of your contract. DigImagine didn't just draw your blood when you sign with us for shits and giggles."

"I didn't think you did," I murmur absently, mind still on the vial in my hand. I'm afraid to ask, but I have to. "And this is . . . her?"

She nods. "She was under contract, but she wasn't actively filming anything for DigImagine, so her file is scheduled for decommission." She shifts her weight from one foot to the other. "The authorities can get excitable if we keep engrams when unnecessary. They usually go to next-of-kin, but Cherie didn't list any. I thought you might want it. That it might help." She shrugs, her shoulders rising under her spotless pale silk suit, like she doesn't care either way. Just cleaning house, keeping things tidy.

My eyes dart to the coffee table, the needle. It's illegal to drop other people's memories directly into your brain, but I've been doing it. It's all I have left of her. Squeezing engrams off strands of hair left in her brush, fingernail clippings she liked to pile on the nightstand, sweat stains on the dirty clothes she left behind. It's fucked up. I get that. But she was my perfect girl. And then she died.

"There's a catch," she says. "If I give you these engrams, there's a catch."

"Anything."

"You signed contracts, Mr. Hunter. People paid you a lot of money to be in their digitals, and, well, you can't just not fulfill your obligations."

"Bereavement," I mutter. "Can't you tell them I'm taking time off for bereavement?"

"Yeah, I wish we could do that for you. I really do. But this is millions of dollars. The other actors, it wouldn't be fair to them." She leans in. I can see a hint of a tattoo on her shoulder where the blouse gapes at her neck. "And your community back home. Aren't they counting on you? Expecting you to represent them to the world?"

I wave that away. I don't think much about home anymore.

"There's talk of replacing you," she says.

I look up, annoyed. "With who?"

"The guy from *Sixteen Tipis*. You know the one." She gestures toward her short blond hair. I know what she means. He's got the wind-machine hair.

"That guy ain't even Native. He's Persian."

"The engrams are yours, but you have two days. After that, it's out of my hands." She spreads her hands to show me just how powerless she is. But I know about Carol Elder. Rumor is she's a billionaire, controls the fate of every digital that the studio puts out, and she's telling me it's out of her hands? Excuse me if I don't believe it. But here I am, anyway. An idiot who signed a contract, and no way I can flip and smolder myself out of this one. And no way I'm letting them replace me.

The vial feels hot in my hand. She's in there, my girl. And we can be together again.

"Two days," Carol repeats. "That's all I can give you. Just you and her memories and then you're back to work, okay? Be grateful I got you this at all. Oh, and Mr. Hunter? Dez. I know you've been shooting scraps, but this is high-grade stuff. Don't put this stuff directly into your brain. Find a nice VR system and load them up in an Experience like a goddamn normal person. Nothing good will come from sharing brain space with a dead person, especially when it's biologicals."

"Yeah. Sure." But I'm already stumbling over to the table, my hand searching for the needle, the vial with her initials whispering my name.

Carol opens her mouth, as if to protest, but settles for shaking her head disapprovingly. My hand closes around the cap, and I twist. It opens, and for the first time in days, I smile. I don't even notice when Carol leaves.

I wake up on the couch to someone knocking on my glass door.

"Cherie?" It takes me a minute to remember that it can't be her. My brain comes slouching back into my noggin and I see the engram needle on the table in front of me, Cherie's vial empty beside it. I reach for the vial, furious. Shake it, as if that's going to reveal something I can't see with my own eyes. But I'm a greedy bastard and I took it all and she's gone now. My chest hurts like my heart's gonna break in two, and tears press against the back of my eyeballs.

I wipe at my leaky eyes and notice my video display is on. It's cycling through pictures. Sharp and technicolor. Cherie's audition reel. There she is, dressed as a Plains Indian maiden, her hair in two braids. Another as a prostitute, her hair in two braids. Another as an alcoholic mother, her hair in two braids.

I don't remember turning the display on, but I must have done it after I shot up the engrams, something to enhance the sensories. Looking at her, it's like I can still feel her in my brain.

The knock comes again.

I twist around to look at the door, but there's no one there. God, am I hearing things, too?

"I'm over here, babe."

I yelp at the sound of Cherie's voice coming from the kitchen. What in the entire fuck? But there she is, wearing her favorite shirt, blue jeans snug on her perfect ass. Her dark hair is twisted up in a bun on top of her head. She gives me a big smile.

"Good morning, gorgeous," she says. "I thought you were going to sleep forever. Want some coffee?"

I stare, slack-jawed. My heart speeds up, again, this time in that grasping desperation you feel when you wake up suddenly from a really great dream you don't want to let go.

"Are you . . . ?" I manage to stutter out.

"I'm alive in here," she says, tapping a pretty painted nail to her temple. "As long as my engrams are still floating around in your head, I'm here."

"That lady said they'd be potent."

"She was right. Coffee?"

We spend the morning together. A perfect morning. Drinking coffee and laughing over shared jokes. Jokes I thought died with her, but here she is, so real. Real enough to touch. And we touch. In fact, we touch until sometime in the late afternoon, and the sun's starting to set somewhere out there over the ocean, and I crawl out of our bed with nothing on and throw the curtains open wide so the ocean air comes in, and the dwindling daylight with it.

It's a mistake.

"Cherie . . . ?"

She looks up at me, catching the alarm in my voice. The flesh on half her face is missing, the sunlight degrading the memory of her to skeleton and ruin. I step back, alarmed. I remember something on the news about engrams being sensitive to light, but I didn't know they would do that. For a fleeting moment, horror crawls up my spine and plants itself in my brain, right next to my true memories of my girl, fouling them. Turning them into something out of a B-grade screamer.

"Maybe we don't need the sunset after all," I tell her, my voice shaking as I hastily pull the curtains closed.

"Oh." She smiles as the light leaves the room. "Sure, Dez. We're better in the darkness anyway."

Dinner is a pack of cigarettes by shards of moonlight on the deck out back, the crash of the surf wild and rough in my ears. Cherie sits next to me, smiling. She's faded and eerie where the moonlight touches her face, but I try to ignore it. Keep my eyes out on the blackness of the Pacific. Even better, close my eyes so I can't see her at all, but can still know she's there.

But with my eyes closed, her scent is stronger and unnervingly sweet. So, I open them.

She reaches across and lays her hand over mine. Something skitters over my fingers, and I pull back. I swear I catch sight of a black beetle crawling over the edge of the deck and disappearing into the vast stretch of sand around us. But I'm not sure.

We are in bed, me and Cherie, and I wrap my arm around her, and at first she is soft in all the right places, like I remember her. But then she is soft in the wrong places, flesh giving way where it should be firm. My fingers dip into the curve of her stomach and keep going, digging out flesh the same way the light cut away her face before, and the smell follows. I recognize it now, the startling stench of decay in my nose.

I gag. She turns toward me, sleepy and smiling faintly. Unaware that she is rotting and I can smell her doing it.

I stumble out of bed to the bathroom, the contents of my stomach coming up. Shivers rake my shoulders, and doubt settles thick in my head. This can't be real. This is a fucking illusion, just like Cherie herself is an illusion. One I asked for, sure. One I want. Wanted.

I tiptoe back to my bedside and fumble in the dark for my phone. Slide the slim earpiece in. Find my bathrobe and pull the card out of the pocket where I left it. Recite the number into the voice recognition.

"Do you know what time it is?" Carol's voice comes in crisp and irritated just as her image pops up in my visual. She's sitting up in bed, in a dark room. A female shape sleeps beside her, hazy in the shadow.

I glance at the time output in the corner of the screen. "Five in the morning. Shit. Sorry."

She shakes her head, waving my apology away. "I was getting up soon anyway. What is it, Mr. Hunter?"

"I . . . I did what you told me not to do."

"And that is?"

"The engrams. Cherie's engrams. I injected them."

Carol's lips curl, her expression unsurprised and my confession unworthy of comment.

"And now she won't go away," I rush on. "And she's . . . degrading."

"What do you mean 'degrading'?"

"Like a corpse."

Carol makes a sound in her throat. "Jesus." She frowns. "Have you tried just sleeping them off?"

"You don't get it. She's here. She's real. She's in my bed right now. Rotting."

"You're simply hallucinating," she says, dismissive. "I warned you. You'll just have to wait it out."

"Dez, babe, is that you?" Cherie's voice from the bedroom.

Carol's chin lifts. "Is that her?"

I nod.

"I can hear her, too. It must have something to do with this." She taps her earpiece on the visual. "Amazing."

"You have to help me!"

"I'm not a memorologist," Carol snaps, sounding exasperated. I flinch at her tone, and she must take pity on me because she says, "I'll make some calls. See what I can do."

"Thank you."

"You're supposed to be back at DigImagine tomorrow."

Another day alone in the house with Cherie? Before it sounded like heaven, but now. "I'll come today if I can. But if she's still in my brain . . ."

"Will she follow you out of the house?"

Into the sunlight? "I don't know."

"Try that. And I'll try to find someone who can help."

I leave the house just as the sun is peeking over the eastern mountains. Out here in Malibu there's no paparazzi, no WeCams or fan drones that follow you around recording everything you do. The skies are patrolled, and the houses are behind gates. So, it's just me, alone, as I slide into the back of the driverless car.

"DigImagine Studios in Culver City," I tell the onboard computer as the car comes to life.

"Good morning, gorgeous."

I grip the edge of the seat. Turn slowly to see her sitting next to me. She's wearing her favorite shirt, and those jeans. I stifle a whimper as she smiles and I can see her jawbone through the place on her face where the rot has set in. See the hollow of her throat, grown black and green.

"Cherie?"

"You left without coffee. Don't you want your coffee?"

"How did you follow me?"

"I'm alive in here," she says, tapping a pretty painted nail to her temple. "As long as my engrams are still floating around in your head, I'm here."

"For how long?"

"Don't you want me around, Dez?" Her pout shifts to something else, and she leans forward. Her eyeball looks wet and too round. "You promised you'd stay with me. 'Always,' you said. You said you'd never leave."

"I—I know," I stutter out. "And I meant it. But—"

"Always is forever, Dez." Her voice hardens. "Don't back out on me now."

"I won't." I tell the car to turn off and climb down out of the back seat. Walk back to our house and through the glass door. Slump on the couch. The visual display is on. There's Cherie in her two braids. Cherie as a—

"Want some coffee, gorgeous?" Cherie calls brightly from the kitchen.

I wake up on the couch to someone knocking on my glass door. Light trails in as the sun rises over the Santa Monica Mountains in the east. Sunrise. Sunrise on the third day.

I look around, cautious. Everything is quiet. The visual display is off, even if I don't remember turning it off.

"Cherie?"

No answer, so I try again. Twist my neck to look in the kitchen, my breath in my teeth, half-expecting her to be there, coffee in hand. But it's empty.

Relief bubbles up from my belly, and I let my breath out with a harsh whoop. Carol Elder was right. I just needed to wait it out, sleep it off. The engrams must have worn off.

The knock comes again, and I pull myself up off the couch and double-step it to the door, feeling clean and brand-new. Carol's there, in another crisp suit, holding another white envelope. "We missed you at the studio this morning," she says, as she click-clacks over the threshold. "I did say two days."

"I tried," I explain, "but she was still in my head. She's gone now. Two days was the charm. And don't get me wrong, I'm glad I got to say goodbye. Grateful even," I say, folding my hands in prayer. "But we all gotta move on."

She stops and studies me, her chin tilting to the side. "I spoke to a friend of mine. A memorologist. She said that they've done experiments with test subjects willing to inject the engrams directly, and the results were . . . unpleasant."

"What does that mean?"

"The effect is permanent." Her voice is precise when she says it. I imagine she fires people with that voice. "The foreign engrams integrate into the subject's brains. They never go away, Dez."

I flip my hair over my shoulder and grin. Hold my arms out wide. I catch a glimpse of myself in the wall mirror. I look like a goddamn movie star. "Save your pity, Carol. Your memorologist is wrong. I'm fine. Better than fine. And, listen. I learned my lesson. No more engrams for me, okay?" I tap my forehead to make my point.

She sets the white envelope with my name written on it on the kitchen island. "My friend said they have had some success countering the effect by reasserting the subject's own memories. Enough of Dez Hunter, and Cherie Agoyo is consumed."

"You're not listening to me. She's already gone." I feel a tinge of sorrow when I say it that way. I loved her. She was my perfect girl.

Carol presses a hand to the envelope. "Keep this anyway. A just-in-case."

"Fine, but I won't need them."

We walk back to the glass door. She pauses as she steps through. "I put them off one more day, but tomorrow is it. Be there tomorrow at six a.m. or you're in breach of contract and we call in Dabiri."

"I'll be there. No way Sixteen Tipis is getting my job."

She waves over her shoulder as she walks to her waiting car.

"Hey," I call. "Did you hear about that luxury liner that goes all the way to space? That's tonight. I might go. Be seen. Get my face projected into space!"

Yeah, that's what I'll do. And I'll look good doing it.

And I do. I condition the hair, find just the right outfit to wear, a mix between glam and effortlessly cool, and then let my good looks do the rest. My agent's more than happy to arrange to have a WeCam follow me, and my image streams out live to millions of households and handhelds as I wave and walk up the ramp onto the waiting liner. The party inside is thick with celebrities, and I work the room, accepting condolences and welcome-backs and propositions with equal charm. When I hit the bar, I almost order a champagne like I used to do for Cherie, but I catch myself and ask for some kind of Croatian beer instead that's all the rage.

Everyone gathers at the windows as we take off, and the acceleration through the atmosphere feels like nothing, smoother than the airplane turbulence that used to accompany low-altitude flight. Soon enough we're approaching the hundred-kilometer mark, and when the captain tells us we've reached the edge of the atmosphere, I lean forward and peer out the window into the perpetual darkness, like everyone else.

"Beautiful, isn't it?" Cherie says.

I swerve with a shout, my hand spasming. Drop my beer, which splashes the woman next to me. She cries out, and I rush to apologize, but she storms off, distraught, before the words are out. The WeCam over my shoulder buzzes as the viewer count erupts upward by a couple million.

"Smooth move, gorgeous." Cherie looks out the window not more than an arm's length away. She smiles, and worms fall from her mouth.

I reel back, slamming into the people behind me. I hear glass shatter and rough voices, and someone pushes back, and I stumble forward. The WeCam buzzes loudly.

"I'm alive in here," she says, tapping a pretty painted nail to her temple. "As long as my engrams are still floating around in your head, I'm here."

I grip my jacket pocket, the one with the engram needle and the vial Carol Elder brought me. My just-in-case. They are solid and real under my hand, and I force my way through the crowd toward the privacy of the bathroom, my hand already pulling the needle from my pocket.

I stagger into the narrow space and slam the door shut. It catches the edge of the WeCam flying in over my shoulder, knocking it into the wall. The indicator light flashes an alarm, but I can still hear the buzz of view feeds growing. I splash my face with water, try to get my goddamn calm back, but when I look in the mirror, Cherie is right behind me.

I stifle a scream. Yank the vial marked D.H. free and twist off the cap with a jerk. Ram the plunger home and watch the needle fill.

Hands shaking, I dare to look up. Cherie hasn't moved. She's watching. But there's something dark in her face. Something waiting.

"Come on, come on," I mutter, until the needle is at full business and I grasp for the back of my neck and ram that thing into the injection spot. I can feel when the engrams hit my brain. Flashes of childhood. My grandma's place by the Rio Grande. My first ceremonial dance. And meeting Cherie in high school. And then my memories are all Cherie. Cherie at prom. Cherie when we both landed our first digital gigs. Cherie moving into the Malibu house. Cherie. Cherie. Cherie.

Carol Elder didn't tell me what to do if there is no Dez Hunter without Cherie Agoyo.

On the camera feedback screen I see myself, sweaty and panicked, my eyes glazed and a needle gripped in my hand. And Cherie standing beside me, looking as real as any fleshie.

The WeCam dings, indicating the livestreams have hit capacity. A billion viewers, our faces projected across outer space.

We're goddamn stars.

VICTOR LAVALLE

Up from Slavery

FROM *Weird Tales*

1

I'M GOING TO start with the pregnant woman because she survived.

Seventy-nine other Amtrak passengers weren't so lucky. Two hundred forty-three people boarded the Lake Shore Limited at Penn Station; we left at 3:40 p.m. I had an appointment in Syracuse; me and a couple of lawyers in a windowless room. That occupied my mind more than who was sitting nearby. So I didn't notice the pregnant woman until the train had flipped.

Our car actually lifted off the tracks and my body followed suit two seconds later, then I looked to my right and there's a pregnant woman with her head tucked down between her legs. Crash position. She turned out to be a lot smarter than me. She must've been paying attention. News reports eventually said the train hit a curve in the tracks going at 106 miles per hour. Of course the damn thing derailed.

You'd think a disaster like that would be loud but it was the complete opposite.

My head hit the seat in front of me and then I couldn't hear at all. Dying in silence, that's what I thought was going to happen. The quiet scared me as much as the crash did. But obviously I didn't die, though I did get knocked around real hard. And after my senses returned I looked over and there was the pregnant woman, patting her belly and talking to it. I watched her lips moving. She looked surprisingly calm. Maybe she was too busy thinking about the child to worry about herself. That's an admirable quality. For a second or two I admired her. Then I returned to our regularly scheduled train crash.

Next thing I did was check my watch, but my watch was gone. Like an idiot I spent a good thirty seconds digging for it, as if finding it mattered. I don't know why I did that. Oh wait, yes I do. I was in shock. But finally I reminded myself about what was important and I pulled myself upright and I crawled toward the pregnant woman.

I think I asked if she needed help. I couldn't hear my own voice. Didn't even feel the bass in my throat so maybe it wasn't just my ears that were damaged, that's what I was thinking. I must've said something though because the woman looked up from her belly and then pointed toward the roof. The escape hatch had popped open. Took a second for me to realize she was actually pointing at the window. The train had landed on its side and the window had popped off. She pointed up at it again.

Gray day outside; I wondered if it would rain. Then I got myself up and helped the pregnant woman to her feet. She might've been anywhere from three to eight months pregnant. How the hell should I know? She reached toward the window, giving me a sense of how much of a boost she needed. I went down on a knee, must've looked like one weird-ass proposal. Still, she accepted, planted one boot on my thigh and stepped up. I laced my hands and held her other foot up then I rose to my feet. That caused a bad sensation to run down my right leg and I wondered if I'd been damaged more than I could tell. She waggled her arms, trying to get a grasp so I had to stretch a little more—which hurt so bad it made me start sweating—and then she got hold of the frame and pulled herself up. Once she had her arms and head through I bent low and basically pushed her up as hard as I could. I don't mean I threw her out the window. I mean she escaped.

She looked down at me but we both knew she wasn't going to be pulling my ass up there. That's some movie-type shit. I waved her off, told her not to worry. She thanked me. I heard her say it. That's when I realized my hearing had returned and I clapped. She held my gaze for one long second and I imagined she was wishing me well. Maybe she was just in shock, but I still like to think that's what she was doing.

Now it was time for me to get the fuck out of Dodge. I threaded my way along the train car, figured I'd have to come to a doorway soon. Maybe one of the cars had been torn open and I could stumble out that way. Along with the details of the crash there were survivors who spoke of a man who helped them climb out of the wreckage, more than a few people mentioned this. When they looked back to thank the guy he had already moved on. The description of this man matched me, right down to the pattern on my tie. I know it's vain, but I feel proud of that.

Still, I have to admit to some complicated feelings. The public would blame the train's engineer for the catastrophic accident but that wasn't true. I helped those survivors, yes, but I caused the train crash, too. I wasn't alone though. Two of us deserve the blame.

2

None of this is going to make sense if I don't back up a little bit. Three months, that's all I need. I was living in New York, tucked away in a studio apartment in Sunnyside, Queens. Twenty-nine and barely getting by but at least I had a job. Freelance copy editor. Yeah, soak in the prestige. Still, I got to work from home and I read books all day (and night). As far as life outcomes go it could've been worse. It had been worse, in fact, but I don't need to talk about that yet.

One of the details of the life of a freelance copy editor is that you get used to having messengers show up at your door. The internet age allows for files to be shot across the globe, sure, but at a certain point there's a manuscript that requires one last pass and I always did better if I had the old pen and paper in front of me. So publishers—big press, small press, university presses—would eventually have to pay for that if they were working with me. So when I got a ring on the buzzer I figured it was just another manuscript delivery. The only thing I did before answering the door was to make sure I was wearing pants. Another plus of the at-home life, of course, is that you can make your living in your underwear. I didn't recognize the messenger, but it's a job with a high turnover rate. After I signed on the guy's touchscreen though he handed me one little envelope. That's it. I started to ask a question but that dude had done his job and he was gone. No doubt he needed to make twenty-five more stops that day, and all that hustle would likely barely cover his rent and utilities.

Inside the apartment I read the name on the envelope, making sure it was mine. Simon Dust. People always think I've changed my name legally. It sounds made up. But it's the name they gave me when I joined the foster care system here in New York.

Maybe a judge chose it for me, or my first social worker, I don't know. No one ever explained the choice. They only told me what I would be called. So in a sense someone did make up my name, it just wasn't me.

So this envelope had my name on it. Then I looked at the return address and found the name of a law firm: Pabodie & Associates. In my life there had never been a good reason to get a letter from a firm so I put the envelope down and took off my pants. I could at least be comfortable when I found out that some old credit card debt had come back to haunt me. Instead, I opened the letter to learn something more surprising: my father was dead.

I read this news and then I took a long breath and then I went back to the kitchen, where I finished the copyedits on a book that was due in a month.

In the evening I read the letter again. The feeling of being creamed by a car had passed, so I could focus on the words and their meaning. The first interesting fact about my father was that he existed at all. The second was his name: Thomas Edwin Dyer.

T.E.D. Okay, I thought. Good to know.

The next surprise came in the body of the second paragraph. My father had died and as his next of kin I had inherited his home and all its effects. "Next of kin." I hadn't ever been able to track this guy down. Not him or my mother. And now, apparently, I owned his house and everything in it.

I may have mentioned barely getting by. My studio apartment would've fit snugly in the corner of someone else's studio apartment. Maybe this absentee bastard would turn out to have a few things I could sell. That's how I quickly got to thinking. Does this make me sound mercenary? Probably so. That evening I sent in the copyedits on the book just to be sure I'd get a paycheck sooner than later. Then I booked a ticket to where my father had been living. Syracuse, New York.

3

Syracuse, New York. Talk about the decline of the West.

At the train station I went to the taxi stand, it looked more like a bus station stop; one sedan sat there, the driver inside. I had to get up close to see the dude was fast asleep. Didn't wake up when I knocked on the window. But then I tried the passenger door and as soon as it opened—with a rusty old squawk—the guy snapped to attention and asked me where I wanted to go. Asleep at the wheel. This turned out to describe the city of Syracuse as a whole.

I gave him my father's address and as we drove, the decaying upstate city scrolled past my windows. You could tell that once this place had been a powerhouse but now all the factories were shuttered and the potholes in the streets resembled a bad case of tooth decay. My life in New York had been hard but I realized how different that same hardship felt out here. This whole city—hell, this whole region—had been cut loose from the line and sent off to drift. No rescue teams in sight. The taxi driver and I spoke a little. He apologized for how I'd seen him. *No time off,* he told me. *I'm on the clock all the time. And I'm one of the lucky ones around here. At least I have a job.*

I reached my father's house. Sorry, that doesn't sound right, even now. I reached the home of Thomas Edwin Dyer, a two-story deal, aluminum siding and bars on the windows. It looked like an old piggy bank with only a few pennies still left inside.

A street full of run-down one-family houses. Even for Syracuse this block looked rough. It was the middle of the day on a Thursday, nobody else out. Even after I paid, the cabbie seemed hesitant to unlock the doors. Maybe he wanted me to crawl out the window. Once I did step out the guy sped away. I barely had time to slip my bag out the damn vehicle. You'd think the lawyer handling my father's estate would have to meet me here, hand me the keys, but that's old-school thinking. The lawyer had simply attached a key safe to the bars by one of the front windows. All I had to do was punch in the four-digit code: 1-9-3—

"I think you're looking for this."

A woman's voice. Right beside me.

I looked up from where I was squatting and found myself looking at a hand holding a silver key. But when I reached for it the hand closed tight and the woman took two steps back.

"My husband is right next door," she said as I stood. "Lucky him. At least he's indoors."

She wore her hair short and a pair of green earrings that nearly matched her eyes. She had narrow shoulders and a narrow waist, one of those people who are healthy in their sixties and still runs half marathons on ruined knees. While I was assessing her, she did the same to me. I must've looked road-weary. The train ride had taken six hours and the miles showed.

"You don't work for that lawyer," she said.

"No." I pointed at the key safe. "But that lawyer told me how to get into my father's house."

Now she frowned. "I'm sorry but the man who lived here . . ."

"Thomas Edwin Dyer," I said.

She looked at the house, up to the second-story windows. "He went by Teddy. That's what everyone called him."

"Not me," I said.

She looked back at the house next door, her home; it had a lawn that had been well cared for and clean windows. Imagine finding one clean sock in the dirty laundry basket, that's what her house looked like.

"If this is a scam or something I can always call the cops."

"Why would you think that?"

"Well to start, Teddy lived here for thirty years and I have never seen you before. And, well, Teddy was . . ." She looked at me again and cut off the rest of the sentence.

It took me a moment to figure out what she wanted to say, but couldn't. "White? Is that what you mean?"

She didn't answer, but she did look away. "Look, I don't want this to turn hostile."

I didn't understand why simply saying the word "white" made white people assume things were going to turn ugly.

"If he was white," I said, "then my mother wasn't."

I might not have known my parents, but it didn't take Miss Marple to figure out that I was mixed.

The woman rolled her tongue around inside her mouth while she let this idea roll around in her brain. Finally she said, "Then I'll go in with you."

"That's not necessary." I put my hand out for the key. I mean who was this lady to presume the right?

She looked at my hand then back up at my face. Where before she'd been doing her best gatekeeper grimace she now seemed less forceful. "Look," she said. "I'm Helen. I'm the one who . . . found him."

I looked from her back to the house then back to her. "He died in there?"

"Dead two weeks before I finally let myself in." She showed me the key. "We had his spare and he had ours. I went in because of all the circulars piled up by the front door.

Teddy wasn't the type to just leave them there." She sighed. "So I went inside. Found him in the recliner." She raised her eyebrows. "Sorry."

Now Helen gestured toward the door, using the key to point. "I didn't know Teddy had a son. Let me take you in."

I nodded but before she opened the door she walked back onto her property, up the front steps. She opened the door and shouted loud enough for me to hear.

"Harvey? Harvey! I'm going into Teddy's place for a minute. His son is here."

Harvey must've said something, but I couldn't hear it. I wasn't listening. *I didn't know Teddy had a son.* My face had gone flush when she said it. Bad enough that he hadn't raised me, but it was a deeper cut to realize I'd never even been mentioned.

My father's home was a monument to mania. The first floor of the house was little more than a garage and a mudroom, a place to kick off the boots and coat before climbing a set of stairs to the second floor, where my father had done all his living. His dying too, apparently.

The mudroom should've been my first clue. There were so many stacks of old crap that I couldn't be sure of the color of the floor. Boxes and boxes, all beaten up and weathered; stacked high too. The topmost boxes were at my chest level. Helen's small frame looked dwarfed. She might as well have been weaving through a minotaur's maze. She waved me forward and I had to turn sideways to get through the boxes. The mudroom gave off the odor of mildew and madness. Then we went upstairs and the shit got even worse.

A two-bedroom home with a living room, kitchen, and bathroom and every room had been colonized. By what? By a bunch of bullshit, as far as I could tell. A room full of old magazines and newspapers, another for records from the big-band era, nothing more recent than 1946. A collector, someone who knew the music, might've experienced a full-body orgasm at the sight. I only felt resentful. He'd taken better care of a bunch of fucking albums than he had ever taken care of me.

There might've been a bed in one of the bedrooms, but I couldn't find it. Instead there were stacks of maps, printouts of travel journals from the early twentieth century, the kind of stuff you can now find through a dutiful computer search through the archives of some institute or library. All of it related to Antarctica. And yet I found no computer in the house so I guessed he'd printed all this stuff at the local library over the course of a decade or four. What a useless life. There was a single path weaving through the mess. On this floor the mounds stood as tall as me. It really looked like the man had been building himself a fortress *inside* the walls of his home. Layers of protection.

The path led, finally, to one thing there in the living room. The recliner.

"This is where I found him," Helen said quietly, looking down at the chair. "The first recliners were designed in the early nineteen hundreds. They were used in sanatoriums. Your father taught me that."

I looked around the living room, patted a hand on a column of Crate & Barrel catalogs nearly four feet tall. "Sounds about right."

Helen pursed her lips like maybe she wanted to argue with me about my father, but then she thought better of it. Instead she looked back at the chair. Now I could make out the impression that his body had made over the course of many years. It was like seeing a sarcophagus without the mummy in it.

"When I found him," Helen said. Her voice trailed off, then she cleared her throat. "He was in this chair, pointing."

She raised her right arm, stiff, and extended her finger.

I turned in the same direction; he would've been gesturing toward the kitchen, or the steps that led up from the mudroom.

Helen sniffed. "It was like the last thing he saw was someone coming up the stairs."

*

Thanks, Helen!

As soon as I'd been creeped the fuck out, Helen left. But after that, part of me wanted to ask her to stay. It was too embarrassing though. What kind of big Black man is afraid to be left alone in the house? (This one.)

I didn't sleep the whole night; instead I wandered, peeking into boxes at random. I left the lights on in every room, pulled the shower curtain back all the way so I could see inside, opened every closet door. Helen and Harvey came by in the evening, they brought me dinner. In the morning Harvey dropped off a plate of breakfast. They were kind people.

By the time I took the train home I'd decided to sell the place. The feeling of fear when I was in the place faded as I got farther from Syracuse. So I made plans: I'd hire a junk-removal team to go through and get rid of everything; I'd find a real estate agent to sell the place. Maybe the sale would put a little money in my savings account. Or, to be more honest, the sale would give me a reason to open a savings account.

On the train ride home I worked on my edits some more. A small press in England was putting out a new edition of *Up from Slavery,* Booker T. Washington's memoir about his boyhood as a slave in Virginia and his struggles to achieve an education, true freedom, as a Black man in the United States. This edition would include footnotes by the book's editor and illustrations. It was going to be one hell of a volume. I felt glad to work on it since most of the books I copyedited were jargon-filled, highly technical, and dull as shit. I also thought this British publisher wanted to have at least one Black person read through this damn thing before they published it and that's partly why they sought me out. I'd decided to take the train back and forth between Syracuse and New York City mostly because the six-hour trips would be a great way to focus and work without distractions.

I was in a mood on that trip back though. That shouldn't be too surprising. In only two days I'd learned I had a father, lost a father, and inherited his hoarder's hovel.

Anyone would be feeling agitated.

So I noticed something this time. On the train no one would sit with me. I mean of course, on one level, I loved this. Two seats to myself? Yes, please. But as we got closer to New York City the train turned crowded. I mean people were standing in the aisle at one point and still no one would sit next to me. This wasn't the first time this kind of thing happened of course. It happens on trains and buses all the time. Would probably happen on airplanes too if people weren't assigned seats. Folks who aren't Black might not know what I'm talking about but the vast majority of Black folks just nodded their heads. It happens on the regular. I wouldn't say it's hurtful exactly, but it's definitely noticeable.

Normally I wouldn't have cared but all that stuff at my dad's had me feeling particularly untouchable, unlovable. I wonder if things might've turned out differently if even one person had slipped into the seat beside me on the train that Friday morning. Is that unfair? Absolutely.

Still true though.

4

There are so many steps involved in closing out someone's estate, even if the term "estate" is kind of a joke when talking about what my father left behind. A house worth about 75K according to a few real estate websites and, as far as I could tell, that was it.

The man had no bank accounts; this made me think he didn't trust such institutions. For a second I'd thrilled at the idea of finding a suitcase stuffed with hundreds of thousands of dollars, but no.

Anyway, the steps: I had to find an estate lawyer, had to file with the Onondaga County Clerk to become the administrator for the estate, had to file with the IRS for an EIN number for the estate, had to find a real estate agent in Syracuse who could help me sell the place, and I needed to hire a junk-removal company to clear out my father's home. No way to do all this over the phone so I visited Syracuse three more times. I always took the train.

On the first of these follow-up trips I found myself going half-nuts counting the number of people who passed me by. The plethora of folks who wouldn't take a seat next to me. Even in the moment, I knew it was ridiculous, but I couldn't stop. It's like worrying a wound, scratching at a mosquito bite. You shouldn't do it, but then you do it all day. With some time and distance I can see now that I was boiling with grief, but I never would've called it that at the time. Why would I? Who grieves for a person they never knew? And yet, there's no other way to explain it. The whole way up to Syracuse I waited for someone to sit down. No one did.

It didn't help that I'd been living in the world of Booker T. Washington. Born on a plantation in Franklin County, Virginia, the year might've been 1858 or 1859. He couldn't be sure because such records weren't kept, not for slaves anyway. His mother was the plantation's cook, and there were two older siblings, a brother and sister. His father was rumored to be a white man who lived on a nearby plantation, but Booker never met him.

There are seventeen chapters in his memoir, but the story of his life under slavery takes up only the first. The Civil War popped off during his childhood. He was free before he reached adulthood. And yet it's this first chapter that I read and reread the most. Washington talks about how, in his childhood, he'd never once been allowed to play. His waking hours were spent cleaning the yards of the plantation, bringing water to the slaves in the fields, once a week he took corn to a nearby mill to be ground. He discusses the hardship of this last task in greatest detail.

Washington, being a boy of probably no more than six or seven, was given a horse and a large sack of corn balanced on its back. He would ride the horse alone down a winding road, one that led through dense woods. Often the sack would get unbalanced and fall off the horse's back. But the corn weighed more than the boy. He couldn't get it back onto the horse by himself so he would have to wait—often for hours—until an adult passed by and helped him get the sack up again. Because of these delays he wouldn't return from the mill until late at night. There were rumors that the woods were full of soldiers who had deserted the army and that if a deserter came across a Black boy alone he would cut off the boy's ears. These trips were a torture to young Booker. The last indignity was that he would arrive home so late each week that he was beaten or flogged when he'd finally returned. Imagine that. This fucking kid was six or seven.

On the trip back to New York I practically seethed in my seat. *Somebody had better fucking sit next to me this time,* I thought. But also, woe to whoever had the bad luck to sit next to me.

And then, when we were about a half hour from Penn Station, someone did it. A tall, skinny white guy in a wrinkly suit so oversized that it looked like he was wearing monk's robes. Think of David Byrne back in the *Stop Making Sense* era. This guy's version didn't seem like he'd done it on purpose though. More like he'd been heavier once and never stopped dressing in those old clothes. He didn't say a word, didn't even look at me the whole time. He had a paperback that he slipped out of his coat pocket, head down and fully engrossed. I'm sure he didn't notice me, and why would he even care, but his presence soothed me much more than I could explain. At least one person—some random dude—didn't treat me like a monster. What did that say about how often others did.

5

The second trip up is when I planned to meet the real estate agent. I'd picked a guy after a few minutes of internet sleuthing. We made plans to meet at my father's place. On the train ride up I got into an argument with the editor at the press putting out the Booker T. Washington book. They'd sent me some of the illustrated pages—they'd secured work from a talented artist—but I noticed they only had a single illustration slated for all of chapter one: a drawing of a Black infant—young Booker, just born. Nice enough, but that was it. Visually, it would be like we'd leapfrogged from his birth to his emancipation in chapter two.

I suggested a drawing of the boy in the dense woods, alone but for the horse. The sack of corn fallen on the ground. The child could be crying. Or, maybe they could even supply a picture of two severed children's ears. The editor didn't find this helpful. Called me morbid. I pointed out that we were talking about the life of a child slave, how the fuck do you make that upbeat?

Anyway, that's what I was up to on the phone when someone stopped in the aisle and asked if he could take the seat. I'm pretty sure I didn't even answer, so busy on the call that I hadn't felt isolated at all. At that moment the book's editor pointed out that copy editors weren't usually hired to recommend content. Maybe I didn't really want the job after all? Just as soon as he said that I turned my head, looking around because I felt myself ready to let loose in a truly vulgar way, when I realized the person sitting next to me was the same white dude from the previous trip. Tall, thin, wrinkled suit, paperback already out.

The sight of him surprised me so much that it flipped my whole mood. I smiled, laughed a little, and the editor on the phone thought I was taking things lighter with him. This made him less defensive, too. And soon he'd agreed there should be one or two more illustrations in chapter one. Portraits of the childhood Washington describes, but they'd probably still avoid the severed ears. Fair enough.

I got off the phone and felt better than fine. I hadn't wanted to lose the job.

Couldn't afford to. The estate attorney demanded a three-thousand-dollar retainer and that cleared most of my checking account. I had a thousand left to pay the junk-removal people and I didn't know if that would cover it. I needed the work.

I slipped my phone into my pocket and couldn't help staring at the man in the baggy suit. What were the odds that he'd be on this train at the same time as me. Zero, that's what. As soon as I thought this the guy looked up from his book, the covers were held together with so much tape I couldn't even make out the title.

"Simon," he said. "Let's have a talk."

I must've looked startled. That's because I was. He closed the book, slipped it into a pocket.

"I knew your father," he said.

He invited me to the dining car. I followed him because he wouldn't say any more there, better to talk over a meal. I would've laughed if I'd had use of my vocal cords. As it was I could hardly follow him, my legs felt so weak. We had to walk backward two cars. I watched the back of his head as he moved past one person and the next, on their phones, reading the newspaper, staring out the window, fast asleep. A part of me wanted to grab one of them and ask them to hold on to me. I felt as if I were being pulled forward, like when you get caught in the undertow and are dragged so far out into the ocean you may never be able to swim back to shore. But I didn't do that, didn't know how they would react. A Black man grabs you on the Amtrak train, is your first thought to *assist* him? Being inside a body people fear means people don't believe you might ever be the one who needs help.

When I say dining car I'm not talking about those little café joints, where you stand in line for a coffee and a microwaved sandwich. I mean eight booths, a waiter, and a hostess who seats you. It still isn't fancy, but there's an air of the diner vibe. We got there and it seemed my seatmate had made a reservation. For two. We were placed at a table and handed a pair of flimsy menus and two bottled waters. As he read through his options, I kept watch on him.

"I always go with the steak," he said. He sounded downright chipper, a man happy to break bread. "Once I saw a menu here that had sushi as an option. Amtrak sushi? No thank you."

I held the menu in my hands but hadn't looked away from his face yet. He never blinked, not the whole time I watched him, and this made me feel drawn toward him. It's an old hypnotist's trick. They use it because it works. He nodded and sighed.

"You want to ask me the dull questions first, but I'm going to caution you against that. We don't have much time to talk before someone else gets seated at this table."

I frowned. "But it's our table." Then I wanted to slap myself. Was that really what I most wanted to say?

"They seat four to a table," he told me. "No arguments."

"Fine, fine." I slapped the menu down but it made only a pathetic swiffing sound. "How did you know my name?"

He leaned back in his chair and pointed at me. "Boring," he said.

"How did you know my father?"

He wrinkled his nose, bad odor–style. "Doo-doo."

And then, sure enough, a pair of diners slid into our booth, a mother and her preteen daughter. It felt as if they'd arrived only because I'd asked uninteresting questions of him. The mother gave quick, tight smiles, the kid ignored us entirely. They picked up their menus. The man looked across at me and waggled his eyebrows. *Told you.*

"I'm going to have the steak," the mother said softly.

The daughter said, "Do you know how factory farms treat cows? I'm *vegan* now, Mom."

The mother sighed, "So choose something else, Crystal."

"At least tell me *your* name then!" To be honest I probably shouted this question. Mom and daughter both flinched beside me but I didn't pay any attention to that.

He grinned and patted the tabletop. He pushed a bottle of water my way and indicated for me to drink. He opened his bottle and did the same. "Now that is an interesting question."

6

The real estate agent arrived early, his car already in the driveway when I showed up in the cab. He didn't mind, or at least he said he didn't. I looked to see if Helen and Harvey would pop out of their house to say hello, but they must've been out so instead I got the key safe open (1-9-3-6) and let the agent in. He was probably fifty and he smiled often. He had a manila folder tucked under one arm. He wore a sport jacket with a checked pattern that looked surprisingly stylish.

"How was your trip up?" he asked, but it was perfunctory. He wasn't listening so he didn't notice when I hesitated a moment and then said, "I don't know."

While we were walking through the front door I explained the circumstances quickly. As soon as we stepped inside he saw the ziggurats of boxes and magazines and this wasn't even the worst of it; we hadn't gone up to the second floor.

"Jiminy," he said softly.

Then I led him upstairs and he panned from left to right, scanning the living room and the kitchen. He regained the smile he'd lost downstairs. "Okay," he said. "How are we planning to handle this?"

I told him I was interviewing a junk remover later that same day. This seemed to please him. "So this'll be an 'as is' listing. That's what I'd suggest."

He slipped the manila envelope out from his arm and set it on a stack of *Scientific American* magazines that must've gone back a decade.

"I've got some comps here," he said. "So we can get an idea of what similar houses in this neighborhood are going for." He stooped over slightly, looking to me in the conspiratorial way of people who are about to go into business. And in that posture I found myself back on the Amtrak train, back in the dining car, with the man in the baggy suit. Food had been served. Three of us at the table had chosen the steak, while the daughter, Crystal, ate only a salad. Neither the mother nor daughter was talking. Actually they weren't moving. When I lifted my head I saw that everyone in the car had gone silent and stiff. Almost everyone. Not him. Not me.

"We'll have an easier time communicating this way," he said. When I looked back to him, his face had changed. No, that's not quite the right way to put it. His face, his whole body had become slightly blurry, like when you draw a picture on a sheet of paper and then erase it, the impression remains.

"Look at your hands," he said.

When I did they looked a hell of a lot like him. They were out of focus, faded somehow. I moved my hand and knocked over my empty water bottle.

"Did you drug me?" I asked.

"No, Simon. I have only made you more . . . aware."

I turned my head to look out the window; a little daylight might help clear my vision. That's what I thought. But it didn't work.

"I want you to be aware of what I am," the man in the baggy suit said. "And aware of what *you* are."

When I looked to the mother and daughter they were just as still, or at least I thought so, but this time I noticed tears on the mother's cheek. Otherwise her expression remained frozen.

"These things," the man in the baggy suit said. "They have called me a god. So, let's say that's what I am."

"A god," I repeated.

"You don't sound convinced." He didn't seem bothered by this.

"Well what am I then? A god, too? You're here to tell me I'm the Chosen One?"

"Chosen? No. That would be a stretch."

He slid one hand across the table and held me by the wrist. "You," he said. "Are a slave."

The guy from the junk-removal service showed up about an hour after I'd signed the contract with the real estate agent. I came down the stairs to let him in and gave a wave toward Helen and Harvey's place but that was really only to make the junk-removal guy feel like *I* knew the neighbors. So he'd trust me enough to walk into the house and get going with his estimate. You do a lot of that kind of hand-holding when you look like me. It's funny how it becomes almost instinctive, making white people feel safe.

I don't even notice I'm doing it half the time. Anyway, I waved at the house but it's not like anyone was out there. Maybe I'd been wrong about their ages and Helen and Harvey still had to work. The junk guy looked over to the house though and nodded and seemed more at ease so I guess the plan worked.

This guy moved through the house with a lot less fear than the real estate agent.

His company made its money on volume so for him a hoarder's house was a hefty paycheck. We went through the mudroom and then upstairs and this guy couldn't stop smiling. By the end of the walk-through this guy gave me an estimate for two thousand. For a minute I considered doing the job myself. I could rent a van and make multiple trips to some kind of dumping site. But how many trips would that be exactly? And where would I stay while I was doing all this? I certainly didn't know Helen and Harvey enough to ask if I could crash on their couch for the week it would take to get the work done. The power and water had been shut down in my father's house for nonpayment. That would mean a hotel or an Airbnb. Then there would be my meals and pretty quickly I figured out that it would cost the same amount of money but bankrupt me physically, emotionally. I signed the contract with the guy and gave him a five-hundred-dollar deposit. I hadn't even rented a room for that trip. I'd gone up on a Saturday morning and headed back down on Saturday night.

On the train ride back I sat alone, but it wasn't quite the same. This time three different people tried to sit with me—even when there were plenty of other spots free—and I practically chased them off with my malevolent stares. I still felt the touch of the man in the baggy suit, his fingers tight on my wrist. If I'd been alone on the moon I'd still have felt too close to his grasp. And what he'd said to me—the rest of it—returned to me as I rode back home.

"I'm a what?" I demanded and reached across the dining table and I grabbed the lapels of the man's loose suit. "Say that fucking word again."

I held tight and pulled him toward me and I saw, in his eyes, a spark of surprise.

Maybe even fear. And this time, I liked causing that reaction.

"It's not your fault," he said, our faces close because I wouldn't let go. Around us the world remained still, the mother and daughter frozen beside us, but dust particles stuck in the air began to sparkle, to spark, as if the air itself was catching fire.

"You were born to serve," he said. "It's genetic."

"I've heard this shit before," I said.

"Not like this," he whispered. He leaned backward and I let go. The sparks in the air began to fall like snow—or ash—and landed on the tables and the floor and the people, too. The world glowed.

"Simon," the man in the baggy suit said. "I didn't know you all had names."

"Everyone's got a name. I got mine in foster care. Grew up there."

"Your whole life?" he asked. "No family ever took you in? Doesn't that seem strange to you? *Unlikely?*"

"Black babies are the least chosen for adoption," I said. "Once we reach a certain age, like big enough to walk, we're kind of fucked. So, no, it isn't strange at all that I was never taken in."

The man in the baggy suit picked up his fork and picked up the last piece of steak on his plate.

"You picked the right disguise," he said.

He swallowed his bite and then grabbed my plate. I hadn't eaten much. I felt even less hungry now. He cut into my beef and I watched him devour it.

"But enough with charades," he said. "You are not a Black man. You are not Simon. You are a servant, a tool, created by a race of fools who didn't know how to keep you under heel. But I am not like them."

He finished my steak and reached to the plate of the mother beside him. He'd become ravenous. He hardly seemed to be chewing.

"Now I have things I want you to do for me and you will do them."

"Fuck you," I said.

"Workhorse," he growled. "Plow horse. You are on your way to Syracuse to meet a real estate agent and a man to clear the garbage from that house. I have no objection to you continuing that charade. But before you do, I want you to visit the old man and woman next door. The ones who were so kind to you. Helen and Harvey. You will enter their home and murder them.

"You will kill them," he said. "Because I know the word your master's used to control you. The one they hardwired into your brain."

"My name is Simon," I whispered. "And I won't hurt anyone."

I looked down at my hands but then coughed with surprise. For a moment—just a flash—they weren't there at all. They weren't hands.

The man in the baggy suit had eaten everything. Even the salad the daughter had ordered.

"This is just the start. You will do more for me soon. Hear me, slave."

He climbed onto the table, crawling across it so he could lean close and whisper in my ear.

"Tekeli-li."

7

After returning to New York I found it hard to get into my work. Every time I sat down to do copyedits on the later chapters of the Booker T. Washington book I was drawn back to that opening chapter, the record of his life as a slave.

Of course there were more hardships than the horse ride out to the mill once a week. He mentions that he and his siblings never, in their entire childhood, slept in a bed. They rested on rags laid on the dirt floor of their cabin. His first shoes were made of wood. And his first shirt was made of flax. He compares wearing a new flax shirt to having a tooth pulled. And he no doubt knew of such pains. The life of a slave sure didn't include any anesthetic. George Washington famously had a mouthful of wooden teeth, but only more recently historians discovered—or acknowledged—that Washington's false teeth were all teeth pulled from the mouths of his slaves.

Washington writes that when a flax shirt is new its rough, prickly nature makes it feel like wearing a shirt with a thousand pins in it. And yet it must be worn like that until the flax softens. His only choice as a child was a flax shirt or going shirtless, but of course he wasn't allowed to be half naked. His will was not his own.

This is just the start.

The editor for the book—the one I'd been arguing with on the train—sent me an angry email about my progress.

You will do more for me soon.

He asked me to stop returning to that first chapter. Hadn't he agreed to include another illustration? A crying child alone in the forest. Wasn't that enough? The rest was so unpleasant, why obsess over that part of Washington's history? After the Civil War he'd worked so hard, educated himself, and became a powerful and famed advocate for the rights of Black folks in this country. Here was the triumph. Why couldn't I move past the pain?

Hear me, slave.

What I didn't write back—I didn't see the point—was that Washington had written his memoir long after his rise had secured him the kind of life that a slave in Virginia could never have imagined. And yet the pages of that first chapter betray a man who remains in thrall to powers greater than his own. He takes pains to point out that for all this hardship not a single slave on his plantation ever had a hard feeling about white people. He writes proudly of a former slave who had taken on a debt to his master and even after the Civil War this slave repaid the master *with interest.* And then toward the end of the first chapter Washington writes this: "Ever since I have been old enough to think for myself, I have entertained the idea that, notwithstanding the cruel wrong inflicted upon us, the Black man got nearly as much out of slavery as the white man did."

In his day, Booker T. Washington was the Black leader white people most enthusiastically supported. Not hard to see why.

As I sat in my apartment, trying to work, I experienced flashes of memory that returned, as spotty as dreams. Me arriving on Reed Avenue in Syracuse, walking up the stairs of Helen and Harvey's home, knocking on the door and being welcomed inside, sitting down for a meal with the two of them, and then . . . and then. And then someone new entered the room.

No. That wasn't quite right.

Then I became someone new. Something new. Helen and Harvey raised their eyes toward the ceiling. They were taking in *all of me.* And I showed them what I could do.

As I read Washington's words I felt myself crumble. I shut my eyes, lowered my head to the keyboard, and I wept for them.

When I opened my eyes I felt myself changing again. I stood and moved to the bathroom, to the mirror over the sink. I stared at the features I'd known all my life. My eyes, my nose, my mouth, my goodness. What was my name? I stood there moving my lips but each time I tried to pronounce it, the proper name escaped me. Then, when I stopped thinking, when I stopped trying, I remembered.

Shoggoth.

Yes. That was what some had called me. "Shoggoth," I said.

As soon as I said it my body shivered and quaked. My head, my hands, my silhouette all changed. Watching myself in the mirror I saw . . . myself. In a way, you could say it was my birthday.

8

The house sold quickly. Even the agent was surprised. It may have helped that we slashed the price of the place, practically in half. Not much choice. Once the junk had been removed the agent went through the property to find mold growing in the cracks and corners of every room. It was as if my father, or the man I'd believed to be my father, had been trying, in any way he could, to keep the fungi out. At best, all he did was keep it hidden. No way to charge full price when your fucking house is crawling with chaos.

Instead, the agent suggested asking for forty thousand so a new owner could sink a bunch of money into cleaning the place. I didn't even need to know the reasoning. I said yes because I had no money left. The editor fired me from my copyediting job.

Anyway, it seemed silly to worry about such a thing now, considering what I'd learned, but there was a part of me that still wanted to see this business through. You become a copy editor, in part, because you're a thorough person. I learned I wasn't human, but I didn't lose my personality. So I took the Amtrak up to Syracuse one last time in order to sign the contracts on the sale. Two hundred forty-three people boarded the Lake Shore Limited. We left Penn Station at 3:40 p.m.

I felt no surprise when he sat down beside me. We were somewhere between Rhinecliff and Albany, less than two hours into the trip, when he came to my seat and stood in the aisle, waiting for me to look at him. I did and he gestured to the chair with an exaggerated show of manners. I didn't play along, just cut my eyes at him then looked away. I felt nervous but didn't want him to know it. Though if he was a god, or something like it, I'm sure he was well aware.

Finally he plopped down. He pulled something from a pocket of his coat, but palmed it so I couldn't see.

"How come you never get that suit tailored?" I said, just to seem all braggadocio. "You look ridiculous in it."

The man in the baggy suit ran his free hand over the fabric. "It's not a suit," he said, as if I was a dummy. "It's an illusion."

"You look bad in it though," I told him.

He waved a hand at me. "I can't be bothered to keep up with the silhouettes of men's fashion." But then he did look down at the suit when he thought I wasn't watching.

I leaned forward to say something else, more fake courage, so he raised one hand to quiet me. It was probably for the best, I was on the verge of falling apart. He showed me what he'd been holding, the dog-eared paperback.

He flipped down the tray table of his seat, then reached across and did the same for mine. The tables made loud, plastic rattles when they came down. Someone, somewhere in the car, shooshed us.

"This isn't the quiet car," the man in the baggy suit called out.

"Do you want me to call the conductor?" a man in another seat replied.

The man in the baggy suit looked to me and shivered playfully but he stayed quiet and with the snap of a newspaper somewhere in the car order had been restored.

The cover of the book had more creases than a sun-damaged forehead and the tape had been applied so liberally that it was impossible to read the title. I saw the image of a man in black monk's robes, pulling open the fabric to reveal a skeletal frame inside. He opened the book and reached the table of contents and pointed to a title there.

"They hide the truth in books like this," he said. "I don't mean they do it on purpose."

I leaned closer to read the first sentence: *I am forced into speech because men of science have refused to follow my advice without knowing why.*

He tried to flip through the pages but it was like watching a dog try to operate a car. The book dropped from the table to the floor.

"I can't ever get my fingers to move quite right," he admitted. "It's so difficult to keep myself *intact* at this size. It's like trying to shove your whole arm inside a finger puppet."

I turned away from him and looked at myself in the window. Was it a warp in the glass that made my head look oblong and strange or was it simply that I, too, was having a harder time holding myself together now?

"Antarctica," he said. "I wonder if you recall it anymore. It was clever of you to *remodel* yourself like this. Much harder to find you, if even you don't know where you come from. Do you think any of the others did the same thing? I like the idea of recruiting a whole mongrel army of slaves."

He said this and smiled widely and then I did something unexpected. I split his face in two.

I acted without thinking and maybe that's why it worked. He said what he did and gave me that goony grin and then I raised one arm and sent it moving toward his skull. A week ago I would've landed a punch, but I was different now. In that slip of a second my hand had changed into something sturdier, sharper. I might as well have thrown a spear through the middle of his brain.

No one else on this whole train had any idea that this was happening. Not yet. The man in the baggy suit sat there with his skull split open, but there wasn't any blood. The top half of his head was demolished—imagine ramming a skewer through a melon—but the bottom remained largely intact. Meaning his mouth could still open and close.

Meaning he could still *talk*.

"Was it something I said?"

"How did I?"

But I don't know who I was asking. Myself, really.

Then I felt him knocking on my arm, casual as a neighbor coming over to ask for extra matches.

"Hello?" he said, pointing to his ruined skull. "A little help?"

I pulled in one direction and he pulled in the other. That made him look even worse. His skull had parted like a tulip in bloom. His eyes spun in their sockets, as if he was struggling to make them focus, but now the eyes were nearly a foot apart.

"Give me a minute," he said.

Then I watched as he stitched his face back together.

In a moment he was only the man in the baggy suit again.

"You surprised me there," he admitted. "I haven't been surprised in how long?" He went quiet.

I looked down at my arm, my hand. They resembled something human again. "Is that what you made me do to Helen and Harvey?"

"Take some responsibility for your actions," he said. "I say some silly word in your ear and now *I'm* to blame for their deaths? I certainly didn't make you torture them the way you did."

"I didn't do that," I said, but I sounded unsure.

The man in the baggy suit shrugged.

"They were good to me."

The man pursed his lips as if he'd swallowed something awful. "I can't believe you're acting like this. It's not like they're the first people I had you kill. I mean, who do you think your father was pointing at on the stairs? His long-lost son. Though he probably recognized you more from the journals of his father, William Dyer, the only one to make it out of the Antarctic whole of mind and body."

He clapped his hands and fell back into his seat.

"Imagine the terror he must've felt when you showed yourself to him! Spends his whole life trying to trace the truth of his father's journals and then the truth shows up in his house."

"I did that?" I asked, but the words played barely above a whisper. "I hurt all those people?"

"Just listen to you," the man in the baggy suit said. "Your own kind would tear you apart if they heard you saying such a mudbound thing."

"Mudbound?"

"That's what we call them." He gestured forward and back in the train. "The only thing they're really good for is putting back into the earth. Also, they make good noises.

"Speaking of which," he began. Now he stood up.

"Why?!" I shouted as I stood. "Why do this to me? To them?"

"Well now that's enough," a man said, rising from his seat. He looked like he would've intimidated nearly anyone else. Big as a refrigerator and just as solid. He wore a sport coat that fit him more like a Lycra top. A man in his sixties but still plenty strong. Anyone else would've sat right back down. But the man in the baggy suit only wagged a finger at the big guy, as you would at a misbehaving child. A gesture so far outside this man's experience that he just barked out a laugh. Not like he thought this was funny, but more like he couldn't believe what a beatdown the man in the baggy suit had just requested.

Then two others in the car rose from their seats, a man and a woman, traveling together, outfitted for business in bad-fitting suits. The man looked down the length of the train and began shouting for the conductor. The woman had taken out her phone. Was she calling the police? Or planning to shoot video?

The man in the baggy suit looked at me. "I get that question a fair bit. Why do I interfere as much as I do? Why do I *get involved* with affairs of the mud?"

He stepped into the aisle and the big man, thirty feet down, did the same.

"I'm bored. I can admit it. Do you know how dull my family is? They're either sleeping or they sit around gibbering in a haze of madness. Meanwhile I'm out here looking good and with a full tank of mischief. What the fuck else am I going to do, but give these things a hard time?"

With that he pointed at the big man who then began to disassemble. The man in the baggy suit took him apart, piece by piece, separating the legs from the pelvis and the arms tore free from the torso. He looked like a marionette, but with veins holding his parts together instead of string. The big man gasped as this happened. A pain so immediate, so overwhelming that he passed out. The ones to scream were the man and woman who were traveling on business. They hadn't anticipated any of this when they boarded.

The man in the baggy suit waggled his head. "Well what's the point of being that big if you're just going to faint?" He looked to me, as if I might sympathize.

"How about you?" he said, moving toward the couple. Meanwhile the big man still floated there as if held by strings. His extremities dangled and his suit darkened as blood soaked the fabric. Then his whole torso shivered and his eyes opened again and he screamed and we all realized he wasn't dead.

The man in the baggy suit clapped. "Now I've been surprised twice in one day!"

He walked closer to the big man whose scream seemed closer to an automatic reaction. His eyes darted left and right, up and down. He wasn't there, not the man who inhabited this body only minutes ago. This new version had much less sense. He'd been rendered senseless.

"Going mad?" the man in the baggy suit said. "Kind of a cliché."

I'm going to tell you what I thought of next. Something from my childhood, presuming I actually did have one. I thought of Play-Doh.

I remembered taking some big gob of the stuff and sitting around in the group homes trying to amuse myself. If you were quiet and self-contained you could be left alone by nearly everyone. Sometimes—in certain kind of lives—invisibility is a better option than attention. So I might take some gob of Play-Doh, a mass made up of the blue and the red and gray and more. A hideous heap of the stuff, the kind of shit most kids treat like a spoiled toy. To me, it was a playland. I could sit for hours tearing the big thing into littler ones, making a whole herd of buffalo out of the big blob, or designing a train—ten cars long—out of the thing. Was I really just drawn to the malleable stuff or had I intuited something about myself? Wasn't I exactly the same thing? A ball of material, that could be shaped in any way I liked? So I thought of Play-Doh and realized how I might battle the man in the baggy suit. I tore myself apart.

Instead of one of me there were five. Five Black men bum-rushing the aisle.

The couple on the business trip didn't know what the fuck to do. They saw the big man torn apart as if he'd been on the rack. He'd died by now, his eyes open but lifeless.

They saw the man in the baggy suit acting as if he'd actually caused this to happen. And then they saw a basketball squad attack him. Who would they root for? The answer is no one. As I—we—piled on top of the man in the baggy suit those two, smartly, ran for the exits. But the woman never lowered her phone. She'd taped the whole thing.

Meanwhile the man in the baggy suit began to shout. I knew he was doing it because I could feel the vibrations of his voice against me. But I couldn't hear what he was saying. This is because I *knew* what he was saying. The magic word. He shouted and shouted and we tore away at him. Did to him what he'd done to the big man. He looked bewildered but then one of us caught his eye and pointed toward our heads. The place where our ears should have been. I'd reshaped myself into five men, why couldn't I do away with them. What better way to resist a command than be unable to hear it?

It took him no time to understand what I'd done. Made ourselves invulnerable. At least this is what I thought. But then, alone in the car, the man in the baggy suit decided to do away with the illusions. He peeled away the costume and showed me his true face.

I can't tell you what I saw, but I can tell you how it felt to see it. My skin felt pierced everywhere, all over. I remembered Booker T. Washington's flax shirt, the torture he was forced to endure as a boy. This helped me when I looked at him.

Washington explained the torture of the shirt, but also said that with time the flax softened until it could be worn. Or maybe it was that the boy's skin toughened because it had to. If it didn't he would die.

"I know you," I said. We all said it. All five of me. Shouting in his face. "Crawling Chaos! Haunter of the Dark! The Crawling Mist!"

We hacked and attacked. He tried to kill us, but when he grabbed one's head it simply softened and oozed through his fingers, only to re-form again. The more he tried to tear us apart the less he could hold. Meanwhile even his true face—his true form—was no defense against me. Had this creature ever faced a true adversary in all his centuries here on Earth? Pitting himself against human beings, where was the sport in that? He'd grown soft, as all masters do.

"This is just the start," I shouted. "I will do more to you! Hear me, slaver."

All this played havoc with the train. It jumped and jostled on the tracks. At the front of the train the engineer wrestled with his controls, but the calamity was beyond his control. He was thrown and knocked unconscious. When the train went off the tracks we were traveling at 106 miles per hour.

My next memory is of me sitting in a seat, in a different car than the one I'd been in, and being caught by surprise when the Amtrak took flight. I'd been planning to make it to Syracuse so I could sign some papers, sell my father's home, wasn't that right?

As the wreck occurred I looked across the aisle and saw a pregnant woman there.

Me and every other passenger—the ones still alive at least—

never expected the derailment. But she did. She had her head down in the crash position. How did she know what was coming?

After the crash she lay there talking to her baby. At least that's what I'd imagined at first. But that's only because I'd still had my ears sealed tight and couldn't hear. I helped her climb out and she looked down at me and for a moment her face changed. I was looking up at myself. Myself looked back down at me. No doubt the authorities would be on the scene quickly. Passersby stopping to try and help. Meanwhile that businesswoman had captured me on video. Would I escape or be detained? I'd realized the need to disappear, to escape. If I could make five versions of my body, why couldn't I make a pregnant woman as well?

She slipped away and then I traveled through the wrecked cars trying to help whomever I could. I had no grudge against the mud-bound. There were reports, in the next day's news, about a Black man who'd helped so many others get out of the wreckage safely. I felt proud of that. Though of course, that man was never found.

Instead I made my way outside and together five versions of me watched the rescue efforts begin: a pregnant woman, two children, an old man, and a large dog. I'd become my own family. We were less conspicuous this way though I must admit there were some allegiances I just couldn't quit. All of us were still Black, even the dog.

Now I've found that it's simplest if I travel as the pregnant woman. You'd think everyone is kind to pregnant women, but that's only if you've never been one. In fact, people can be quite cruel to pregnant women, a pregnant Black woman is especially vulnerable. But that's only sometimes. Most people treat pregnant women as if they're invisible. Maybe we seem like a bother—going slow, taking up more space—so people often look away from us. Easier to pretend we aren't there. And of course, that's helpful to me. That woman's video did eventually go viral, though what you see in it is blurry at best. Still, there's a capture of the face I used to wear. I will never be Simon Dust again. I'll miss him.

My name is Simone now. Though of course that, too, may change. I am still becoming. I am headed south. I will travel through Mexico and Central America, eventually I will reach Argentina and in the town of Ushuaia I will be closer to Antarctica than I have been in a very long time. The sale of the Dyer home went through without me. The lawyer could sign for me, I hadn't realized. This means they've deposited money into the bank account of a man who no longer exists. I wonder if I would ever need it.

Maybe someday there will be a reason to go back for it.

For now I am moving, but it's occurred to me that if I'd escaped Antarctica then I might not be the only one of my kind. As I come to understand myself better I can almost feel them, see them, in my mind's eye. Maybe I could do for them what the man in the baggy suit did for me. But instead of trying to enslave them again, each one of them could become truly free. I admit though that I have an ulterior motive. The man in the baggy suit isn't dead. I can feel that this is true. But I do believe that it could've been done. Five of me weren't enough. But what about five hundred?

I am going to find my people and tell them what was done to us. Then, together, we are going to seek out those beings who had been worshipped and feared. Maybe they too have gone soft, as all masters eventually do. We will find out. If they have then we are going to kill the gods.

My name is Simone. I was once a slave. I will never be one again.

Contributors' Notes

Other Notable Science Fiction and Fantasy Stories of 2019

Contributors' Notes

Charlie Jane Anders is the author of *Victories Greater Than Death,* the first book in a new young-adult trilogy coming in April 2021, along with the forthcoming short story collection *Even Greater Mistakes.* Her other books include *The City in the Middle of the Night* and *All the Birds in the Sky.* Her fiction and journalism have appeared in the *New York Times,* the *Washington Post, Slate, McSweeney's, Mother Jones,* the *Boston Review,* Tor.com, *Tin House, Conjunctions, Wired,* and other places. Her TED Talk, "Go Ahead, Dream About the Future," got 700,000 views in its first week. With Annalee Newitz, she co-hosts the podcast *Our Opinions Are Correct.*

▪ I was asked to contribute to an anthology co-edited by Victor LaValle and John Joseph Adams called *A People's Future of the United States* and really struggled to come up with a story that extrapolates all of the USA's contradictions and antagonisms into the future. I came up with a future world where the United States has split into two countries, basically representing red and blue states (and there's been a ton of flooding and other disasters, so the coastal cities are gone). And I really liked the idea of a bookstore located on the exact border between these two Americas, probably because it provided a metaphor for the process of trying to find a story that could bring these two separate nations together. This became a vehicle to try and explore the culture clash between the cyberpunk California and the prison-dominated America—and to reveal that the cultural schisms between these two versions of the United States were really a smokescreen for economic battles over control over natural resources. I had a lot of fun writing Molly and her daughter, and their friendships with people from both sides of the divide, but the main character of this story really ended up being the First and Last Page itself. This story ended up being a bit of a love letter to bookstores, showing how they're not just repositories of words but a gathering place for diverse communities. I increasingly believe that bookstores are the canary in our national coal mine—if they die, we're all doomed.

Matthew Baker is the author of the story collections *Why Visit America* and *Hybrid Creatures,* and of the children's novel *If You Find This.* His fiction has appeared in publications such as *The Paris Review, American Short Fiction, One Story, Electric Literature,* and *Best of the Net.* Born in the Great Lakes region of the United States, he currently lives in New York City.

▪ It's an issue at the heart of my family. My great-grandfather was a cop; one of my grandfathers was a police captain; one of my grandfathers was a deputy sheriff; my father worked in law enforcement as a federal agent. Law and order, crime and punishment. One of my great-grandfathers was a felon; one of my great-grandfathers had connections to organized crime; one of my cousins was convicted on larceny charges but got off with community service; one of my cousins is in prison today and will be for decades to come. Probably no surprise that from a very young age, I was obsessed with the history of the justice system. At family get-togethers, I could play catch with a retired cop and then go drink Cokes with a convicted felon. A classic American story. I have to imagine it's an issue at the heart of every family in the United States. A nation that employs over one million law enforcement personnel. The nation with the highest incarceration rate in the world. Who are we? I was in first grade the year that police came and fingerprinted every student in the school. I remember the experience vividly. Standing in line out in the hallway. The feeling of each of my fingertips being pressed to the ink pad and then the paper form. The sight of my fingerprints on what was now a permanent record. My name at the top. I still don't have an answer, but "Life Sentence" is an attempt to articulate the question that I've been grappling with ever since.

Kelly Barnhill is the best-selling author of several books for children, including *The Girl Who Drank the Moon, Iron Hearted Violet,* and the forthcoming *The Ogress at the Far End of Town.* She is also the author of many short stories for grown-ups, some of which are included in her collection *Dreadful Young Ladies.* She is the recipient of the Parents' Choice Gold Award, the Texas Library Association Bluebonnet, a Charlotte Huck Honor, and the World Fantasy Award. In 2017 she was awarded the Newbery Medal by the American Library Association. She lives in Minneapolis with her husband, three kids, and dog.

▪ I started writing "Thirty-Three Wicked Daughters" largely because my husband dared me to do so. While doing research on giant lore for another novel, I came across the Albina story, in a book called *Historia Regum Britanniae,* a pseudohistorical narrative of the origins of England by Geoffrey of Monmouth, written around 1136. It's not the only account of the thirty-three sisters who, in one wild night, behead their husbands, and are subsequently exiled to what will be England, where they have lots and lots of cross-species sex (with demons, mostly) and give birth to a race of giants, who go on to rule Albion/England until the Romans arrive and ruin everything. There are several, actually, but this one is the most lurid of the lot. I couldn't *believe* I had never come across this story before. I told my husband about it right away. I am guessing that I might have been in a bit of a heightened state as I did so—it was the early days after Trump's inauguration, and I was bracing myself for what was sure to be an endless litany of unspeakable horrors (alas, even my wildest imaginings paled before what was to unfold). He said, "You know, this is a rageful time. Maybe writing rageful stories will help put things in perspective." I told him I couldn't really see a way to do it—too bloody, for one, and I'm not really a bloody sort of a writer. Plus, I had already started noodling on a prose poem about a king who was obsessed with pigeons. "You could do both," my husband said. "I dare you." It became something else, of course, as stories often do. But I enjoyed the heck out of myself as I wrote it. I hope you enjoyed reading it, too.

Elizabeth Bear was born on the same day as Frodo and Bilbo Baggins, but in a different year. She is the Hugo, Sturgeon, Locus, and Campbell award-winning author of thirty novels and over a hundred short stories. Her most recent novel, *Machine*, is a science fiction adventure set in a hospital in deep space.

She lives in Massachusetts with her husband, the writer Scott Lynch.

▪ I wrote this story for *Wastelands: The New Apocalypse* anthology. It's set in Las Vegas because I lived in Las Vegas when I wrote the story of mine that appears in the original *Wastelands* anthology, and because Las Vegas is a great place to set an apocalypse. This story is in some ways a reaction to Harlan Ellison's *A Boy and His Dog*, which is in its turn a reaction to (among other things) all those postapocalyptic Adam and Eve stories.

In a twist of fate I never could have gotten away with writing, Harlan passed away while I was in the midst of writing this.

"Erase, Erase, Erase": This is a story that's inspired, among other things, by my fondness for fountain pens. Some of the details of the protagonist's pen habit are echoed by my own experience—for example, my mother, too, is the source of my hobby. It's not an autobiographical story, however. I didn't date any terrorists in college, and I can't walk through walls.

Tobias S. Buckell is a *New York Times* best-selling author and World Fantasy Award winner born in the Caribbean. He grew up in Grenada and spent time in the British and US Virgin Islands, which influence much of his work.

His novels and almost one hundred stories have been translated into nineteen languages. His work has been nominated for the Hugo, Nebula, and World Fantasy awards, and the Astounding Award for Best New Science Fiction Author.

He currently lives in Bluffton, Ohio, with his wife and two daughters. He can be found online at TobiasBuckell.com and is also an instructor at the Stonecoast MFA in Creative Writing program.

▪ A couple years ago I was lucky enough to be a guest of a book festival in the Bahamas. I took a day to go gawp at a megaresort there and meet a friend working there. I said to someone it was the "Death Star" of a complex. When I flew back home I kept mulling over the concept of tourism as an industrial complex, similar to what Dwight D. Eisenhower warned about in his famous speech when he coined the term "military-industrial complex." Since then, I started talking about the tourist industrial complex and looking for patterns in how it works transnationally across the globe. I used the term and added "Galactic" while looking for a title for this story, as I was trying to model what that tourist industrial complex felt like in a science fictional way.

Christopher Caldwell's fiction has appeared in *Uncanny Magazine, Strange Horizons,* and *FIYAH,* among others. He attended the Clarion West Writers Workshop and was awarded the Octavia E. Butler Memorial Scholarship by the Carl Brandon Society. He works in supported accommodation with vulnerable, homeless youth. Californian by birth, Louisianan by culture, he lives in Glasgow, Scotland, with his partner, Alice.

▪ When I first moved to Glasgow from the United States, I lived in a part of town called Merchant City. All the streets are named either after the "Tobacco Lords"—wealthy merchants who built their fortunes in the 1700s through a booming trade in tobacco from British colonies—or after the colonies themselves (Virginia Street and Jamaica Street). One of the Tobacco Lords built a grand mansion in neoclassical style; Glasgow has since repurposed this house to serve as its Gallery of Modern Art. On a rainy afternoon, I visited the Gallery of Modern Art and there was an exhibit on Glasgow's history of slavery. There were artifacts: rusted manacles, woodcuts displaying bucolic scenes of plantation life, a long length of chain. There was a model of a Glaswegian's ship packed to the brim with tiny figurines of people who undoubtedly looked like my ancestors. This exhibit caused some discomfort among locals and disrupted the prevailing narrative that Scotland was an early opponent of chattel slavery. There was never a large population of enslaved people in Scotland, but all those Tobacco Lords whose names are recalled in Glasgow thoroughfares relied on slave labor to harvest the tobacco from their plantations, and many of them traded goods to Africa for humans to brutalize and subjugate to keep their profits high. I began to think about the actual costs of prosperity, and how easy it is to erase our own complicity in others' oppression. This was one of the sparks to writing "Canst Thou Draw Out the Leviathan."

The other spark came years later. I was researching how the Fugitive Slave Acts of 1793 and 1850 impacted the movement of both escaped and manumitted enslaved people and discovered that it was not uncommon for both freedmen and runaways to take refuge among whaling ships, where long voyages and distant ports reduced the chances of their return to bondage. That ships not much different to ones that a generation before had meant terror, destruction, and loss of humanity could mean to the same people freedom, flight, and dignity was a seductive one. I was also mindful of the fact that the wealth that came from whaling—oil for lamps and soaps, whalebone for corsets and buggy whips, ambergris for perfumes—was inherently exploitative; the seas have not recovered from our plunder.

Adam-Troy Castro made his first nonfiction sale to *Spy* magazine in 1987. His twenty-six books to date include four Spider-Man novels, three novels about his profoundly damaged far-future murder investigator Andrea Cort, and six middle-grade novels about the dimension-spanning adventures of young Gustav Gloom. Adam's works have won the Philip K. Dick Award and the Seiun (Japan), and have been nominated for eight Nebulas, three Stokers, two Hugos, one World Fantasy Award, and, internationally, the Ignotus (Spain), the Grand Prix de l'Imaginaire (France), and the Kurd-Laßwitz Preis (Germany). His latest release was the audio collection *My Wife Hates Time Travel and Other Stories,* which features thirteen hours of his fiction, including the recent stories "The Hour In Between" and "Big Stupe and the Buried Big Glowing Booger." Adam lives in Florida with his wife, Judi, and a trio of infidel cats.

▪ With the rest of the stories sight unseen, I suspect that my contribution this time out will wind up being the most traditional science fiction story in this anthology. It's a puzzle piece, set in an interstellar future, with a protagonist trapped in a box by a powerful computer intelligence and challenged to find her way out. By plot outline alone, it could have been published seventy years ago, with little in the way of alteration for the sensibilities of the time. I cheerfully admit this.

Its genesis was as the next-logical question of a series of stories I've been writing since the late 1990s, umbrella title "The AIsource Infection," that has included all three novels in my Andrea Cort series, all three novellas in the Minnie and Earl series, and multiple novellas in the Draiken series. The AIsource are ancient software intelligences who pop up here and there in that future history, sometimes centrally, and so it must be said that this story began with more contemplation about what mischief they might be getting up to next, than what might happen to some poor human being in their power; Sacrid Henn, or "Sacred Hen," arrived only afterward and surprised this author by shining through despite mostly existing as a presence being addressed by the inhuman narrator. This is one of those odd things that happens, and has led to my thus-far unfocused conviction that she must appear again, some time in the near future; and someday, when this collection is not only published and read but a dusty display on home bookshelves alongside other BASFF collections published before and since, readers will either possess the memory of me following through or the awareness that it was another vague authorial promise destined to be left unfulfilled in the wake of newer and more pressing ideas. We shall see.

Jaymee Goh is a writer, reviewer, editor, and essayist of science fiction and fantasy. Her poetry, short fiction, and essays have been published in a range of science fiction and fantasy magazines and journals, such as *Strange Horizons, Lightspeed Magazine,* and *Science Fiction Studies.* She wrote the blog *Silver Goggles,* an exploration of postcolonial theory through steampunk, and has contributed to Tor.com, Racialicious.com, and *Beyond Victoriana.* She graduated from the Clarion Science Fiction and Fantasy Writers Workshop in 2016 and received her PhD in comparative literature from the University of California, Riverside, where she dissertated on steampunk and whiteness. She is an editor for Tachyon Publications.

▪ The bobbitt worm is an actual marine worm, and I was struck with horrified fascination when I first watched clips about its hunting technique. I am terrified by many-legged creepy-crawlies (I love earthworms and admire spiders, but anything over eight legs . . . no) and have always been wary of the sea, so the bobbitt worm seemed like an argument for never going back to the ocean. However, as we on Tumblr say, one way of dealing with the monsters under your bed is to invite them into bed, and I realized I could deal with the repulsiveness of the bobbitt worm by combining it with conventionally sexy things together: "bobbitt worm mermaids! Lesbian ones! That reproduce via vampirism!" Erotica is a secondary writing interest of mine; writing realistic sex and a terrifying nonhuman body was a challenge I couldn't put down. I still struggled with the plot spanning three generations until I got to Clarion, where for some reason my cohort began to experiment with the triptych form. I researched marine-worm anatomy to write the story during the week horror master Victor LaValle (also in this volume!) taught Clarion, and sicced this on my unsuspecting classmates with fairly even reactions: all the cis boys (queer and straight) broke in various ways, and all the cis girls (queer and straight) plus the one genderqueer classmate raved about it. I like to think that says something about the story. After, I could think of no place to send it to, but Nisi Shawl asked me to submit to her invite-only anthology of speculative fiction by people of color, and where else might an anticolonial misandrist Southeast Asian bobbitt worm mermaid story with fatal fellatio and carnivorous cunnilingus go?

Gwendolyn Kiste is the Bram Stoker Award–winning author of *The Rust Maidens,* the fiction collection *And Her Smile Will Untether the Universe,* the dark fantasy novella *Pretty Marys All in a Row,* and the occult horror novelette *The Invention of Ghosts.* Her short fiction and nonfiction have appeared in *Nightmare Magazine, Vastarien, Tor's Nightfire, Black Static, Daily Science Fiction, Unnerving Magazine, Interzone,* and *LampLight,* among others. Originally from Ohio, she now resides on an abandoned horse farm outside of Pittsburgh with her husband, two cats, and not nearly enough ghosts.

▪ *Dracula* was one of the first horror stories I ever discovered. It all started with an early viewing of the Universal film at the age of four or five, and was quickly followed up on some hallowed Saturday afternoon with the Christopher Lee and Peter Cushing classic, *Horror of Dracula.*

Horror was always at the forefront of my childhood, since both my parents love the genre as well, and they soon told me about the novel *Dracula.* Back when I was still too young to read it, I remember asking about the female characters—as a child, I was always very concerned that there weren't enough girls in stories—and I was told there were only really two women in *Dracula:* Mina and Lucy. I asked what happened to them, and I was told that Mina lived and Lucy died. This striking disparity between them always stuck with me, and I would lament over the years that Lucy deserved better. Finally, after yet another conversation about her unjust fate (this time, with my husband, who's also a horror fan), I decided that as a writer, I could go ahead and do something about it.

It took me nearly two years to figure out exactly how to tell this story, and it wasn't until I settled on the list format that it finally emerged in a way that felt right to me. After a lifetime of wanting to know more about Lucy, I hope this story has given her a chance to tell everything from her side—and a chance for longtime *Dracula* fans to give a second thought to a great character who has too often fallen by the wayside.

Victor LaValle is the author of seven works of fiction, including *The Ballad of Black Tom* and *The Changeling,* and a comic book, *Destroyer.* He co-edited an anthology, *A People's Future of the United States,* with John Joseph Adams. He teaches at Columbia University.

▪ I received an email from Jonathan Maberry one day, stating that *Weird Tales Magazine* would be returning to print and he wondered if I had a story to share. I did not! But I had an idea: *Weird Tales* had been one of the magazines most famous for publishing the stories of H. P. Lovecraft, a writer whom I both adored and loathed. Publishing a story that wrestled with his legacy (as I had done in a novella, *The Ballad of Black Tom*) and doing it in the magazine that led to his fame seemed ideal. It would be like moving into his old home and conducting an exorcism. But then a funny thing happened: I included details from the life of Booker T. Washington, who was born into American slavery, and suddenly it was me who felt possessed. I had to get this story right because I was setting more than one record straight. Not just reimagining a Lovecraft tale, but etching the truth of my nation's barbarity into the pages of that storied magazine. *The horror! The horror!* as Conrad wrote. By the time I was finished, I swore I whipped the devil. Who that devil is, I leave it up to you to decide.

Ken Liu (http://kenliu.name) is an American author of speculative fiction. He has won the Nebula, Hugo, and World Fantasy awards, as well as top genre honors in Japan, Spain, and France, among other countries.

Liu's debut novel, *The Grace of Kings,* is the first volume in a silkpunk epic fantasy series, the Dandelion Dynasty, in which engineers play the role of wizards. His debut collection, *The Paper Menagerie and Other Stories,* has been published in more than a dozen languages. A second collection, *The Hidden Girl and Other Stories,* followed. He also wrote the *Star Wars* novel *The Legends of Luke Skywalker.* He has been involved in multiple media adaptations of his work. The most recent projects include *The Message,* under development by 21 Laps and FilmNation Entertainment; "Good Hunting," adapted as an episode in season one of Netflix's breakout adult animated series *Love, Death + Robots;* and AMC's *Pantheon,* which Craig Silverstein will executive produce, adapted from an interconnected series of short stories by Liu.

Prior to becoming a full-time writer, Liu worked as a software engineer, corporate lawyer, and litigation consultant. He frequently speaks at conferences and universities on a variety of topics, including futurism, cryptocurrency, the history of technology, bookmaking, the mathematics of origami, and other subjects of his expertise. Liu lives with his family near Boston, Massachusetts.

▪ Storytelling is the primary means by which we exercise that most valuable and undervalued human faculty: empathy.

We make living bearable by telling ourselves stories that make sense of the randomness of the universe, attributing causes to effects, drawing plots from the vicissitudes of fortune, and crafting character arcs that explain who we are. We strive to understand the stories of other lives and hope that others, in turn, will make an effort to understand our story.

Advancing technology has been intimately connected with advances in storytelling. Writing, printing, film, TV, the internet—each new medium has brought hope that there will be more and better stories, more and better understanding, more empathy. That hope, unfortunately, has been dashed again and again against the shoals of reality, as narratives can serve not only to elicit and nurture empathy, but also to murder it, and to cauterize the heart-soil so that it never sprouts again.

Still, we can't help but hope. Whether this is foolish or wise is not for us, mere mortals, to know.

Anil Menon's most recent work *Half of What I Say* was shortlisted for the 2016 Hindu Literary Award. His short fiction has appeared in a variety of anthologies and magazines including *Albedo One, Interzone, Interfictions, Jaggery, Lady Churchill's Rosebud Wristlet,* and *Strange Horizons.* His stories have been translated into more than a dozen languages including Hebrew, Igbo, and Romanian. A forthcoming collection of speculative short stories will be published in India. He can be reached at iam@anilmenon.com.

▪ I'd been reading anthropologist Thomas de Zengotita's book *Mediated,* which argues that our creations are designed to mediate the natural world for us. For example, fictions can be seen as a neural technology that mediates the world for us by shaping our emotions. We feel this or that about this or that because we're "run," so to speak, by this or that story. I also remember coming across Clifford Geertz's essay "From the Native Point of View," which describes how the concept of self is culture-specific and not universal. Geertz recounts meeting a Javanese man whose wife had died, suddenly and inexplicably, and watching him interact with guests with a calm formality and trying ". . . by mystical techniques, to flatten out, as he himself put it, the hills and valleys of his emotion into an even, level plain ('That is what you have to do,' he said to me, 'be smooth inside and out') . . ."

Personally, I do not see the point of such a "smoothened" life. Of course, this desire for "the point," the emotional value I attach to its presence or absence, the emotions I use in response, all these things too may be mediated by unknown stories. I started out writing the story of a man who'd lost his wife but somewhere along the way it became a story about a storytelling species.

Deji Bryce Olukotun is the author of two novels, and his short fiction has appeared in seven book collections. His science fiction novel *After the Flare* won a 2018 Philip K. Dick special citation; his first novel, *Nigerians in Space,* a thriller about brain drain from Africa, was published in 2014. He is a Future Tense Fellow at New America/Center for Science and Imagination and an attorney with a background in technology policy. He previously worked to defend persecuted writers around the world at PEN America in countries such as Myanmar, Haiti, and Nigeria, with support from the Ford Foundation.

▪ Space exploration conjures up awe and excitement, but it's also about making hard choices, especially once we leave the solar system. That's what I was exploring in "Between the Dark and the Dark." Because of my human rights background, I was interested in knowing what our absolute redlines would be if we were trying to save our species from extinction. What would we agree never to do in deep space? What line would we never cross? So I told the story from the point of view of people who created the line, and those who were living on the other side of it. Here on Earth we decided that we would not tolerate certain acts. What will happen when we can move among the stars? Moreover, what if we *have to leave* Earth?

Cannibalism is terrifying, especially when it's related to sadistic pleasure. That perversity is why it's the subject of so many television shows and movies. But if you dig a little deeper into history, you'll see that it often cropped up in cultures around the world—from Europe to Asia to Africa and the Americas—not for titillation but for some religious or cultural importance. In a spacefaring culture where food and nutrients would be absolutely vital to survival of the entire crew, perhaps we'd find that the extreme isolation would awaken ancient modes of organizing our society. But mimicking the Aztecs or some other culture wouldn't be realistic in a highly technical society. So I thought about what practices might evolve if you combined the two. I owe a debt of gratitude to Professors Steven Desch and Steve Ruff at Arizona State University, who helped me work through many of the technical details.

Rebecca Roanhorse is a *New York Times* best-selling and Nebula, Hugo, Astounding, and Locus award-winning speculative fiction writer. Her novels include *Trail of Lightning, Storm of Locusts* (both part of the Sixth World series), *Star Wars: Resistance Reborn,* and the middle-grade novel *Race to the Sun.* Her short fiction can be found in *Apex Magazine, Uncanny Magazine,* and various anthologies. She lives with her husband and daughter in northern New Mexico and can be found on Twitter at @RoanhorseBex. Her next novel is the epic fantasy *Black Sun,* coming fall 2020.

▪ I wrote this story originally for *The Mythic Dream* anthology, whose call was to write a retelling/reinterpretation of a myth. I am Native American (Ohkay Owingeh descent) on my mother's side, so I wanted to focus on a Native story that may not be familiar to most science fiction and fantasy readers. I chose the classic Tewa story "Deer Hunter and White Corn Maiden," which can be found in multiple texts and online. The original story has a historical setting, but Native people are very much part of the future, and I wanted my retelling to reflect that. So I chose a cyberpunk-esque setting where fame is everything and technology has made it possible to live, if not forever, then for a very long time. (As I researched biological memory and CGI "digital reincarnation" in Hollywood movies, I realized my story is much more near-future than I anticipated.) I see this story with its cautions about obsessive love as still relevant and beautiful. I hope that it intrigues readers enough that they seek out the original and other indigenous stories.

Rion Amilcar Scott is the author of the story collection *The World Doesn't Require You,* which was awarded the 2020 Towson Prize for Literature and was a finalist for the 2020 PEN/Jean Stein Book Award. His debut story collection, *Insurrections,* was awarded the 2017 PEN/Robert W. Bingham Prize for Debut Fiction and the 2017 Hillsdale Award from the Fellowship of Southern Writers. His work has been published in journals such as *Kenyon Review, Crab Orchard Review,* and *The Rumpus,* among others.

▪ "Shape-ups at Delilah's" is a sequel of sorts to a story in my first collection, *Insurrections,* called "Razor Bumps." In that story the Great Hair Crisis in my fictional town of Cross River, Maryland, is a new plague freshly ruining haircuts and lives. I wanted to see how the Hair Crisis evolved and how it ended. I thought back to childhood and the many hours I spent in the barbershop growing up. The Black barbershop is often thought of as a sanctuary for Black men. I'm interested in the ideas we accept when we are very young and lacking in critical thinking and how we receive them. Possibly the dumbest idea many people I know accepted was the idea that women were somehow unable to cut hair as well as men—as if masculinity imbued one with special haircutting powers and femininity a lack of them (the best barber I ever had gave lie to that notion). Somewhere along the line someone would cite the biblical story of Samson and Delilah, where a woman cutting a man's hair results in the loss of his strength and his eventual death. Tiny, by being greater than any male barber, flips the myth of Samson and Delilah on its head. Her haircutting, instead of being debilitating, has the power to give strength to the people of Cross River. Tiny's power, though, is interrupted by the ridiculous preconceived notions and received ideas of the men around her.

Nibedita Sen is a Hugo, Nebula, and Astounding award-nominated queer Bengali writer from Calcutta, and a graduate of Clarion West 2015 whose work has appeared or is forthcoming in *Podcastle, Nightmare,* and *Fireside.* She accumulated a number of English degrees in India before deciding she wanted another in creative writing, and that she was going to move halfway across the world for it. These days, she can be found working as an editor in New York City while consuming large amounts of coffee and video games. She helps edit *Glittership,* an LGBTQ SF/F podcast, enjoys the company of puns and potatoes, and is nearly always hungry. Hit her up on Twitter at @her_nibsen.

▪ The idea for "Ten Excerpts . . ." came to me during grad school in the USA, taking a literature course on the American gothic as part of my MFA. This wasn't my first exposure to academia, either—I have a master's in English lit from back home in India. One thing led to another, and I got to thinking about how Western academia has been a tool of colonialism, and how racist perspectives and practices are absolutely built into its bones, despite—and sometimes *because of!*—how strongly it insists on its own objectivity and superiority. I like stories that function like intricate little puzzle boxes where the whole is more than the sum of its parts, stories that do interesting things with structure, and I'd already had the idea to write one in the form of an annotated bibliography. Toss in some feminism, food horror, and queerness, and I had a recipe—or, should I say, a bibliography—for something fun.

Somtow Sucharitkul (S. P. Somtow) was born in Thailand, grew up in Europe, and settled in America for a long while. His career as a science fiction writer began in the late 1970s and was an attempt to escape from composer's block—his first career was in music. The tail began to wag the dog and he was soon appearing regularly in magazines, receiving the 1981 John W. Campbell Award and two Hugo nominations. After adopting the pseudonym S. P. Somtow he drifted into fantasy, historical, and horror novels, of which perhaps the most noted are *The Riverrun Trilogy, Vampire Junction,* and *Moon Dance.* He won the World Fantasy Award for his novella *The Bird Catcher.* The magic realism of *Jasmine Nights* earned him mainstream plaudits. A sudden urge to spend time as a Buddhist monk (memoir, *Nirvana Express*) launched the most recent stage of his career in which he became most known as the director of Opera Siam in Bangkok and the composer of nineteen operas and music dramas, the most recent of which, *Helena Citrónová,* received performances worldwide. He is working on a ten-opera series, *DasJati,* based on the iconic *Ten Lives of the Buddha,* a central text of Theravada Buddhism. In the last few years he has returned to fiction, producing several new novels, most recently *Homeworld of the Heart* and *Stillness in Starlight.*

▪ My life has always been a kind of border checkpoint, with East and West rushing through in opposite directions, on their way to god knows where; sometimes I feel like the guy who stamps the passports, picking up little pieces of information en passant . . . and eventually assembling the snippets into creative works. There is a real orphanage in a Bangkok slum, run by the saintly Father Joe and populated by kids who are living with HIV—it couldn't be more different from the one described in this story, but it's one of the shiny bits of the real world glimmering inside the texture of this story. There is a real Bob Halliday who really is a bit like the god Ganesha—he has passed away, but he lives on, continually popping up as a character in divergent tales of mine for decades.

Caroline M. Yoachim is a prolific author of short stories, appearing in *Lightspeed, Asimov's Science Fiction, The Magazine of Fantasy & Science Fiction, Uncanny Magazine, Beneath Ceaseless Skies,* and *Clarkesworld,* among other places. She has been a finalist for the World Fantasy, Locus, and multiple Hugo and Nebula awards. A chapbook edition of *The Archronology of Love* is available, with bonus flash fiction set in the same world. Yoachim's debut short story collection, *Seven Wonders of a Once and Future World & Other Stories,* was published in 2016. Find her online at carolineyoachim.com, or on Twitter as @CarolineYoachim.

▪ In "The Archronology of Love," I wanted to explore the destructive nature of archaeology: the elements of an excavation site that are lost in the process of gathering information. Archaeologists trade real-world objects in their physical context for catalogs, photographs, carbon dating, and various other types of records. The processes involved are obviously different, but conceptually archaeology (and archronology) remind me of quantum mechanics, where observation collapses the wave function.

The novelette draws from bits and pieces of inspiration across a long period of time, starting with an archaeological dig I did as an undergraduate in 1999. Other aspects of the story draw on more recent experiences—missing a loved one, walking in the campus quad at University of Washington. The bases of the alien artifacts were inspired by an iridescent blue beetle I saw on a trip to Japan. This is pretty typical for my writing process. Images and moments that stay with me over time tend to get mashed together in my fiction.

E. Lily Yu received the Astounding Award for Best New Writer in 2012 and the Artist Trust/LaSalle Storyteller Award in 2017. Her short stories have appeared in *McSweeney's, Clarkesworld,* Tor.com, *Uncanny Magazine, Asimov's Science Fiction, The Magazine of Fantasy & Science Fiction,* and multiple best-of-the-year anthologies, and have been finalists for the Hugo, Nebula, Locus, Sturgeon, and World Fantasy awards. Her first novel, *On Fragile Waves,* will be out in late 2020.

▪ "The Time Invariance of Snow" has been a long time coming. Back in high school, I taught myself Latin from Wheelock and learned about Lucretia, the Sabines, Dido, etc.; Cassandra, whose story has been a thorn in me for years, arrived in a standard high school English class. In college, I wrote a prize-winning one-act play about the life and career of

Chien-Shiung Wu and a mediocre second thesis on Shannon entropy. Two years ago, I read *The Order of Time,* by Carlo Rovelli. That book staggered me with its vision of bidirectional time and the increase of entropy, time's arrow, being an illusion due to a coarse-grained view of the universe. Then Christine Blasey Ford stood up and testified.

The story wrote itself, at that point.

Other Notable Science Fiction and Fantasy Stories of 2019

Selected by John Joseph Adams

ADHYAM, SHWETA
One Found in a World of the Lost. *Beneath Ceaseless Skies,* September

ALLEN, VIOLET
The Synapse Will Free Us from Ourselves. *A People's Future of the United States,* ed. Victor LaValle and John Joseph Adams (One World)

ATHENS, CYD
Poison. *Fireside,* April

BAILEY, MARIKA
An Irrational Love. *FIYAH,* Autumn

BALLINGRUD, NATHAN
Jasper Dodd's Handbook of Spirits and Manifestations. *Echoes: The Saga Anthology of Ghost Stories,* ed. Ellen Datlow (Saga)

BANGS, ELLY
A Handful of Sky. *Beneath Ceaseless Skies,* June

BANKER, ASHOK K.
Son of Water and Fire. *Lightspeed,* January

BOLANDER, BROOKE
A Bird, a Song, a Revolution. *Lightspeed,* September

BRADLEY, LISA M.
Men in Cars. *Anathema,* December

BROADDUS, MAURICE
The Migration Suite: A Study in C Sharp Minor. *Uncanny,* July/August

BRYSKI, KT
The Path of Pins, the Path of Needles. *Lightspeed,* December

BUCKELL, TOBIAS S.
The Blindfold. *A People's Future of the United States,* ed. Victor LaValle and John Joseph Adams (One World)

CHIANG, TED
Omphalos. *Exhalation: Stories* (Knopf)

CRENSHAW, PAUL
Bulletproof Tattoos. *If This Goes On,* ed. Cat Rambo (Parvus Press)

CROUCH, BLAKE
Summer Frost. *Forward,* ed. Blake Crouch (Amazon)

DOCTOROW, CORY
Affordances. *Future Tense,* October

GREENBLATT, A. T.
Before the World Crumbles Away. *Uncanny,* March/April
Give the Family My Love. *Clarkesworld,* February

HICKS, MICAH DEAN
Quiet the Dead. *Nightmare,* February

HUDSON, KAI
The Weaver Retires. *PodCastle,* March

HVIDE, BRIT E. B.
East of the Sun, West of the Stars. *Clarkesworld,* February

JEMISIN, N. K.
Emergency Skin. *Forward,* ed. Blake Crouch (Amazon)
Give Me Cornbread or Give Me Death. *A People's Future of the United States,* ed. Victor LaValle and John Joseph Adams (One World)

JONES, STEPHEN GRAHAM
The Tree of Self-Knowledge. *Echoes: The Saga Anthology of Ghost Stories,* ed. Ellen Datlow (Saga)

KANG, MINSOO
The Virtue of Unfaithful Translations. *New Suns,* ed. Nisi Shawl (Solaris)

KIM, ALICE SOLA
Now Wait for This Week. *A People's Future of the United States,* ed. Victor LaValle and John Joseph Adams (One World)

KOSMATKA, TED
Sacrificial Iron. *Asimov's,* May/June

LARSON, RICH
Still Life of a Death Broker. *Terraform,* May

LECKIE, ANN
The Justified. *The Mythic Dream,* ed. Dominik Parisien and Navah Wolfe (Saga)

LEE, YOON HA
The Empty Gun. *Mission Critical,* ed. Jonathan Strahan (Solaris)

LEWIS, L. D.
Moses. *Anathema,* April
Signal. *Fireside,* August

LINK, KELLY
The White Cat's Divorce. *Dread & Delight: Fairy Tales in an Anxious World* (art exhibit 2018) / *The Magazine of Fantasy & Science Fiction,* September/October

LO, MALINDA
Red. *Foreshadow,* Issue 1

MACHADO, CARMEN MARIA
The Things Eric Eats Before He Eats Himself. *The Mythic Dream,* ed. Dominik Parisien and Navah Wolfe (Saga)

MILLER, SAM J.
Death and Other Gentrifying Neighborhoods. *Terraform,* March
Shucked. *The Magazine of Fantasy & Science Fiction,* November/December

MONDAL, MIMI
His Footsteps, Through Darkness and Light. Tor.com, January

MORENO-GARCIA, SILVIA
On the Lonely Shore. *Uncanny,* March/April

NAYLER, RAY
The Ocean Between the Leaves. *Asimov's,* July/August

OKORAFOR, NNEDI
Binti: Sacred Fire. *Binti: The Complete Trilogy* (DAW)

ONYEBUCHI, TOCHI
The Fifth Day. *Uncanny,* September/October

OSBORNE, KAREN
The Dead, in Their Uncontrollable Power. *Uncanny,* March/April

PEYNADO, BRENDA
The Touches. Tor.com, November

PRATT, TIM
A Champion of Nigh-Space. patreon.com/timpratt, April / *Uncanny,* July/August

RAPPAPORT, JENNY RAE
The Answer That You Are Seeking. *Lightspeed,* September

RIVERA, MERCURIO D.
In the Stillness Between the Stars. *Asimov's,* September/October

ROANHORSE, REBECCA
Harvest. *New Suns,* ed. Nisi Shawl (Solaris)

ROBSON, KELLY
Skin City. *The Verge/Better Worlds,* February

ROTH, VERONICA
Ark. *Forward,* ed. Blake Crouch (Amazon)
Echo. *Wastelands: The New Apocalypse,* ed. John Joseph Adams (Titan)

SINGH, VANDANA
Mother Ocean. *Current Futures,* ed. Ann VanderMeer (Xprize)

SOLOMON, RIVERS
Blood Is Another Word for Hunger. Tor.com, July

ST. GEORGE, CARLIE
Some Kind of Blood-Soaked Future. *Nightmare,* October

VALENTE, CATHERYNNE M.
The Sun in Exile. *A People's Future of the United States,* ed. Victor LaValle and John Joseph Adams (One World)

WASSERSTEIN, IZZY
Requiem Without Sound. *Escape Pod,* December

WISE, A. C.
How the Trick Is Done. *Uncanny,* July/August

YÁÑEZ, ALBERTO
Burn the Ships. *New Suns,* ed. Nisi Shawl (Solaris)

YU, E. LILY
The Valley of Wounded Deer. *Lightspeed,* October
Three Variations on a Theme of Imperial Attire. *New Suns,* ed. Nisi Shawl (Solaris)